Erebus Unleashed

Genesis Planet Book 2

Kate Glass

Beartown
Press

PRAISE FOR PERSEPHONE RISING

Fast-paced and engaging! Persephone Rising *by Kate Glass delivers a gripping tale of survival, secrets, and the bond between siblings in a crumbling future Chicago. Perfect for fans of dystopian adventure.*

—Millie Copper

Author of the bestselling speculative series Havoc in Wyoming.

For Howard, whose advice and support have been invaluable

Sometimes letting go is how we save ourselves.
-Helen Johanssen

New Chicago

2073

1

Solast

The space shuttle's retractable stairway grumbles and groans outside the airlock—a sound that drives cobwebs of sleep from Sol's eyes. She gasps, sits up, and rips the sleep mask from her face. Her heart jolts. Fear fires adrenaline through her body. She's the only one who ever lowers the boarding stairs into the aerospace museum's parking lot. Someone's coming.

She scrambles from her bunk, grabs bedding, shoes, the pot she pees in, and her tiny aloe plant. Sol runs for the cargo bay. Outside the hull, boots thunder an alarm. She drops her things on the bay's floor, dislodges the panel at her feet which hides the compartment where she keeps her meager possessions, and slides inside. She pulls the plant, pillow, shoes, and blanket in behind her. Sol lies flat and nudges the panel back into place. It settles with a *snick* just as voices erupt in the corridor.

When Sol first saw this ship, she'd known if she could get inside, she'd be safe. Well, safer than living in some cardboard-and-tin vagrant shack. The prototype space shuttle gleamed and sparkled like a multi-faceted sapphire—or maybe a featherless bird—neck tapering to silver beak, its lightweight landing gear tethered to a concrete pad. Panoramic windows overlooked the parking lot. LED lights outlined unfurled wings that could be folded to fit compact spaces.

She'd renamed the J-Bird C Class ship the *Blue Goose*. Someday, NASA would collect the loaned solar ship, but for now it belonged to the aerospace museum. Or to Solast Bahri, depending on how you looked at it.

Now she doesn't feel so confident in her choice of homes. Who could be out there? Maintenance workers? Officials from NASA? A tour group? Had she left anything in the cabin? Would they sense her hiding like some piece of forgotten freight in the hold?

She holds her breath as the intruders enter the cargo bay. Shadows jump through slits where the panel fits into metal flooring. Voices murmur excitedly. They sound too young to be NASA officials. *Shh!* Someone warns. Someone else laughs. Shoes scrape across aluminum. The strangers stay in the cargo bay for maybe half an hour, leave, then come back again. Sol dares not sneak off the shuttle during the interim. Outside, the sun's a spotlight, the risk of exposure too great. And she has no idea where they've gone on the shuttle. For all she knows, she would be in their line of sight.

She settles into the narrow compartment, adjusts her pillow, and bides her time. She's good at it. Hasn't she been waiting to exact her revenge on Anton Cheverra for years? Even though her cramped muscles scream for release, she stays quiet and tries to sleep until her usual waking time of midnight.

She only partially succeeds. For a while, thoughts rush through her brain like rabbits chased by dogs. She imagines what-ifs and worst-case scenarios. But as minutes drift into hours and the noises outside the bay continue, her rabbits retreat into their holes. Sol tires of thinking and worrying, and she dozes.

The cargo compartment shudders beneath Sol, startling her awake. For a moment, dreams meld with reality. She's inside a coffin, buried deep underground, forgotten by everyone. Then the nightmare fractures, and reality breaks through. She remembers the trespassers. Is it midnight yet? She checks the Skinpad glowing beneath her forearm's epidermis and frowns. Nine o'clock.

The aluminum floor judders. The *Blue Goose* groans. Vibrations pound a rhythm along Sol's backbone. The shuttle's *moving*, but how? Realization strikes like a PulseLock gun to the skull. *Those young scrulls are stealing my home!* Yet it's *not* her home anymore. It's a trap. A cage. Maybe even a death sentence.

She catches the panel's straps inches from her nose and braces against the sarcophagus-like enclosure. Intense pressure pushes her back and doesn't let up for what feels like minutes. She fights unconsciousness. Pain shoots along her temples, and the chamber pot knocks into her head. Just when she thinks she might pass out, invisible weights lift. Silence wraps around her. Sol shifts, and her body rises like a helium balloon until she bumps into the panel above.

Feccing pisspot bloody thieves! She slams a hand against the hard aluminum and fights down panic. Her brain scrambles for an explanation and doesn't like the one it finds—that the prototype has broken free of its moorings and lifted into the black. But how? Why? She felt so safe here. *And* she'd made progress finding Anton, the man who murdered her father eleven years ago.

Now he's on Earth, and she's in outer space. It's an idea too big to wrap her head around. Her nemesis, growing smaller and smaller, until any idea of exacting revenge against him blinks out, and she's left hollowed. Empty. Without her retribution, who is she?

Sol shakes off despair. She's in space. Big deal. A shuttle that flies *out* of Earth's orbit can fly back. Not by itself, of course, and certainly not with *her* in the pilot's chair. Yet *someone* is flying this vessel. She simply needs to convince that person to take her home.

Anger twists in her throat, and something between a scream and a sob bursts out. She muffles the cry with a hand and bobs against the compartment's sides. The aloe plant skitters along the panel. She catches it and holds it next to her crucifix which floats, leashed to its chain. Adrenaline sharpens her foggy brain. *I need a weapon.* But first things first. Even if someone's waiting for her in the cargo hold, she's getting out of this compartment.

Sol braces her legs and pushes up with a free arm. The cover pops loose and floats away until the straps catch it. She gathers her leg muscles beneath her and launches upward. Her arms cartwheel. The plant goes flying. Nylon brushes against her fingers, and she grabs hold of a wall harness securing a tub that hadn't been there before. Whoever stole the prototype wasn't planning on a quick joyride. They meant to leave Earth for who knows how long.

Strapped-in containers and crates clutter the cargo hold. Sol presses the compartment panel back in place with an awkward combination of legs and one-armed maneuvering. Hells. This nil gravity. She already hates it. A quick look around reveals she's alone, at least for now. Recessed lights illuminate the small bay, which has curved sides and a shiny metal floor.

The thieves flying the *Blue Goose* don't know about Sol, but what will happen when she's discovered? They won't take her back to Earth. These people are on the run. They've made off with NASA's premier science vessel, a boat that hasn't even made her virgin run. This shuttle must be worth millions of credits. The crew lurking somewhere above will be desperate, without morals, and possibly skilled fighters.

She's a skilled fighter, too—dangerous even without a gun. But she's one woman against how many? Plus, in zero-g, a physical encounter could go sideways in a flash. Sol had heard multiple voices, multiple sets of feet. Not good odds. If they overpower her, they might throw her out an airlock.

She wedges her plant between a strap and a plastic bin, then glances around again. Past the new clutter, the room's main features are air vents, handholds attached to pale gray walls, and the hatch leading out of the hold. Weightlessness plays spin-the-bottle with her stomach. She tastes acid and swallows hard. No way is she throwing up in this vacuum. She imagines the blue-green orb of Earth dropping away and swallows again. At almost six feet tall, Sol isn't tiny, but right now, she feels as small and helpless as a bug.

Think, Solast, think. You've been in plenty of tight spots before.

A voice answers back, *But never in outer space.*

Canned air rushes through the vents. The *Blue Goose* purrs against her palm where she presses it flat to the wall. This ship was supposed to be a *model* aircraft, secured in place at the museum's entrance to draw visitors. How did the thieves get it to fly? *Easy. The ship is a* working *model, a completely solar-operated shuttle that's been soaking up rays for months.* Other questions aren't as simple to answer: Where are they headed, and who's in control of the ship?

Best to find out, and the sooner the better.

Sol clings to handholds and peeks inside boxes but finds no weapons—only blankets, crackers, towels, and other random items thrown together in a hurry. She discovers a crate of bottled water, grabs one, unscrews the lid, and attempts to drink, no small feat in zero-g. Next, she devours a packet of jerky and some of the crackers. Only a few escape and float away.

Her belly settles and head clears. Sol runs a hand over her bristly scalp. The thieves will think she's a scrull. Some homeless leth-head. Does she care? *You're stalling. Get on with it.* Hand over hand, Sol uses the railings to leave the hold and travel down the narrow passageway.

She pulls herself past six tiny cabins, three on each side of the corridor, and peers into an open area half the size of the bay. Despite the quiet, she fears the presence of others. Sol scans the couches, dining table, and chairs anchored to the floor. Her gaze skims over a large vid screen built into one wall and moves on to the kitchen area, its appliances unused, spotless, *waiting*.

Feeling exposed, she hurls her body through the commons area and along another corridor. She flies past the escape pods and into engineering, a space filled with the humming, incomprehensible innards of the *Goose*. Pipes, cables, and mysterious machines fill the ship's belly, but no people jump out at her. They must all be on the bridge.

Back at the commons, a free-standing titanium stairway leads to the *Goose's* top level. Sol pulls herself up, hand over hand, legs floating behind like jellyfish limbs. Dread grows with each foot of progress. No way can she fight these people. No way can she avoid them. Once they spot her, she'll need charm and negotiating skills, neither of which she has.

Voices drift into the stairway, and Sol pauses. Two males. Two females. Four thieves, then. They sound like kids. Rich kids stealing her boat on a dare? Rage buzzes behind Sol's eyes. The *Goose* is hers!

Only it's not. Just a way station on her journey to finding Anton and exacting revenge. He's her target, not these hoodlums. She can handle them, has handled much worse in her years as a street rat in New Chicago.

Sol pokes her head above the stairway and surveys the scene. A young man of maybe eighteen sits in the pilot's chair, the seat swiveled to reveal his profile—defined cheekbones, a shadow of beard, and dark, tousled hair. In the co-pilot's chair lounges the other male, even younger and the picture of a credit-flush kid with his slicked-back hair, pinky ring, and expensive silk shirt. A young woman with caramel-colored tresses that slither through the air like snakes holds onto the pilot's seat back. *Medusa,* Sol thinks with a grim smile. The girl's back is to Sol. Her jeans and tee are faded, cheap like the pilot's clothes. She's not quite as tall as Sol.

The female behind the co-pilot's seat, however, wouldn't top five-four even if she piled her waist-length braid around her head like a crown. This short one turns and spots Sol peering at her. A string of invectives spew from her mouth. The others stiffen, and more heads jerk Sol's way. She draws breath, gathers what little composure she has, and pulls herself past the stairway and onto the bridge. Pushing off with her feet, she reaches for a wall railing, fumbling before she snatches it. Any try for dignity vanishes. Her legs flail and head bumps against the curved viewport. Sol's curses mingle with the short girl's. She eyes her enemies one by one and finally settles on the girl with the colorful language, the one wearing a mechanic's jumpsuit grimy with oil stains.

Nil gravity becomes Sol's friend. The thieves remain tethered in place, unable to rush her. The mechanic girl doesn't speak, but silver eyes stab at Sol like glass shards.

The flyaway-hair female Sol thinks of as Medusa demands in icy tones, "Who are you, and how did you get on our ship?"

Sol's gaze slides toward her. *I should have thought up a story.* She clears her throat. "My name is Solast Bahri. And who says the *Blue Goose* is your ship?"

"The wh—?" This from the slick-haired rich boy.

"The *Blue Goose.*" The name sounds silly, said aloud. Still, Sol stiffens her spine and plows on, "I was here first, and I named her. She's blue, and she flies. What's hard to comprehend?"

"You're a stowaway," the taller girl states. Hazel eyes flicker over Sol's oversized black hoodie, frayed joggers, and combat boots, then return to her face.

Sol knows what Medusa sees in that shaved head, scarred cheek, skeletal frame, and haunted umber eyes which mark her as homeless. She tilts her chin. "I'm not a leth-head."

They stare at each other while the rest gawk. Sol lets go of the railing with one hand and pulls up her sleeve to reveal the Skinpad implant used by anyone with enough credits to afford it. She almost loses her grip and struggles to regain a precarious perch next to the wall.

The girl's eyes widen. "Why would someone with a Skinpad be camping in this shuttle?"

"It's safer than the parks," Sol spits out.

Medusa nods like she gets this, but why would she? A Skinpad glows beneath her own forearm. On the other hand, those clothes aren't lux.

Sol takes a stab at negotiation. "I worked as a nurse in a public clinic until it closed a couple of years ago. They gave me the Skinpad for my job. I tried living on the streets, but it's dangerous, so I borrowed the prototype. I wasn't hurting anyone. I'm no thief." *Not like you.*

Medusa's stare hardens.

The rich kid rolls his eyes. "Right. You're Saint Teresa come to life."

"Look, I don't care what you all think you're doing, taking the *Goose* on this little jaunt. I just want to get back to Earth. That's all."

The boy in the pilot's seat turns fully around to face her, almost making Medusa lose her hold.

"Elio!" the girl yelps.

He grabs her arm and holds on. Their wide mouths and warm skin tones mark them as siblings.

Elio says, "The only way back to Earth is through the airlock."

"Not true," Sol replies. "There are three escape pods. I can just …"

"No. We aren't losing an escape pod so you can head to the nearest police station and report us. Forget it."

The others nod.

Great job negotiating, Sol. She worries her crucifix with a thumb.

The caramel-haired girl sucks in a breath, then expels it like she's searching for equilibrium. The air pulses, thick with tension. "Look, my name is Clera. My brother is Elio, as you probably caught. She's Mila, and that's Juke." She nods toward the others in turn. "First off, we won't be headed back to Earth, maybe ever. Second, we don't know you and don't trust you, which leaves us at an impasse. We have several hours before we arrive at the U.S. Space Station, and in that short time, we have to figure out what to do with you for *all* our sakes. I'm asking you to go sit in one of the cabins while we do that."

The word *but* hovers on Sol's lips. Instead, she blurts, "How do you know I won't just steal an escape pod on the way past them?"

Juke's long fingers drum across the co-pilot console. "There." He leans back in his chair and eyes her sideways with sharp, bright eyes. "Thanks for the heads up. I've just disabled them."

Stupid. Why didn't you take a pod in the first place, idiot? Were you really that curious to find out who'd ruined your life?

Clera continues in an annoyingly calm voice, "You'll go into the first cabin on the left and close the door so we can consult up here in private. I'll come find you when we've decided what to do. Look, we aren't your enemy. We don't want trouble, but you've put us in a bind." Her expression softens into a pleading look. "Please, Solast."

"It's Sol," Sol snaps. She clamps down on the inside of her cheek while her brain scrambles to catch up to the situation. Do these young people really think they're going to be received with open arms at the U.S. Space

Station? They won't be. All of them will be arrested. She will, too, unless they have some plan she doesn't know about. They've gotten this far, so maybe they do? Otherwise, everyone aboard the *Goose* is cooked.

"Fine," she spits out. "I'll wait below."

2

Clera

For a minute, no one says anything. They watch Sol until the stowaway disappears down the stairway. Clera holds up a hand and counts to one hundred in her head, then asks, "Juke, is there a way to tell if Sol's where I told her to be?"

"Um." He leans forward and studies various screens. He flips a switch and speaks into a mic. "Sol?"

After a pause, one sharp syllable pings back. "Yes?"

"Lock her in," Clera mutters.

Juke taps on another screen. "Done."

Clera releases a held breath.

Her brother Elio whistles low between his teeth. "She's going to be pretty mad."

Clera shrugs.

For a single moment, life was good. She and Elio had escaped the gang, Second City, which had dragged her brother into its war with the Steelheads. She'd bribed him out of jail, then had the brilliant idea to steal NASA's prototype solar shuttle when the ship they originally planned for their escape from New Chicago crashed. To fulfill their dream of a new life far from planet Earth, Juke hacked them into the starship *Calliope*'s manifest, and they were cleared to dock at one of her last berths and join a group of two thousand pioneers headed through a Martian-made wormhole called the ARH. Beyond that lay a new solar system and an unspoiled, Earth-like planet.

Vishnu, with its green oceans and lush landscapes, awaited them along with a new life. Elio's Arcade training on the shuttle sims would ensure they reached the U.S. Space Station where *Calliope* was docked safely. And perhaps his aviation skills would secure him work in the security and defense division aboard the starship. Mila, with her mechanical prowess, would obviously join a maintenance crew. Hopefully, Juke could find work in the tech department, and Clera? Well, they'd called her their leader, and she *had* come up with the plan to steal the prototype, but ...

She shakes off this thought. Somehow, she'll prove herself useful. Her work at Fadel Arboretum and Greenhouses didn't last long but might secure her a place on *Calliope*. Zavi Fadel was kind to get her that job. Clera's heart constricts. Such thoughts veer into dangerous territory, especially since Zavi was hired as the director of *Calliope*'s Biosphere. If anything, she and Elio must avoid him once they board the starship. He thinks they're still on Earth, and he knows she's just a Slummer, not some rich exec able to afford this trip. He'll realize they stole the museum's shuttle and might turn them in. She can't risk that possibility.

Clera realizes the others are staring at her as if for answers. She clears her throat. "Well, obviously we shouldn't throw this Sol person out of an airlock."

Mila crosses her arms. "We can't trust her. Did you notice how she's dressed? Like some Second City gangster. Where did she get that scar, I wonder? And why shave her head?"

"Hey, now," Juke interrupts. "Maybe she favors girls. Nothing wrong with that, darling."

The others roll their eyes. Clera still isn't used to Juke's flamboyant, over-the-top comments, though without his exceptional tech skills, none of them would be here. Despite his young age, Juke's a genius with computers. She turns to her brother. "What do you think?"

Elio frowns at her. He's grown so much in the last year that he hardly resembles the boy who once snuggled with her to read stories. "She's a problem we have to solve quickly. We can't trust her, but we can't kill her or lock her up permanently, either. At least, *I* think that would be cruel. Plus, we'll be on *Calliope* in a few hours."

"Right." Clera pushes a strand of floating hair away from her face. "And only four of us are expected, not five."

"There's nothing for it." Juke sighs. "I'll have to add her to the manifest."

Clera asks, "Won't that seem odd to the crew on the starship? To add someone when the shuttle is already out of atmo?"

Juke shrugs and taps agile fingers on his leather seat rest. "Depends. It's quite possible that Command has bigger fish to fry than worrying about the passenger list for a single shuttle."

A ball of worry expands in Clera's stomach. "We're already taking risks just flying NASA's solar prototype anywhere near *Calliope*. She *will* stick out. Hopefully, that tractor beam can suck her into our berth before anyone glances out a viewport and notices those distinctive solar panels."

Juke scoffs, "You all worry too much. Our ship is a speck in the black. With all the drones and other craft flying about, no one will notice."

Clera scans her crew: Elio, their pilot, Mila, the mechanic, and Juke, the teenage tech wizard. She has faith in their ability to trick their way aboard the colonists' transport. Clera nods to herself. "You're right. We always knew there would be risks, but we've already made it farther than we thought we could. Our stowaway puts a wrench in the plan, but we can deal with her. Maybe she'll even prove useful if she really has nursing experience."

Mila snorts. "She doesn't look like any nurse I ever went to."

Clera reminds her, "Sol said she's been on the streets for a couple of years, which means cleanliness and flashy clothes weren't high on her agenda."

"Well, I don't trust her." Mila, always forthright, scowls.

"No one does, pumpkin." Juke pats her shoulder. He might be the only person who can get away with showering such endearments on Mila, but then, they've known each other for a long time.

Clera reasserts herself into the conversation. "No one has to trust her. If we're lucky, we can dump her at the space station, and she can catch some NASA flight back to Earth." She considers this, then admits, "I doubt NASA will go for that, though. Plus, dealing with the station attracts attention to us, something we absolutely can't do. So it's more likely our unwilling guest will be with us for at least seven months, until we arrive at Mars." She pauses to let the others digest this. By their alarmed looks, she knows they hadn't yet realized Sol might be a long-term problem.

Her brother growls, "Well, hells. And things were going so well for about ten minutes."

"Right." Juke claps his hands. "We'd better get to know this woman, lay down some ground rules, get our story straight before we set sail across the black."

Again, they're all looking at Clera. She sighs. "Fine. I'll talk to her, try to feel her out, set down some rules and red lines, and tell her if she messes up, we'll have to reconsider the airlock idea." Clera bites her lip. "Which would be a bluff." She eyes her brother sternly. "And I'll be sure to explain that it's to her advantage as much as ours not to draw attention to the '*Blue Goose*,' as she calls it."

"The name *is* kind of catchy." Juke shrugs.

Mila snorts again.

Elio grins, breaking the tension. "If anyone can negotiate with a stowaway, it's you, sister. Mila will just piss her off, I'll lose my temper, and Juke will probably proposition her." His smile fades. "But someone should go down with you. What if she attacks you? Holds you hostage?"

"I'll just talk to her through the locked door."

Elio nods. "Well, be careful anyway. Don't let her trick you."

"Right." Clera wants to savor his concern, but there's no time. She addresses Juke. "Get her added to the manifest quickly, and let me know if you have problems."

"Uh, what was our nurse-turned-gangster-turned-stowaway's full name again?"

"Solast Bahri. B-A-H-R-I, I suppose?"

"Weird first name," Mila murmurs, obviously determined not to like their newest problem.

Juke turns back to his console and starts typing. "I'll just call her Sol Jones. Easier to spell."

Clera regards Mila with thin-pressed lips. "You and this Sol person aren't going to be a problem, are you?"

"Big ship, isn't it? I'll just stay down on green deck, lounging by the pool, while you all deal with our visitor."

"Haha," Elio smirks. "Am I invited? Sounds like a great place for a tryst."

Mila catapults herself onto his lap, and he plants a long kiss on her lips.

Clera grimaces. "Do you two mind? I still haven't gotten used to my little brother having a girlfriend, and you're supposed to be flying a ship right now, Elio."

He snuggles Mila against his chest. "Hey, I put in the coordinates. There isn't much else to do."

"Well, watch for stray asteroids or space junk." Clera swirls a hand in the air.

Mila and Elio laugh, then look at her like they're waiting for something. She shakes off her reluctance for the task ahead. Time to confront the stowaway. Clera pulls herself from handhold to handhold until she reaches the stairway. Laughter follows her awkward descent down to the main level.

This is ridiculous, Clera thinks as she misses a railing and careens into the couch in the commons area. The shuttle *should* come equipped with gravity boots. She hopes NASA stocked it with basic equipment even though it was only on loan as a promotional centerpiece for the museum, not as a craft prepped to fly into outer space. After a lot of bumping around and hauling herself along handrails, she finds what she's looking for in a set of lockers just inside the engine room. Beneath sleek, microfiber spacesuits, rows of helmets, and face masks, pairs of identical black boots line up with toes pointing toward the wall.

Clera checks the bottom of one boot to make sure they really are magnetic, and her spirits lift when her guess proves correct. She awkwardly slips her feet into a pair. The footwear feels two sizes too big, but at least the boots pull her feet flat against the metal walkway. Red buttons adorn the sides. Pressing them causes inner padding to inflate and cocoon her feet. The boots are still too long, but she can't slide around inside them.

She practices walking. It's like wading through sticky syrup, a slow process yet better than bouncing off walls. Pushing her toes against the top of her boot makes the magnets click off. Bearing down makes them reengage. Clera takes three pairs of footwear to the base of the stairway. Laughter drifts above her. She smiles and sets the boots down, not letting loose until pressure activates the magnets. Let the others make their way to them like she had to.

Next, she removes her go-bag from the cargo hold and chooses a cabin. She tucks the bag into the single cabinet, rummages for a hair tie, and secures her hair in a ponytail. Clera glances around curiously. She only had a brief look at the cabins during their self-guided tour a few hours ago. Can so little time have passed? She frowns and clomps to a porthole so she can stare outside. Earth isn't visible, just a swath of stars—a million tiny penlights pointing the way through the black.

Besides the cabinet, her room contains a bolted-down desk, chair, and bunk with additional straps to secure her during sleep. That's about it. Not much of a home, but better than some she's had. A vision of the abandoned apartment building she and Elio lived in flashes before her eyes. Rat droppings, dust, hanging wires, and that saggy bed ... This is an improvement, though she misses her adopted stray cat, Duro. Petting his soft fur had settled the panic that used to consume her.

But I'm better now, Clera tells herself. *Not a coward. Not someone who hides in her novels while real life passes her by.*

She gathers another pair of grav boots and approaches the locked cabin door next to hers. Clera firms her shoulders and knocks.

After a moment of silence, a muffled voice says, "Come."

"I can't. Juke locked you in."

The mumbled reply sounds like a curse.

"You'll have to speak louder."

Sol's annoyed tones drift through the polymer panel. "This is stupid. Just unlock the feccing thing and come in."

"My brother thought you might take me hostage. Or, I don't know, murder me."

"Well, I won't."

Clera stares at the door. Sol is right. If they're going to live together for months, they need to trust that their stowaway won't harm them. Once they dock with Calliope, will keeping her locked up even be practical? "Promise me you won't hurt me or try to leave."

"Where would I go?" comes the grumpy reply, followed by a sigh. "Sure, I promise. I was a nurse, for fec's sake. I *healed* people. I didn't murder them."

Clera taps a message to Juke on her Skinpad and waits. She imagines the crew consulting or maybe sending down backup, but no one appears. The lock clicks, and a message pings. It's from Elio.

Tell the stowaway that if she harms you, I *am* throwing her out the airlock.

Clera punches the open button, and the door slides into the wall, whooshing shut after she steps in. Sol lies strapped in on the bunk, arms pillowing her head. Her eyes find Clera, but she doesn't move. Clera holds out the extra pair of grav boots. "I discovered these in engineering."

Interest sparks in the woman's eyes before she represses it.

Clera hands her the boots. "They'll adjust to your foot size."

Cautiously, Sol sits up. She manages to release the bed straps and propel her feet inside the grav boots.

"Push that button on the side if they're too big."

Sol does so, and her eyes widen. She plants her feet on the metallic floor and turns to face Clera. "Thank you."

Encouraged, Clera sits on the one chair and nods.

She's still wondering what to say when Sol asks, "Clera, right?"

"Clera Diaz." Clera tucks her palms beneath her thighs and swallows.

"So, can we agree that I have just as much right to this ship as you do?" Tension radiates through Sol's clipped words.

Clera doesn't reply immediately. She studies the older woman, who must be thirty-ish? Though sometimes street people look older than they really are. A pink scar runs beneath Sol's left eye almost to her mouth. Otherwise, she appears unmarked. She's too thin, but if she grew her hair out and cleaned up, she might be pretty. Those almond-shaped eyes indicate Asian blood, and her skin tone is just a shade darker than Clera's. "How long have you been living on the prototype? What's your story?"

Sol blinks, and her shoulders relax an inch.

She was expecting an ultimatum or threats right off, but I've given her a chance instead. Clera remains still, like she would with a wild animal. No sudden moves.

After a pause, Sol says, "I was born a Slummer to factory workers. My father and I left New Chicago when I was ten and lived in a commune in the Barrens. I trained to be a midwife there, but after my father died, I returned to the city and worked for the execs in the sewers until I got a better job at a public clinic. Then it closed, like I already said."

Did her voice tremble on those words, *my father died*? Clera admits, "My brother Elio worked for the execs, too. He said it was horrible."

A brief nod.

"How old were you when you returned to New Chicago?"

"Twenty."

"And now you are ..."

"Twenty-eight. Why? Is this ship only for teenagers now? Is stealing the *Goose* some crazy stunt by a bunch of kids playing grown-up?"

"What? No!" Clera shakes her head vehemently. "We're more like you than you know. Elio and I were Slummers, too. These Skinpads"—she holds up her arm, "—are brand new. Juke said *Calliope* would never let us stay without them. The colonists would know we were low class." She juts her chin. "We're joining the pioneers headed to Vishnu."

"So, you're a bunch of dreamers hoping for adventure. New planet. New lives. Just like the old ones never happened."

"Sort of. But, well, no! Obviously, the old ones did happen. And what's wrong with wanting something better?" Clera grinds her teeth, then forces herself to relax. "Elio and I were left homeless not very long ago. Leth suppliers accidentally blew up their lab and our apartment along with it. Our mother was killed in the explosion, and we found ourselves on the streets. I know what being homeless feels like. So does Elio. But since then, we've pulled ourselves out of the gutter and made friends who've helped us."

"Helped you steal a shuttle."

"Normally, I'm not a thief, but we had to get away from the Second City gang. Elio got mixed up in—never mind. It's not important. Mila was a mechanic at the aerospace museum and knew about the shuttle. Juke is the hacker who just added you to our manifest, hopefully without the crew aboard *Calliope* noticing."

Sol's eyes narrow. "Why would you add my name to your crew?"

Clera raises her eyebrows. "What else were we going to do? We can't show up at the starship with an extra person on board. It would attract too much attention. Someone might start asking questions about the rest of us. We're heading to Mars, and from there we're going through the wormhole to Vishnu."

"But I can't go to Mars, let alone some far-off solar system! I have to get back to Earth. There are important things to do there."

"Like what?"

Clera's honest curiosity must sound like doubt because Sol's back goes rigid. "None of your business," she snaps.

"How are you going to hitch a ride home? Ask NASA to take you back when we reach the space station? Just walk up to an astronaut and say, 'Hey, I accidentally stowed away on a shuttle that just docked on *Calliope*. Could you give me a lift back to Earth?'"

Sol's sulks, "I was in the middle of concocting a story when you barged in."

Clera reaches for patience. "Look, if you just stay with us until Mars, there are a couple of communities there. Work. A new life. And if you still want to go home so you can accomplish this thing that's so important, you can save money for a berth on a flight back. I don't suppose those happen every day, but people *do* go back. It's not like the old days when a trip to the red planet was a one-way ticket."

Sol bites her lip. "How long?"

"Juke thinks about seven months to reach Mars. I don't know how long you'd have to work to earn enough credits for a return trip. But I do know that the underground city of Arsia Mons is almost complete, and there are lots of job opportunities there."

"So why aren't you and your friends staying? Why trust some old Martians to make a wormhole that's safe for space travel and won't kill you before you can settle on Vishnu? The first ship that tried that was never heard from again, right?"

Clera squirms. "Communications don't seem to work outside our solar system, so no one knows what happened to *Loki* or *Lycka*, the Swedish ship that just passed through the ARH. But probes came back, and they brought plenty of encouraging information about Vishnu."

Sol snorts and rubs her arms. It's a nervous gesture, and Clera guesses she isn't as sure of herself as she makes out.

"Look, if you don't want to be stuck on Mars for years while you arrange a berth home, maybe Juke can help you out. Unlike the rest of us, he's a rich kid. His parents run a super church, and his allowance plus the credits he makes hiring out his computer skills have made him pretty flush."

"Why is he leaving Earth, then? Sounds like a lux deal."

"Not everyone is concerned only with credits. I don't know much, just that he wasn't happy living with his parents. Maybe his reasons for running away aren't so different than yours for going back. You're on a mission to what? Change something in your life that can only be fixed on Earth?"

"Something like that." Sol glares at her.

"Okay, then. Become part of our crew until Mars. When it's safe, we'll help you get back to New Chicago." Clera doesn't know if she can keep such a promise, but she hopes so.

"What makes you think you won't be caught as soon as you dock with *Calliope* in your stolen shuttle?"

"Juke's fixed things so we won't." Clera hopes she projects more confidence than she feels.

"And you trust him?"

Without hesitation, Clera answers, "Yes, I do." It's one of her better lies. She looks Sol in the eye and hopes her brother's flashy friend—a high school kid she's only known for a few days—*is* trustworthy.

"Fine. I won't give you away."

Clera ducks her head to hide her relief. Then she rises and walks toward the door, pausing a few steps away to regard Sol with crossed arms.

She opens her mouth to speak, but Sol jumps in first. "I have some rules to lay down if we're going to be flight-mates for seven months. First, I want this cabin all to myself, and no one barges in without knocking. Second, I don't like being told what to do by a bunch of kids."

"I'm twenty-one, and so is Mila. No one ..."

Sol speaks over her. "And third, I'm willing to carry my weight, but you don't get to ask questions I don't want to answer."

"Fine. But we have rules, too. No fighting, drugs, or any sort of violence will be permitted on the shuttle. Just like us, you aren't allowed to enter any cabin except your own, and no stealing. Finally, unless the authorities confiscate this ship, she's mine and my crew's now. Not yours. No one takes orders from you."

Sol gets up and approaches Clera, two inches taller and perfectly positioned to take her hostage and strike a more advantageous deal with the others. Clera glares at the other woman and tries to hide her unease.

But Sol simply holds out a hand. After a moment of hesitation, Clera shakes it. "One last thing," the older woman adds, her grip tightening. "We quit calling this boat the 'prototype.' She's the *Blue Goose*, and that's final."

Clera huffs out a surprised laugh. "Fine, then."

"Tell the others." Sol releases her.

Clera steps back. The cabin feels too small to hold them both. Solast Bahri's anger fills all the space, but it's not directed at her. More at ... circumstances. Maybe they'll even be friends once Sol comes to terms with her new situation. She's full of contradictions yet not dangerous, Clera senses. A softer version of their new crewmate chose that silly name for the shuttle. A more vulnerable Sol survived the Barrens and the death of a parent. And was she really trained as a midwife? There's much more to the stowaway than what shows on the surface, and Clera's curious. If all goes well, she has seven long months to navigate this prickly woman and possibly, just possibly, make her a real part of their crew.

At the door, she glances back at Sol. "You know, once you have time to think, what seems like a disaster now might look differently. You were hiding out in a shuttle, homeless and, I'd guess, down to your last credit.

Whatever ties you to Earth—maybe it's time to let go. Your life lies ahead of you, not in the past. That's the lesson I had to learn."

Clera exits the tiny cabin before Sol can argue. Her hands shake from the encounter. She leans against the wall until the trembling eases. She isn't used to dealing with conflict, but she'd better *get* accustomed to it since the others seem to think she's their captain. Fingers crossed—Elio, Mila, and Juke will approve of the deal with Sol. If not, they're welcome to take a turn at negotiating. With a heartfelt exhale, Clera makes her way back to the bridge.

3

Solast

Sol wipes furious tears from her cheeks. How has she been reduced to a blubbering mess when just days ago she'd been so optimistic? In a stroke of luck, she'd discovered Anton's whereabouts at the bar, Smoke and Blues. If only she'd taken her chance with him then, not waited. Regret tangles with anger, and her stomach roils like a simmering stewpot. When was the last time she felt at peace? Happy? Despite what Clera says, moving on isn't an option. Sol will never find peace and joy until the man who murdered her father has disappeared permanently.

She doesn't want to think of Anton or the past, but her mind has other ideas ...

Things hadn't been going well since the last contagion. Her father, Ridge Bahri, sickened but recovered, though a stubborn cough persisted. Soon after, he began sharing his dissatisfaction with Anton's leadership. *Our leader speaks of equality for all, then takes extra for himself. He speaks of saving Earth, then hunts in the off-season and leaves a motherless fawn to die."* Before long, Father's opinions became her own.

She'd been fifteen then, practically an adult by the commune's standards. Anton began training her and other teens in martial arts, shooting, and hand-to-hand combat. Soon after, the group's midwife, Cress, took Sol on as an apprentice. Sol loved foraging for medicinal herbs, binding small wounds, and delivering babies, but she worried Father's break with the commune might morph into something more dangerous. Her philosophy was to lay low. She didn't trust Ridge Bahri to share that sentiment.

When Cress died from an infection, Sol took over her work. Meanwhile, Father sank into depression. He didn't have an outlet like she did. Misery not tempered by satisfying work increased his disillusionment with the Earthers and came to a head that fateful day she turned seventeen.

They'd been sitting at a communal table with the others. It was Feast Day, but grasshoppers and drought had plagued the harvest. Still, Anton stood and toasted everyone with the moonshine he distilled behind his house. "The earth belongs to the earth! She gives what she will, and on this day, we show gratitude for it!"

Sol's father straightened. His fists clenched, opened, clenched again. Finally, he rose and spread his palms across the oaken planks. "Gratitude for what?" He swept an arm to indicate the meager foods spread before them. A couple of women jumped up and scurried away, sensing trouble. Sol caught her father's arm, but he shook her off.

He drew a shuddery breath, voice strengthening. "This is no feast. You are no leader. Spurning all technology has led us to spurn ourselves!" His gaze swept the thirty or so people left at the table before returning to Anton. "Your misplaced beliefs have led us to live like animals in the wilds. Once I believed in the Earther cause, but now I see how naive I was. *We* were. Your family toils endlessly for you, Anton, and you take more than your share. There is no equality in this camp." He addressed the others again. "Look inside your leader's house. You'll see an excess of meat there! And a solar heater manufactured in New Chicago's factories!"

Anton nodded to several of his men, who edged toward her father. Sol tugged on his arm, but he paid no heed to her or the guards closing in on him. His face twisted into something unrecognizable. Fear cramped Sol's stomach, yet she stood up, too, and palmed a paring knife from her healer's belt. Ridge Bahri raised a fist and slammed it down, then stepped away from the bench. He stomped toward Anton, and she followed on his heels. Sol doubted Father even remembered she was there. His glazed eyes saw nothing but injustice. No one but Anton Cheverra.

The men grabbed her father's arms and thrust her away. They accompanied him to the head of the table and left her forgotten. No one saw the threat in her.

Anton's goons positioned her father before the Earther leader. Father didn't even struggle, just stood tall and indomitable in front of the man they'd known was dangerous for a long time. Not a messiah but a thug with a silver tongue. *Step in! Say something to save him!*

Before words could form, Anton bellowed, "How dare you betray me? Betray these people?" He whipped a hunting dagger from the leather sheath at his side. The rage in his voice stunned Sol into silence. *Our leader's true self emerges at last.*

Anton's jaw worked. His eyes turned into bits of obsidian. The blade flicked out, winking in the sun. It swept toward her father and slashed sideways. Blood bubbled across Ridge's neck. He put a hand against the gash, and crimson gushed between his fingers.

Sol gasped, her world collapsing. Father swayed, tilted, surrendered to gravity—felled like an axe-severed tree. The men holding him drew back. They stood ten feet away, equidistant from Anton. Sol raised her knife and hurled it. The blade thudded into Anton's shoulder, and a dark circle bloomed across his shirt. His eyes widened in surprise.

What have I done? Yet the sight filled Sol with dull satisfaction.

Her father choked out, *"Run!"* His last word to her.

She hesitated.

Anton bounded forward, bloody knife held aloft. He reached her before the stunned guards could react. Fingers clutched her sleeve. His weapon was a blur of steel filling her vision. Fire seared her cheek as she twisted away and left Anton holding an empty jacket.

She'd wanted to stay. Fight. Protect her dying father somehow. *Save him!* But Sol fled into the woods.

More reaching fingers, the guards this time. They'd waited a moment too long to assist Anton. Now they couldn't catch her. Sol was a monkey. A breath of wind. A wraith. Skinny but quick. And Anton was injured.

Hands clutched at her, but she dodged and squirmed and slipped through the noose. Sol darted into the woods, weaving between tree trunks and pumping her arms. Her legs were long as a man's, frame much lighter, muscles toned. Eventually, the sounds of pursuit faded. Sol hid deep in a thicket that night and tended the gash on her face. An inch higher, and she'd have lost an eye.

Sol comes back to the present. Fleeing saved her life, but she can't forgive herself for abandoning her father even though logic tells her he was already a dead man. She couldn't have beaten Anton. He was more experienced in combat and twice her weight. Rationalization doesn't soothe the guilt, though, just fuels her desire for revenge. Anton stole the last of her family, and now she'll steal what matters most to him. Not the Earth, but himself.

The memory cuts like a fresh wound. She refuses to forget even though remembering hurts. Without her thirst for revenge, why go on? She never planned to start a family or reach old age. Even her dream of becoming a healer has faded.

The grav boots feel like weights dragging her down, but they allow controlled movement. She practices walking around the tiny cabin while she thinks about her conversation with Clera. In another life, perhaps they'd have been friends, but not in this one. Her deal with the "captain" is a means to an end, a way to lull these thieves into letting down their defenses. Once the *Goose* reaches the U.S. Space Station, she's gone.

No way is Sol traveling clear to Mars. By the time she got back to Earth—if ever—who knew where Anton might be?

For the moment, she needs these criminals. Even she can see the importance of docking on the starship as a crew member, not a stowaway. Hopefully, the slick-haired kid can make that happen. He doesn't look like an experienced tech genius, but she doesn't resemble a trained nurse, either.

Sol glances down at her outfit and wrinkles her lip. Where did Clera say she found the boots? In the engine room? Maybe Sol can snag a change of clothing there. She peers into the corridor, finds it empty, and steps out of the cabin. The shuttle hums like a living thing, and she's glad it got to fly—if only it hadn't taken her with it.

Lockers line the left side of engineering. Machinery and piping fill the rest. One storage unit reveals padded spacesuits obviously meant for spacewalks, not navigating the interior of the shuttle. A second locker contains grav boots, a rack of helmets and gas masks, and more suits, but these are made of some clingy black material similar to gymnast leotards.

Sol finds suits to fit her lanky frame. The NASA emblem decorates the right breast, and tugging to remove it doesn't work. Sol shrugs. She'd better tell those kids on the bridge to get changed so they don't give away who they really are.

4

Clera

Clera edges around the boots she left sitting on the stairs and climbs. Voices float into the stairway. Elio sounds defensive. "... can do it! Clera might look puny, but she's got a backbone."

Mila argues, "This scrull isn't the kind of person she's dealt with before, Elio. Did you see the look in her eyes? She's been through things the rest of us can't imagine." He starts to argue. She overrides him. "I know you were Slummers who lived on the streets, but only for months. Sol has been out there for years, and before that, the Barrens. Who comes back from that? I'm telling you that our stowaway is a killer. She'll say what she has to in order to survive, then stab us in the back."

Juke chimes in, "It's nothing against Clera, hom. Just facts. People from the Barrens are worse than gang members, so I've heard. It's survival of the fittest out there. You learn to be vicious, or you die."

Clera clunks onto the bridge. Three heads swivel at the racket. All her crew remain just where she left them.

"Whoa, girl," Juke whistles. "That's some fancy footwear."

She walks toward them to exclamations of "Grav boots!" and "Where did you find them?"

"They were in the engineering lockers. There's clothing there, too, and we're going to need it. Elio and I don't look like space travelers in our jeans and tees."

"I hadn't thought of that," Mila admits, frowning down at her work clothes. Of all of them, she appears most like what she is, an aeronautic mechanic. Clera wonders if billionaires like Dec Gaston, the guy who sponsored the shuttle lottery Elio hoped to win, will shed their silk suits for spacewear. Even if they don't, Juke might pass muster, but she and her brother won't.

Juke says, "*Calliope* doesn't seem to have noticed that I added Sol to the manifest, so maybe we're okay. ETA to meeting up is an hour or so. I agree with Clera. We'd better change into those fancy boots and find spaceman clothes to match."

"Not so fast," Mila objects. "First, I want to know how your meeting with Sol went, Clera."

Mila will be hardest to convince Clera made a trustworthy deal with Sol. Clera maneuvers closer, frowning. "Our stowaway really wants to return to Earth, though I can't imagine why. And yes, I tried to pry it out of her, but she's not easy to talk to."

"No doubt," Elio half-laughs. "Still, did she see reason, or are we going to have to throw her outside?" He sounds almost serious.

Clera hesitates. Can they trust Sol? "I think I convinced her that it's in no one's interest to get noticed. Contacting some official about hitching a ride home will really raise eyebrows since some colonists waited years for approval to come on this trip."

"Good. Good." Juke rubs his hands together.

"And I laid down a few basic rules about privacy, stealing, and being a team player." Clera pauses, then reluctantly adds, "Sol laid down a few rules of her own, too, mostly that we respect her privacy. Oh, and she wants us to call the ship the *Blue Goose*."

This last statement raises a chorus of protests from the guys. Elio scoffs, "Sounds like some children's fable. How are we supposed to be taken seriously with a name like that?"

Clera replies, "The ship has some scientific identifier, doesn't it? That's all *Calliope* will recognize. The *Blue Goose* is just what we'll say among ourselves. It's an easy compromise that doesn't hurt anyone."

Surprisingly, Mila chimes in, "She's right. And I like it. Makes this boat feel kind of homey, you know?"

Clera expected more of a fight from their opinionated mechanic. She rushes on, "Once we reach Mars, Sol is determined to leave us and somehow find a ride back to Earth. I promised her we could make that happen."

The others hate this idea. "How are *you* going to do that exactly?" Elio asks.

"I don't know how *we* are doing it, but we'll have seven months to make a plan."

"So, basically you lied to her." Mila smiles.

"Well, yes."

Elio rises but keeps a hold on Mila when she starts to float off. "Nice job, sister. I didn't know you had it in you to fib. Now let's go find us some proper clothing. I'm itching to get into a pair of those grav boots so I can look like a proper spaceman."

Juke grunts, "Not me. I have a feeling no one will recognize me without my swank wardrobe."

"I wouldn't worry," Mila tells him. "Even without posh clothes, your personality would shine through."

The others discard their shoes for the grav boots Clera left them, and she shows them how to adjust sizing. Once they reach engineering, she finds the black jumpsuits. They change, secure their old clothes and shoes in the lockers, and stuff their feet back into the boots. Mila glances down at the NASA emblem. "What about this?"

Elio pulls a pocketknife from the jeans he discarded and carefully cuts the threads holding their patches on. Clera does the same for his suit, then collects all the emblems and old clothing. "These are going into the disposal bin. I've thought about it, and we need to get rid of anything that ties us to our old lives."

"But Clera!" Juke objects.

Elio tells him, "You're a spaceman now. Embrace it. Personally, I'm looking forward to saying goodbye to Mila's baggy work clothes. I like the new ones much better."

She slugs his arm but grins.

Clera finds the incinerator and recycling bins in the kitchen area while the others choose cabins and rush to unpack crates and boxes. She doesn't encounter Sol, and no one speaks of her as they make their way back and forth down the hallway. Juke returns to the bridge to monitor the *Goose*'s progress, Mila disappears into the engine room, and for a moment, Clera and her brother are left alone next to an open kitchen cabinet Elio just stocked with canned ravioli and crackers. Netting attached to the shelves holds everything in place.

"Seems like we brought the wrong sort of food," her brother says. "Don't spacemen eat packets of liquid goo or something?"

Clera shrugs. She leans against the counter and folds her arms. "Weird, isn't it, that it was just you and me for months, and now, suddenly—" She can't finish. She smiles almost wistfully.

Elio searches her face. "You know Mila will never replace you, right? What I have with her is different than what you and me have. We've been family for two decades. We know things about each other no one else will ever know. Nothing can break that bond."

"You're right, Elio. It's still you and me against the world. That world has gotten bigger, sure, but so has our family."

"You mean Juke and Mila?"

"Maybe even Sol, someday. Providing we can convince her we aren't the enemy. If she really has medical skills, she might prove useful."

"Hmph. Good luck cracking that nut. I just hope she doesn't murder us in our sleep."

Loud footsteps interrupt their conversation, and Sol steps into the commons area. Clera thinks, *No one is going to be sneaking up on anyone on this boat. How much of what we just said did she hear?*

Elio nudges Clera and nods to Sol's jumpsuit.

Clera beckons her closer. "Glad you found the suits. We're dumping anything from our old lives into the bin. Elio can remove the NASA patch with his pocketknife."

"I already thought of that," Sol answers. "While you were busy, I threw my old things into the recycler. There wasn't much."

Elio squints. "What's that around your neck?"

Clera studies the thin silver chain and dangling crucifix. Her Grandma Buela wore something similar.

Sol rubs two fingers across the shiny metal. "It's just a cross. I'm not throwing it out, so don't ask."

Elio holds up his hands and looks to Clera.

She shrugs. "Is it anything someone could use to tie you to your old life?"

Sol looks down and doesn't answer immediately. "Once, maybe," she mutters. She tucks the cross under her suit, and her voice resumes its already familiar husky tone. "But not for a long time. The crucifix won't give us away."

Clera nods slowly. Did she just witness Sol without her armor? Only for a couple of seconds, yet it's a start.

Juke's voice floats out of an intercom. "Hey, people. You'd better get up here pronto."

Elio and Clera exchange looks. His face mirrors her own excitement and fear.

Sol brushes past them. "Great. Just great."

5

Clera

When he sees them, Juke slides from the pilot's chair into the co-pilot seat. Elio takes his place, and Clera and Mila stand behind him to watch a tiny dot grow through the viewing glass. Clera forgets about Sol as the speck grows into a cluster of arrays and modules. A painted American flag decorates one of the larger ones. Girders stretch from the station to the starship *Calliope*, tethered with smart clamps. The huge vessel dwarfs the station tenfold. A few workbots flit about like flies, adding finishing touches.

A shuttle drifts toward the behemoth and settles into a concave niche near *Calliope's* curved belly. From this distance, the ship reminds Clera of a giant whale. The bridge is a tiny hat atop the whale's head, while near its tail, a transparent ring rotates slowly. Four rows of tiny, circular windows stretch from bow to stern. A hangar bay yawns open like a gaping mouth below the ship's nose.

"Amazing," Juke breathes.

"Feccing hells," Sol mutters. She moves in close to view the starship and ignores the rest of the crew.

A pleasant female voice startles them. It drifts out of speakers set into the flight consoles. "Good afternoon, passengers aboard J-Bird C Class Science Vessel. Welcome to the American starship, *Calliope*. In approximately five seconds, a tractor beam will override your navigation system and pull you into berth 235 on Blue Deck. Please do not attempt to assist in this process except to retract your wings. Simply sit back and enjoy the ride. Once you have docked, remain aboard your craft until an official arrives with your welcome packet and further instructions."

"So far, so good," Elio mutters.

The ship jolts, and Clera and Mila grab onto the pilot's chair. Juke leans forward, while Sol stays near the glass, still as stone, face drawn into a grimace. They made a deal, didn't they? But can Sol be trusted? It's not too late to confine her to quarters—or is it? Clera's friends aren't fighters, nor do they possess weapons. Like *Calliope*'s AI said, this is a science vessel, not a prison ship. No, she'll just have to trust Sol to behave.

The starship grows inexorably larger until it blocks out the blackness of space in the viewscreen. Details along the hull take on definition. The concave niches become holes mostly plugged with shuttles that have already arrived. The *Blue Goose* rotates sideways. Elio does something on his console, and her wings tuck in. She glides snugly into an empty slot. There's a grating sound, a loud click, and the cessation of movement. Out the radiation-proof glass windows, pale gray walls hug their shuttle so tightly Clera doubts the *Goose*'s distinctive solar panels will show much.

She breathes out the tension of the last few days, but it comes rushing back when she glances at Sol. Despair dominates their stowaway's expression. Clera walks toward her, meaning to say something. The movement draws Sol's gaze, and a blank look slides across her face.

Before Clera can open her mouth, Juke whoops.

Elio pumps a fist in the air. "We did it!"

Mila leans down to kiss him.

Clera tells them, "We may as well go below. There's only one way out, and that's through the main hatch. I hope this 'official' comes along soon. I'm anxious."

Elio rises. "Don't worry, sister! The hardest part is over!"

They troop down to the main level, shooting wary looks at Sol, who trails them, keeping her distance. Elio, Mila, and Juke settle on couches in the commons area. Sol leans against the wall, arms folded, and Clera stands nervously, not wanting to sit, just wanting … what? To know if Zavi Fadel stands just outside in *Calliope*'s corridors without any notion that she's here? After he got her that job at his grandfather's arboretum and greenhouses, they'd become close. Not quite girlfriend and boyfriend, but definitely more than pals.

Before their relationship could blossom, Zavi's grandfather procured him the directorship of *Calliope*'s Biosphere, that rotating wheel capable of creating its own gravity and providing extra sustenance for the colonists. He couldn't pass up the promotion. She understood that. She really did. Yet part of her wondered if he'd wanted to get away from her. Especially after she'd been forced to admit Elio's and her connections to the gang, Second City.

She'd had no part in Zavi's world on Earth. Could she belong to it now? Or would he immediately report her when he discovered she'd tricked her way aboard the starship? That didn't *seem* like Zavi, but how well did she really know him? Clera couldn't take the chance. She'd followed Zavi Fadel into outer space, but he was just as unreachable here.

Clera comes back to herself, shakes off a familiar sense of loss, and moves closer to Sol. "Are you all right?"

The tall woman starts. "Why wouldn't I be?"

"I saw how you looked when the tractor beam drew us in." Clera glances at the others, but they seem occupied with each other. She closes the last steps between herself and Sol, whispering, "If you've changed your mind and plan to tell the official who's about to come knocking that you want out of this journey, forget it. Tens of thousands of people failed to secure berths on *Calliope*, and Command will know something's off if you say you made a mistake. That's bad for all of us, including you. If we get caught, you're going down with us."

"Maybe." She blinks. "Or maybe if my story's good enough, they won't believe I'm with you. They'll think I was some innocent bystander, perhaps an inspector who had too much to drink the night before and passed out in the cargo hold. Who only woke up when it was too late."

Clera hisses out a breath. "You're wrong if you think it's so easy to catch a ride from the space station. Shuttles to and from Earth are few and far between. They're reserved for scientists, not tourists. No one is going to want you along." She hopes this is true, anyway.

"Why are you such an expert?"

"I read. I read a lot." Clera hesitates. Sol's glaring at her, yet she can't help adding, "Mostly fiction, but nonfiction, too. Lately, at least."

Sol rubs her crucifix through the moisture-wicking fabric of her suit and regards Clera with an inscrutable expression. "Look, I have nothing against you kids—other than the fact that you stole my boat and forced me to go somewhere I didn't want to."

"Not your boat. Ours," Clera seethes between clenched teeth.

"Whatever." Sol shrugs. "Seven months is a long time. The year or more it might take to book passage home from Mars, then travel another seven months to get back, is *too* long."

"What's so important that you'd risk imprisonment? Because I warn you that if you attract attention to us, we will tell these officials that you're one of us. Not some drunken inspector. Not a stowaway. One. Of. Us. And which story seems more believable?"

Clanking sounds cut her off. The lights flicker. *Calliope*'s AI voice floats down to them. "You are now connected to *Calliope*. Your mooring is secure, and my life support systems have integrated with yours. Power down your shuttle if you have not already done so. An official will be arriving shortly."

Clera turns to the others. They stare back with alarmed looks that make clear the argument with Sol hasn't gone unnoticed.

Elio glances from one woman to the other. "Is everything all right?"

Clera shrugs helplessly, then blurts, "If anyone asks, Solast Bahri has been part of this crew from the start. She panicked when we left atmo, but we have full confidence that she will recover fully once she has her work assignment and becomes accustomed to her new life aboard *Calliope*. She'll be quite willing to take a psychological eval if necessary."

"Um ... okay?" Juke says.

Mila scowls. "If you blow this for us, stowaway, there won't be anywhere you can hide that I won't ..."

Sol interrupts, "... zip it, mechanic girl. You have no idea who you're dealing with. Mind your own business, all of you, and I'll mind mine."

"Clera?" Elio breaks in. "I thought you two had come to an agreement?"

"So did I. Well, I hoped, anyway." She clenches her jaw, then unclenches it. "Just do what I said, and we'll be fine whether or not Sol cooperates."

Elio heaves a sigh and rises. "I'll go up and make sure we're properly shut down and roll out the stairs for our visitor. Be right back." He casts a wary look at Sol and departs.

Clera heads to the exit hatch. A few moments later, the stairway outside rumbles down, and soon after that, a knock signals the official's arrival. Clera gathers her composure and opens the door.

Standing before her is a blue-uniformed, middle-aged man with a receding hairline. He smiles and hands her a pile of darker blue jumpsuits similar in style to the ones they're wearing. Clera moves aside so he can enter, leads him to the others in the commons area, and invites him to sit.

The man declines and pulls a tablet from his pocket. "This won't take long. My name is Jans Albright. I'm the under-steward assigned to berths 200-300 on Blue Deck. First off, which of you is the pilot of this shuttle?"

Everyone but Sol clusters around the under-steward. Elio raises his hand. Clera clasps the jumpsuits tightly to still her trembling limbs.

The under-steward ticks off their first names and positions on his tablet—including Sol's—without batting an eye. Juke listed her as a trained medic and himself as a technical specialist. He named Clera "captain," which makes her want to laugh. Or vomit. At any moment, she expects Sol to burst out with some wild plea to go home. Then Clera will have to lie again, not her best talent, and who knows …

She shakes her head, realizing she missed what this Albright guy just said.

"… synching with your Skinpads so I can download all the rules and regulations we expect you to follow aboard this vessel. There. Finished. Please review the information listed under the orientation tab."

"Will there be a test later?" Juke jokes.

Jans Albright regards him without a return smile. He runs a hand through his remaining strands of hair, clears his throat, and continues, "*Calliope* is scheduled to depart in two days. Within twenty-four hours, you'll be receiving your work assignments, which begin once the ship launches. In exchange for work, colonists receive weekly allotments of food, toiletries, and other miscellaneous items. You are expected to wear your assigned jumpsuits whenever you emerge from your shuttle. There are four decks. The top deck, White, contains the bridge and Command quarters. The next lower deck, Red, houses the armory, training gym, mechanics, medical, research, the brig, and escape pods. Your deck is Blue, the colonists' deck. Beneath you is Orange Deck, where the cargo holds, engineering, reactors, engines, cooling and recycling are situated.

"You'll find Blue Deck is arranged like a small city. The shuttles of most colonists reside here and will act like apartments. Down Blue's wide corridors you'll find such luxuries as restaurants and bars, clinics, religious spaces, classrooms, laundromats, and even a theater at the bow end."

"What about that rotating wheel aft of the ship?" Elio asks.

"Ah, yes." Albright brightens for the first time. "That is the Biosphere, and the only area aboard ship where you can dispose of those clunky grav boots in lockers and enjoy a walk among green orchards and gardens in full gravity. The Biosphere is accessible via all four decks and never closes to the public. Our chief psychologist recommends a daily dose of the parks to offset any dark moods that may result from our prolonged stay in space. And regular exercise will be essential to prevent muscle atrophy and bone deterioration. This exercise is best accomplished in the weight rooms of the Biosphere."

The man winds up his spiel with a harried sigh and wheels to depart. Clera follows him to the exit hatch, where he holds up a hand as though warding her off. "If you have questions, please refer to the orientation module on your Skinpad. Forgive me, but I'm much too busy to linger. Expect details on your job assignments by tomorrow. No credits are required for enjoyment of *Calliope*'s many amenities, only hard work." He bobs his head and eases out the door.

As she reenters the commons area, Clera hears Elio saying, "Hells. I had about a million questions." He pouts and taps his Skinpad.

She turns to Sol. "Thank you for not making a scene."

Mila says, "You see? Life aboard this boat is going to be so much better than anything you could have imagined on Earth. Just give it a chance."

Sol bites her lower lip and says nothing.

Words slip from Clera's mouth before she can think better. "Life isn't all about pleasure, though, is it? Sometimes you have to let go, no matter the cost."

Sol grunts and whirls away from them. She shoots over her shoulder, "I'll be in my cabin."

Clera watches her retreat, then sighs and tells the others, "I'll go make us a celebration dinner." *Of crackers and energy bars*, she doesn't add. *And be sure to gulp them down quickly before they float away.*

6

Solast

It's hard to pace in magnetic boots, but Sol does her best in the box-like cabin. Out the porthole, the starry expanse has been replaced by neutral gray walls. She feels trapped and curses herself for not storming after the under-steward while she had the chance. He probably wouldn't have listened anyway. Too busy. He'd said *Calliope* would depart soon. She's got precious little time to figure out a way onto the space station and beg a ride home.

Sol slumps on her bunk. Who is she kidding? She's going to Mars. *Make the best of it, Sol.* She wavers between her innate fatalism and stubbornness. The stubbornness wins out, will always win out, because who is she without that dedication to vengeance? Just a homeless Slummer without family or career, likely to die on some random street corner ... or in outer space.

A different official from the Steward's office proves this wrong the next day. He's young, has a spring in his step, and excitement rolls off him. He appeared at the hatch while everyone but Sol was eating breakfast at the galley table. She rose early and attempted to swallow food in zero-g while alone in her cabin where she couldn't be laughed at, but she emerged when she heard voices.

She rushed—well, clomped—down the hall in time to witness the young man saying to Clera and the others, "… job assignments should be showing up on your Skinpads just about … now. Keep in mind that you have one more day to orient yourself aboard *Calliope* and find where you should report after we launch. Work is a requirement. As I'm sure Mr. Albright mentioned, those who slack will lose access to amenities such as food and water. Of course, only as a last resort." He bounces on his heels and passes out electronic wristbands in varying colors. Red for Elio and Juke, orange for Mila, and a multi-colored band for Clera. Sol steps forward, and the huddle parts for her. The bouncy official smiles and hands her another red bracelet. He says, "These are your passports into any service provided aboard ship. Use them to do laundry, eat out, reserve a locker in the Biosphere, attend the theater—you get the idea. If you lose yours, fill out the replacement form on your Skinpad under 'Steward's Office,' and a new bracelet will be sent. Any questions?"

The others snap the bands around their wrists, *click, click, click* as magnetic clasps connect. Sol clenches hers in a fist while the man glances at each of them. His eyes linger on her balled hand before they slide away. He clears his throat. "Have you all read your rules and regulations packet under Orientation? If not, be sure to do so before nine a.m. tomorrow. Though our departure should prove smooth, all passengers are required to buckle in until the AI, Matilda, gives the all-clear."

"Matilda?" Elio echoes.

"The female voice you heard when you first came within beam range?" The man shrugs and looks a bit sheepish. "We call her Matilda. Bit of a joke among the officers. These AI constructs do begin to seem like old friends after a while." His eyes flash across them again, then settle on Sol.

"Keep in mind that we are a small, tight-knit community, and order must be maintained. *Calliope* does have a security division as well as a brig, not that any of you will ever see its interior, I'm sure." He grins. "Well, I must be off! Much to do today."

The man turns and exits the hatch. By the time Sol pushes past the others to follow, the under-steward has already left their berth. Sol hurries after him into a warmly lit corridor that stretches into the distance, and the door slides shut behind her. Similar doors line the right-hand side of the hallway. Red buttons glow to the left of each. A scattering of colonists amble past, dressed like clones in the blue jumpsuits and black boots.

Sol brushes into a tall man's shoulder but doesn't stop to apologize, intent on catching up to the under-steward. "Sir? Mr. Ah—Sir?" She grabs his arm.

He spins about, eyebrows raised. "Oh, it's you. Is there a question you forgot to ask?"

"I don't need a wristband. I've made a terrible mistake, and I need to get back to Earth."

His shiny face dims. "But we're launching soon. I'm sure you went to a great deal of trouble to procure your berth. Why, thousands of people weren't able to ..."

"I know all that," she interrupts. "But there's been an emergency. A—a dying relative. I can't go to Mars, after all. I'm sorry. What should I do to return home? Could you help me contact the space station? Perhaps—"

He's shaking his head. "Did you read the literature we sent before approving your passport? You signed the dotted line, so you must have. There were multiple warnings about backing out after a certain deadline, which is now well past. I suggest, as you are obviously in some distress, that you visit the mental health office on Red Deck. Counselors there can help ease your mind. A map in the *Calliope* app on your Skinpad will show the way."

"But I …"

"I really am quite busy." The man's lightbulb smile returns. He pulls away from Sol and tips his chin. "Have a wonderful day." He hurries off, punches a door code, and disappears inside a berth.

Angry tears prick Sol's eyes. She blinks them away and stares blindly at the closed door where her last hope fled. A glowing number winks at her. Berth 238.

A deep voice speaks at Sol's back. "Are you all right?"

She whirls around, a jumbled mess of emotions. She has no idea what to do.

The man before her is so tall she has to look up to meet his eyes—an unusual occurrence. He's lean, clean-cut, with brown eyes and a firm mouth. A touch of gray frosts his hair. His forehead wrinkles in concern.

Sol doesn't need this stranger's pity. She straightens her shoulders. "I *will* be all right if I can just get off this feccing ship."

He nods like he understands. "I suppose space travel isn't for everyone."

Sol expected him to tell her what a great opportunity jumping through a wormhole to an unknown solar system is, or rave about the lux life aboard ship, but he doesn't. He just stares at her as though waiting for something. That look sets her off balance. She knows she should respond, yet words fail her.

"I'm Oskar." He doesn't hold out a hand to shake, just continues to regard her with unreadable eyes.

She stares back, defiant, not giving away anything, even her name.

"If you visit the med bay on Red Deck, you can schedule an appointment to remove that scar. Everything is free here."

The suggestion startles her. She reaches up to touch the familiar curved line that stretches across her cheekbone. Who would she be without it? What would she be? "Thanks, but no thanks. I like my face just fine how it is. Excuse me."

She edges around him and continues down the hallway. Sol imagines those puppy dog eyes following her progress and sighs when she turns into a bisecting corridor.

She taps the *Calliope* app on her Skinpad and brings up a map of the ship. She orients herself, then strides off in the direction of the lifts. Identically dressed people, all as well-groomed and sparkling as Oskar, shoot curious glances her way. She guesses that scar makes her stand out. Her buzz cut can't help, either. Maybe she should take that tall man's advice.

No. Removing the scar would be like removing her father, his death, and everything he stood for. Erasing the past through plastic surgery means saying goodbye, and Sol can't do that until Ridge Bahri has been avenged.

She takes a lift to Red Deck. Crimson track lighting along the floors reminds her where she is, just as the blue lights on Blue Deck screamed, *This is home now.* She checks the map again, then navigates to the Security and Defense Headquarters, meeting hardly anyone along the way. Those people fly the shuttles, so maybe they can get her to the space station.

The lieutenant who greets her has "frown" set as his default expression. "Military shuttles aren't for civilian transport," he barks. Sol knows intractability when she sees it. Swearing beneath her breath, she turns back toward the lifts. Forget the Steward and all his underlings who are too busy to assist her. Forget the shuttle Nazi. She'll go straight to the top. When she reaches White Deck and tries to pass through a closed portal labeled "Command," however, Matilda's annoyingly calm voice informs her, "Access denied."

She remembers the wristband still clenched in her hand and reluctantly fits it around her wrist. She holds it up to a scanner next to the door, yet the voice only repeats, "Access denied."

What to do now? Sol closes her eyes and breathes long and slow, like on the training field with Anton before a fight. But she can't fight this. She retraces her steps to Blue Deck, where the Steward's Department has its office. The woman at the front desk isn't interested in her plight. She can't believe anyone would seriously want to get off *Calliope*.

Sol finds a lounge area filled with graphite-epoxy tables and chairs—attached to the floor like everything else—and sinks down far away from other occupants scanning Skinpads and sipping drinks through straws. She rests her head in her hands. A headache has formed behind her eyes. She pushes aside the pain and repeats a familiar mantra: *You'll find your way out of this. You always do.*

Only there isn't much time.

She remembers what the perky stewardling said about work assignments and taps on her Skinpad. A message from *Calliope* titled "Work Assignment" appears: **Solast Jones. You are receiving this work assignment ahead of schedule. Report to Medical Clinic 2D on Red Deck on October 31, 2073, at 11 a.m. for training as a medic.**

Jones? Not Bahri? She snorts. Juke must have concocted that fake name when he entered her into the manifest.

A thrill runs through Sol. She quickly smothers it as a betrayal to everything she's worked for since leaving the commune. But the chance to practice nursing again! To learn from these high-class doctors aboard a starship! She stops herself. *Remember your purpose. When you were young and naive, that purpose might have been to save people in the Barrens, but then everything changed. You are the angel of death, and you are coming for Anton Cheverra.*

7

Clera

Any minute, Clera expects Security to demand entrance to the *Blue Goose*. They'll ask questions like, *Why does one of your crew wish to go home? What made you decide to leave Earth? How did you obtain your berth? What connects you to each other? And wait a minute. How did you manage to afford a shuttle anyway?* None but Juke are rich, and his parents probably have an APB out on him by now.

She never should have trusted Sol. That handshake meant nothing. Clera's certain that when Sol hurried after the under-steward, she planned to beg him for help getting off *Calliope*. The others had stared after their stowaway with raised eyebrows until Juke said, "Let her go. She's got issues to work out. And if she doesn't come back?" He shrugged. "Well, it's been a bit awkward, hasn't it? Maybe she'd be happier bunking elsewhere."

Mila and Elio are so wrapped up in each other that nothing can pop their bubble of happiness. It's only Clera, aways the worrier, always expecting disaster, whose stomach ties in knots. *Please let Sol return without dragging some uniformed official with her.*

They open their job assignment messages in a moment of silence. A burst of relief replaces Clera's dismay. She's to report to the Biosphere tomorrow. Her supervisor in the Care and Harvest Division is a woman with an impossible name—Kristolin Bjorndottir. The work should be similar to what she did at Fadel Arboretum and Greenhouses.

Elio bursts out, "Yes! I'm in Defense and Security. Hope that means I'll get to fly."

Mila sneers, "They've labeled me 'Assistant Mechanic.' Bet I know more than the chief. Oh, well. At least I'll be in the right department."

"How about you?" Elio looks at Clera expectantly.

A smile breaks across her face. "Biosphere."

He starts to congratulate her, then hesitates. "Zavi Fadel is the director, right? Do you think that'll be a problem? I mean, if he starts wondering how a bunch of low-class scrulls made it onto *Calliope*?"

"I hope he won't betray us," she replies slowly. "But it might be best if I avoid running into him. The Biosphere covers all four levels, so it shouldn't be hard."

"I thought maybe you and he—" Elio falls silent. A frown crinkles his brow. "Sorry, sis. I know you really liked him."

"It's not as if our relationship would have gone anywhere with me stuck on Earth. We should all just be grateful to have decent work. Anything extra is frosting on the cake."

"That's a good attitude." Mila squeezes her shoulder.

Juke snorts, drawing their attention. Red tinges his cheeks. He bites out, "They put me with Environmental Control and Life Support. Maybe the tech department was full. Probably they have no idea about my skills since I couldn't exactly tell them when I filled out their stupid forms."

"That rots," Mila sympathizes.

Elio adds, "So you start there and transfer when an opening comes up. We've got less than a year in these jobs, anyway. After we're through the wormhole, who knows what will happen."

Clera nods. "That's right." But Juke's usually ebullient face has clouded. After an awkward silence, she adds, "I think I'll go explore the ship, maybe collect a food allotment if I can figure out where to do it."

Mila wraps an arm around Elio's waist. "Good idea, Clera. Elio and I are headed out, too. I can hardly wait to take a look at the innards of this boat."

"Nerd," Elio retorts, grinning. They exit the hatch together, and Clera turns to Juke. "Want to come along?"

He shakes his head. "Go. Don't worry about me."

She hesitates, sorry for Juke. Without him, they wouldn't be here. She wants to tell him this, to offer comfort, yet she doubts he'll accept it, so she follows the others.

The *Goose*'s steps lead down to a portal that opens onto a corridor. At the entryway, she looks over her shoulder. Glints of ceramic blue show behind her, but the berth's curved roof hides much of the prototype's distinctive solar sides. *Good.* She steps out, loving how she blends into the pedestrian traffic in her clingy blue jumpsuit. The multi-colored wristband sets her apart somewhat, but she wears it like a badge of honor. Now she understands the unique coloring, since the Biosphere opens onto all decks of the ship. Mila's orange band puts her on the lowest level in engineering, while Elio's and Juke's put them beneath the bridge on Red Deck.

And Sol? Maybe she'll get such a great assignment she'll change her mind about wanting to leave. Probably wishful thinking, yet Clera determines to set worry aside and enjoy this day. She wants to relish her new role of colonist. No one knows she used to work at the Perkine Skinpad Factory, that she schooled out at sixteen without graduating, that she was homeless for a time. No one except Zavi and her crew, that is. She can't think of Zavi without her chest pinching, so she shoves thoughts of him to the back of her mind.

The passengers wandering down the hallway come from all nationalities, and snatches of foreign tongues drift through the recycled, temperature-controlled air. No one gives her a second look as she navigates the metallic path. Blue track lighting indicates the deck level in case someone as directionally challenged as Clera forgets. She brings up *Calliope*'s map on her Skinpad and heads to the nearest market—there are several on Blue Deck. How did she ever survive without a computer glowing beneath her forearm? You didn't even need a library if you had one.

She remembers her trips to see Mrs. Moriarty at the local branch growing up, how the old books and the librarian's friendship helped her survive in a world meant to put down people like her. Such bittersweet memories carry her into the market, which is really a large alcove filled with aisles of food, mostly in pouches and freeze-dried containers, though there's a small section of fresh fruits and vegetables secured in plastic holders. *And there will be more, thanks to people like me*, she reminds herself with a smile.

Signs glowing at the end of each aisle remind shoppers of their weekly allotments. Clera gathers as much food as she can, an exorbitant amount compared to what she's used to. She nudges a hover cart to a checkout kiosk and watches the person ahead press her Skinpad against a glowing red square. A robotic voice approves the "purchase," and then it's Clera's turn.

Heart racing, she imitates the previous shopper. Will someone recognize her for the Slummer she is? The thief? But the scanning device pings, and the robotic voice tells her, "You have reached your weekly allotment, Clera Diaz. Manage food carefully so you don't run out before next week. Thank you for shopping on Blue Deck."

Well, managing won't be a problem. She's always been good at that, which is probably why the others insist on calling her their leader. Unless it's because it was her idea to steal the *Blue Goose* when their original choice, *Beatriz*, blew up.

Clera returns to the shuttle with her cart, leaves it bobbing at the bottom of the stairs while she unpacks, then pushes a button to send it floating back toward the market. Juke and Sol aren't anywhere aboard, so Clera works alone, then finishes uncrating the last bit of hastily packed luggage from Earth. This done, she stands in the commons and looks around.

Silence envelopes her. How drastically her life has changed! It's like a dream. Holding onto that thought, she sets off to further explore her new home.

Blue Deck's grid-like layout simplifies navigation even for someone like Clera. The ship smells synthetic and new. It's hard to imagine New Chicago's grit ever touching these pristine surfaces. The blue-banded colonists probably maintain the shops and entertainment kiosks, the theater and plaza-like areas. For a spaceship, *Calliope* feels surprisingly roomy. She supposes the rich taking this trip—those like billionaire Dec Gaston—would tolerate nothing less.

A crowd gathers at the theater near glitzy signs announcing showings for the week. Curious, Clera jostles among onlookers until she spots a model-thin Asian girl hanging on the arm of none other than Dec Gaston himself—founder of the Arcade franchise that gave Elio his start flying shuttles. The couple aren't dressed in blue jumpsuits but in shiny, high-class smartsuits. Clera recalls how Gaston rigged the lottery Elio had hoped to win so that Gaston's newest girlfriend, Yara Okiro, could accompany him to Vishnu.

Anger fills her, but she reminds herself it doesn't matter now. A few white-uniformed men and women armed with PulseLock guns hop off a nearby lift and head toward the crowd. She's seen similar weapons on

New Chicago's streets. The pulse technology disrupts electrical signals in the body, paralyzing victims. She shivers as the armed security forces push through the crowd. Clera falls back with the rest. The security team huddles around the billionaire and Yara. Maybe they won't get special treatment aboard *Calliope*, after all. She smirks, imagining him and his girlfriend garbed just like her. Unremarkable equals.

Clera heads back down the corridor, drifting through vast hallways until she reaches a set of bulkhead doors. "Biosphere," proclaims a sign in elegant lettering above the portal. Excitement makes her palms sweat. She scans the long list of rules looping through a vidscreen on the adjacent wall, then scans her arm and enters. *Calliope* will know she's here, how long she stays, and what sorts of activities she engages in. The ship will know if she litters, destroys the vegetation, steals an apple—not that she would.

A tube-like passage with railings curves into the Biosphere. The instructions outside called it a "transition tube" designed to gradually increase centrifugal rotation until it aligns with the Biosphere's imperceptibly spinning axis. The walls are lined with large, transparent panels that provide views into the biosphere and showcase its lush flora. By the time she steps through another set of doors into an anteroom, her body has acclimatized to gravity again. She finds she can remove her heavy grav boots and store them in one of hundreds of lockers that line the walls. She receives a receipt on her Skinpad noting her locker number. As mass reclaims her body, Clera's stomach lurches, then settles.

She steps out onto a gravel path. The man-made gravity feels a bit lighter than Earth's. One step forward carries her two feet. She leaves the ground an extra second before touching down again.

Paths wind through orchards and gardens. An advance cadre of colonists must have joined *Calliope* months ahead of launch to establish so much greenery. Two passengers play frisbee in an open field. A bell rings behind her, and she moves aside to let a hoverboarder pass. Many colonists have ventured here on this last day before work begins. Some hold hands as they stroll, while others enter and exit the extensive exercise rooms that house rowers, ellipticals, treadmills, and other devices Clera can't name.

She keeps expecting to see Zavi but never does. Relief mixes with disappointment. This place could make her forget caution. She doesn't *want* to hide anymore. Near a warehouse-like structure, chickens peck at corn kernels. Farther off, some kind of shimmery forcefield stretches between cubes set at four corners of a stand of saplings. A portable fence? Above, the projected image of the sun sinks into a clump of pink clouds. The dome looks exactly like Earth's sky. Clera gives herself over to *Calliope*'s wonders until she grows hungry enough to leave.

The others are already home by the time she arrives. Mila and Elio have cooked up a feast of freeze-dried roast, potatoes, and canned carrots contained in covered, disposable dishes. Everyone except Sol already sits around the galley table, but even the taciturn stowaway shows up as they dig into the food. Utensils seem impractical here, so they use their fingers.

Sol sits down at the far end of the table. The others eye her with mouths half-full. Clera swallows, clears her throat, and invites their new crew member to move closer.

"I'll stay where I am."

Mila frowns at Sol, picks at her potatoes, then looks toward Clera. "Thanks for getting food. Where did you explore today?"

Clera mentally thanks the mechanic for breaking an awkward moment. "The Biosphere, mostly." She cracks her container and picks out a piece of beef while Elio launches into his and Mila's adventures.

Once he pauses for breath, Clera turns to their unusually quiet hacker. "How about you?"

He shrugs. "I checked out my new workplace. It's just like I thought. I'll be crawling through vents while you all enjoy your lux assignments."

"Hey, I wouldn't call them lux," Elio protests. "Who knows? I might be assigned MP duty and be in charge of arresting you criminals when *Calliope* discovers we aren't here legally."

Clera breaks in, "Don't joke about that. It's not funny."

He only raises an eyebrow and adds in a drawn-out voice, "Sooo, did you stumble across Zavi in the Biosphere?"

"No, and I doubt I will. That place is huge."

"Still—" Elio lets the word hang.

Mila adds, "If you do come across him, you might need a story at the ready."

Clera nods. "I'll think on that." Not wanting to dwell on Zavi, she turns to Sol. "No luck on escaping from the starship?" She keeps her tone light, but Sol scowls at her anyway.

"Obviously not, and you don't need to worry that I've given us away. No official would even see me. Guess I'm stuck with you until Mars."

"Hey, we aren't so bad." Elio spreads his arms. "You'll get used to us."

"What's your assignment?" Mila asks Sol.

"Medic," she replies shortly, then goes back to eating like her last meal was a week ago.

Juke groans. "You see? Even our stowaway gets a better job than me, and you all wouldn't even be here without my brill tech skills."

"We appreciate you, hom, even if no one else does," Elio replies. "Just hang in there, alright? Things will get better. I noticed there's an Arcade down by the theater."

Clera thinks about adding that she saw Dec Gaston and his girlfriend there, then changes her mind. She doesn't want to remind her brother of that devastating moment when his dream of flying to the stars was ripped from him by the cheating billionaire. They made it here anyway, so best to move on.

By the time dinner finishes, even Juke has recovered some of his spirit. Sol's silence felt uncomfortable, but Clera can't blame her. Maybe she just needs time to adjust to her new circumstances. Clera resolves to speak to her in private, to feel out her state of mind and offer comfort if she'll take it. She doesn't trust their stowaway—not because she's rough around the edges but because she seems so unhappy. Unhappy people make rash decisions that could affect everyone on the *Goose*.

8

Solast

Sol hears her name. She thinks about pretending she didn't but quickly discards that idea. She might as well confront Clera, self-proclaimed "captain" of the *Goose*. At her door, she turns to see the younger woman clumping toward her. "Yes?"

"Can we go inside?" Clera looks both ways down the empty hallway.

"How long will this take? I'm tired."

"Just a minute … in private … unless you want this conversation interrupted by the others."

Sol ushers Clera into the cabin. "What am I in trouble for now, Captain? Did I unknowingly break one of your rules?"

"No." Clera wraps her arms around her waist as the door clicks closed.

Sol leans against it and resists folding her own arms. "Well?"

"When you followed that official earlier, you looked like you were on a mission. I suppose you wanted to ask him how to get off *Calliope*. Did you?"

"I'm still here, aren't I? Just like I promised, I gave no one away. That was our deal."

"So, he refused your request." Clera's brows knit. "Or like you said earlier—he wouldn't even talk to you at all. Too busy, I suppose."

Sol doesn't like how close Clera's come to the truth. "Maybe."

"Look," Clera sighs. "You might actually like us if you give us a chance. It's going to be really awkward having dinner every night with you glowering at us from the other end of the table."

"Not for me."

"I don't believe that." Clera's arms fall. She looks around the spartan room, gaze landing on the one photo Sol saved when she ran from Anton. It lies on the bed, tucked beneath a harness strap, folded and faded. It's one of those carnival booth photos with old-time clothes and forced poses. She'd had it in her pocket that day—where she always kept it. In the photo, she'd been five, her mother a few months pregnant and happy, not knowing she'd die in childbirth. They'd *both* been happy.

Sol moves to the bunk and collects the photo, pressing it against her stomach.

"Your mother?" Clera asks.

Sol bites back a sharp retort and nods tersely.

"I sometimes still miss mine like she died yesterday. Elio and I fought to stay out of the homeless parks after we lost her and our home. When the chance came, we did what we needed to make a new life for ourselves."

Sol reminds herself that this girl is no friend. She's someone who lit Sol's plans on fire with a blowtorch. "Then you should understand why I was hiding out in the shuttle."

"Oh, I do!" Clera offers a tiny smile. "If we'd thought of it, Elio and I would have done the same. Instead, we ended up in a condemned building in Slavland."

"Slavland?" Sol clamps down on the word too late. Her curiosity betrays her.

"Over in West Town. We didn't know that the Second City gang considered it their territory and us their new recruits." She shrugs. "We were desperate. We stole a shuttle. If I'd had any idea you were aboard, I would have warned you."

Sol sees the truth in this but needs someone to blame. Shifting blame to Clera and her friends allows Sol to believe *she* hasn't messed up, that sleeping in the *Goose* wasn't a big mistake. Yet it was, and that's on her. "Why are you here?"

"I guess I was worried you'd given us away somehow, maybe without meaning to. We've made it this far, but I keep thinking our luck can't last. I'm used to things getting worse, not better."

I know what you mean. The words almost slip out. Sol finds she's crossed her arms after all and unfolds them. "Well, you don't have to worry about me. But socializing with the crew wasn't part of our deal. If I feel like staying apart from the rest of you, that's what I'll do."

"Of course!" A dimple appears in Clera's cheek. It transforms her face from mousy to almost pretty. "We'll respect your privacy. I just knew I wouldn't sleep tonight until I'd spoken with you."

Silence falls between them. Unsaid words hover in the air, yet she only says, "Is that all?"

Clera clears her throat and nods. "I'll leave now."

After the door closes, Sol sits on the bed and tilts the old photo so it catches the light. Her mother looks down at her fondly while her younger self stares wide-eyed at the camera. *Anna.* That had been her given name. Sol recalls so little of their time together. Clera should feel grateful she held on to family for so long. Sol speaks in her head the words she'd wanted to tell the girl. *I know what it feels like to lose someone you love, just like you. So hold on to what you have left because once everyone is gone, the darkness finds space to move in.*

During the next hours, Sol does her best to find a way off the ship. She even attempts to steal an escape pod, but her wristband won't let her through a locked portal. How does this feccing ship expect people to eject during a real emergency? Finally, Sol corners Juke in his cabin. The posh rich kid looks just like everyone else now except for a diamond earring glittering in his right earlobe and that shiny, pomaded black hair.

She pushes her way in and does her best to put him at ease even though that isn't her strong suit. He edges toward the door.

"Wait! I just want to talk, not hurt you!"

"Right." The cockiness he displays in front of the others has vanished. "What if I don't give you what you want, though?"

"Is talking really so dangerous?"

"You *want* something. Why else would you be here? Not that I'm not sought after for my charming conversation." Juke tries to smile but can't quite pull off nonchalance.

"Please. I don't mean to get you in trouble or draw attention to the *Goose*. Just help me get to the U.S. Space Station. Hack something or whatever you do."

He frowns at her and finally says, "And then what? You think it will be easy to persuade them you have to get back to Earth immediately? Sure, they'll send you away when it's convenient for them, most likely in handcuffs. How will that work out for you any better than staying here in comfort? What's your job assignment again? I bet it's better than mine, anyway."

Distracted, she can't help asking, "What did they give you? I wasn't really listening ..."

"Nothing in tech, darling." He clenches his jaw, then continues, "They said that department filled up months ago when I wrote back to complain, so I'm stuck with Environmental Control and Life Support. I'll probably end up scrubbing filters or recycling excrement."

Sol winces at the thought of this kid who's probably never known a hard day's labor stuck cleaning out *Calliope*'s guts—before she reminds herself that she couldn't care less about the thieves who stole the *Goose*. "Please," she grits out.

"No." His hand finds the door button, and the panel slides open. He steps into the corridor and gestures for her to leave. What good will attacking him do? Besides, she doesn't want to hurt Juke. Not that she cares about him. She just isn't used to being the aggressor. Defense and running away are more her style.

So that's it. Sol returns to her bunk, removes the boots, and straps herself in. It's late, but the ship murmurs, never sleeping. Now would be the time to cry, yet she stares at the ceiling, dry-eyed, numb, defeated. Sometime after midnight she finally dozes, awakening the next morning to Matilda's annoying voice announcing through the *Blue Goose*'s speaker system, "Attention, colonists. Please strap in aboard your shuttles. *Calliope* departs the United States Space Station in fifteen minutes. Congratulations on becoming some of the first humans to travel to a new solar system and colonize the green planet of Vishnu."

Some of the first. Of course. Norway's *Loki* passed through the ARH over a year past, and Sweden's *Lycka* left months ago. They haven't been heard from since, so maybe Sol is headed to her death. She might as well be, since without her revenge, what does she have? Once they depart, her only hope lies on Mars. Maybe if she gets a job there and saves for a year or more, she'll be able to afford a return trip to Earth. Maybe.

Matilda reminds those aboard twice more to buckle up. When the ship finally fires its fusion engines and pulls away from the steel girders that tether it, she barely notices. Their anti-climactic departure creates barely a ripple of sound or vibration. The AI informs everyone that launch has been successful, and they are on their way to Mars. Cheers erupt outside her cabin. She clasps her hands over her ears.

⸺◈⸺

Sol arrives at the clinic on Red Deck ten minutes early, dressed in her new spacesuit and fighting back an excitement that feels like an abandonment of her goals. She's cleaner than she's been in ages. The chemical shower on the *Goose*, like all her systems, has somehow been integrated into the starship. "Chemical shower" is a misnomer, though. The experience felt more like cleaning her body with a damp, astringent washcloth and a trickle of water. It couldn't come close to the gush of rapids pouring over her skin in an early summer creek—but at least she's fresh, skin tingling. This plus clean clothes lend her an air of confidence she really shouldn't feel. Was she ever that hoodlum girl in the oversized hoodie? Or was it just a guise to get her where she needed to be? Where Anton was.

He's gone, so she might as well embrace this job and learn what she can from it. She loved working at the New Chicago clinic those few brief years, loved helping the midwife, Cress, in the Barrens, too. Now she's got a chance to reclaim those experiences. *Careful, or you'll start sounding like Clera.*

The lobby of Clinic 2-D is composed of a waiting area and counter. Someone has already tried to add character to the place by attaching shiny acrylic images to the walls, some depicting peaceful forest scenes, others with titles like, "Are you feeling bloated? Exhausted? Nauseous? You may have ..." Fill in the blank. A receptionist at the front desk directs Clera down a hallway lined with doors on both sides. She enters an office the size of a closet. An Indian man in a turban with dark-fringed eyelashes and neat hands invites her to take a chair in front of his desk. Though he appears little older than Sol, a list of degrees and awards parade across the wall behind him. He rises to shake her hand, then settles himself.

Sol slides into a proffered chair. Like all furniture outside the Biosphere, it's bolted to the floor—an annoyance, as her long legs bump against the front of the desk. Nervousness flutters in her belly. She feels like a fraud only posing as someone versed in medicine.

"I'm Doctor Hassan Chandra," the supervisor tells her. "They've put me in charge of this clinic. On Earth, I worked at Fort Cambell in Kentucky, and I received much of my training on the battlefields of the Middle East. Since you've been assigned to a Red Deck facility, I'm guessing you also have experienced heavy duties in the field." He glances at his Skinpad, brow creasing. "Though your records are quite scanty. I'm seeing two years at a clinic in New Chicago? And before that, you were …"

"… training just outside the city gates, mostly with a midwife, though I also learned general family medicine from her."

"Outside the gates." His eyebrows rise. "No wonder they assigned you here instead of to one of the milder clinics on Blue Deck. Don't get me wrong. We're cleared to treat cases of flu and norovirus, but there's a reason they put this clinic next to the Security and Defense training grounds."

"*Calliope* is expecting a fight?" Curiosity bubbles up, but she quells it.

"You never know. We're heading into uncharted waters, plus military training isn't risk free. I've been aboard for a month and already witnessed a fighter collision."

Her eyes widen. "*Calliope* has fighter aircraft? With guns? Like in the old movies?"

Dr. Chandra flashes a white smile. "Exactly. Sometimes I feel like I'm part of a space opera novel just by being here. And perhaps I am. *We* are." He sits forward and taps his forearm. "I'm sending you a link to download the clinic system's app. It'll have your work schedule and training modules inside. Also a contact list and employee expectations. Be sure you read through them this week."

"Training modules? As in there will be tests?"

"Is that a problem?" Her supervisor folds his perfectly manicured hands. They match a white lab coat so far unstained by chores of the day.

"No, of course not," Sol assures him, yet she wonders how her education will stack up to that of the other nurses'. She attended primary school in New Chicago but probably received a better education out in the commune, where volunteers took turns holding classes. She hasn't read a book since she left. Does she still remember how? *Duh. You already read the information that steward guy sent. You'll be fine.*

Dr. Chandra stares at her with a tilt to his head. Did he say something while her thoughts drifted in outer space? *Ha! Everyone's thoughts are in outer space now.* Her accidental smile feels out of place in this conversation, so she quickly follows it up with, "I'm excited to get started."

"Good." He reaches into a cabinet behind him and pulls out a thick belt with multiple compartments hanging from it. He hands it over. "You'll wear this while on duty. I'll have Nurse Sadiki explain what everything is for. Oh, and stick this in the sheath." He turns again and rummages. When he twists back around, he's holding something that looks alarmingly like a handgun, only it's slimmer, and liquid floats in a transparent tube where perhaps a bullet cartridge would rest.

She wraps the belt around her waist and buckles it, takes the gun, and tucks the device into a sheath. "What is it?"

"You've never seen a knockout gun?"

"Um, not really." Sweat breaks out on her brow, and she hopes she hasn't given herself away for the fake she probably is.

"Well, the clinics in lower-class neighborhoods of New Chicago probably couldn't afford them. Very handy for emergencies where you need to render your patient unconscious quickly. For example, in cases of extreme pain, shock, or hysteria. Sometimes people do more damage to themselves when they panic than the original wound does."

"I see." Sol conjures up a nod and a smile.

"I'll just buzz Sadiki in. She's been here about three weeks and comes from a hospital in Paris. Her English is quite good, however. I don't think language will be a problem. She'll train you, and you'll spend all your time with her until you pass your modules. Only after that do we allow nurses out on the floor alone."

There's a knock, and a fortyish black woman with braids wrapping her head in a coronet peers in.

Dr. Chandra beckons, and Sol gets up to greet her. The doctor introduces them and wishes Sol luck. Sadiki follows her out, grav boots providing a tenor beat to the soft swish of her lab coat. Sol spends the day learning what the various tools and vials in her utility belt are for as well as how the knockout gun operates. Patients remain few, Sadiki proves forbearing and kind, and Sol's doubts sink into the background while she learns her way around this new job. By the time she leaves, *revenge* and *despair* sound like foreign words stolen from someone else's life. She reminds herself that her stay here is only temporary. The mission is still the same. Kill Anton. Avenge her father.

9

Clera

Clera's steps are light as she stows her grav boots and follows directions on her Skinpad to a cluster of enclosed gardens and a greenhouse on the far side of the Biosphere. She's so glad to work in close-to-regular gravity, so grateful to be back among growing things. That is, until she meets her supervisor, Kristolin Bjornsdottir. "Call me Kris," the woman says right off. She looks Clera over with narrowed eyes as though searching for flaws. Her name suits her. Kris wears a crisp white apron over her jumpsuit, ice-blond hair scraped back in a chignon, eyebrows tamed into thin lines, and lipstick in a pale pink shade. A French manicure gleams on her polished nails. She could be twenty-five or forty.

They meet at one end of the greenhouse in a warehouse-type room filled with plastic crates. Long tables strewn with stems and dirt fill the space. "This is the processing room, where we pack vegetables and fruits to send to the markets and restaurants," Kris tells her. "And you are Clera Diaz, I presume? What is your background?"

Clera tells her, and the woman frowns. "That's all? Please reassure me you at least have a botany degree? Or biology? Environmental science?"

Clera wants to lie but can't make herself. She shakes her head. "No. I'm a fast learner, though. Reliable. Prompt."

Kris flicks away the words with a flutter of her weaponized fingers. "So is everyone here if they want to keep receiving food allotments. How did you get aboard, anyway? You must know somebody." She turns, apparently not expecting an answer. Lucky, since Clera doesn't have one.

The Care and Harvest supervisor walks Clera through the warehouse, introducing her to other non-smiling workers along the way. Kris shows her where the garden tools are stored and drills her on the importance of "... picking up your area. We want no sloppy workers here." The tasks appear similar to ones she performed at the Fadel Arboretum and Greenhouses. If only this Kris person leaves her alone, she might enjoy work in the Biosphere.

Kris interrupts the thought with a snap of her fingers. Clera's already noticed how the woman shows off those impractically long nails as much as possible. The supervisor tells her, "Your daily work will be posted on your Skinpad. If you have questions, I'll be in that office over there." She points at a door on the opposite end of the warehouse from the crates. "Our job here will be essential for the health and well-being of the colonists, so I expect you to take it seriously. There are no lowly jobs aboard *Calliope*." Kris finishes like she's quoting a pamphlet. "And I expect a strong work ethic, cleanliness, and efficiency above all else."

How is Clera supposed to stay clean working in the dirt? Her heart drops when she recalls her last boss—Mr. Harris—the fat, jolly director who believed in her before he even knew her. Zavi's recommendation had been good enough for him, but there's no Zavi to help her now. Judging by how big the Biosphere is, she doubts avoiding him will be difficult. His offices might not even be on this level. She tries to feel relieved, yet regret sneaks in. Everything here reminds her of a relationship that can never be. Maybe she shouldn't have been so happy about her work assignment.

There's nothing to be done, though, so Clera settles into the task of checking that tomatoes in the garden are receiving enough water from the automatic system. Being a Perkine Skinpad Industries employee was a much worse job. While she can't be outside in the Biosphere, at least a fake sun and wispy white clouds move across the radiation-shielded glass disguised as blue sky. Animated birds fly past, making her smile.

Clera's left alone to check tasks off her app list as she completes them. She finishes everything by quitting time. Of course, she skipped lunch and breaks. She didn't want to ask Kris about them on her first day. Besides, she wouldn't have completed the checklist if she paused, and then what? Clera doesn't want to find out.

Kris checks on her as she's hanging up her apron in the workroom. "That goes in the laundry. Can't you see it's filthy? You'll get a fresh one every day."

Clera bites her lip to avoid saying, "You might have told me," or "A couple of dirt smudges isn't 'filthy.'" She'd assumed a starship would want to conserve water even if they recycled it. Remembering the trickle of water in the *Goose*'s shower, she frowns, then summons the courage to ask after all, "I skipped breaks and lunch today. What are the rules about those?"

"There's a break room next to my office. As long as you finish the tasks on your list, you are welcome to pause as much as you wish." Kris' smile reminds Clera of a feral dog's barred teeth. "You will receive two free days during the week. They occur on a rotating schedule. Check your app for them."

"Thank you."

Kris nods, then looks ruefully at her clothing. "I really must fly. I'm meeting the Biosphere director for dinner tonight at one of the new restaurants. The managers have just finished a redesign to make it a copy of *La Paris* in San Francisco! I really wish we were allowed to wear our own clothing. Of course, in nil gravity, a dress wouldn't be too practical, would it?" Her laughter tinkles like glass.

The inane words are lost on Clera. She heard only one thing. Her supervisor has a date with Zavi.

Her Zavi.

No, not hers. And who's she kidding? He never was.

———◦◦◦———

That night at dinner, Elio entertains them with descriptions of the Red Deck training grounds. He goes on and on about laser guns, smart armor, and state-of-the-art training sims. Finally, Mila puts a hand on his arm. "Elio." Only one word, and his monologue trickles to a halt. He grins sheepishly.

Wow. Clera never had that kind of power over him. She's happy he's doing well, happy he has Mila. But there's that pang again. It used to be him and her against the world. Now he has all he's wanted, and she has ... Clera shakes off self-pity and finishes the thought ... *a new life. You've got a brand new, sparkly clean life, and you should be grateful.*

Juke's voice interrupts her inner monologue. "Well, that's great for you. Want to hear about my day? It was all training, too, only not like any sim you've ever played. I learned how to change air filters. Oh, and I got to crawl through ducts cramped enough that if I were claustrophobic, I'd have lost my shit. Hey, that's a thought, actually. Maybe they'll transfer me if I can come up with some condition." He turns to Sol, seated in what's becoming her regular place at the far end of the table. "You think as a nurse you can get me out of Life Support and into Communications, or anything else, really? I'd do what you do if I could have one of those belts you're wearing. What is that, anyway?"

"Looks like they gave you a gun, too," Elio adds, "only you don't have to return it at the end of your shift."

Sol sucks down a mouthful of pouch stew. "It's a knockout gun to put patients to sleep. I'm on call twenty-four-seven and have to keep the belt on me."

Clera prods, "How did your first day go?"

A tiny smile creeps onto Sol's lips before she straightens them into her customary scowl and shrugs. "Glad to have work again."

"What else is in the belt pouches?" Mila asks, craning around the side of the table to catch a glimpse.

"Pills, medicines, bandages. Just what you'd expect."

"We'll be glad to have you here if we ever get sick," Clera tells her.

This receives a tiny nod. Sol's trying hard to keep her distance, but surely, even she can see that flying out on *Calliope* is a step up. Not a disaster but an opportunity.

Once dinner is finished and Mila has wrapped up a "riveting" description of the engine room with no one willing to shut her down, Clera catches Sol before she heads into her cabin.

She barely brushes the woman's arm, yet Sol still jumps away as best she can in grav boots. "Seems like you should be happy, but you don't seem to be. I mean, isn't your job perfect for you? Or maybe it's the people in the clinic who ..."

"My co-workers are fine," Sol interrupts. She looks like she might say more, then doesn't.

"What was so important back on Earth that you'd want to be there even now? You had no real home, no friends, no job, no credits."

"But I had a purpose, Clera." The words tumble out.

"Which was?" Clera leans forward. Maybe she's finally getting somewhere with her sullen crewmate.

"Mine alone to know." Sol stalks off.

Clera stares after her. She pushed too hard, too soon. Maybe Sol needs space. It's a shame, though. Sol might not need someone to confide in, but Clera could use a friend. That used to be Elio, but he and Mila are so wrapped up in each other there's no room for her. Despite living in close quarters with four other people, she feels more alone than ever.

Elio has moved on. So has Zavi, apparently. Just weeks ago, they were practically girlfriend and boyfriend, and now he's dating someone else? Can she let go so easily? She doesn't blame him. He thinks she's still on Earth, and there's nothing to hold him back from forming a new attachment. But with Kris the Ice Queen of all people? Maybe Clera shouldn't judge from first impressions, yet *really*?

She rubs her temple where a headache is forming and moves down the corridor. She has work tomorrow and should try to get some sleep.

10

━━ ◆ ━━

Solast

The Red Deck clinic has three nurses: Sol, Sadiki, and Nora, a solid, middle-aged woman from Indianapolis with an English accent. Like Dr. Chandra, she worked at a hospital and has two decades of emergency room experience. The next few months are packed with learning, and the other nurses are patient teachers who never question Sol's experience or qualifications. Though she answers their curious questions about her past with brusque vagueness, her tongue loosens and defenses drop with every day that passes.

She aces the first training module with a hundred percent score. Dr. Chandra calls her into his office and congratulates her, his only criticism that her bedside manner could use improvement. "It's good to let the patients know who's boss, but a little empathy and interest in their lives is its own sort of medicine." He folds his beautiful hands and looks soulfully into her eyes. "How are you doing, Sol? Perhaps this reluctance to engage with patients results from trauma you yourself are still dealing with? If so, we have free counselors who are very good."

No, she assures him, she's perfectly happy. Mentally fit for her job. The thought that she could lose it frightens her into trying harder to be friendly with patients. The other nurses notice and increase their efforts to draw her into the comfortable companionship they seem to share.

One day, Sol catches Sadiki studying her face while they eat yogurt pouches in the staff room. "How did you get that scar?"

Sol's fingers slide to the shiny pink skin of her cheek. She should have prepared for this question. Everyone aboard is so clean cut, healthy looking, unmarked. She hates that she stands out. "It was an accident when I lived in the Barrens at a commune. Life was hard and accidents common in the rurals." It can't hurt to admit this, but what they can't know is that her commune was led by an Earther, son of a Mexican drug lord, recently added to the FBI's most wanted list for terrorist activity. She learned this when she searched the feeds for signs of Mons Vega, or Anton, as she knows him. There's been little. The Earther cultists haven't made headlines lately—odd since they were quite active just before she left on *Calliope*.

Sol recalls getting caught up in one of their rallies. It was the first time she'd caught sight of her quarry in all the years of searching. She'd spotted Anton again in the bar, Smoke and Blues, before bad luck thwarted her plans for retribution. Now, it's hard not to appreciate her new job, food security, and even the camaraderie among her crewmates. She's softening toward them. Oh, she's definitely softening.

A picture of Sol's father floats into her mind. Tall and muscled, like some superhero out of legend, yet gentle, with soft brown eyes and huge paws for hands. Sol inherited her mother's eyes, hard agate that reflects a stubborn personality. The picture wavers, fades, and guilt stabs at her. *I'm sorry, Father. Truly, I haven't forgotten you. Your death will be avenged.* Yet the words feel empty.

Nora's voice brings her back. "You know, we can fix that scar. It's a simple outpatient surgery. You'd be healed in a few days, and all healthcare is free aboard *Calliope,* as you know."

Sol touches the mark. Who would she be without it? How would she remember that girl she was? Remember her father? She shakes her head. "No, thank you. I'm used to the scar."

Sadiki grins. "It does make you look a bit badass. Kind of like a pirate. Fits your personality."

"You think of me as a badass? Or a pirate?" Sol lets her own grin answer, not holding back for once.

"Definitely," sedate Nora agrees. She glances at Sadiki. "Though that isn't a description I would have used."

"Oh, lighten up." Sadiki elbows her friend. "You know it works for her."

Does it? Sol thinks a badass should have abs of steel and biceps like iron balls, yet hers feel flabby since she's been in space. She should use the weightrooms in the Biosphere. Maybe today she'll start.

But later a message from the Steward's office pings on Sol's Skin-pad, and she discovers she's been assigned to attend an orientation class in the Blue Deck theater this evening. Command is prepping the colonists for their arrival on Vishnu. Throughout the seven-month trip to Mars, presenters are scheduled to speak about everything from survival skills, basic wound care, plant life on the green planet, to homebuilding from kits stored in *Calliope*'s massive holds. Since Sol doesn't plan to venture through the wormhole, she'd skip the classes if they weren't mandatory. However, the message warns absenteeism without good cause will result in reduction of allotments.

Sol takes a quick shower after work, sucks down a packet of beef soup, and heads for the hatch, where she runs into Clera, who says, "Oh, we must both be scheduled for tonight's training. Am I right? Should we walk together?"

Sol hesitates but sees how awkward it would be for one of them to follow the other down *Calliope*'s vast corridors like strangers who don't know each other. On the other hand, Clera sets Sol's nerves on edge with her constant worrying. The need to keep her friends safe from the imagined danger Sol poses grates like sandpaper.

Sol doesn't hate Clera or anyone else on this ship. That's the problem. The farther from Earth they travel, the harder it is to remember what she's lived for since her seventeenth birthday. For a long time, there was nothing *else* to live for. Now, though, she finds it difficult to dislike her berthmates and impossible to loathe a life of security and a job she loves.

"Sol?"

She starts, realizing she never answered Clera, who stands uncertainly at the top of the stairway.

"I promise not to interrogate you. Really. I won't even talk if you prefer. It just seems silly not to walk together."

Sol shrugs and nods.

Others assigned to tonight's class fill the wide hallways. It's Sol's second lecture. The first was jaw-droppingly boring. Tonight's might be more interesting. The topic is Ancient Martian Civilization, the presenter someone named Dr. Lehmann. He holds his degree from Berkley, taught at Yale, and helped excavate the Martian ruins found under Arsia Mons, so he's one of the very few colonists who's ever been out to Mars.

Again, Clera interrupts her thoughts. "So, how are you doing? I mean, have you decided life aboard a starship suits you after all, or …"

"Didn't you just make me a promise?" Sol softens the words with the hint of a smile.

"Oh. Sorry." Clera falls quiet.

Sol eyes the younger woman sideways—notices the slump of her shoulders, her lackluster facial expression, and can't help asking, "What about you?"

"Me?" Clera's head jerks up. "You're asking me?"

"Well, yes." Sol waits.

"Everything is wonderful. Elio's happy, we're away from the gangs, and we have a safe place to stay and plenty to eat."

"But ..."

Clera looks straight ahead. "I can't stand my supervisor at the Biosphere. She's like some glamorous ice queen who looks down on absolutely everybody. She sends out these task lists that have to be completed before you clock out for the day, and they leave no time for breaks. I've been losing weight because I skip lunch. But that's not the worst—" Clera trails off.

"What is?" Sol can't help asking.

"Never mind." Clera shakes her head.

"You'll feel better if you get it out, believe me."

That draws a laugh. "Oh, really? This from someone who's kept up an air of mystique ever since we left Earth?"

"An air of mystique? You speak like a romance novel."

"I read a lot. And what would you know about novels, anyway?"

"I can read." Sol dials back the defensiveness in her voice. "Anyway, we're talking about you." They break apart to swerve around a slow-moving couple, then drift close again.

"I don't know if you overheard us talking in the *Goose*, but we're a bit worried about Zavi Fadel. He's the director of the Biosphere. More importantly, we were sort of seeing each other at the greenhouse where I worked on Earth."

"I don't see the problem."

Clera sighs. "Zavi knows my background, my lack of education, connections, wealth." She lowers her voice. "What he doesn't know is that we stole a NASA shuttle. He doesn't realize I'm aboard *Calliope*, and we all worry that he might turn us in if he discovers it."

"Vindictive, is he?"

"Not at all!" Clera inhales a sharp breath. Her hands clench.

Sol waits curiously. It's nice to be the one prying into someone else's life for a change.

"I just … it's especially hard because … well, my supervisor is seeing him."

"You mean dating?"

"I think so. She brags sometimes about how she's going here or there with Zavi. It's hard to endure, especially when I want so badly to see him myself but can't."

Sol considers this and finally says, "If this Zavi has moved on so quickly, maybe he's not worth your time."

"Right." Clera purses her lips, then repeats more forcefully, "You're right! Why can't I just be happy? Grateful for what I've got? You know?"

Sol has asked herself that question many times during the last months. She almost blurts, *I definitely do,* yet holds back. She's always shied away from people. It's a flaw, maybe, but also necessary self-protection. Everyone she's loved is gone. If she lets herself like Clera, maybe she's condemning the younger woman to the same fate. Something horrible will happen to her, and it will be Sol's fault, however illogical that sounds.

"What?" Clera regards her quizzically.

"Nothing. Just that I can relate. It's easy to think the worst, to look on the dark side, because then you can't be disappointed. Hope is harder. More dangerous."

"Exactly."

They fall silent as the crowd condenses before the open doors that lead into the theater. White-suited stiffs from Command scan their Skinpads as they enter the foyer, then the echoing, half-circle room filled with tiers of cushioned chairs. A lit stage stands at the far end. Clera grabs Sol's arm as others jostle them. "Let's sit up front so we can see better." She starts down the aisle, hauling Sol after her.

"I bet you were always the goody-two-shoes student who chose the desk at the head of the room," Sol grumbles but allows herself to be led.

They settle into seats five rows from the stage. The lights dim, and a tall man with a rolling gait emerges from behind a panel. Three vid screens positioned high on the walls light up with identical slides that read, "The Martian Chronicles."

"Clever," Clera whispers in Sol's ear.

"What?"

"The name of his presentation. It's taken from Ray Bradbury's *The Martian Chronicles*. You never read it?"

"No," Sol answers, barely listening. The presenter has her full attention. That lanky build. Those mild brown eyes. The touch of gray in wavy hair and permanently worried expression. She only met him once when she first arrived on the ship. Now she recalls how he was the first to tell her she could get her scar removed. Sol fingers the taut line of it and remembers that day Anton sliced her, then winces away from the memory. Oskar Lehmann had been—unusual. He'd taken her swearing in stride, then suggested she see a counselor. That memory stings a little. She wishes she'd had more self-control.

Oskar Lehmann. Doctor Lehmann. Here he is again, but he won't remember her. She's only a lowly clinic nurse. He's probably forgotten her outburst. Forgotten her.

Dr. Lehmann scans the audience. His eyes reach her, pause, and she swears he *recognizes* her. His expression doesn't change, though, and he turns to the podium where a laptop computer rests. He taps on a mic pinned to his suit. It's a smartsuit, not a jumpsuit like the rest of them are wearing. He *looks* smart.

Oskar clears his throat and shifts nervously. "'We Earth men have a talent for ruining big, beautiful things.' Ray Bradbury said that, but he also said this: '... at base, science is no more than an investigation of a miracle we can never explain, and art is an interpretation of that miracle.' So are humans the destroyers, or are we the preservers, those who recognize miracles and try to hold on to them? It's been my life's work to become the latter. And the Martian ruins below Arsia Mons are one of the biggest miracles I've ever seen."

A hush falls across the room. He continues, "During my presentation today, I'll show you the beauty of Martian artifacts, the brilliance behind their technology, and share the little I know of their time on Mars millions of years ago. What they left us, as you know, has propelled this ship toward the red planet and will catapult us into a new solar system. It may even offer a means to save our people left behind on Earth."

He pauses, lets this sink in. No one stirs or even coughs. The lecture proves fascinating. Oskar recounts events which led to the earthquake that revealed the hidden tunnels—an ancient Martian underground network—and disabled the cloaking device that hid the manufactured wormhole, or ARH. He shows slides of Martian artifacts: pottery with dragon-shaped designs, strange metal machines whose purpose remains inscrutable, stone murals bearing marks that could be language. He ends with the mysterious vanishing of an advanced Martian civilization. How did these aliens meet their end? Did they die out or leave Mars?

As Oskar's words trickle to a stop, Sol realizes she hasn't moved or thought of anything besides the images his deep voice evokes. He's held her spellbound. Only as applause erupts does she come back to herself.

His eyes don't find her again.

11

Solast

The exercise room, with its free weights and bot-like machines that work muscles, stretch stiff joints, and massage fat from flabby midsections, is almost empty. Sol made sure to show up early in the morning, an unpopular time, apparently. She studies various torture devices before settling on the free weights. The pain of lifting lulls her overactive brain. *Pain focuses the mind,* Anton used to say during training sessions at the commune. There'd been a handful of teenagers in attendance, those hoping to join Anton's hunting parties or move up in the little community's ranks. "Equality for all" was the commune's motto, but that fanciful notion didn't really exist, did it? Surely not in Anton's world, where he got the best housing, the best food.

Concentrate on the pain, not the past. Sol brings a dumbbell to her chin. Her muscles object, so she reduces the weight and tries again. *Better, but you should be able to lift more. You're getting soft.* She works out until the gym fills. Then she sanitizes the weights, grabs a hand towel, and wipes sweat from her face. She drapes the towel around her neck and looks up.

Shock freezes her in place. She tries to blink away the hallucination standing in the entryway, but he refuses to disappear. Feccing hells! He's *real.* Not fantasy or wishful thinking. Not some doppelganger. Anton.

His hair has grown since the last time she saw him in Smoke and Blues talking with the exec. No Earther tattoos proclaim what he is. With enough credits, ink removal's easy. Just a simple outpatient surgery like the one for her scar. Her scar! Will Anton recognize it? She presses the towel against her cheek and shrinks behind a treadmill. An overweight man puffing his way to nowhere keeps her hidden while she stares at her nemesis.

In many ways, he's the same. Stocky body, ruddy complexion, so bland in appearance you'd walk by him on the street without a second look—unless you stared long and hard into his eyes. Their fathomless black depths burn with a fanatic's passion. At least she always thought so. How do strangers see him? How did her father when they first met and he charmed Ridge into joining the Earther movement?

And how in seven hells is Anton *here*? She sifts through memories and comes up with an answer in snatches of an overheard conversation in Smoke and Blues. *It will be in your account by Monday ... And that other thing you promised? ... You can count on us to get it done. We aren't faithless ... Do we have a deal or not? ... I don't get why someone so into saving Earth would want to ... The paperwork has already been processed, and you should have a receipt and directions on your Skinpad by tomorrow morning.*

Sol slips into a side room filled with rowing machines. From there, an exit propels her onto a walking path in the park. Whoever controls the skyscape—probably AI Matilda—has decided a pale half-moon should hang next to the sun. A hawk streaks past it. Sol struggles to slow her racing heart and jogs back to the lockers. She changes from a tee-shirt and shorts into a spacesuit and retrieves her bag and grav boots. Her shaking hands have trouble pulling them on. Any second, she expects Anton to show up and recognize her. Back in the commune, he'd been everywhere at once. You couldn't escape his eye once he suspected you of something.

And there was no evading punishment for betrayal.

Sol exits the Biosphere and melds into a crowd of workers headed for morning shifts. She's glad for the anonymity of their identical blue jumpsuits. Work starts soon, so she'll have to hump it if she wants to shower first. Her mind flips back to Anton's meeting with the exec. It's important, but why? As she walks, puzzle pieces shift and snap into place.

Her first conclusion: Anton paid off a powerful exec back on Earth, probably someone with NASA connections, to worm his way onto *Calliope*. His fortunes must have improved dramatically since their commune days, but hells, that was over a decade ago, so no telling how many credits he's culled from gullible followers by now. Second, and more importantly, why would Mons Vega, Earth's Protector and the Enemy of Technology, want to fly out with *Calliope*? It's a bad look for him, isn't it? Goes against everything he stands for, unless ...

What if Anton has sabotage in mind? He's grown powerful indeed if he thinks he can beat *Calliope*'s security forces. Elio brags about state-of-the-art weapons and the quality of officers pulled from the United States' best military academies. Still, Anton had years of training with the Barrens as his fighting grounds. Before that, there were rumors he grew up in Mexico, raised to serve as bodyguard to his drug lord father, nicknamed The Chemist. More rumors he'd fought his way north after his family's compound was bombed and his parents murdered.

Anton himself could have made up this story. All she knows for sure is he's smart. He understands how to manipulate people, and he's patient. A thinker. If he has some nefarious plan to bring down NASA's colonization program, he's been refining its details for years. Sol can't just run to Command and blurt her suspicions without attracting unwanted attention. The officials would never believe her, anyway. They'll see Anton as some forty-something lucky winner of a lottery meant to enlarge *Calliope*'s gene pool. He won't be *Cheverra* now. A hacker like Juke almost certainly baptized him with a new surname, something innocuous like *Smith*.

What's his job assignment? Can she find out? Sol's not thinking like someone whose only goal is to return to Earth. One random encounter has thrown off everything she thought she knew. Again. Here she is, and here he is. No longer does she need a lift home. Wherever Anton resides *is* home.

Until he's dead.

Suddenly, Sol's all-in on this journey. With any luck, she can find justice for her father before they dock at Arsia Mons. Only then will she consider a return to Earth.

◦

She's on duty with Nora today. The motherly, fifty-year-old woman is stocking bandages in the storeroom when Sol arrives two minutes late. Nora doesn't comment, just smiles and continues her work. Sol slips on a lab coat and approaches her.

"Yes?" Nora pauses with her hand on a box of gauze. They mostly fix wounds with glue-all, but sometimes old-fashioned supplies work better.

"Do you remember how you mentioned the clinic could repair my scar?"

"Of course. You've changed your mind?"

Sol nods.

"No problem. Just navigate to 'Medical' on your Skinpad and sign up for the surgery. Dr. Chandra will do it. He's very good." She flushes.

"Great. I'll do that."

Nora asks, "What made you change your mind?"

"Huh? Oh, I decided you were right. I might as well take advantage of the free medical while I can. Who knows what will change once we reach Mars."

"You mean Vishnu, don't you? The red planet is just a pitstop."

"Oh, right."

Nora looks at her quizzically.

Sol forces a smile. "Sorry. My mind is elsewhere today."

"Maybe there's another reason you want the cosmetic surgery? A new man, perhaps?" Nora winks.

Sol's used to the older woman's love of soap opera drama by now. She suspects the nurse has a million bodice-ripper romances stored in the entertainment app on her Skinpad. A face flashes before her eyes—craggy, with puppy dog eyes and a perpetually worried brow. Oskar Lehmann, the well-spoken archeologist. Sol shakes away the image. "I'm not into men," she blurts to forestall any more prying on Nora's part, though who knows. The nurse might be just as interested in Sol's love life if she *was* dating a woman.

Nora pats her cheek. "You'll be so beautiful once Hassan fixes you! You'll be able to have any man ... I mean woman ... you want."

— ◆ —

Day 13

I consumed the last freeze-dried food pouch several days ago. Since my stranding on Vishnu, I have experimented with various recipes using native flora and fauna (such as there is of it). My family back on Earth might be surprised to discover that I enjoy these culinary adventures. Survival depends on finding nutritious, non-toxic foods to consume, but I also aim to create delectable meals. Well, palatable, at least—

What follows is a list of three staple Vishnuan ingredients ...

Sorry. Feeling poorly. Possibly a reaction to alien bacteria or a virus that my body hasn't developed a resistance to yet. Will finish this entry once I've recovered.

-N.J.

12

Niklas

Vishnu. The Green Planet. Named for the Hindu god who protects and preserves the universe. Second planet from the red dwarf star, called Kali after the Hindu god of blood. Niklas Johansson can hardly believe he's here at last.

He stares up into a teal-colored, cloudless sky. Kali, a larger and redder star than Earth's Sol, shines brightly down. At least a dozen alien rings identical to the Martian ring near Deimos litter the heavens. It's unexpected. Intriguing. An indication that there may be more habitable worlds scattered across the galaxy, reachable thanks to Martian technology. Only before they were Martians, what were they called? And is Vishnu the genesis planet from which their civilization sprang millions or even billions of years ago?

Niklas imagines humanity spreading: expansion rather than contraction, rebirth instead of a pyre. Hope rises in his chest. He's proud to be part of something so big. *Lycka* is the second ship to reach Vishnu, assuming *Loki* arrived safely. His team of biologists has been on the lookout for signs of Norway's *Loki* since they arrived. Like his own starship, *Loki* lost contact after passing through the wormhole. They'd hoped to find her circling the planet but haven't seen the massive ship. Still, maybe *Loki*'s colonists are wandering around down here. They should have constructed a community, yet where is it? Had the Norwegians landed on the other side of the planet despite what their settlement plan indicated?

Water shushes at Niklas' feet. He stands on a white sand beach. An emerald sea pushes up against the horizon. If not for the color, he could have been at his parents' summer home in Greece, where he spent many happy hours swimming as a child with his cousin, Zavi.

Zavi. For the tenth time since passing through the ARH, Nik messages his best friend, but like always, the words fall into the ether, unreceived and unanswered. Something keeps the quantum messaging app from working even though distance shouldn't matter. Theoretically. He's a biologist, not a physicist, and doesn't understand the mysteries of quantum mechanics. He likes his field. It's grounded in the physical, in things he can feel and see. The cool water at his feet or the rocky gray cliffs erupting to his right. Waves pound against rock, a sound so familiar that homesickness grabs at him.

Niklas sends *Lycka* Command a message. It goes through, but no one answers, again, which is odd. He frowns at his Skinpad. The anti-radiation perma-spray which coats his skin shimmers. Could the spray be affecting communications somehow? He can't think of another reason the ship won't answer, but this is the fifth instance of radio silence. His team has been on-site for several days. They deployed in the first shuttle, and he expected a second group to follow, yet no other shuttle has streaked down from the dot that is *Lycka*. She's still up there, her trip through orbit visible in the dark. She creeps past like clockwork, a sight that should reassure him. It doesn't.

Shuffling footsteps make Niklas turn. His pilot, Dana Adere, slogs toward him through the sands. "Niklas, everything is ready."

"Have the others returned from their mapping expedition?"

"Not yet." At Niklas' frown, she hurries on, "But Ben checked in a bit ago. No sign of *Loki*'s crew or any human life. No animal life, either."

"And no crash indicators? Burn marks? Nothing alien?"

She smiles at this. "By that you mean nothing human, I take it? You're already going native." Dana's golden hair, a shade darker than his own curly locks, falls straight to her shoulders. She's taken to wearing it down. For him, maybe? Normally, he'd be interested. She's pretty in an athletic kind of way, but he's too worried right now for distractions.

"We should get used to seeing ourselves as Vishnuans. Vishni?" He grimaces. "Dr. Ghatak really should have chosen a different name for this planet. Something easier to pronounce."

"If we don't get someone on the horn soon, we might as well rename it, as there won't be any going back to Earth, and no one will care what we call this place, anyway."

"Don't talk like that. It's way too soon to imagine everyone left on the starship has just"—he flicks his fingers to mimic an explosion, "—vanished. I'm sure it's an error with the communications system. Still, we need to find out. We only have enough supplies for two more days if we're careful. The second crew was bringing cargo for a more permanent camp." Dana already knows this, of course. Saying it aloud helps him think.

Ever tactful, she waits patiently until he speaks again. Beautiful *and* smart. "Maybe we'll get the answers we need once we dock the shuttle in the hangar bay on *Lycka*. I hate to show up unexpectedly, but we tried to warn them we were coming." He hesitates. "Just in case there *is* something wrong up there, maybe some weird virus that has put everyone down for the count, you do have enough gas masks for the three of us as well as protective suits, right?"

"Of course." She becomes all business. "Adrian just double-checked everything."

"I'm putting him in charge once we board. I might look like a military-trained stud, but science is my field, not security and defense." He grins and shrugs, hearing how his tongue-in-cheek humor comes off.

Dana grins back and raises her eyebrows. She doesn't call him out on the "stud" remark. They both know he's strong, not to mention six-two and an exercise fanatic. That's not ego, just facts.

"Let's go," Niklas says.

13

Clera

While Clera trims dead leaves off plants in the gardens, she tells herself that overall, things are going well. Grow-lights strung above her head envelop her body in warmth. The false sky is a cloudless blue today. Classical music wafts from hidden speakers along a nearby walking path, and the air smells green and fresh. After months aboard *Calliope*, her crew has settled into this new life.

Elio returns to the *Blue Goose* every night with news of his latest sim test score or with a demonstration of some martial arts sequence. Mila, too, seems to love her job in engineering, though she's been a little pale, a bit quiet. Perhaps she caught a cold despite the meds they take to boost immunity and strengthen bone. She called in sick today, emerging from the cabin she shares with Elio only to grab a bagel and vanish again. When Clera asked Elio if anything was wrong, he only shrugged. "She'll be better tomorrow, probably."

Then there's Juke. Clera misses his over-the-top endearments a surprising amount. He speaks little about his job in Environmental Control and Life Support. She asked him last week if he put in for a transfer, and he nodded yes, then added, "There's a long waiting list for Communications and Tech. Probably those jobs went to people with college degrees, not scrulls like me."

"You're brilliant!" Clera objected, and the others—minus Sol—chimed in. This seemed to cheer him enough that he made a few jokes about his work crew. Venters, he called them. Clera feels for him. Her own job isn't making her as happy as she thought it might. She imagines Zavi, tucked away in some office, unaware of her existence aboard *Calliope*. If he knew, would he care? Or has he moved on with Kristolin Bjorndottir?

Most of her dismay over her job stems from Kris. The woman's condescension makes Clera grit her teeth. Kris frequently leaves her office so she can "observe" Clera and her coworkers. The women on Clera's shift, Maya and Lin, hiss, "Incoming!" every time they see that office door open. Though they all suffer under Kris' micromanaging eyes, Clera feels her supervisor's disapproving gaze most often. Like a cold wind, Kris wafts into Clera's area and frosts over any happiness before she blows away again.

Clera finishes the leaf job, checks it off her list, and heads to the warehouse for fertilizer. The day is almost over, her footfalls a tired plod. She skipped lunch again, but she'll grab an energy bar from a stand along the walking path when she clocks out. She's just taken the container of fertilizer from its shelf when Maya groans from the table where she's preparing seedlings for transfer. "Incoming!"

Kris bursts from her office in a flurry of plumage. Clera squints at the feather-edged white leather jacket draped across her boss' shoulders. Before she can hide, the supervisor flashes taloned nails and calls out, "Oh, Clera! I'm leaving a little early to meet Zavi, but I wanted to speak with you first."

Reluctantly, Clera meets her midway down an aisle, still clutching the fertilizer. Maya murmurs, "Good luck," as she edges past.

Kris launches a familiar barrage of questions at her. "Did you cross everything off your list today? I noticed that yesterday you missed tagging a couple of the apple varieties in the orchard. We can't have that! Tasks left half-done don't count."

Clera missed *nothing* on yesterday's list, and all the apples were labeled. But arguing only works against her, so she ignores the criticism. "I just need to fertilize the tomatoes in the far plot."

"Well, good. That will take half an hour, though, and there's no overtime pay on *Calliope*!" Kris titters like she made a joke, yet her eyes remain the frigid color of polar ice. Ice Queen fits the woman perfectly. Unlike Maya and Lin, Clera only uses the title in her head, though she feels vindicated whenever she hears the others voice it.

"I'd better get going, then." Clera forces pep into her voice.

Kris doesn't let her pass. "Do you like my new jacket? Technically, we're only supposed to wear those awful blue jumpsuits, but some of us get special privileges."

"I'm surprised you can find anywhere to buy one aboard the ship." Lots of shops litter the maze of corridors on Blue Deck, but they mostly sell standard food items or decorations to make the shuttles homier.

Kris' voice falls to a whisper. "The black market, dear." She puts a claw-like finger to her lips. "Don't tell anyone."

Clera manages to nod instead of gag. She's about to say, "Excuse me," and slink past that voluminous jacket when the warehouse door opens. A man stands silhouetted in its frame. Kris pivots and calls out, "Dr. Fadel! Over here!"

Clera's world collapses. Worktables, plants, co-workers—everything fades into a blizzard of white. Her mouth drops open for a moment before she clamps it shut. She presses the fertilizer container into her midsection, and her eyes fasten on that form in the doorway. He moves inside, takes on definition, and becomes Zavi Fadel. Same startling blue eyes and dark blond hair, though cut shorter than she recalls. Same lithe frame and same mobile mouth, frozen in shock when he spots her.

He ignores Kris. His gaze fastens on Clera in a moment of recognition that stretches like a rubber band—farther, farther, until it will surely snap. When it does, will his expression morph into disbelief? Disappointment? Suspicion? Betrayal? Or "E" for "All of the above."

They might as well be alone in the warehouse. Each footfall brings him closer, and she wants to turn and run. That or bolt toward him and throw her arms around his shoulders. She's terrified of him and desperate to touch him at the same time.

Kris' voice pierces the fog. "Dr. Fadel?" There's a tiny hesitation in it. She's noticed how her boyfriend only has eyes for Clera. *Boyfriend.* That's right. There will be no salvation. No reason for Zavi not to call Security and expose her.

He blinks. His eyes shutter as he glances at Kris. "Nice jacket," he remarks absently before his attention returns to Clera.

The supervisor butts in, "Oh, you like it? I picked it out just for tonight."

Her words pull his gaze away again. "For the work meeting? Are you sure that's appropriate?"

Zavi wears the simple blue jumpsuit they all do. It clings to his frame in all the right places, emphasizing muscles built up during the months of the physical therapy he needed after an air rail accident that crushed his spine. His grandfather paid for a new, bionic spine and for Zavi's new lease on life.

Pink spots emerge on Kris' cheeks, and Clera almost feels sorry for her.

"Work meeting?" Clera can't help repeating Zavi's words. "I thought you had a—"

Kris interrupts, "Hadn't we better be going, Dr. Fadel? We wouldn't want to be late."

And isn't he "Zavi" to you? A niggling suspicion surfaces that Kris may have misrepresented their relationship. But why? Just to have something to brag about? Another one-up for an insecure woman fulfilling a job assignment she considers beneath herself?

Zavi's deep, gentle voice breaks into Clera's thoughts. He looks only at her as he says, "But—I thought you were still on Earth."

Kris' head jerks from one to the other like a marionette's. "You two know each other?"

"I ... I ..." Clera scrambles for an explanation but can't find one. She should have prepared a story. "It's ... complicated." She casts a quick glance at Kris to find her staring open-mouthed.

Zavi glances between them and seems to gather his wits. "Of course it is, and here isn't the right place for long explanations." He smiles tightly. "But we should have that conversation—later, if that's all right with you, Clera?"

"Of course," she squeaks past lips gone dry with fright.

"I'll look you up on the community chat later." He glances at her covered forearm. "Unless ... but of course you have a ..." His eyebrows knit, and he trails off. His blue eyes hold a mixture of puzzlement and—could it be hurt?

Oh, no. Zavi. Please, please don't hate me. She pushes her mouth into a smile. "Yes, please do."

He searches her face, then turns and walks away, followed by Kris in her ridiculous jacket.

Please do? Seriously, Clera. You sound like some prim and proper spinster from the nineteenth century.

Maya appears at her elbow. "Who was that?" she breathes, round-eyed.

"Just a man. The director of the Biosphere."

"He looked like he knew you."

"Well. Maybe he did." Clera wills back tears. "I have to go." Without glancing at Maya, she rushes outside.

Has she ruined everything for her crew, or will Zavi keep her secret? Other questions rise past that one. *Will he forgive me for stealing a shuttle and coming here, then avoiding him? Not even trying to salvage our relationship? How badly have I hurt him?*

Strangely, that question bothers her most.

In a daze, she finishes her last task, ticks it off the horrible list, and heads home. She skips grabbing the energy bar. Suddenly, she's not hungry.

⸺⟡⸺

"Zavi knows, Elio." Clera stands in front of her brother's cabin door waiting to come in so they can sit down and have a real conversation.

But he says, "Mila still isn't feeling great. Better stay in the corridor to talk. No sense in getting sick."

He closes the portal behind him and regards her reddened eyelids. "Are you okay? What did he say to make you cry?"

"Let's go into the commons. My feet are killing me."

She leads him to the galley table and sits across from him, relieved they're alone. She sighs.

"Well?" Elio looks at her with concern. "If he threatened you—" Angry color suffuses his face.

"No, of course he didn't!" Clera clutches her brother's wrist. "He was in shock. And we weren't alone. We barely said two words to each other before he had to leave with my supervisor for a meeting."

"Did he give you away?"

"No." She sighs again, deeper this time. "Though Kris knows we've met. I can't imagine what story he'll concoct to explain that, but I'm sure she'll be asking. She led me to believe she and Zavi were dating."

"If so, he sure got over you quick." Elio adds sheepishly, "Sorry."

She shakes her head. "It's fine. And I thought they were together, yet now I have doubts. I get the impression she really likes him, but it's possible she's only a work colleague as far as he's concerned." Clera releases Elio and rubs her temple where a headache is forming.

"Sure that's not wishful thinking?"

"Could be. I don't know. All he said was that we should talk and that he'd message me on community chat."

"Okay, so what's your story?"

"That's what I need to talk to you about. I suppose we should gather everyone. If Zavi decides to betray us, it won't just be my life on the line."

"What can they do to us at this point? Throw us in the brig?" He bites his lip. "Oh, hells. They *could* throw us in the brig. And from there into some jail on Mars."

Clera's chest tightens, an old warning sign of an impending panic attack. She counts and breathes until the feeling passes. With the relaxing of tense muscles comes clarity of thought. She won't scramble to invent a story Zavi won't believe anyway. "I'm telling him the truth."

"But ..."

"I have to. Anything else will sound crazy, unbelievable, and he's been hurt enough already."

Elio slams a fist against the tabletop. "I'm not worried about Zavi's feelings." He softens his voice. "I mean, he did help you bust me out of jail, but Clera! He's a loose cannon. Also a rule follower, I bet. He won't like that we broke the law."

"You barely met him," Clera chides, yet Elio might be right. They only knew each other for several months before she left. How well does she understand Zavi's mind? His motivations? His code of right and wrong? "We'll eat dinner when Juke and Sol get here, then break the news."

Elio frowns, then nods.

Clera rises. "I'm going to the head. You're on chef duty."

"No problem." He grins, worry falling away. "I picked up Italian at that little shop near the theater. Feels like stealing, doesn't it, not having to pay? We'd better enjoy it while it lasts!"

"Right."

On that ominous note, she heads down the corridor.

14

Clera

Mila meets Clera at the door to the head, face pasty and hands trembling. She holds a bag they use for waste.

"Oh, hello," Clera greets her.

Mila bursts out, "Oh, no! Not again!" and pukes into the bag.

"Elio hoped you were getting better, but it doesn't look like it."

"It comes and goes." Mila draws a quivering breath. "Sorry." She puts a hand on the wall. Color rushes back to her face. "I'm better now. Don't worry."

"Do you have congestion? Fever?"

"No. Just the feccing nausea. For over a month now."

A suspicion forms in Clera's mind that she wants to brush off but can't. She counts backward, and alarm raises the hairs on her skin. She glances both ways to make sure no one's listening, then leans close. "Mila, is there any possibility you could be pregnant?"

"What? No!" Mila starts to say more, then stops. A thoughtful look descends on her face. "I mean, I got a patch from the public health clinic in New Chicago maybe a year ago. Or was it longer? I forget."

"How long do the patches last? I've never had one."

"You're supposed to re-up every year. There were budget cuts, though, and the clinic stopped its reminder emails. But I've been taking that med cocktail they give us on *Calliope,* and I thought it was supposed to include pregnancy blockers."

"Yet if you were already pregnant …"

Mila pales. "The chances of that weren't very high, were they? Elio and I had been together less than a month."

Clera recalls sporadic sex ed talks from public school. She echoes a soundbite they drilled into her. "It only takes once." Seeing Mila's panicked expression, she adds, "You did say you wanted children with my brother."

"Not yet! I mean, what will happen to us if I have to admit I messed up? Isn't there a rule or something about not having children? Not until we're settled on Vishnu, anyway. Will I lose my job? Maybe they won't even let me go through the ring!"

Clera squeezes her shoulder. Though petite, Mila's personality dominates any room. She hates to the mechanic shrinking like a violet exposed to midday sun. "Listen, Mila. We'll talk to Sol, have her sneak you anti-nausea meds and pregnancy vitamins from her clinic if you're pregnant. And you should stop taking the med cocktail right away, just in case it does include pregnancy blockers."

"Oh, gods. Do you think it could have damaged my baby? Maybe the stowaway will know. She was a nurse, right?"

"Don't worry yet. We don't even know if you're pregnant. Have you missed a period?"

"Maybe." Mila's voice sinks to a whisper. "I just thought it was all the changes in diet and gravity. I mean, didn't you see a difference in your flow once we got here?"

Clera shakes her head. "No. But we need to be sure so we can make a plan." She drops her hand and calculates. "If I'm not mistaken, we'll have started construction on a permanent colony before you're due. So that's good."

"How will I hide a belly the size of a blimp?" Mila glances down at her flat stomach.

"Does engineering supply coverings, something like the apron I wear or Sol's lab coat, to protect your jumpsuit from oil stains?"

"Yes." Mila straightens. "And they're roomy. I can hide a pregnancy in that. But if I stay out sick much longer, someone will get suspicious."

"Let's speak with Sol. Maybe she can take care of your symptoms. And let's find out if our suspicions are even justified." Clera taps her chin. "And Mila, you might want to stop referring to our medic as 'the stowaway.' We're going to need her help."

"Right. Of course." Mila shakes her head like she can't fathom this new reality. Her eyes, clear as a winter sky and shiny with a trace of tears, stare into Clera's. "And thanks. I know you and Elio are close, and you might feel like I stole him from you, but—"

"Nonsense. I'm glad to see my brother so happy. And if you do have a baby on Vishnu, it's probably going to be the first. By then, a very welcome miracle for every colonist. After all, they'll want us to make more humans once we land, correct?"

Mila smiles. "You're right. Of course you are."

Before they part, Clera messages Sol for a list of items to snag from her clinic. She's relieved to get the reply a minute later.

It won't be a problem. Short and to the point. No drama. No hesitation. Clera likes their surprise crew member more and more.

She calls a meeting after dinner, stomach roiling. She's keeping Mila's possible pregnancy a secret from everyone—even her brother—until they know more, but she can't hide the fact that Zavi Fadel has discovered them.

Juke slides into his seat and immediately complains that he's sick and tired of wearing grav boots everywhere.

"So are we all, hom." Elio slaps him on the back. "Once we reach Mars, maybe you'll be able to change into lighter boots."

"Still sounds uncomfortable and style-less. I miss my suede loafers. By the way, when did you become the font of all knowledge? Thought you hated reading."

"I don't hate it. It's just hard for me. The words swim. But the guys and I talk during trainings. I've found out a few things."

Sol breaks in, "Are we still having a meeting, because if not—"

Clera's glad for the interruption. *Let's get this over with.* "I saw Zavi." She blurts the words before she can change her mind.

Four heads swivel toward her. "Um," Juke ventures. "Did he see you?"

She meets her brother's gaze. Though he already knows, he's still tense. Questions and worry spark in his brown eyes. Only Elio has met the director of the Biosphere. Only he has some idea who Zavi is. Not just the privileged son of a pharmaceutical CEO and philanthropist but a flesh-and-blood person who helped them. Tearing her eyes from her brother, she sweeps a look around the table. "He saw me. We spoke, but only briefly. He said he'd message me and we'd get together."

"Did he seem mad?" Mila asks. "Or suspicious?"

"I'm not sure," Clera admits. "Shocked, mostly. We weren't alone. My supervisor was present, so we couldn't really talk. I didn't have a story ready. I should have, but I didn't."

"*We* didn't," Elio adds. "All of us—well, most of us—knew that Zavi might become a problem, yet we didn't plan for it."

Mila says, "Just how close were you two?"

A flush creeps up Clera's cheeks. "Not as close as you and Elio. He'd broken things off with me after his grandfather persuaded him to take the director position. Flying out to colonize a new planet was more important than ... us." She swallows.

Sol says, "Then he shouldn't care that you've managed to find your own way aboard. Or that you never contacted him once you did. He should be happy for you."

"The thing is ..." Clera sips water through a cup specially designed to keep liquids from floating away. "He's not like us. I'm sure he's never broken the law. His moral code might not let him keep this quiet. He's got a top position aboard *Calliope* and no obligation to protect a girl he only knew briefly on Earth." *And only kissed a couple of times.*

"He wouldn't do that." Elio folds his hands atop the table. "Zavi cares for you. Even now. I know he does. When you meet him, just explain ..."

"Wait, she's going to tell the director of the Biosphere that we stole a NASA shuttle and hacked our way into *Calliope*'s system?" Juke's eyes go wide. "I thought maybe we were gathered here to decide on a story. To line up our facts."

"Making up an explanation does seem like a good idea," Mila agrees.

But Elio frowns. His face turns stubborn, and Clera knows he'll support her despite his own doubts. "No. Clera's right. A made-up story will have holes. Zavi's no dummy. He'll know something is up, and then he'll feel angry. Betrayed."

"Maybe even ready for some retribution," Sol adds ominously.

Clera frowns. "Zavi isn't like that. He's kind. Reasonable. And he knows how desperate of a situation Elio and I found ourselves in."

"Sounds like you're in love with him," Mila comments.

Juke adds, "Sure you haven't lost your perspective, darling?"

"It doesn't matter!" The words explode with more emotion than Clera intended. She reigns in her feelings with difficulty. They've been building like a powder keg ever since she reached *Calliope*. The stress of knowing Zavi was aboard and wanting to see him, yet not wanting to, has stretched her to this breaking point. She inhales a breath before continuing, "Zavi has moved on. He might be ... according to Kris, my supervisor ... dating her."

Sol's raspy voice cuts through the clamor of discussion. "Clera and Elio are right. If you can't make up a convincing story, better to stick with the truth. Let her meet him and try to explain. See what he says. We'll go from there. There are no good options, only less bad ones."

We. Sol called herself one of the crew. Did the others catch that? Clera smiles gratefully but adds, "This isn't just my decision since it affects us all. Should we take a vote?"

Mila raises an eyebrow. "Well, you and Elio and Sol are all for telling the truth, so majority rules, I guess."

Juke shrugs. "Go for it, girl. And may love triumph over being a stickler for the law."

Clera thinks about messaging Zavi but chickens out. What if he despises her now? What if he's with Kris, after all? What if he can't abide rulebreakers and regrets ever getting involved with a Slummer like her?

15

Solast

Mila surprises Sol by asking her to remain in the cabin while she takes the pregnancy test. It's not a traditional "pee in a cup" kind but a state-of-the-art blood prick like they only do in doctor's offices. Mila perches on the bunk and waits for the strip's red or green light. It was easy for Sol to steal the supplies Clera requested. Too easy. Everyone trusts her at the clinic. They don't know her past, and she's been a reliable employee.

"Positive," Mila croaks. She bursts into tears, then wipes them away and flashes a dimpled smile. Apparently, mood swings have already kicked in.

Sol sighs in relief when sunshine breaks across the mechanic's face. Comforting people isn't her forte. "Okay." She nods briskly to mask her worry. If this pregnancy gets out, it'll draw unwanted attention. She hands Mila a bag of meds. "Take the prenatal vitamins every morning along with food and the anti-nausea pill." She'd found the medicines tucked away on a back shelf of the clinic and supposes this made sense. Once *Calliope* passes through the ARH, women might be encouraged to pop out babies.

She contains her grimace. That idea seems so ... patriarchal. But even in this day and age, some things remain solely the domain of women.

"Thank you so much." Mila takes the bag. "You know, I didn't like you at first. Everything was going off without a hitch until you showed up."

Sol's hackles rise, but Mila rushes on, "That was before, though. Now I get why you might have been hiding out in Uncle Bas' shuttle."

"*NASA's* shuttle."

"Whatever." Mila waves this away with a grin.

Sol persists, "I wasn't exactly hiding out. Just trying to avoid being raped or murdered in one of the parks while I slept."

"I get that." Mila rises and tucks the pills into a storage locker, her back to Sol as she continues, "It was brill, actually, to think of the prototype. Way more comfortable, too. I was continually having to clear out homeless belongings from the old shuttles in the yard we kept for tours. My uncle ignored my advice about investing in better security."

Mila turns in time to see Sol's nod of acknowledgment. Sol releases a breath she feels she's been holding for weeks. "Well, I'd better be going."

Mila's voice stops her at the door. "Why were you so set on staying on Earth, anyway? Shouldn't you see snagging a berth on *Calliope* as an incredible piece of luck?"

"One minute I was napping in the cargo bay. The next I was bumping my nose against a floor panel and trying not to vomit as the ship shook her bones loose passing out of Earth's atmosphere."

"Would have freaked anyone out." Mila's dimples emerge. "I like how you describe her."

"Huh?"

"The *Goose*. You used the word *bones* just now. I think of these ships as living beings, so our shuttle having 'bones' rings true for me."

Sol raises an eyebrow. "Next you'll be saying we're kindred spirits."

"I wouldn't go that far." Mila mimics the eyebrow, then adds, "But seriously, once you were past the shock, why not embrace this journey? You've been cold as ice for months."

"Maybe I'm just shy."

The eyebrow inches higher. "Right. I'm not buying that. Taciturn, maybe. Sullen, sure. Not shy."

"Gee, thanks."

Mila shrugs. "I call them as I see them."

Sol steps into the corridor, hesitates, and turns back. She has no idea what makes her confess, "I have a score to settle."

"Oh!" Mila's mouth purses in thought. "I can see why you'd be mad at us in that case. We screwed up your plans."

"You could say that." Sol draws the words out, only half believing them as she thinks of seeing Anton in the weightroom. *If not for a bunch of thieves, Mons Vega would have been beyond my reach forever.* She doesn't say it aloud. The crew wouldn't condone murder, and that's what she's intent upon committing. What they don't know won't hurt them. She hopes.

———◇———

Sol studies her new face in a hand mirror and runs a finger along the nu-skin which blends smoothly with her epidermis.

Dr. Chandra knocks before stepping into the post-op room. He fiddles with something in his lab coat pocket and beams. "How did I do?"

"It's like I never had a scar," Sol whispers. If only the memory of that day could be erased so easily.

"I don't understand why you never had it fixed on Earth."

An honest answer like *Slummers can't afford plastic surgery* won't suffice. "I thought I wanted to keep it—as a reminder." She focuses on her reflection in the mirror. Her hair has grown into a pixie cut. Minus the scar and with the weight she's gained aboard *Calliope,* she looks almost pretty. Refined. Upper class. "It was an accident on a playing field. The man who gave it to me died. The scar was my only reminder left of him. But I've started a new life, so maybe it's time to move on."

The lies remind Sol of something Clera said when they first met: *Maybe it's time to let go. Your life lies ahead of you, not in the past.* Those words seem prescient now she knows Anton is here. Once she kills him, she'll be able to finally say goodbye to Father and settle into a new life. First, though, she must *find* Anton again. In New Chicago, he was a needle in a haystack. Here, she has a good idea where to look.

Some "blue-bands," as the colonists call them, manage the shops on Blue Deck. Stores that began as identical-looking restaurants, bars, and grocery shops have developed individual flavor. One such place caught her attention recently while she waited for a lift to Red Deck. "Mixed Drinks and Music" now reads, "Smoke and Ashes."

Smoke and Blues ... Smoke and Ashes.

Sol forgot about the lift and turned to stare while her mind traveled back to a sooty street in downtown New Chicago. At the time, regret and anger had kindled inside her. She'd felt like a lit fuse about to blow. But now?

Standing in the doorway a week later, her thoughts settle. This is the place. Anton will see the resemblance to his old hangout and come here. The round tables and platform at the back of Smoke and Ashes mimic that other bar, just like the dim lighting and dark décor do. The hallway where she overheard Anton's deal with the exec is gone. No glasses clink, and no blues music plays, but it's early. The music might start later, and as for the clink of glass—there is no glass on *Calliope*, just the lidded polymers she sees everywhere. Also, no alcohol. Too flammable. *But he'll come here.*

Slipping inside, Sol orders a faux whiskey at the bar and looks around. It's dinner time, seats filling with off-shift workers. Their blue jumpsuits blur into one homogenous lump. Only a few people defy dress codes with jewelry and jackets. No one can ditch the grav boots, though.

Sol wants to blend in. It's been eleven years since Anton knew her as the traitor Ridge Bahri's daughter from that commune in the Barrens. Has she changed enough to avoid recognition? A few lines frame her eyes now, and she carries herself like a woman who's gone toe-to-toe with life and survived. She was just as tall at seventeen, though with long hair. And, after Anton sliced her, she had the telltale scar.

Sol touches her cheek and studies the crowd while she sips her drink. It burns going down just like whiskey. She coughs, but no one notices. The women and men at the tables chat and laugh and occasionally swear, intent on their conversations. Most wear red wristbands like hers, not surprising since Red Deck encompasses many of *Calliope*'s work divisions. There are a few rainbow bands from Biosphere, though, as well as a scatter of whites from Command, so this place must be doing well.

The barkeep sets a covered metal dish on the magnetic bartop. Sol reaches into the hole on the side to grab a handful of nuts. She slides them into her mouth without any floating off. She's getting better at this anti-grav stuff. Juke wanders in clutching the arm of a man made entirely of muscle, and Sol freezes mid-swallow to observe them. Juke's companion has a square face, wide mouth, and beard-shadowed jaw. A cleft chin tops off this impressive display of testosterone. Though Sol only saw him once on Earth, she recognizes him.

No surprise. Every detail of that night in Smoke and Blues is imprinted upon her brain. She pretends to stare at her cup but studies Juke and his friend beneath her lashes. Definitely the same guy. When Anton left that hallway at Smoke and Blues, he'd joined a bunch of Earthers at a table. There had been an older, steel-haired man, a voluptuous woman and her equally voluptuous companion, a slight, scholarly guy with sandy hair, and this one. The looker. Someone who could have been peeled from a billboard advertisement for aftershave. Of course, she recalls him. Who wouldn't?

Juke and his friend take the last two chairs at a table filled with Red Deckers who greet them with hearty slaps and cheers. Sol looks for Earther tattoos on their necks, but they don't have any. No one could get aboard *Calliope* with such a mark. Tattoos might be easy to remove in a high-end Earth clinic, yet that still doesn't explain how Anton's followers slipped aboard—unless he arranged their passage along with his own departure.

A chill runs through her. *Of course he did. But how many? And why?*

Excitement replaces fear. She's on the right track. Anton will show up any minute, and she'll follow him, learn which berth is his, and then—. Her thoughts lurch to a stop when Juke spots her and calls, "Sol! Come say hello!"

She winces at his use of her name. This is the old, jovial Juke, the one she'd barely met before he received his rot job assignment and turned sullen. He wraps one arm across the hunk's shoulder and beckons with his cup. Maybe the walking, talking cologne ad explains Juke's high spirits. Sol frowns and sidles over. *This is a chance*, she tells herself. But what if Anton shows up and recognizes her? She wants to stay in the background, not be drawn into his crowd.

Juke offers her the last remaining seat, and unable to find an excuse, she slides into it. He raises his voice above the conversation around them. "I didn't expect to see you here."

"I drink," she offers shortly.

Juke points. "This is Jo-Jo, R.B., Orion, and Muff." He pats his companion's shoulder. "And Anvil."

Anvil. That figures.

"And this is Sol," Juke tells them. Her name again. A curse rises to her lips. If she's lucky, Anton won't know her face anymore, but he might know that name.

She thinks fast. "No, not Sol. I'm Hanna. Sol was just a kid name I used on Earth, kind of like Sunny, you know?"

R.B., a short, stocky guy with huge biceps, says, "Sure, we know. We all left names behind, too. Took on ones with more meaning."

Sol wonders what possible meaning "R.B." could have yet doesn't ask.

She keeps her eyes on Juke and repeats with emphasis, "Hanna." It's close to her birth name, Anna, but different enough to pass inspection. Where is Anton, anyway? And what'll she do if he shows? She doesn't trust herself to meet him face to face. Her rage simmers too close to the surface. She's got to be smart, not reckless.

Juke tilts his head at her, a curious expression in his eyes. Yet he doesn't question her. Jo-Jo, a well-built woman with flashing black eyes and a nose ring, makes some joke, and conversation moves past and over Sol. Orion, the guy with the bowling ball head, orders another round of drinks. Muff uses her Skinpad to pay for the round. She looks like her name, a soft, doughy female, mid-thirties, with brown eyes and lank brown hair. Anvil is the only one Sol remembers from Anton's old crowd.

She studies the entrance for him when she isn't watching Juke. His new friends seem to be part of his Life Support crew. Venters. It's great Juke's made friends, but these guys? Is only Anvil an Earther, or are they all? Beefcakes rests a proprietary hand on Juke's leg, and they lean close to each other, obviously in the throes of first love. Just great.

She puts up with their raucous jokes and work talk as long as she can, then rises and says she has to be going.

"No," Jo-Jo whines, acting sloshed even though drunkenness is a physical impossibility.

"Come back again," R.B. chimes in, and the others nod.

Sol turns to Juke. "We'll talk later."

There's a pause before he purrs, "Sure, *Hanna*."

16

Solast

Before Sol reaches the exit, someone cups her elbow and breathes hotly into her ear. "Going so soon, beautiful?"

She rolls her eyes, fights for calm, and pulls away from the man. He looks like a bouncer—all muscle and no brain. One of Anton's men? No reason to think so. Anton might not even frequent this bar. "I'm not interested."

"Why not?" The man holds out his hands. "I'm a nice guy, and look." He waves a white-banded wrist. "I'm high up in Command."

Huh. If this guy only knew how *less* desirable his rank makes him. She wants to stay far away from anyone connected with laws and rules. Besides, Sol hasn't considered romance or sex since she was a teenager. Once she left the commune, her life focused on survival. Well, mostly. A doctor at the health clinic briefly caught her eye, but then the clinic closed. That chapter of her life ended.

The man stares at her while she daydreams. "Thinking about it now, aren't you." He nods like he's wise to the ways of women.

She wants to knock his head off. Instead, she scans the room for an excuse to get away. Her gaze falls on a back table where a man sits alone sipping a drink. It's that speaker from her first class, the archeologist. She turns to the guy beside her. "Um, no thank you. I have a boyfriend." She points Dr. Lehmann's way.

"Him? Isn't he too old for you? Sure you don't want someone young and fit like me?" He flexes a bicep and grins.

Repelled, Sol edges around him with a mumbled, "Sorry," and heads toward the archeologist. Once she reaches his table, she glances back, but the other man's eyes still track her. She slides into the chair opposite the lecturer and flashes an apologetic smile. "Hi. Do you mind if I join you for a minute? I told that guy gawking at me by the bar that you're my boyfriend. Sorry to disturb you. I was trying to avoid a scene."

Dr. Lehmann's eyebrows rise. He looks past her shoulder, then back to her, and their eyes meet. His are the mild brown she remembers, crinkled at the corners. A five-o'clock shadow follows the contours of his jaw. His nose is long and narrow, his forehead high. Brown hair tinged with gray around the ears waves neatly across his skull.

"You decided to stay aboard *Calliope*." He hesitates. "Or you weren't able to find a way off."

She likes his rumbly voice—deep as a well and somehow calming. "The second," Sol admits. "And I can't believe you remember me. We met so briefly in the hallway after boarding. That was months ago."

"I never forget a face. I'm Oskar, by the way, in case *you* forgot." He sips his drink, gaze steady on her.

"Solast Bahri. Sol for short."

"Named for the sun."

"It's a spirit name. I was born *Anna* but chose *Solast* when I was twelve. Most people in my group picked names with meanings. Mine ... well, it just came to me. But that table over there thinks I'm Hanna." With a nod toward Juke's friends, she adds, "So don't call me 'Sol' too loudly. Long story." The words must sound crazy, and she can't help grimacing.

Oskar doesn't seem perturbed. He focuses on her cheek. "You took my advice, after all, and had scar removal surgery. They did a good job, though I find myself agreeing with you that scars aren't always a bad thing. They give one character and serve as reminders of things best not forgotten."

She feels her face warm beneath Oskar's perusal. He sees too much, and his observations land too close to truth. "Perhaps I would have received less unwanted attention if I'd kept it."

He cocks his head. "No. You would be a beautiful woman either way. It wouldn't have mattered." The words sound like flirting, yet his expression remains serious.

She smiles nervously and picks at her wrist cuff. Compliments unnerve her, so she changes the subject. "Why were you sitting all alone here, Oskar—Lehmann, right?"

"Yes. Professor Lehmann, technically, but please don't call me that. Just Oskar. And I enjoy solitude. My office is small. I don't interact much with co-workers, and I know few people aboard *Calliope*, but that's all right." He shrugs and sips. "Like I said, I'm content with my own company."

Sol remembers her fake whiskey and tips it back. The drink offends her taste buds, and she sets it down again, frowning.

Oskar smiles. "Not the same, is it? Just something to do and a place to be, after hours."

"Right." She'd much rather remain in her cabin than be surrounded by noise and bustle, but she doesn't add that.

"I get tired of the four white walls of my shuttle. It's NASA's shuttle, really, and it doesn't feel like home. I'll admit I've done little decorating. Maybe that would help."

"NASA flew you up to *Calliope*?"

"I'm the ship's top expert on Martian civilization. I'm serving as consultant to the Command division and, well, teaching a few classes."

"Yes! I went to your class. It was very interesting." Sol leans forward, realizes how eager she must look, and pushes back again.

"You are kind, but I believe everyone was forced to attend, so you needn't compliment me. I'm sure many are complaining about their off hours being taken up with these learning modules. Especially those classes that don't relate directly to topics such as survival on the surface."

"You're wrong. My crewmate and I were both fascinated by your talk. How can colonists not want to know about the Martian technology that created the ARH and is the reason they *get* to colonize?"

He shrugs and swirls the liquid in his cup. "Technology isn't my area, really. Culture is. The past. In my twenties, I worked in the field on Mars, and I've studied many of the Martian artifacts uncovered after the quake that shut down the cloaking device shielding the wormhole."

"What did you do on Earth?"

"Professor at Yale. You?"

"I was a medic at a public health clinic. And I birthed babies in the Barrens."

"You lived in the Barrens?"

"I shouldn't have told you that." Her hand tightens around the cup.

"Why not?"

"It's a part of my life I'm trying to forget, and I'd rather you didn't mention it again." She regrets the sharpness in her voice yet doesn't apologize.

Oskar leans forward and peers at her like she's one of his specimens. "You are a puzzle, Sol Anna Hanna." His lilting murmur makes her wince. "You lived in the wilderness, then somehow made your way into ... where?"

"New Chicago," she mumbles.

"Then worked at a clinic where I'm certain the pay is low. Yet you managed to obtain a berth on *Calliope*. That's pretty remarkable."

"I won a lottery to get aboard." The lie comes easily, but Sol doubts he believes her. Coming to his table was a bad idea. She likes this Oskar, though. He exudes comfort like a thick winter coat or a ... *Good gods! Snap out of it!*

She's drawn to him. That's a fact. Best to nip this attraction in the bud, yet she doesn't rise.

Oskar remains silent for a moment. Sol's palms are sweating by the time his mouth quirks and he finally speaks. "I think you might be a spy." He ticks off reasons on his fingers. "Many aliases. Has traveled in dangerous places. Seems extremely lucky. Those are great characteristics for a spy."

"I'm just a nurse on Red Deck. Sorry to dash your hopes."

"You think my hopes are dashed? Do I have hopes?" A crease forms at the bridge of his nose while he considers this. Finally, he says more to himself than to her, "Maybe I do." A note of surprise lifts his words.

Sol decides to end this conversation before it spirals out of control. "Is that brute at the bar still staring at me?"

Oskar squints past her shoulder. "He's found a new conquest. They have a table. And the group of folks who only know you as Hanna seems to be getting up."

"Good." Sol sighs, then remembers she was going to catch Juke. "I'd better follow them."

That eyebrow again. "To spy?"

A laugh bursts out, surprising her. "Of course not! I used the wrong words. One guy at that table is my shuttlemate, and I want to warn him away from another guy he's with."

"The male model with the chiseled jaw."

"Well, yes." Again, she can't help grinning. The rusty movement comes more easily, like a gear freshly lubricated with oil.

Oskar reaches a big hand across the table. She takes it without thinking. His fingers envelop hers, and warmth travels up her arm. "I'd like to see you again." He says this earnestly, with no innuendo.

"How ... how old are you?"

"Does it matter?" Disappointment colors his question.

"No! No. I was just curious."

"Thirty-eight. And you must be ... eighteen?"

"I don't look that young, but thanks. And yes, I'd like that. To see you again. Maybe." Why do words tumble out of her mouth like thrown jacks? Though it's a bad idea, she nevertheless exchanges private messaging numbers with Oskar. At least he doesn't make her commit to a date. She'll have time to make up some reason she can't meet. Perhaps he'll be glad. Dating a "spy" might prove risky for both of them.

———◆———

Juke's friend Anvil parts with him soon after the other Venters disperse down various corridors along Blue Deck. Sol hurries to catch up. Juke's still staring dreamily after Beefcakes when she calls him back to earth with a whack on the shoulder.

He jumps. "Hey!" And his eyes turn wary. "What do you want? Another shot at an escape pod? I don't think they're designed to deposit people back on Earth from this distance."

"Thanks, but no thanks. I've resigned myself to life aboard *Calliope*." She falls into step beside him.

"Good for you, girl. Easy to do when you have the sweet job you always wanted and a place to call home."

"You have a place to call home, too," she reminds him. "And your job in the ducts won't last forever."

"True." He eyes her sideways. "What's gotten into you, Sol also known as Hanna?"

She keeps her gaze on the path ahead. "I have reasons for that name not to get around outside the *Goose*, all right? Thanks for going along with me."

He stops in the middle of the hallway. A group of colonists split like water around rocks to miss him. "Are you in some kind of trouble beyond trespassing on NASA shuttles? Something that could get the rest of us noticed?"

"Nothing like you think." She takes his arm and urges him to keep moving. "Nothing against the law. But that guy you're hanging with? Anvil? I've seen him before. Did he tell you he's part of a cult called the Earthers?"

Juke allows himself to be led but gapes at her. "How do you know that?"

"He's from New Chicago just like you, right?"

"Yeah. That's how I got to talking with him. He's on my crew. Anvil worked in tech for the execs and saved up money for a berth."

"Anvil looks more like a male prostitute to me."

"Doesn't he, though?" Unoffended, Juke goes dreamy-eyed.

"Hey, snap out of it! This man isn't who you think he is."

"How do you know him, then?"

"Well, I don't really *know* him," she admits. "Last time I saw him, it was at a similar bar, and he was with a bunch of Earther cultists. Those people are dangerous. He's gotten rid of his tattoo, but look closely on his neck. Maybe there's some remnant. Or ask him and see what his reaction is, but don't bring me into it."

Juke turns forward so only his profile shows. Sol drops his arm, yet he seems content to continue walking beside her. Without his silken shirts and polished shoes, he looks vulnerable. Sympathy nudges her heart.

"Look, I get that you've had a hard time, believe me. But Anvil isn't the answer."

"What you say doesn't even make sense. Why would an Earther book out on *Calliope*? Those people hate tech. They think it's the main thing destroying the Earth. 'The earth belongs to the earth' and all that."

"Yeah. And it's 'Earthers'."

"What?"

"Earthers. Plural. I've seen at least two I recognize."

"Were you one of them, then?"

"Not for long. And I'm not telling you about it, so quit looking at me like that. All you need to know is that these guys can't be up to anything good on *Calliope*, and if you stick with Anvil, you'll become involved."

"Thanks for the concern, *dar*ling." Juke adds an extra dose of irony. "But I'm finally having a little fun on this trip, and your story doesn't hold weight. Not without details. You've done nothing to make me trust you. I've got to have reasons why I *should* trust your words before I take your advice."

"Why would I lie?"

He lets that settle. "You might think you really saw Anvil and this other guy among Earthers in New Chicago, but people look alike, you know. Ever thought you might be a little paranoid?"

"Of course I am. That doesn't mean I'm not also correct." They've reached their berth. Sol glares at Juke. He seems like such a kid, especially when stripped of his fancy clothes. His manicured eyebrows and clipped nails are almost perfect. Only one tiny scar—a mere scratch—mars his smooth skin.

Juke's eyes widen. "Hey, you fixed your face! I should have noticed at the bar. It looks good."

"You're changing the subject."

"Yep." His mouth forms that crooked, devil-may-care smile she remembers from the first day she met him. He was a tech whiz then. A hacker genius. Not some glorified janitor. She knows how it feels to come down so far.

Sol sighs. She's done what she can. Maybe this crush will die its own quiet death without further interference. She fingers the crucifix tucked beneath her jumpsuit and offers a prayer to saints she barely remembers. "Don't forget, you can call me Sol aboard the *Blue Goose*, but if I see you out with those scrulls, either ignore me or call me Hanna."

He salutes her and opens the portal. "No problemo."

"Wait!"

"Yes?"

"You put my name into the manifest as 'Sol,' right? Maybe I should be listed as 'Hanna' on official channels. Is it too late for that?"

"Probably not. I doubt anyone would notice."

"Could you change it?" She hates asking and feels her cheeks burn.

Juke just shrugs. "Sure, *Hanna*. I'll do it tonight."

After he leaves, she rubs at her temples and groans. Why didn't she think of changing her name before? The whole clinic knows her as Sol. That's the problem with lying. Once you start, you create a web of confusion. Lies lead to more lies, and suddenly …

Oh, well. There's nothing she can do about the past except cross her fingers and hope no one discovers her duplicity.

17

Clera

A message pings on Clera's community chat. Adrenaline fires through every nerve when she sees it's from Zavi. He's left an invitation to join his private account. Her finger hovers over the link, but she doesn't tap it. Maybe she's afraid, or maybe she's just being cautious ... probably the former. He already knows she's here, so there's no use ignoring him. She needs to get her story straight, though. Sure, she told the crew she'd be honest, yet *how* she explains herself matters.

Elio steps into the commons area, whistling. It's getting late. Everyone except Juke is back on the *Goose*. He's been gone a lot—more hours than work can account for. Yet he's more cheerful, too, so perhaps she shouldn't worry. Her brother grabs an energy bar from its cupboard slot and flops down beside her on the couch. "Hey, sis. Did Mila tell you?"

"Um, no. Tell me what?" She pulls her sleeve over her Skinpad and Zavi's message.

"Mila's pregnant." Elio focuses on opening the food packet while he speaks. She doubts he's as relaxed as he sounds.

"I thought maybe she was—I asked Sol to get a test from the clinic. So how are you feeling about it?"

He takes a bite. "I don't know. Happy? Scared? Worried? Take your pick."

"But you're not going to abort this baby."

"Hells, no." He chews and finally looks at her. "Mila's really excited. And she thinks if she wears her work coat outside the *Goose*, no one will notice until after we break through the ARH. Once we start building a colony, she'll probably become a hero. Her name will go down in history as being the first human to give birth outside the solar system."

Clera nods slowly, not surprised at their decision. She recalls Mila saying she wanted to have babies with Elio, and that was at the *start* of their relationship. "Did you tell Juke?"

"Not yet. I thought you should be first to know."

Her brain switches gears. "Have you spoken much to him lately? You know Juke better than anyone but Mila. He seems more like his old self."

"I think he has a boyfriend. Someone on his work detail. Love is making that job more pleasant for him."

"Anyone you've met?"

"No. I suppose he'll tell us more when he's ready."

"He wouldn't be doing anything illegal on the side, right? Like practicing his old 'tech skills'? I know he misses that life, yet I worry he could get caught. I mean, we wouldn't be here without those skills, so I feel bad saying that, but—"

"Hey." Elio squeezes her thigh. "You're taking this leadership thing pretty seriously. Relax a little. We've made it this far, and we'll make it through the wormhole. After that, we're home free."

Are we, though? She buttons her lips and quells her doubts.

The next day at breakfast, Mila officially breaks her baby news to everyone—meaning Juke—and explains how she'll hide the pregnancy. She claims to feel better, thanks to Sol's meds, so that'll help. Juke looks around the table and jokes, "I'm the last to know, aren't I. Well, cheers to both of you anyway. Can I be Uncle Juke?"

Mila and Elio share a look that excludes everyone else. Clera rubs at an ache along her breastbone. Her brother's happy, building a life with someone. That's all that matters.

Juke breaks into her thoughts. He stares at Sol but speaks loudly like he's addressing them all. "Hey, Sol, nice fix on the scar. Maybe you have a new boyfriend you want to impress?" His mouth curves into a teasing grin.

"No," she answers shortly with her typical glare. Does Juke receive an extra dose of vitriol?

"Okay, then," he titters.

"You look great," Clera tells her. Elio and Mila nod their agreement. When did Sol find time for plastic surgery?

Sol stares down at the table and mutters, "It was free, so why not? The scar was making me stand out, and you want to keep this crew under the radar, right?"

More nods. Sol's shoulders unhitch. They finish breakfast and trickle out to meet the day. Clera can't forget her message from Zavi but shoves it to the back of her mind for now.

⸺◆⸺

Nothing seems to have changed at work except that Maya gives her a curious stare before leaving the warehouse to check cucumber seedlings in the gardens. Kris is as officious and micro-managing as ever, but before long she disappears into her office. Clera catches glimpses of the Ice Queen through the cracked door while sorting seeds at a worktable. She's happy to see her supervisor focused so intently on her tablet.

There's no time to look at the community chat, and she'd be breaking one of Kris' rules if she did. That afternoon, a new message glows briefly beneath the micro-wicking of her sleeve, but Clera keeps working. She's just following protocol, not avoiding Zavi. Right? Later, as she cleans her workspace, Kris appears at her elbow. Clera startles when she turns to see the woman standing there with folded arms.

"Are you done for the day?" Kris asks.

"Almost." Clera looks around to reassure herself everything is in order.

"You haven't been answering your messages."

"I thought we weren't supposed to."

"That rule's for private ones. Work messages are obviously allowed. Dr. Fadel wants to see you in his office."

Clera feels herself blanch.

Kris' lips form a satisfied smile. "If you're in trouble, don't expect me to bail you out. Zavi and I are close, but I'd never presume to interfere when it comes to work."

Clera bites back a retort. Why bother? She finishes wiping her table, checks *Calliope*'s map for directions to Zavi's office, and heads to the Red Deck level of the Biosphere.

She expected his workspace to look homey, with plants and pottery scattered throughout, yet sterility rules. There's a desk, chairs, and a conference table. Large windows overlook the paths and orchards outside. Though he's in charge, no secretary or reception desk occupy this space. His title, "Zavi Fadel, Biosphere Director," appears on a placard beside his door.

Clera drew a calming breath before entering, but she's already edgy again. Zavi sits behind a shiny new desk that places a wall between them. She feels like a student called to the principal's office. Maybe she *is* in trouble, for all she knows. She perches on a seat and tucks her feet beneath the chair. Clera left her grav boots in a locker and feels naked without them.

Zavi laces his fingers together and regards her with fathomless blue eyes. They were the first thing to attract her back on Earth. Azure as the sky, warm as sunshine. "You didn't read my message."

"I was busy at work today. Kris doesn't let us use our Skinpads until after hours. Sorry. Am I in trouble?"

He blinks and doesn't answer right away.

She feels his gaze searching hers and forces her features into a blank mask.

"Should you be? In trouble?"

"I don't think so. No. Definitely not." This isn't going well. She pictures Elio rolling his eyes. Clera just told her first lie, and she's *so* bad at it.

Zavi looks like he's waiting for more of an explanation but hates to ask for one. She can't help him. Anything she says will make her sound guilty. Finally, he sighs. "I called you up here to offer you a job."

"What?" Her heart stops, then restarts double time. Confusion clouds her brain.

"You can't be happy working for Ms. Bjorndottir downstairs." At her stunned expression, he adds, "The Ice Queen?"

"You call her that, too?"

"Doesn't everyone?" He almost smiles.

"Kris has been bragging that you two are dating. I thought you were going out to dinner when we first met, not to a work meeting."

"Ah." His intense gaze relaxes. "I'll have words with her about that."

"Oh, no. You'd only get me yelled at. She's hard enough to work with as it is."

He cocks his head. "If you accept my job proposition, that won't matter. Kris rarely comes up here."

"You mean I'd be working in research with you?"

"I could use another assistant. We're going through data from the *Pioneer* probes and attempting to replicate some of Vishnu's flora. Does that sound interesting?"

"Oh, yes!" She feels like she did back in the Boba Tea Cafe, with Zavi Fadel offering her an interview for a greenhouse job. Clera pulls herself back to the present. "I don't understand why you would offer me such a position. Don't most people in research have college degrees?"

He shrugs. "It's not required, and I know you'd be a reliable employee."

"But ... but ..."

"It's simple. You seem unhappy working for Ms. Bjorndottir, and I can fix that. In return, you'll help ease my burden. I know you, and there are very few people aboard *Calliope* I can say that about."

"Aren't you wondering how I even came to be here?"

Silence reverberates between them.

His folded hands show white at the knuckles. "It's enough that you're here," he finally mutters, staring into space. "Maybe someone helped you. Perhaps in exchange for something. I don't know. It's not my business."

"If you're suggesting I gave myself to some man in order to get a berth, you don't know me very well. Besides, when exactly would I have arranged all that? Between saving my brother from being deported to the Barrens and saying goodbye to you before you left me?"

"It wasn't like that." He squeezes his eyes shut, then opens them. "My grandfather wanted this for me. You know that. I owed him, and he trusts me to help set this new world on a better path than the one that has ruined Earth. I couldn't turn my back on that."

"I know." Her outrage deflates, replaced by something tender. Something that aches inside and makes her want to touch him. She clenches her hands in her lap. "I'm glad you took this job. And I know you must be wondering how I'm here. But maybe you really don't want to know. If I tell you—"

"Don't, then."

"What?"

"If knowing will put me in a bad position, perhaps I'm better left in ignorance."

Clera swallows. She wasn't expecting this. "So where does that leave us? Employer and employee?"

"I'd like to take you to dinner."

"Oh." Her heart pounds. Her blood races. "Um, like a work dinner?"

"Like a date." He unlaces his hands and sits back. The hint of a smile traces his lips again.

"There isn't some policy against such things?"

He shrugs. "Not that I'm aware of. I'm in charge here, you know. I have no boss."

"Right." Clera can't meet his eyes. What would Kris say if she knew? She'd be furious, for sure, and imagining that decides Clera. "Okay. When and where?"

"I have a place in mind. I'll message you if you share your private chat."

She rises. "When do I start my job here?"

"Tomorrow, if that works. I'll let Kris know." He rises, too, and comes around the desk. He hesitates, then takes her hands. He stares at them while he speaks. "When I saw you down in the warehouse, I couldn't believe it. When I blinked and you didn't vanish, I guessed I wasn't hallucinating ... and something in me lightened. Since I left Earth, life's felt so *heavy*. I haven't heard from my cousin, and Grandfather has been ill. My work here is lonely. Challenging, yes. Interesting, yes. But solitary. Then you appeared like some kind of miracle."

Zavi looks up, gaze intense and filled with hope. *He doesn't know what I've done to get here.* She disentangles her hands and steps back. "Zavi—"

"If you don't feel the same, or if you've met someone new, please tell me now."

She shakes her head. "I haven't met anyone," she replies in a strangled voice. So much more wants out, yet the words clog in her throat. "Thank you," she manages. "For believing in me."

He nods.

Clera backs away. Those blue eyes watch her until the door closes. Later, she accepts the link that connects them in private chat.

18

Clera

Despite Zavi's dinner date offer, he doesn't message her with a "when and where" that week. Instead, he lets her settle into the Biosphere's research department. She's got her own small office, her own desk, her own tablet loaded with data from the *Pioneer* probes. He shows her around a high-security greenhouse and gives her a special key card to gain entrance. Inside, under grow-lights and encased in protective coverings, his team produces facsimiles of flora found on Vishnu. They've given the plants names like *toxifera* and *nutrivine*, but Clera's favorite is *emerald kelp*. The bright green, long-fingered plant floats in a hydroponic vat filled with special water that imitates seas on the green planet.

The other two assistants, introverted men with little sense of humor, patiently answer her many questions that first week. They wear protective gear and masks around the alien plants, and they teach her concepts such as scientific method, control groups, and the importance of taking meticulous care and copious notes.

Zavi stops by with instructions for new experiments to conduct. He explains to Clera that while the Biosphere's regular gardens help feed the colonists, the plants in this lab may save their lives on Vishnu by providing new medicines, protections against foreign pathogens, and sustenance that thrives on its home world. For the first time in her life, Clera feels a part of something important. Crucial, even.

Finally, Zavi's message pings on her Skinpad—an invitation to dinner at a South Korean restaurant on Blue Deck. Clera remembers her friend, Soo Yun, who worked at the Boba Tea Cafe and introduced Zavi to her. It makes sense for him to choose a Korean restaurant. Nostalgic. *Something lightened in me when I saw you.* What does he want from her?

Calligraphic lettering lights up the front of the restaurant. Clera arrives five minutes early, but Zavi's already there. He beckons her in, and a petite Asian girl seats them in a booth beneath painted silk tapestries. A waitress hands them old-fashioned printed menus, magnetized to stick to the table. Without its ambient decorations, this place could be any eatery on Blue Deck. Still, "eating out" makes her feel almost like she's on Earth. She supposes Command wants to keep the colonists happy and reassured with such reminders.

"You seem deep in thought."

Zavi's voice jolts her back to the present. The past week has lulled the nervous flutter she feels whenever she encounters him. He's been professional, kind, and most of all, uninterested in how she came to be here. In his place, she'd want to know—unless he doesn't care. Yet he *did* ask her out ...

"I'm so confused," she mutters.

His brow furrows. "About?"

"Us. Thank you for giving me a job—again. But you should be feeling something besides pity or sympathy for me. I thought you'd be angry. Disappointed." She squeezes her eyes closed. "Hurt," she whispers.

When she looks at him again, he's ruffling the menu and clearing his throat. "Maybe we should just stick to ordering food right now. I'm not ready for deep conversations yet."

"Right." *And yet you asked me out.* She swallows back all the things she wants to say and simply replies, "I *am* grateful. And seeing you lightened something in me, too."

His frown eases. He glances around. "This place was supposed to remind you of the Boba Tea Cafe, but they aren't much alike. There are no funny masks on the walls and no boba tea."

She smiles. "And no kimchi special."

"I will aways miss that."

Clera's shoulders relax. "I wonder how Soo Yun is doing out in the government-sanctioned commune." She'd gone there with her family to reunite with an estranged sister before Clera left Earth. At the time, her loss heaped another desertion onto the growing pile. Clera's mother. Zavi. Her friend from the factory. Only Elio hadn't disappeared from her life.

If Zavi notices she's lost focus again, he doesn't comment, only says, "She probably isn't any worse off than if she'd stayed in New Chicago. That cafe was going to shut down soon anyway."

"And then you'd have had to find a job for her, too."

"Ha. Maybe."

The waitress shows up. They order food by pointing at photos attached to unpronounceable names. She takes the menus and departs.

"I hope I'm something more than a savior to you."

Another U-turn into dangerous territory. Yet she wants to be honest and open. More than that, she has no desire to hurt Zavi, so she answers, "Of course you were. Are. You can be both, you know. The hero who rescues people as well as someone I ..." She falters.

"You what?"

She'd been about to say *love.* "... care about."

"I care for you, too." His gaze softens. "That day with the fireworks celebration for President Bendurin's birthday, I'd gone looking for you, but you'd vanished from the bungalow. Finally, I found your old apartment building—or the empty lot where it used to be—and sat across the street for hours on a bench. My shuttle flight got moved up, and I had to leave the next day, wondering all the while what you thought of me. Hoping you'd be okay. I'm not surprised that you were. You're stronger than you think."

Clera imagines Zavi watching the fireworks and wonders if he glimpsed the flash of the *Blue Goose* as it streaked through Earth's atmosphere on a mad dash toward a new life. She almost tells him the truth, but the words don't come, and maybe that's best.

They compare experiences arriving on the starship until Zavi's spicy barbeque and Clera's glass noodles and vegetables arrive in their nil-grav containers. They eat with their fingers and drink plain tea. Comfortable silence falls across the table. Finally, Zavi wipes his mouth, tucks the napkin into a slot for waste, and asks, "Are you enjoying working with Stark and Barak in the lab?"

"Oh, are those their names?" She quirks an eyebrow at him. Images of the nearly identical, soft-spoken men form in her mind. She can only tell them apart because one is bald and pale, the other topped with a mop of salt and pepper hair.

"Not the best company, are they? I inherited them from the guy who was supposed to be up here running the Biosphere. He and Stark and Barak started preparing the special greenhouse months ago. Lots of Biosphere workers joined the crew early. At least my other assistants don't care for drama or one-upping anyone."

Clera tucks her used dishes into the slot. They whoosh away through a tube leading under the floor. "I thought you were the first choice to run the Biosphere."

"Oh, no. I don't have the credentials for a job like this, nor the experience." He flushes with embarrassment. "I must admit that I'm a good example of rich privilege, though I had nothing to do with promoting myself for the job or paying off anyone. That was all Grandfather, like I told you before."

"All that matters is you're here." She reaches out to touch his hand but pulls back just in time. That intimacy feels like crossing a line.

Zavi doesn't seem to notice. "You see, Grandfather and Dr. Gatak are old friends. He's the engineer who named the red dwarf solar system we're traveling to and helped design this ship. He brought in Dr. Aman, a renowned botanist, and Grandfather put up quite a bit of money for this journey. Anyway, they became close friends, and when Dr. Aman got sick and couldn't make the trip, my grandfather convinced him to let me take his place. Being young is an advantage here. You don't see many people even Stark's and Barak's age aboard *Calliope*."

"And they don't resent you being their boss?"

"I suppose they would if I were incompetent, which I'm not." He grins wryly. "Besides, do they seem like the kind of guys to harbor resentments? They just want to be left alone to conduct their experiments."

Clera nods, knowing he's right. "But surely some people in the Biosphere feel differently."

Zavi shrugs. "My job, like I said, is pretty solitary. What do I care if a few passengers I don't know stare daggers at me or make snide comments about rich kids behind my back?"

In his place, *she* might care. She's always worried too much about what others think. Another way they're different—besides their upbringing, education, and probably a bunch of other things. Yet she's still drawn to him like he's a puzzle piece and she's the puzzle—like he's a missing part of herself.

"What are you thinking?" He reads her emotions too clearly. She sees it in the smile behind his eyes.

"Just that we aren't much alike, yet we always seem able to carry on a discussion anyway."

"I don't want to date someone who's my clone." He grimaces. "I spend enough time with myself as it is."

"Are we dating, then?"

"Do you want that?"

The answer should be easy, but Clera ponders it. The secrets she keeps make everything complicated. "I want to spend time with you. Maybe I should tell you—"

He interrupts by covering her hand with his and saying, "Not yet. Let me just enjoy getting to know you again without the burden of things that might … that could …"

"Burden." She latches onto that word. "I'm a burden."

"You're deliberately misinterpreting me." He holds her hand tightly when she tries to withdraw and leans forward. "We have time. Not everything has to be talked out and decided tonight."

Is he right? She's unsure, yet he's offering her an easy out, and she takes it. "Alright."

He lets her go.

"When you find out I'm secretly a spy sent by President Bendurin to infiltrate this ship, you'll be sorry."

Their laughter mingles. Doubts lurk in the shadows, though, at least for Clera. She has to tell him and soon—whether he wants to hear the truth or not.

— • —

Day 24

I've recovered from a nasty but short-lived cold. This entry picks up from the Day 13 entry concerning my three staple food sources on Vishnu:

Aurora Blossoms - Palm-sized, luminescent flowers that grow in sunlit clearings, open by morning, and close at sunset. Sweet, floral tasting, and packed with vitamins. Also multi-colored like the aurora borealis at its best ... and beautiful.

Thorny Shield Bark - An all-too-common bush found in Vishnu's forests, quite annoying to hike around, but stripped of its thorns and chopped, this shrub provides zest for salads. Additionally, the thick base contains a tangy, sweet liquid rich in nutrients.

Kelp - (Yes, I know. Not a poetic or original name.) This plant, found in undersea groves, provides an abundant, easy-to-preserve food source chocked with vitamin A. If salted and hung to dry for several days, it will last a solid month if not more. My skin has turned green from eating so much of it (an exaggeration).

P.S. I realize my "scientific journal" has veered into the personal. Forgive me. Dry observations were never my forte, and since no one may ever read these musings, who the helv cares?

-N.J.

19

Niklas

The shuttle rises from a broad, sand-packed beach. Niklas watches the landscape diminish as the ship pushes into turquoise-stained skies dotted with alien rings. Cliffs and lush, vivid forests fall away on both sides. The emerald sea stretches toward a distant horizon. No birds dot the skies, just like no animal life seems to inhabit the forests. This bothers Niklas, but he keeps his worries to himself. They have more immediate problems, such as why no one on *Lycka* is answering messages.

Beside him, Adrian stretches his legs into the aisle. He's a shorter, stockier version of Niklas, clean-shaven, with a buzz cut and a barrel chest. His nose was broken and never fixed, so he must like his brawler look. Niklas can see why—it only enhances the tough-guy image—useful for a security officer.

Once they break atmo, Dana locks in a route to catch the orbiting starship, and *Lycka* comes into view an hour later. Niklas tells the pilot to hail her and continue hailing her until she responds. Dana taps in a flight path to keep them trailing the big ship, then does as instructed. Nik tells himself to relax but doesn't succeed.

"*Lycka*, do you read?" Silence. "*Lycka*, do you read?" More silence.

He turns to the security chief. "Adrian, can you hack into the security cameras aboard the ship?"

"No need to hack. I have top clearance. This close to her, there shouldn't be interference." He fiddles with his Skinpad, frowns, fiddles some more. "You'd better look at this."

Niklas leans over Adrian's shoulder as he displays the black and white footage on his arm. *Lycka*'s empty halls look deserted. Adrian taps some more, and new views of various decks come up. In the entertainment commons, bodies slump over tables. In the gravity-rich workout room, treadmill belts cycle beneath bodies that seize and shiver with the movement. "*Helv*." He rarely swears, but the expletive seems appropriate. "What has happened? Can you switch decks? Go to the command center. I want to view security footage in the hangar bay, too."

"What are you two seeing back there?" Dana snaps through the helmet mic.

Niklas describes the scene in terse tones. "Bodies everywhere. Like people were caught unawares and died without having time to react. How can that be on a ship as state-of-the-art as *Lycka*?"

"Gas." Adrian closes the screen and pulls his sleeve down. "Only thing I can think of."

Niklas nods thoughtfully. A chill runs down his spine. "An accident?"

Adrian shakes his head. "Unlikely, yet not impossible. No system is foolproof."

"Sabotage, then? But why would anyone do such a thing? What would they have to gain?" Scenarios scroll through his brain. He settles on the most likely. "Could someone on Earth have been sending a message? Someone who missed out on the chance to come along, maybe?"

"A case of sour grapes?" Dana chimes in with a snort.

Adrian's eyes narrow. "No. The ship was checked top to bottom several times before takeoff. Every system from life support to propulsion was cleared. The AI saw nothing amiss, and neither did human eyes. Not even a stowaway mouse could have managed to join us without *Lycka* knowing about it.”

“What about luggage in the storage bays?”

“X-ray machines scanned everything that came on. Any sort of suspicious canister would have been flagged.”

“What about gas in solid form, something that might react to air and change composition?”

“Hmm.” Adrian has no answer.

“Shite,” Dana mutters.

“Helv,” Niklas curses again. “We’re donning gas masks and the protective suits before anyone steps out of the hatch. Once we’re ready, Dana, take us in.”

Dana leaves the shuttle on auto pilot while they dress, check each other’s gear, strap on oxygen tanks, and test the audio communications embedded in their helmets. Niklas rarely dons such heavy suits. The close-fitting design gives him mild claustrophobia. He takes deep breaths and repeats the mantra, *You’ll be fine. You’ll be just fine,* before signaling Dana to dock.

She takes back manual control and eases them into the yawning bay beneath the bridge. Track lights blink reassuringly and light their path. At least *Lycka* still breathes, even if her passengers don’t. The ship glides to a stop, and docking clamps engage. Niklas directs Dana to use the shuttle’s sensors to pick up problems outside even though their capability is limited.

“Negative.” Dana confirms what Nik suspected. They’ll have to go out with handheld equipment as they did planet-side and test the air.

Nik sighs, fogging his faceplate. He grits his teeth, gathers the handheld sensor, and tightens his work belt, which contains scientific gear needed to gather data on Vishnu. He tries not to think about the people he knows on board—acquaintances who may very well be dead.

Adrian grabs his arm before he reaches the hatch. "I'll go first." The security man's voice sounds tinny in the earpiece.

Niklas nods to him, and Adrian opens the hatch.

They clunk down the gangway and stand in the hangar. A few small vessels sit empty and still as though ready for a launch that will never come. Nik directs his team to fan out and test the atmosphere. There is none, of course, but they do it anyway. They find no sign of human life, a fight, or damage to the hangar bay. He waves them toward an airlock.

Once they seal the door, canned air hisses in through vents, and an ultraviolet light ripples down their suits to sterilize any foreign microbes they might have tracked inside. The AI announces, "You are cleared to exit the airlock. You may remove your breathing apparatus." Nik only wishes he could. This spaceman rot isn't for him. Past the airlock, his grav boots continue to anchor him. Limp bodies, similarly anchored, sway like car lot balloons. The dead colonists might be dancing to a tune only they can hear if not for their sightless eyes and gaping mouths.

The second level contains defense quarters, an armory, hospital, and sub-command centers, so plenty of corpses crowd its corridors. They haven't decomposed yet, thank goodness. Dead eyes watch him pass, and his heart rate ticks up. He reminds himself that he's a scientist and these poor people only specimens to examine. The bodies show no sign of violence. No blood or abrasions. He recognizes no one so far, thank the gods.

Niklas tests the air on the second level. A red light flashes on his sensor, and a screen reads, "Warning. Poison gas detected. Do not remove breathing masks." The others stare at their sensors with the same stunned expression he must be wearing. Helv. He hates being right. He taps on the sensor device for details. Words scroll across the screen.

Soporon-D is a synthetically manufactured, crystal-based substance originally produced by Russian labs for military use, but the crystals have proven too unstable for practical application, and the Siberian research facility producing the toxin was shut down in 2045. The crystals must be vacuum-packed in special bags made expressly for this purpose, as exposure to any gas or liquid causes a chemical reaction. In such a case, the crystals revert to their original gaseous form within seconds and attack the nervous systems of living entities within range.

There is no known antidote to Soporon-D poisoning, and death will occur within minutes of exposure depending on the size and weight of the carbon-based life form. Soporon-D has been banned by the World Health Organization and is illegal in all countries except Kazakhstan. Standard military grade face masks do protect against this lethal substance.

"Well, at least that's good news." Niklas' voice rings with irony.

"Shite," Dana whispers.

Adrian just grunts. "Poor sods. They never even knew what hit them."

Niklas examines the facial features of the nearest corpse more closely. "His skin is bloodless, but no vessels have ruptured, and the whites of his eyes are clear. He's not gritting his teeth, though I don't know the time of death. Rigor mortis may have eased. Looks like this stuff kills quickly, at least. Not much time to suffer."

"What are we going to do, Dr. Johanssen?" Dana's voice sounds strained, and she hasn't addressed him this formally since they started training together for their Vishnu mission.

He considers his options. Really, there's only one. Get rid of the gas. If they vent the ship, hopefully the poison will be blown into space. "We need to get up to the bridge," he tells the others.

Niklas tries not to look at or touch the bodies, which stir with their passing. On the bridge, more bodies await them. Dana nudges one aside and slides into the pilot's chair. "*Lycka*'s been on auto pilot since before we left on our mission. Makes sense. The ship only needed to maintain orbit until we took her back through the wormhole."

"How much fuel does she have?" Niklas asks.

Dana punches buttons, then exhales an exasperated breath, muttering, "I'm only trained to fly shuttles, fec's sake." She turns a knob on her helmet, and her voice suddenly broadcasts, "Hey, *Lycka*, how much fuel is left?"

The AI responds in its placid tone, "Four to five thousand hours of fuel remain without solar assist."

Starships like *Lycka* weren't built to land on planets. They're too huge. The plan had been for *Lycka* to unload her crews, make sure all was well with the colonists, then travel back through the wormhole. If needed, some passengers could return with her. Niklas flips his broadcast switch. "Hey, Ms. AI. I need you to vent this ship."

A pause. "Venting *Lycka* will result in the death of all passengers not wearing spacesuits and helmets."

"*Lycka*, can your systems show you how many human life forms are alive on this boat?"

"One moment, please." While they wait, Adrian shifts and bumps into a corpse. It drifts toward Nik, who pushes it away. He uncaps several vials from his kit, waves them about, then caps them again and puts them in his belt. Hopefully, he's collected some of the poison.

The AI voice returns. "There are three live human life forms aboard *Lycka* at this time."

"Doesn't that seem a bit odd to you? Vent the ship. We're all wearing spacesuits."

"I will need a top commander's authorization for such an action."

Niklas fumes. This is why he hates AI. As advanced as it gets, its thinking remains binary just when you need it to reason like a person the most. He strides among the floating bodies until he recognizes the captain by his distinctive black brows and the four-star insignia on his suit. Gritting his teeth, he searches the man for some kind of ID. Adrian holds the captain still until Niklas' gloved fist emerges from a breast pocket with a magnetic card reading, "Top Security Clearance."

"Over here." Dana points to a large monitor embedded in the pilot's console. "Every time *Lycka* speaks, the screen lights up, and there's a slot just underneath."

"Good work." Niklas shoves the card into the opening. "Here is your authorization, *Lycka*. Now vent the ship."

"This action requires double authentication."

"In what form?"

"Retinal scan."

Groans echo through Niklas' headset, his own among them. He nods to Adrian, who clasps the floating captain around the waist and hauls him to the console. Dana points to the retinal scanner, and Nik helps Adrian hold the lifeless head close enough that a red laser can ripple across one staring eyeball.

"Access granted," *Lycka* says. "The ship will vent in one minute. It will take twenty-five hours and thirty-three minutes to restore life support once venting is complete. Please strap in."

After it's done, Niklas instructs the others to gather what supplies they can. He visits the Biosphere, where skylights opened the gardens to the sub-zero temperatures of space during the vent. Black and withered stalks march in neat rows. Zavi would hate seeing this. *Zavi*. Niklas straightens. Sickness gathers in his belly. What are the chances *Lycka* wasn't the only ship sabotaged? *Loki*'s status is a mystery, but *Calliope* will reach Mars in a few months.

I've got to contact Zavi and tell him what happened here. Nik sends a message. Just like always, it disappears into the void. **Not deliverable at this time.** The same thing happens when he tries contacting an officer he knows on Mars. Hopefully, those messages will go through eventually. With luck, what happened to *Lycka* will remain an isolated event.

Some bodies were sucked into the black when the ship vented, but plenty remain. Nik and his team don't have the time or energy to dispose of them right now. In the end, they take replenishment supplies to the shuttle and prepare to depart. Niklas left a video message on the bridge explaining what happened just in case someone reaches *Lycka* before she loses power. Once that occurs, she'll fall from orbit like a slow-diving bird until she crashes through Vishnu's atmosphere. Then she'll metamorphose into a flaming phoenix, break apart, and crash into the planet. Nik winces at the thought of losing her. She cost trillions, and her destruction will devastate his country.

Adrian surveys the hangar, then turns to Niklas. "Are you going to alert the rest of the ground crew?"

Nik looks from Adrian to Dana. They've held up remarkably well considering some of the dead were probably friends of theirs. His, too, though thank the stars, he still hasn't recognized any bodies they passed in the corridors. The people he's closest to are right here and down on the planet—those he's trained with for months. "Let's wait until we set down," he says.

They trudge up the shuttle stairs to the main hatch. Niklas pauses at the top. If he forgot to collect something important, they can always return. In fact, they'll need to in order to bring down the supplies necessary to build a colony. They've got plenty of time. *And way less people to provide for than anticipated*, he reminds himself wearily.

With a heavy heart, Nik ducks inside the shuttle.

20

—— ◆ ——

Solast

Sol catches Juke with Anvil in their shuttle's commons even after she warned him away from the Earther. She orders Anvil off the *Goose,* and once he's gone, she whirls on the red-faced hacker. "No outsiders aboard this boat."

"That was not okay." Anger replaces Juke's usual relaxed charm. His eyes spark, and his hands shake.

Sol doesn't care. "That guy is dangerous. He was an Earther when I saw him in New Chicago. Have you asked yourself why he's even here? It doesn't make sense."

"Maybe you're mistaken. Did you know him in the city? Lots of people look alike."

"Not that many can pass for a supermodel hunk."

Juke deflates at this description and almost smiles. "I thought Earthers wore those round tattoos with spears going through them. He's clean. Every single part of him." He smirks.

"Tattoos can be removed, just like scars."

Before either can add more, Clera walks in. She's been weirdly absent-minded lately. Something's up with her, too. More than the transfer to her Biosphere job can explain. She says, "Are you two fighting? I heard you down the hallway."

Sol faces her. "*Captain* Clera, please inform this boy that he is not allowed to bring strangers onto the *Goose*."

"Anvil isn't a stranger to me." Juke clenches his hands.

"Anvil?" Clera echoes.

"Right. *Anvil*." Sol rolls her eyes.

"He's my boyfriend," Juke tells Clera. "The only good thing to happen on this fell trip. Have a heart."

Clera frowns. Sol's relieved to see her looking sharp rather than dreamy-eyed. "It's not a good idea to have anyone outside the crew here, Juke. Remember how we decided to keep a low profile? Can't you meet somewhere else? Maybe his berth? We'll arrive at Mars soon, then go through the ARH, and after that things will be different. Until then ..."

"Right. I get it. Sure. I'll stay away."

"Hey, we don't mean *you* ..." Clera starts, but he speaks over her.

"If Anvil isn't welcome here, neither am I. Think I'll miss dinner tonight."

"Oh, come on," Clera calls after him as he huffs off. A few moments later, they hear the *Goose*'s exit hatch open and shut.

Clera turns to Sol. "He's not himself." She bites her lip. "I hope he doesn't do anything foolish." She shakes away whatever thought's causing her brow to wrinkle. "And how is Mila? Have you looked her over lately? Is she taking her meds?"

"Yes, she certainly is," Mila calls from the corridor. A moment later she steps into the room.

Sol eyes her patient's petite form. Mila's stomach has thickened, but too many desserts could account for that as easily as a baby. If there's one thing Sol feels competent at handling, it's pregnancy. Midwife Cress from her old commune taught her the kind of lessons you don't forget. "The baby is growing like it should. I heard a strong heartbeat when I examined her." She focuses her gaze on Mila's face. "You're feeling him kick now, right?"

Mila glows. "Sure am. It's weird. But great. Definitely, great."

"Only one heartbeat?" Clera asks Sol.

"Just one."

"That's enough!" Mila plops down on the couch. "I've gotten away with wearing my protective coat all right. If I look like a bowling ball in a couple more months, though, that won't be so easy to hide."

Clera pulls an apple from a bin in the kitchen area and crunches into it. She takes the other end of the couch, while Sol perches on a straight-backed chair. "What were you saying about this Anvil character?" Clera asks.

"He's an Earther. I recognize him from living in New Chicago. You both know about them, right?"

"It's a cult." Mila picks at a grease stain on her coat.

"Could you have been mistaken, Sol?" Clera says.

"No." The word whips out. "No," she repeats more softly. "I ran into him with a bunch of other Earthers at a bar in New Chicago. They had these distinctive tattoos." She remembers the demonstration and Anton speaking atop a marble fountain. The way his followers chanted his words back at him sent chills down her spine.

"You should tell someone in Command," Mila advises. "Or I can have Elio mention it to his boss."

"There's no proof. Let me handle this," Sol replies.

Clera and Mila shoot her uncertain looks which she ignores. Truthfully, she couldn't care less about "handling" Anvil. He's like a mouse in a snake's den. She hasn't seen Anton in the Smoke and Ashes bar yet, but she'll eventually encounter him again, figure out his habits and where he lives. Then she'll "handle" *him*.

Without the head, the snake will die. Then mousy Anvil won't be a problem.

Oskar doesn't message her on her private account, so maybe he's decided against seeing her again. Why does this idea make her heart sink? They have nothing in common, and a romantic entanglement will only distract Sol. Furthermore, she's dangerous, and he's a nice guy. He doesn't deserve to carry her baggage.

Sol has passed all her medic modules, is competent with the knock-out gun, and understands her medical belt supplies and their uses. Nora recommended ending her trial period, and Dr. Chandra called her in to congratulate her. Sol feels half guilty and half pleased. She's a fraud, not some reputable nurse from a city clinic on Earth.

A thief. A vagrant. An angel of vengeance.

Does it have to be that way? Sol remembers her father falling, his last desperate look that begged forgiveness, pleaded with her to run, get out, save herself. So that's what she'd done. Luckily, it had been spring, not some cold, dead of winter month. Still, she almost froze that first night hiding in a thicket while Anton's goons passed her by. She had no blankets, no supplies, and was forced to drink stream water. The crucifix and folded photo of her mother—those mementos she kept on her always—had been saved. They were her only comfort as she sobbed herself into restless slumber.

Once she discovered another commune, things got better. She stole a backpack, bedroll, and water jug from that ragtag group. From another small band, she pilfered vegetables in an early garden. Eventually, she found a government-sponsored commune near the city gates that agreed to take her in if she served as midwife and nurse. She became Hanna and stayed with them for almost three years.

A close call with Anton's nomadic group had spurred her to leave. If not for that brush with her past, she might have remained in the Barrens. Instead, she'd bribed her way into New Chicago, where she could remain safely anonymous. That was the city's only perk. She missed the open country, rolling fields, and bright stars after New Chicago swallowed her up.

Sol's mind wanders the foggy corridors of the past until the clinic receptionist clears her throat and says there's a patient waiting with a bloody bandage on his hand.

"Send him in."

When Oskar appears in the doorway, she starts in surprise. Her gaze cuts from his face to the dark stains on a gym towel wrapped about his fingers. "Hello," he says.

The receptionist leaves them. Sol moves past her patient and clicks the door shut. "Have a seat on the table, please."

"Is that the only greeting I get?" He smiles around a grimace of pain.

Sol collects antiseptic, medi-glue, and a smartwrap. The hardest thing about her job was learning to deal with nil grav while treating patients. Everything must be secured so it doesn't float away. Any bodily fluids that hit the air are quickly sucked into a biohazard container. Vomit is especially disgusting to deal with.

Sol gathers her defenses as carefully as she gathers supplies. She steels herself and turns. "Hello, Oskar. I wasn't sure you'd be happy to see me."

He folds his lanky frame onto the papered table and regards her with raised eyebrows. "Why not?"

"You said you'd like to see me again, but I never heard from you." She winces at the accusation in her voice and hurries on, "It's fine, really. I was just confused. Maybe you'd like another nurse? I can page ..."

He grabs her wrist with his good hand. "Of course not, Sol. Or Hanna? But we're alone in here, so ... Sol."

She stares at the place their skin meets. Warmth travels up her arm and infuses her whole body. Heat climbs her cheeks.

He lets her go, and she backs away. "I'm terrible at dating, obviously. It's been such a long time. I was distracted by my job, and well, that's an excuse." He shakes his head ruefully. "Once I got home from that bar, I started to doubt myself. I mean, why would a young, beautiful woman want to date an old guy like me?"

"You're only thirty-eight," she reminds him.

"You remember that?" He stares at her with those warm brown eyes. Even though several feet separate them, electricity jumps across the space.

Sol shakes off Oskar's spell and reminds herself he's a good man who must be protected. If Anton ever recognizes her, people she's close to could become targets. *He won't know you. He's seen you in the gym and didn't give you a second look.* She banishes the thought and focuses on Oskar. "What happened to your hand?"

He glances down, looking surprised to see the blood-soaked towel. "Oh, that. I play battleball on an intramural team. Some guy on the other side forgot to remove a wedding ring. It sliced me. The cut isn't as bad as it looks, but I might need your fancy glue to stop the bleeding."

Sol moves close to unwrap the towel. The ring opened the thin epidermis on the back of Oskar's hand. She wipes blood away with an antiseptic cloth, tucks it into the bio-bag that attaches to her belt, and pinches the wound closed while she traces a line of medi-glue across the cut. She throws the sullied towel into recycling and the used wipe into the bio-hazard bin, then stows her supplies.

Oskar says, "You're very efficient at this job. Do you enjoy it?"

"I do." They stare at each other.

"Will you tell me where to go if I ask you out now?"

"You can always try me." And there it is. All her promises to protect him down the garbage chute.

"Will you have dinner with me tomorrow night at the swanky little Mexican place near the theater?"

She shrugs, helpless against the charm Oskar unknowingly exudes. "Sure. Six o'clock? I'll meet you there." The place sits right across from Smoke and Ashes. Maybe she'll show up ahead of time and watch for Anton.

21

Solast

Sol arrives early and loiters in the corridor outside Smoke and Ashes. It's a slow night. No Anton. No Juke or Anvil. Nobody she recognizes.

Oskar speaks behind her. "You could have gone inside. I have a table reserved."

"Oh, I'm not thirsty."

"What?"

"Right. You mean the restaurant, not the bar." Sol's brain unscrambles while Oskar observes her with a bemused expression. She explains, "I was watching for one of my crewmates. I told him he was hanging out with the wrong crowd, but I don't think he listened to me."

"I remember. The Venters at the middle table. The ones you didn't want to learn your real name."

"Venters?" As soon as she says it, Sol remembers the nickname for workers in Life Support and Maintenance.

Before she can answer her own question, Oskar supplies, "Those lucky lottery winners who work in the ship's guts. I mean, they do more than clean scrubbers and monitor the innards of the ship, I suppose, but the name has stuck."

"Hmm." He probably considers *her* one of the "lucky" scrulls to win a berth. She shoves away the thought. "Do you remember everything you hear?"

"Pretty much." He steers her into the Mexican place.

Oskar gives his name to a hostess, who ushers them into a tiny booth. Vintage mariachi music wafts from hidden speakers. Except for that, the managers haven't done much decorating other than place multi-colored lantern lights overhead.

Sol asks, "Do you have a photographic memory?"

"I've never been tested, but I'm observant and have good recall. My job requires it."

"Of course." He's a professor. A scholar. And she's never been to college, never even graduated from high school. Still, she refuses to feel intimidated.

A kiosk on the wall lights up, and they punch in an order of enchiladas and chili rellenos. Margaritas arrive in the covered sippy cups used everywhere. The drinks taste like sugar water and lime juice tinged with salt. Sol grimaces. "Once we get to Mars, I'm going to require a real mixed drink if they have them."

"Better chance of that on Arsia Mons than aboard *Calliope*," Oskar agrees.

"That's right. You've been to Mars."

"I didn't visit the bars much. I lived above ground in the Mars One colony. Have you heard of the gold towns during booms in the Wild West? Well, imagine that, only take it down a peg or two. That was Mars One. You couldn't eat anything without getting a mouthful of dust. But the food was all freeze dried, so it didn't really matter."

"Yum." Sol takes another sip and decides the drink isn't so bad.

Oskar shrugs. "When I became an archeologist, I knew what I was in for. Work in the field is often rough. Nothing like living in the Barrens, though. How did you come to be there?" He ignores his margarita and focuses all his attention on her.

Sol doesn't want to lie to this man. She swishes liquid around her mouth, swallows, and considers. "I was born in the tenements of New Chicago to factory workers. I don't remember much about my mother. She died in childbirth when I was five. So did the baby." She plays with the rim of her cup. It's easier to talk if she doesn't look into Oskar's eyes. "My father never really recovered. He started attending these Earth First meetings when the Earther movement was just getting started. They gave him something to focus on besides loss, I suppose. But he got sucked in like lots of others, moved us to a commune in the Barrens when I was ten." All that was before Anton took over Earth First and transformed it into something darker. Before the Earther movement washed up on foreign shores, and before it became a weapon.

"And then?"

She glances up. "At twelve, I took a spirit name. I know. It sounds like some cult thing—but it was a cool ceremony, and I liked getting to choose my own name. I was at that age when kids are trying to form their own identities."

"Indigenous people often followed that same custom. The Earthers only borrowed a long-standing tribal tradition."

"Well, anyway, that's when I became Sol. At the commune, we only used the names we chose. No last names. No reminders of the past. We were baptized into new lives. I learned to work hard and live off the land out there. It wasn't all bad. At fifteen, the midwife who helped with our sick started training me as her assistant."

"You never went to college?"

"She trained me," Sol repeats, prickling. Will Oskar look down on her now that he knows her low origins? How little in common they share? And why does it matter so much? Her chin ratchets up a notch.

Oskar nods. "Field work is always the best education. What then?"

Her shoulder muscles loosen. "I left at seventeen after my father died, hopped from commune to commune until I made my way back to New Chicago and got a job at a public clinic." She won't tell him how she worked in the sewers first, how the clinic let her go when funding was cut, how she roamed the streets for years searching for Anton. How her father died.

He doesn't ask for details, just says, "You must be pretty competent to have survived out in the wilds for so long, at least if the rumors about the Barrens are true."

"They are," she replies shortly. At his curious look, she adds, "I learned to fight from a martial arts expert in my commune." It's the one favor Anton ever did her.

"I'll remember not to make you angry."

Just then the waitress shows up with their food, steaming beneath translucent lids and covered in melted cheese and red sauce—almost like real Earth fare. They dig in, and companionable silence descends. Sol's glad she shared her past with Oskar. Well, dressed-up parts of it anyway. If he knew she aimed to become a murderer, he might lose his appetite. She chews, swallows, and asks, "What about you?"

"Me?" His fingers hover near his mouth, a rolled piece of tortilla pinched between them.

"It's only fair you lay your past on the table."

"But mine is so ordinary. I'd bore you."

"I'll be the judge." She waits.

He finishes his last bite and pauses so long she's sure he'll remain a mystery man. But then he speaks. "I grew up in Sacramento, only son of scholars, went to college, interned in my twenties, went back to school for my PhD, and I've been at Yale ever since. Well, until NASA came calling and offered me this chance to be their Martian Expert in Residence."

"Why would they do that? What made you so special?"

He shrugs, not meeting her eyes. "I might have published a few papers that got some acclaim. Accepted a few awards."

"You're famous. A prodigy. And you're only thirty-eight. You must have been *very* young when you started university."

That forces a laugh out of him. "Sixteen. They moved me ahead on an advanced track. And I'm hardly famous. Only in my field, and it's a narrow one."

"Did you want to leave Earth?" Sol wipes her mouth and tucks the soiled napkin into her covered tray.

"Never really considered it," he admits. "But the timing was good. I ... I wasn't doing well, and NASA's offer gave me a chance to reset my life, if you will."

So, he has secrets just like her. She should let them lie, yet she can't help asking, "And that's all you want to say on that subject?"

He smiles sadly. "I didn't want to burden you with the darker bits. We're out to dinner. Protocol says to keep things light on a first date, right?"

"I don't think that's a hard and fast rule, but what do I know?" She refuses to release him from her stare.

Oskar sighs. Words pour out in a fast stream. "A few years ago, there was a flash flood, and my wife and son got caught in it. The car was swept away, the bodies never found. It was hard to come back from."

This isn't what she expected. Now she wishes she hadn't forced revelations that might cause him to remember his pain. "I'm sorry."

He shrugs. "I'm better now. The worst part is the guilt." His gaze flits away from hers. He clenches his jaw, then admits, "I wasn't a great husband and father. My job took me away too much. Sometimes I was attending conferences, sometimes consulting or on a dig. I'd do things differently if I had another chance."

"Would that mean sacrificing your career?"

"Probably. You can't have everything, though. You have to make choices."

Sol knows this truth all too well. Hasn't she chosen to pursue justice over having a family, a home, a life?

After dinner, Oskar walks her to the *Blue Goose*. When they reach her berth, he says, "We'll be arriving at Mars before too long. My life is about to get very busy, but I'd like to see you again. I'd like to show you the Martian ruins in the caverns under Arsia Mons. If you're interested, that is. I realize my field isn't something everyone finds as fascinating as I do."

"I'd like that," Sol hears herself saying even though she should stay away from this man. He might be an excavator, yet he takes nothing from her. Instead, he fills the hole inside. Maybe she's tired of keeping people out, weary of the constant battle her life has become.

Oskar smiles, shifting from foot to foot like he doesn't want to go. Impulsively, she leans up and brushes a kiss against his stubbly cheek. He turns at her touch, and their lips meet for a second, then two. He pulls back and clears his throat. "I should go."

She watches while he walks away, his long-limbed frame somehow graceful even in grav boots. She touches her mouth. When was the last time she kissed anyone? How old had she been? Sixteen? And had it ever felt like this?

22

Clera

Clera promised herself she'd tell Zavi how she came to be aboard *Calliope* yet never finds the perfect opportunity. He doesn't push, and their mostly platonic dates continue as the starship approaches Mars. Light banter, a few parting kisses, but nothing like the rare, passionate exchanges they'd shared on Earth. Perhaps he only wants friendship now. She's almost convinced herself of that—not that she's okay with it—when he calls her into his office after work one day.

"I'm supposed to present a learning module next week in the theater," he begins without preamble. "And I could use an assistant. The talk will be more meaningful if I can bring in live specimens. Can you help?"

The thought of standing in front of people on a stage makes her insides turn over, but what can she say? She's a sucker for anyone in need. Besides, preparing for the class will give them extra time together. "Of course."

They spend the next week planning the presentation, hovering over a monitor in Zavi's office, then roaming the special greenhouse to select alien plants. There are four presentations, one per night. Zavi looks frazzled, hair tousled and shadows beneath his eyes, when Clera meets him on the evening of the first lecture. They steer a hover cart loaded with the plants through the corridors and into the theater auditorium. These learning modules could have been broadcast onto shuttle channels, but Command wants the colonists to mingle, socialize, get away from their shuttle-craft. It's the same reason all the shops exist. Some psychologist probably recommended that Blue Deck's structure mimic a small town's.

Clera helps Zavi set up his holographic visuals and arrange examples of Vishnu's flora in the order of his outline. Her job is, literally, to hold up various plants when he nods to her, but she's nervous anyway as colonists stream into the auditorium. Her brother waves from the back, and she acknowledges him with a slight nod. She turns to Zavi and brushes a hand across his tense shoulders, though what she really wants to do is smooth his hair. "You're going to be great."

Distracted blue eyes find her. "Most of these people don't want to be here. What do they care about botany?"

She shakes her head. "Not true. They'll be living in close quarters with these plants soon enough, and they'll realize it's important to understand their uses—and their dangers."

"I hope you're right. I had a dream last night that I was standing up here naked, and then the crowd started throwing rotten tomatoes at me. As if that would even work in zero gravity."

She gets stuck on the word *naked* and barely hears the rest of what he says. "I wouldn't have thrown fruit at you." *I'd have stared.*

"Thanks." He grins, and her heart flip-flops.

Zavi begins his lecture with a joke that lands well. Scattered laughs make him relax his stance, and he seems perfectly at ease as they proceed. He warns his audience about toxic plants and explains how to identify the "good" plants that might provide stable food sources. A hush falls over the crowd. Clera alternates her attention between holding up each specimen as Zavi explains it and watching the rapt audience.

When they finish, enthusiastic applause breaks out. Colonists engage in animated discussions while they file out. Elio gives her a thumbs up, then disappears into the crowd.

"A success!" Clera announces once they're alone.

"With your help. Thank you."

She returns his smile, hesitates, takes a leap. "After we put things away in the Biosphere, will you walk me home?" He has no idea which berth is hers. That's how stilted their relationship has become. How distantly polite. Does he want it to stay that way?

But Zavi replies, "Sure," as he carefully lifts a yellow-striped plant and places it under grow lights on the cart. They add the other plant specimens to the cart and head out. Clera proceeds Zavi through the corridors. It's growing late, and the hallway stretches vast and empty before them. They return the plants to the Biosphere, then veer back to Blue Deck. The closer they get to the *Goose*, the harder her heart pounds. After a few banal remarks, Zavi falls silent.

When they reach Berth 235, Clera forces a hearty, "Here we are," out of her suddenly dry mouth.

"Here we are," Zavi repeats.

"I want you to come in."

"Won't I disturb your crewmates?"

"Not this late. Elio, Mila, and Sol will all be in their cabins. Juke may or may not be home. He's taken to staying at his boyfriend's berth sometimes." She frowns, remembering their last encounter, then shakes off her worry.

"You've made more friends since we left each other on Earth."

Clera presses her Skinpad to the scanner, and the portal slides open. "Come on." Hoping he'll follow, she tromps up the metal stairs that lead to the hatch. Zavi's boots thud reassuringly behind her.

Once they've entered the *Goose*, Clera glances down the corridor to make sure they're alone. She gives him a tour, pointing out the forward bay, cabins, head, engineering, and commons in whispered tones. She leads him to the bridge, where they can talk normally and without interruption. They exit the stairway and enter the vacant heart of the *Blue Goose*, where wide windows stare out on gray walls, and leather command chairs sit empty. Clera slides into the pilot's chair. After a moment's hesitation, Zavi claims the copilot's seat. "You're going to tell me how you acquired this boat, aren't you." His mouth forms a straight line. A look of resignation—or perhaps trepidation—ripples across his face.

"I think it's time. I can't maintain this ... this charade of friendship, of let's pretend, anymore. I trust you to keep what I'm about to say to yourself, no matter what you think of me after. There are other lives at stake besides mine."

"Fair enough." He leans back and folds his arms.

Clera closes her eyes, takes a few deep breaths, and wonders where to start. Finally, she begins on Earth, with Elio and her fleeing to Juke's posh estate, enlisting his help in a daring plan to steal the shuttle, *Beatriz*, which was about to land at the aeronautical museum for its retirement. She details Juke's part in hacking NASA's space program, obtaining Skinpads for Elio and herself, and joining them as payment for his help. "That's where Mila comes in," she adds.

"But didn't *Beatriz* explode before she could touch down?" Zavi asks. Clera can't tell by his tone if he's disappointed, repulsed, or sympathizes with her so far.

"Right. That's when I decided we'd steal the prototype solar shuttle parked in front of the museum instead." She takes all the blame for herself. After all, the theft of the *Blue Goose* was her idea, and she has no regrets.

Zavi digests her words in a silence that stretches too long. Finally, he asks, "Where does this Sol person come in?"

"We didn't realize she was hiding out in the shuttle, using it as an alternative to sleeping in the parks, until we broke atmo, and it was too late."

"So now she's a part of your crew, also."

"Yes." She watches him for signs he'll betray them, but his face remains unreadable. "We were desperate."

Finally, he nods, sits forward with elbows on knees, and closes his eyes. "Zavi?"

They blink open.

"I'm not going to apologize for doing what I had to in order to get us away from New Chicago's gangs and give us a chance at a better life. Say something."

"I suspected you might have committed a crime, yet part of me hoped you'd simply lucked into winning one of the last berths open to the general public. I don't know. Maybe that billionaire who ran Elio's lottery had a change of heart and decided to play fair. Perhaps Elio was called in and informed he'd won after all."

"If it had been that easy, I'd have told you when we first met aboard *Calliope*."

"I know."

"I was afraid you'd discover me on the ship, and you'd turn us in."

"You really thought I might?"

"Maybe. I couldn't take the chance."

"You don't know me at all." Is that anger in his voice? Distaste to discover she's a thief? Or disappointment that she didn't believe in him enough to find him as soon as she docked on *Calliope*?

He gets up, so she rises, too.

"I need time to digest all this."

Her heart sinks, but she manages a tight, "Of course."

Neither moves for a moment. Clera wants to say the words to make him stay. They don't come. "I'll see you out."

⁕

She moves through the next few days in a numb state. Zavi doesn't contact her, and he stays away from her cubicle-sized office in the Biosphere. At first, she was disappointed, angry, and sad by turns. Now, as they close in on Mars, there's nothing. She's a void. A black hole. And she likes it that way.

No security forces come to arrest them, so Zavi's keeping his word, at least. Messages from Command and the Steward's office begin to zing across her Skinpad: explanations of how they'll disembark, expectations for the week they'll remain at the underground city, suggestions on sight-seeing activities to pass the time while they're there. And, of course, loads of messages about the big celebration in the Biosphere to occur the night before *Calliope*'s docking at the space station that hovers above the red planet.

A message pings from Zavi—finally—but Clera ignores it. As long as she doesn't answer, she can hold onto the numbness that coats her like anesthetic.

Day 31

The mushrooms erupted for the last time two weeks ago. I couldn't write of them until now. The painful memories they evoke stay with me still, but as this journal is meant to be scientific (ha!), not personal, I will attempt a dispassionate description.

Toximycelium Giganteus or (common name) Doomscap Fungi

Doomscap fungi are notable for their remarkable growth and reproductive strategies, particularly their unique response to rainfall.

Upon the cessation of a rain shower, typically within one minute, Doomscap fungi exhibit rapid emergence from the ground. These fungi reach heights of approximately six feet and display a distinct, rubbery gray surface mottled with blue smudges.

During the eruption, the fungi release clouds of toxic spores, which are dispersed by wind currents over considerable distances, potentially extending for miles. This spore cloud presents an ecological hazard, as the toxicity of the spores has been observed to kill fauna which have not developed genetic modifications to combat them.

After a period of one to two hours, the fungi undergo desiccation due to exposure to sunlight. They shrivel and retract into the ground, leaving disturbed soil as the only evidence they existed.

-N.J.

23

Niklas

Niklas decides to break the news of *Lycka*'s demise to the other five team members in person, but no one appears as they clamber down from the shuttle. Wrongness permeates the air, yet the camp remains as they left it—tents pitched, crates scattered about, the fire a pile of damp ash. He instructs everyone to keep their protective gear on. A few puddles indicate that rain fell while they were away. Niklas looks across the sands for the bright green suits of his crew.

Not finding them, his eyes drift downward, then toward the forest. Loamy earth up an embankment shows signs of disturbance—as though giant rodents dug holes there. Fresh mounds dot the spiky tree line. Adrian grabs their fire poker and stalks to the broken ground. He prods and pokes, but no alien moles burst forth. No snakes slither from dens to attack him. The breeze wafts its sweet scent across a landscape devoid of mammalian life. Could there be life *beneath* Vishnu? Maybe that's why they've spotted no animals?

"Bendu! Cara!" Dana cups her hands around her mouth and repeats the call. Only the wind answers. "Zedon! Lana! Cal!" Still nothing. Adrian tosses the poker aside and shakes his head at Niklas. Whatever broke through the earth has come and gone. A threat, sensed but unseen, pounds a warning against his temples. If this threat isn't imagined, they may be well and truly helved.

Niklas scowls. *Idiot. The* Pioneer *missions took samples and found this planet's air quality acceptable. It can't be that. Of course, science has been wrong before …* His gaze shifts to the seven-foot, waxy-leaved shrubs that border the strip of open land between sea and interior. Maybe the others are on a scouting mission. If they'd run into trouble, they'd radio someone. He's being paranoid. Still, he can't ignore a creeping dread.

Nik walks to the line of greenery and peers between thick branches. Here, too, the earth has been disturbed. He steps carefully around the holes and finds the path his team carved using a machete bot. Sweat trickles down the side of his face. He unclips his scanner and tests the air. A red message flashes across the screen. *Unknown substance identified. Possibly toxic.* He stiffens, then barks a warning through his radio com.

Nik's alarm escalates as he continues walking. Soon he catches sight of a green suit and bursts into a clearing. He skids to a halt, heart leaping into his throat.

The missing crew members lie in contorted positions, faces frozen in agony, eyes bulging and mouths open in silent screams. Hands claw like talons. Body postures indicate involuntary spasms—a horrible way to die. "Get over here now. Keep your masks on. Follow the trail," he orders through the com. Five bodies. Everyone they left behind. Dead.

A haze passes over Niklas' eyes. He glances everywhere at once, muscles tight with panic. His fists bunch, ready to fight back against—what? The very air? He doesn't scare easily, yet he's panicking now. Vishnu feels not like the planet of hope but the planet of fear and despair.

He's both a risk taker and an eternal optimist—exhaustively happy according to his family—and these qualities have served him well in his scientific career. Experiments fail more than they succeed, and sometimes you've got to take risks to make advancements. Yet he's never faced this dire a challenge. This level of death. And other than Dana and Adrian, he's totally alone.

The others appear in Nik's periphery vision. They gasp and run forward to kneel next to the bodies. Dana lets loose a single, sharp cry, but it's big, buff Adrian who breaks down. Nik turns his com off to block the ragged sobs. He gives the man privacy to grieve for about a minute before switching their radio link back on. Then, in clipped tones, he tells Adrian, "Get ahold of yourself, soldier. There will be time to mourn later. Right now, we need to run tests, figure out what killed our friends."

He uses the field equipment on his belt to examine the air sample he took from *Lycka*, then joins the others near the bodies, where he takes tissue and blood samples. Like Niklas, the others use scanners to run tests, then convene away from the dead to compare notes. "It was a neurotoxin that killed our friends," Dana mutters. "Maybe the same one that did in the people aboard *Lycka*."

"No," Niklas amends. "Look at the results from my *Lycka* sample. The toxin released aboard the starship has been identified as So-poron-D, harmless in crystalized form but toxic once it reacts with nitrogen—the main component in the air we breathe."

"This planet has a nitrogen-rich atmosphere, also." Adrian frowns.

"But look." Niklas shares the data gathered from the samples taken off the dead crew. "The AI can't identify the toxin that killed our friends. Sure, it attacked their neural pathways, yet that's where the similarity ends. There's no indication it was ever in crystalline form. *Or* gaseous. This is something new."

"Not surprising since we're not on Earth," Dana murmurs sourly. "But you'd think all those scientists who studied Vishnu might have had some idea what we were in for here." She glares at Niklas, eyes flashing. "No offense, Nik."

"None taken." Again, darkness threatens to overwhelm him, but he drives it back. He *must* be the leader. The one who doesn't crack. "Let's test the air again. And collect samples from the leaves on these shrubs and from the earth as well. After that, we'll take care of the crew."

When all the tests Niklas can think to run show no remaining toxins in air, leaf, or dirt, he orders helmets off and heavy suits stored in their rucksacks. He's happy to shed the extra clothing. Vishnu's day compares to Earth's, and its star, Kali, burns high above them, heating the atmosphere to a comfortable twenty-seven degrees Celsius. Clouds gather on the horizon, a dark gray bank that promises more rain later, but for now, they've got good weather and should make use of it.

Adrian only removes his suit after watching Niklas and Dana do so with no ill effects. They haul the dead back to the camp, strip them of equipment, and make a pyre. Nik would rather bury the bodies, but the disturbed ground makes him wary of digging. If there were dangerous creatures about, the smells of burning and smoke might call them close, yet nothing moves across the lush landscape. Was it always so, or did the strange poison in the air—here, then gone—cause mass extinction?

Normally, Niklas loves a tough puzzle. Not today. Not with the taint of burning flesh in his nose and white bone gleaming through flames. Dana takes his hand, then Adrian's, and they stand before the fire, linked by loss and sadness. Terrified, too. Or is that only Nik?

Afterward, he runs through the data regarding Vishnu that he downloaded on his Skinpad before they passed through the wormhole, but no answers come. He glances at the clouds, decides there's time for a quick swim, and heads down the beach toward gray cliffs and foamy surf.

Swimming always makes him feel better, helps him think. If there's an answer, he'll discover it flat on his back while this planet's buoyant waters cradle him. He'd better find an answer soon. Zavi is somewhere between Earth and Mars, and Nik can't contact him until he passes through the ARH. Still, he adds another message to the long string of "undeliverable at this time" before diving in.

24

Solast

Tomorrow. Mars. Sol should feel relieved, not excited. Mars was supposed to be the end of the line, but once she exacts her revenge, she *could* continue on to Vishnu. Maybe she and Oskar can share a future. It's the first time she's considered life post-Anton, and a heaviness inside her lifts. Too soon to make plans, though. The weight room remains the only place she's seen her nemesis. He vanishes like a ghost when she tries to follow him. The Smoke and Ashes idea has been a bust, too.

At least she has a plan for how to defeat Mons Vega. Her knockout gun should render him helpless—a less risky choice than hand-to-hand combat. Anton taught her everything she knows about fighting, but he's bigger, stronger, more experienced. Age doesn't seem to have slowed him down. He hasn't gone to flab.

A hubbub outside the workout area breaks into her thoughts. Three men gather around a prone figure on the path. Sol's training kicks in, and she darts forward. "Move aside. I'm a medic." She shoves the closest man out of the way, glances from the woman on the ground to the men, and freezes. Anton stares directly at her. She feels blood drain from her face yet can't look away even though he might recognize her.

But he only studies Sol blankly, then tells his companions, "Back away and let her work."

They obey, and Sol kneels next to the unconscious woman to feel for a pulse. Finding none, she pulls a resuscitation device from her belt. It pumps air into the woman's lungs like a bellows, making her chest rise and fall, yet life doesn't return to the woman's eyes. After the prescribed time, Sol removes the mask. She checks her patient's pulse again and calls it. "She's gone."

The woman looks to be in her thirties, with short-cropped red hair and a nose ring. Sol doesn't recognize her. She might be another Earther if she's with Anton. How many did he bring aboard, and why? Does Sol care as long as they don't get in her way?

One of the guys with Anton says, "What happened? She was just walking along, and her body went sort of limp."

Sol selects a scanner from her belt and runs it over the woman's body, lingering on her skull. "Blood clot in her brain." She glances at the three men hovering above her and explains, "Aneurism."

"Hells." Anton runs a hand through his dark hair.

Sol shivers. He doesn't recognize her. Thank the gods she had that scar removed, that her hair's cut short, that she's aged a decade.

Anton sighs. "Just what I need. Now my Venter crew will be one short, and no one wants a transfer into Life Support and Maintenance."

"It won't matter that much longer," one of his companions says.

Anton's attention jerks away from the dead woman. His eyes flash, and the speaker shuts up.

What did he mean? Just that we'll be through the ARH and on to Vishnu soon? Or is something else going on? Before she can think better, words fly unbidden from Sol's mouth. "I might want a transfer onto your crew."

Their gazes turn her way. She scrambles to her feet. Can they hear her heart hammering? See past the cool facade she's barely maintaining?

"Why?" Anton tilts his head like she's some curious specimen.

"I ... I'm tired of being a medic." The lies get easier as they unravel. "I'm always on call, and it's stressful. My rich patients are never grateful, and they treat me like a scrull."

"You think anyone will say 'please' and 'thank you' in Life Support?" Anton scoffs. The others chuckle.

"Well, no," Sol admits. "But I like physical work. And I'd like to see the parts of this ship that no one else does."

Anton's eyes narrow. "Where are you from?"

Sol forces her body to stay relaxed and resists the urge to swallow hard. "New Chicago." *Stay as close to the truth as possible.*

There's a moment of hesitation before Anton nods. "I thought I heard a trace of accent in your voice. What did you do there?"

Is this an interview or what? Anton might be a crew chief yet surely doesn't decide work assignments. "I worked in a public clinic and won a lottery spot on *Calliope.*" In a flash of genius, she adds, "I didn't really want to come, but my mother put in for me, and when I was actually picked, she insisted I follow through. She's dying of cancer, and her last wish was for me to escape from the city and start a new life. Personally, I think we should all stick around on our home planet and try to fix it, not run away." *Too much, Sol.*

Something flickers, then settles in Anton's gaze. "Fine. Give me your contact info, and I'll have someone get in touch with you."

She does so, then messages the medical division for body removal.

"Thanks for the help," Anton says. His companions echo his words. He holds out a hand.

Her skin crawls, but she takes it. She could pull a scalpel from her belt and end him right here. *Dumb idea. How did knifing him last time go?* Besides, he's already drawing away. She studies Anton as he retreats with the others. *Better watch your back. I'm coming for you.*

Adrenaline evaporates, leaving her shaky, and Sol settles onto a bench and rests her head in her hands. *What have you done? The clinic job was the best you've ever had. You made friends there. You finally had a life.* She wants to cry and pump her fist in triumph all at once. Sure, it's a big sacrifice to leave the clinic. Yet she's used to sacrifice, and if Anton can get her transferred to his crew, she'll have more than a tiny chance in hell of getting him alone. Of course, if she loses her job, she'll have to give up her med belt and the knockout gun. *Not if you steal an extra from the storage cabinet first.*

———◦———

Later that day, the transfer goes through. So fast! Someone's probably afraid she'll back out if they don't accept her request immediately. Is a Venter's life really so distasteful? *Doesn't matter*, she tells herself and tries hard to believe it. What will Oskar think? What excuse to give for rejecting such a great job? And why does she care so much?

Everyone aboard *Calliope* has a week's vacation on Mars before they depart for the ARH. A message from Life Support informs Sol that she's scheduled to report to the maintenance department on Red Deck for training a few days before Calliope heads to the ARH. Anton Smith is listed as her immediate boss. Smith? Really? Finally, she's gotten what she wanted. So why is she scared? And, if she admits it to herself, a little depressed?

Dr. Chandra calls her into his office. He regards her gravely from across his desk and asks her a single question. "Why?"

So he's already been notified, too. Tears well up. Humiliating, hot, and hard to hide. She can't answer right away. Finally, she chokes out,

"I appreciate everything you've done for me here. This has been the best job—"

"Then why?" he repeats.

The fabrication she's prepared dies on her lips. She sucks in a breath. "There's a good reason, I promise you, but it's my own. Someday, if everything works out, I hope to return to nursing."

He sighs heavily, pushes to his feet, and offers his hand. Sol rises also, leans out to grasp it, and meets his eyes through the film of water building in her own.

"If you're in some sort of trouble, I might be able to help."

She withdraws. "No trouble. Just ... just something I need to do."

He frowns. "I can't imagine what sort of mission you'd have in Life Support and Maintenance. You realize they'll likely have you crawling through ductwork and cleaning scrubbers, right?"

"Yes."

He sighs again. "Maybe, once we land on Vishnu, you'll reconsider nursing as a career. You have a lot of talent." He doesn't even add, *though your manner with patients could use some work.*

"Thank you." She holds her head high and walks to the waiting area, where the receptionist, Sadiki, and Nora form a gauntlet. Sol endures hugs from each. They murmur their regrets, while she murmurs back apologies and all the other inane things people say during goodbyes. Vague words like, "It wasn't anything you did ... I loved working with you ... thanks for everything ..." What she'd told Dr. Chandra was the vaguest thing of all: *There's something I have to do.* At least that's the truth. She escapes from the clinic without uttering a single falsehood.

Determined to celebrate along with the rest of her crew, Sol dons the second-hand party clothes Clera found for her at a shop on Blue Deck. For once, passengers won't be required to wear identical blue jumpsuits to the celebration taking place in the Biosphere. *Calliope* drifted into the docking framework attached to the Mars space station a few hours ago. Special shuttles will ferry people to the surface in the morning. Then Mars rovers will transfer them to temporary housing below the surface in the bustling city of Arsia Mons.

Tons of tours, restaurant adverts, and tips for successful stays have been flashing across Sol's Skinpad all day. She ignored them but opened a private message from Oskar. He wants to meet up tonight at the Biosphere party. How to tell him she's no longer a medic. To explain something unexplainable. She could say nothing, yet he'll find out eventually.

She closes the message. Once she gets her thoughts in order, she'll send a reply. Maybe. Yes. Of course, she will.

An hour before the party starts, she still hasn't thought of one. Her crew gathers in the *Goose*'s commons, the guys in smartsuits Elio procured through a connection on Red Deck, the women in glittery jumpsuits. Sol's is a black-sequined affair which leaves one shoulder bare and shows off her flat stomach and long legs. Clera chose a salmon-colored, bell-bottomed outfit for herself with a v neckline that exposes the shadows between her breasts. Mila wears a loose-flowing silver outfit which matches her gray eyes.

Elio whistles when the three of them emerge from the corridor. He draws Mila against his side, kisses her cheek, and growls, "That's my girl."

She squirms away and stares crossly at him. "I look like a whale."

Sol doesn't think so. Though she's starting her third term, Mila's added weight could be chalked up to overeating too much good food on *Calliope*. Her cheeks have filled out, and her fingers are swollen, yet she glows.

No one knows Sol's no longer a medic, not even Clera. Sol managed to steal some precautionary meds from the clinic's storage unit along with the knockout gun before she turned in her med belt. She'll continue to oversee Mila's pregnancy despite losing her job.

⸺◆⸺

Colored balls light the Biosphere's paths, and the ceiling imitates a Terran night, with a full moon hung among a glitter of stars. Half the colonists have ditched their drab spacewear. *We could almost be on Earth*, Sol reflects as she follows the others out of the transition tube and stows her boots. Juke veers away like he's got somewhere important to be—no doubt involving Anvil. Will Sol have to work with that man now?

Elio and Mila wave goodbye and head toward a dance floor set up on a playing field. Musicians tune up at one end on a temporary stage. Clera turns to Sol. "Well, here we are." She shifts from foot to foot and nervously twirls a lock of hair.

Sol's glad to have company. She's galaxies out of her comfort zone, just like Clera, and is about to ask her crewmate if she wants a drink when an unfamiliar woman approaches. She waves to Clera, whose eyes light up. "Maya!"

She's young, vibrant, and dressed in one of the familiar blue spacesuits. She hugs Clera and says, "We've missed you!"

Clera returns the embrace. "I've missed you, too." She nods toward Sol. "This is my berthmate …"

"Hanna," Sol hurries to fill in.

Clera looks confused but then smiles widely. "Is Lin here with you?"

"Right over there." Maya points. "Can you join us? We'd love to hear about your new job."

Clera glances at Sol, who's quick to shake her head. "You should go. I'll be fine."

"You're welcome to join us," Maya says.

Sol has no desire to be the third wheel. She nudges Clera. "Go on. I'll find you later."

Clera protests half-heartedly, but another nudge convinces her. Sol moves off and wanders through the crowds. The atmosphere is half carnival, half night club. Not that she'd know much about either. She pauses at a kiosk selling cotton candy and buys a bag just for something to do. Maybe she'll stroll for a while, listen to the music, then slip away.

The thought makes her sad. For a brief time, she had crewmates, work friends, a potential boyfriend. But at this moment, she's as solitary as ever. Seems like everyone from the *Goose* has paired off, and she never did answer Oskar's message, chicken that she is. The memory of their kiss comes back to her. His lips soft, parting in surprise, lingering for just a second. Her blush. His sheepish look. A moment so ordinary yet so extraordinary, too, because it was Sol and Oskar. Two people who never should have met. Fate brought them together, and fate is pulling them apart.

A deep voice calls her name. She whirls, and there he is. Oskar. In the midst of a thousand-plus people, he's managed to locate her. His slim-cut suit accentuates his rangy form. His hair has been slicked back, but one curl wants to fall across his forehead. Sol waits for him to reach her, mind racing for what to say.

He stares down at her, frowning. "You didn't answer my message. Does that mean I should leave you alone?" She blinks, unprepared for such bluntness. He rushes on, "I thought maybe that kiss ... that we were sharing something ... but it might have been my imagination. I'm not good with people. You have to tell me if you want to be left alone."

She almost smiles. "I don't want that." And she's never uttered a truer statement. She licks her dry lips and watches his eyes fall to her mouth.

"Why didn't you write back?"

"It's ... complicated."

He hesitates, then takes her arm and steers her toward the apple orchard. Picking a bench set beneath overarching branches, he pulls her down with him. He surveys the slinky black outfit and grins. "You look like a supermodel in that get-up. Like you should be at the Grammys, not here." His gaze flits across the trees, then returns to her.

"Clera found it for me."

"I should thank her."

He's flirting. Even after she ghosted him. She can't help the lift of her mouth. "I'm sorry I didn't answer you. It was wrong. I was trying to think up what to say, and then I didn't say anything at all."

His frown returns. "You can be honest with me. You don't have to make up stories to let me down easy. I totally understand if I'm too old for you. Too boring. Too ..."

"You aren't boring!"

His grin is self-deprecating. "Just old."

Her voice falls to a murmur. "I don't care about that."

"What, then? Is there someone else?"

"Hells, no. It's that I—" *Tell him, Sol. Say it.* "I quit my job."

"What? Why?"

"I can't tell you that. It's a secret. Well, sort of a secret. If you knew everything ..."

He squeezes her hand. "You can trust me."

She shakes her head but lets her palm remain in his big, warm one. "You should stay away from me. I don't want to put you in danger, and hanging out with me could be a death sentence."

One eyebrow rises. Oskar's grip tightens. "If you're in trouble, we need to go to Security and tell them."

"It's nothing they can help with, believe me." She looks into his puppy dog eyes and silently begs for understanding. "Just trust me, okay? I needed to take on a new work assignment until we reach Vishnu. By then, everything will be different, and hopefully the danger will be gone."

"You aren't planning something illegal, are you?"

And she tells her first lie. "No. Of course not." But she can't look at him. It's an amateur mistake.

"I like you." His voice wraps her in its magic, and she wants to blurt out everything about Anton. She shakes off his touch and stops herself just in time. Revealing her mission would be selfish. Knowing too much won't keep Oskar safe. It might even kill that warmth in his gaze when he looks at her. So perhaps not telling him *is* the selfish choice.

"I like you, too. Please, let me do this thing, and as soon as it's safe, I'll get in contact with you. I promise."

"You already have a new job assignment?"

"In Life Support and Maintenance."

He utters a disbelieving sound. "Why would you go there?" Then he holds up a palm. "Right. You can't tell me. Or you won't. I might look like a nerd, but I can take care of myself." When she doesn't answer, he speaks again. "Will *you* take care?"

She smiles a little at that. "I'm not on a suicide mission. And I know how to fight. I lived on the streets of New Chicago."

"Right. You worked in a public clinic, but ..."

"I was homeless for a time. I didn't want to tell you. Believe me when I say I'm a survivor."

"You thought knowing you'd been homeless would turn me against you? There's no shame in it." One finger runs feather-soft down her cheek, and she shivers. He looks thoughtful. "You weren't an addict, were you? If you need help, they have meds here, but then you know ..."

"No." She clutches his fingers to stop him. "Not that. Please, trust me."

"I'm worried."

Her heart constricts, then expands painfully in the area of her breastbone. Her father was the last person to worry for her. To care for her. She thought she didn't need that, didn't want it, yet now she's not sure. "Oskar, please." Helpless, she leans toward him and wraps her arms around his back. His shoulders contain more muscle than expected, and his heart beats a quick rhythm against her cheek. She wants to stay pressed to his chest. Instead, she says, "Let me go. I'll come back to you if I can."

It takes willpower to push away before Oskar can stop her. A helpless expression clouds his eyes. Sol walks backward, making the connection between them last as long as possible. "Goodbye," she mouths.

He calls after her, "I wanted to show you the Martian ruins."

She hears him—but turns away and pretends she didn't.

25

Solast

Sol passes a tiki bar made of bamboo and palm leaves adjacent to the dance floor, where a bartender in a flowered shirt hands out mocktails. Round tables decorated with floral tablecloths and rose-filled bowls dot the area. Colonists mingle, find seats, and sip drinks beneath the ambient lighting. A deep voice calls, "Hey, you! Hanna!" Her fake name on Anton's lips lands like a missile. *Hanna*. Thank the gods her self-given name isn't on the manifest. Thanks to Juke, *Hanna* will appear in any shipboard messages.

Anton and his followers take up two tables littered with drinks. Juke's there with Anvil, the workout gym guys, plus Venters she recognizes from Smoke and Ashes. *My new crew*. She forces a smile.

"Come join us," Anton beckons.

Finding no plausible excuse not to, she wedges herself between him and a dough-faced woman with red-lidded eyes. Juke's gaze meets hers from the next table. He blinks in surprise, and she shoots him a warning glare, then turns back as Anton introduces her to people she's already met. Weeks ago, Juke made these same introductions, and she warned him about his friends. Now here she is—an apparent hypocrite—but right where she needs to be.

Sol's pale seatmate, Muff, glances at her with sorrowful eyes. "You're Juke's friend."

She clears her throat and wishes she were somewhere else. "Was the woman who died outside the gym *your* friend?"

"She was more than a friend. She was my soulmate." Muff gulps her drink, then adds, "I should have known something was wrong. She kept having these headaches, but she refused to go to a clinic. We Slummers aren't used to getting help from anyone."

Anton's voice pulls Sol's attention away. "It's all in the past, Muff. We're free from all that now."

What does Anton mean by "free"? Free from Earth, or free to enact some nefarious Earther plan? She summons blankness into her expression. Anton isn't looking at her, though, just absentmindedly tapping his Skinpad. Finally, he glances up.

Twice he's studied her now, yet his eyes still betray no recognition from their days in the Barrens. Has she changed that much? Has he forgotten the killing that marked her deeper than any scar? That pivotal moment which drives her life? Part of her *wants* him to remember. But that's foolish.

A familiar rage pushes against Sol's self-control. Sure, it's been more than a decade, and she was just a kid, but still. How dare Anton's murdering her father not mark *his* life? Anton accepts her presence and her manufactured name with a nod and turns toward the tall, skinny man on his other side. Creek, she thinks.

Muff taps her arm, then hands her a drink. It tastes like rat piss. Some weak, nonalcoholic brew. Even on a night of celebration, this fell ship doesn't supply the real stuff. What she wouldn't give for a whiskey, yet she thanks the woman and sips. It's something to do while Muff reminisces about her dead "soulmate" and Sol tries to decide when she can leave without attracting notice.

Fifteen minutes later, Juke taps her on the shoulder. "Wanna dance?"

Sol searches for Anvil. "Where's your boyfriend?"

"Already out there." He points.

Anvil gyrates with several other crewmates from his table. The band's music blends pounding drum cadences with electric guitars and synthesizers. It's noisy, wild, unfettered.

"I'm not much of a dancer."

"Come on, darling." He tugs on her arm while leaning down to whisper, "We should talk."

She lets him pull her up. Her mind feels sluggish, like there really was alcohol in that drink. It's must be the stress of Anton's nearness. Juke heads toward the portable flooring laid over short-trimmed grass and packed with dancers. She follows him to the far side until they're hidden behind a wall of bodies.

Sweat stink mixes with perfume. The raucous song ends, and a slower one starts. Juke propels her close, one arm firm on her lower back, the other mid-spine. She lets him confine her, too curious to object.

His breath warms her ear. "What are you doing?"

"Turning in meaningless circles to the beat of a sappy tune?" She focuses on the dancers without really seeing them.

"Don't play dumb. Why are you with Anton? Why did you transfer to Life Support after all the horrible things I've been saying about it? Are you spying on me?"

"What? No! Not everything is about you."

"Then why?"

"That's my own business." Her sharp retort shuts him up. The music swells, filling the void of conversation for a few seconds. "By the way, thanks for putting *Hanna* on the manifest. You haven't taken my advice about Anvil."

"He wants me to join them. The Earthers. Apparently, they're holding secret meetings after shift."

She lets this sink in. A scrap of remembered conversation resurfaces. When that woman collapsed on the path, Anton said he'd be one crew member short, but his companion replied, "It won't matter for much longer." Because ... why? They'd reach Vishnu soon? Or was some planned sabotage about to change everything? *That* might explain why NASA haters would join *Calliope*'s colonists.

"Sol?" Juke stares at her.

Her breaths come shallow and fast. *Sabotage makes sense.* She leans close and shares her theory with Juke.

She expects him to scoff, but he doesn't. His lips thin while he considers. "You really think that's why they're aboard? If so, what are they waiting for?"

"I don't know, but I'm going to find out." She worries her lip while she thinks. "You should join the Earther movement, and you should invite me along."

"Anvil—" Juke falls quiet, his mouth turned down. "I really like him."

What can she say? She really likes Oskar, too, yet there are bigger stakes at play than either of their relationships. *Bigger than my own revenge.* It hurts to admit this. Even if she gets the chance, she can't kill Anton yet. Not until she discovers what he's up to.

Juke's despair must be catching. It washes over her, but she shakes it off. "Hey. Can I count on you to help me, Juke? If Anvil isn't involved, we'll be saving him, too."

Juke snorts. "And what are the chances of that?"

Almost none, she thinks yet doesn't say. Instead, she pulls him closer to murmur, "You aren't alone, even if things don't work out with Anvil. Remember that."

He pulls away, surprise etching his face, then suspicion. "Sol, you do have a soft side, and here I thought you were all angles and bones."

She flashes a savage smile. "Oh, I'm very pointy. Just get me into an Earther meeting, and I'll have your back. I promise."

He shakes his head. "You are one crazy woman to leave your cushy clinic job for the glam life of a Venter."

"Someone has to play Supergirl and save the day." She arches a brow at him.

Juke laughs. "Ain't that the truth."

26

Solast

Sol's in one of the first groups shuttled down to the surface of Mars. Finally, a use for the puffy spacesuits tucked away in an engineering locker on the *Goose*. After the short flight, a rover with thick treads transports her, Clera, and a dozen other colonists from the landing pad along a rutted road that trails into a tunnel. The dusty cliffs of Arsia Mons tower above. In every other direction, pitted, rock-strewn hills of naked soil stretch to the horizon. Clera edges closer to Sol. She looks nervous even through the thick facemask of her helmet. Butterflies flutter through Sol's stomach, too, but she puts on a brave face.

The tunnel ends at a huge cavern filled with transports and bustle. They pass through an airlock and follow signs saying it's safe to remove oxygen masks. Huge blowers pump an oxygen-nitrogen mix into the hub of smaller branching tunnels. Despite not wearing grav boots, Sol discovers she can walk without floating away, though she bounces into the air several feet with every step.

Their group is directed down a side tunnel into a stadium-sized cavern filled with cots. No glam hotel for *Calliope*'s colonists—at least not for people like her. Sol drops her pack and helmet on a bed and looks toward Clera, who's glancing around and wrinkling her nose. "This place reminds me of a homeless shelter Elio and I stayed in once, only the walls there were cinderblock, not stone."

"At least we're off the ship for a bit." Rows of identical cots stretch off into the gloom. "Think our stuff is safe to leave here?"

"Yes," Clera replies. "I mean, this isn't exactly New Chicago, is it? These people were vetted. Not a scrull among them. We should be safe."

Sol wants to disagree. She barely stops herself from blurting out everything Juke and she discussed last night. No use worrying Clera since she can do nothing about the Earthers. Sol strips off the bulky spacesuit, then suggests, "Let's go check out Arsia Mons, yeah? The city, I mean. Not the mountain." If someone wants to steal her toothpaste, good for them.

"Great idea." Clera discards her suit. They press past another group of arriving colonists as they backtrack to the transport hub. Clera forgets caution and pushes off too forcefully. A gasp escapes her lips as she rises a foot off the ground before dropping. Sol catches her arm and helps her recover her footing. She laughs—a scratchy sound like maybe she's forgotten how. She points to a sign with directions for reaching the underground city. A rolling rubber tread like airports used fifty years ago carries them down a hollow tube of reinforced rock. The tread runs the other direction, too, carrying people and packages up to the surface. LED lights illuminate their path. The air smells of dust, and heat bars attached to the tunnel walls only partially mitigate the cold.

The walkway deposits them into another vast cavern with a ceiling ten stories high. Some kind of bioluminescent lifeform clings to the rock-hewn surfaces and sprinkles light across the city of Arsia Mons. Whirring fans create a constant hum. Vines with no visible light source cling to railings and walls, and fountains set into shelves of red rock splash and spray. Sol forgets her goose-pimpled flesh and gasps in wonder.

Walkways crisscross the cavern floor in a grid pattern. Like the Anasazi Indian ruins of long-ago Earth history, shops, stairways, and balconies pock the cavern walls. More moving walkways transport people from place to place. The locals dress in a hodgepodge of colors and styles, from henna-died saris to crisp white turbans, to earth-toned, pajama-style leggings and tunics. They regard the spaceship visitors in their one-piece jumpsuits with open curiosity.

Sol feels light as a feather. She grabs a railing and jumps from the tread. Clera imitates her move, gasping and giggling. They walk in circles to admire the newly constructed town. "It's amazing," Clera breathes.

"Can you imagine living here full time, though?" Sol watches two black men wearing beanies and work boots push a pile of crates onto the rolling walkway. The men jump on behind them with grace born of practice. "I'd miss the sunlight after about two minutes."

"Me, too." Clera sighs. "I'm glad we're going on through the wormhole." She eyes Sol sideways. "You are continuing our journey, right? Or do you still want to find a ride back home?"

"Not anymore," Sol admits. She's grown to like Clera despite their rough start. It'd be nice to confide in her, yet Sol doesn't dare. The less she knows, the safer she'll be. "I've made my peace with leaving Earth. I've also changed work details, just so you know. But it won't keep me from helping Mila when it's time. My new assignment is only temporary."

"What? You left the clinic?"

"For a bit." Sol avoids Clera's searching gaze. "Please don't ask questions that will only put you at risk."

"You haven't given up on whatever it is that made you so mad to leave Earth, have you? Yet *something's* changed." Clera's lips purse. "You've discovered something new, or made some plan, or, I don't know, met someone. Just tell me whatever you're up to isn't going to get us all in trouble."

She's closer to the truth than she knows. Sol *has* met someone—or rediscovered him, anyway. She chalks up another lie. "I promise," but she keeps her fingers crossed.

Mars uses credits similar to Earth's, so the Steward's office has allocated everyone temporary accounts filled with enough money to get them through the week. Sol and Clera climb one steep stairway, then another, until they reach the highest level of Arsia Mons. Sol isn't even out of breath. She weighs less on the red planet, and she feels strong. They enter a cafe, order drinks and pastries, and pick a spot on the veranda that overlooks the city. The table and chairs are constructed of familiar white polymer, but the view is so alien that Sol leans over the railing to soak it in.

Clera bites into a flaky crust. "If you fell over that, maybe you wouldn't even die, just drift down gently to land on one of those ant-like people below us."

"I don't know. There's still quite a bit of gravity. Maybe if I were a gangster, I'd have to think up a better way to kill my enemies than by throwing them off rooftops."

"Um, I guess? Do your thoughts always veer off in violent directions?"

Sol sits back and smirks. "If I say 'yes,' will you abandon me here and go find someone else to eat with?"

Clera thinks about this. "Nope. I'm okay with violence as long as you're on my side."

"I am." Sol means it, too. Somewhere between home and Mars, she's come to see the *Goose*'s thieves as compatriots, not enemies. Maybe that's a mistake. Once you care for people, you're tied to them, and if they leave you—she cuts off the thought.

Clera points to the faint outline of Sol's crucifix. "You play with that necklace a lot. What is it to you?"

Sol pulls the chain from under her suit. It winks beneath the lamp attached to their table.

Clera says, "A crucifix. My Buela had one like that."

"Buela?"

"My grandmother. She lived with us. She's my abuela, *grandmother* in Spanish, but Elio and I found Buela easier to say. She died several years ago in one of the flu epidemics."

Sol frowns at the cross. "This was my mother's. I don't remember her well. She left it to me before she passed."

"How did she ..."

"Childbirth complications."

Their eyes lock. They aren't so different: Slummers born to factory workers and destined for poverty. But Sol's determined to make her own destiny. Once Anton is destroyed, she'll go back to nursing, maybe even start her own clinic on Vishnu. Anything will be possible. Anything at all.

Oskar appears in her mind's eye. She bends over the railing again and searches the streets below. Is he down there somewhere looking up? Can he see her? Hear the words she never spoke to him? *Yes, I'd love you to give me a tour of the old ruins.*

Two days later, she decides to explore them on her own.

———◆———

Sol stares down a silent tunnel. She's left the city's bioluminescent glow lights, vertical gardens, and splashing water structures behind. Gone is the gabble of a multilingual society that claims many nations—or none. Gone the transactions, commerce, and chatter. It's quiet here, like the Mars of old.

The last tour group headed this way half an hour ago. Perhaps she'll catch up with them, perhaps not. Oskar hasn't messaged her, and she wants to be alone anyway. If she's honest, she's looking for the ghost of his younger self. Searching for the twenty-something scholar, the burgeoning academic, a young man who lopes colt-like down tunnels, all legs and curiosity and passion for life.

Maybe Oskar was never like that. Perhaps he was always quiet, humble, and a bit sad. Will she ever know? His disappointment in her decision to quit the clinic might spill into general disillusionment. He'll retreat into his office, bid her a silent goodbye. At least the Earthers will never connect Sol to him if her plans fail. That would be best. Definitely.

So why does she torture herself thinking of Oskar? She hastens her pace as if she can outrun his memory. The tunnel branches. She thought there would be signs, but she supposes tourists rely on tour guides to get around down here. Oh, well. She turns left.

The air handlers barely stir her hair. At some point, will breathable oxygen run out entirely? Does it even work like that? If she'd stayed with a tour group, she wouldn't need to worry. Still, track lighting guides her steps, offering some reassurance. She can't be that lost. Another ten minutes without finding ruins, and she'll turn back. Ahead, a tiny light gleams like a firefly. Sol squints. Her breath hitches, and she hesitates, uncertain. Go back, or keep on?

The pinprick becomes a lantern, and suddenly the silhouette of a man looms from darkness. "Hello?" a familiar voice calls. "Are you lost?"

Sol's breath whooshes out. "It's me, Oskar." She hurries forward.

He holds the lantern high. It illuminates the rough tunnel better than the track lights. He looks past her as though searching for others.

She tells him, "I'm all alone."

He frowns. "Why?"

She scrambles for an explanation but can't find one, so she lies. "I got distracted, and they left me. It's all right. I prefer to explore on my own."

He steps close to her. "No. That's a bad idea. It's too easy to lose your way down here. Didn't the tour guide warn you to stay with the group?"

She squares her shoulders. "I thought *you'd* offered to show me the old ruins, but you haven't messaged me."

"I didn't think you were interested."

"Well, I am. *If* there are even artifacts to see. All I've noticed so far are boring rock walls." She leans against one, hands spread across the cold stone at her back, and resists the impulse to shiver.

He laughs, and the tension between them snaps. "That's because you left the group. Come this way, and I'll show you petroglyphs uncovered when the tremors first started."

Together they backtrack, turn at an offshoot she missed, and arrive abruptly at walls covered by red-inked drawings. They could have come from Neanderthal dwellings if not for the fantastical shapes they depict—something like Chinese dragons and very long-legged humanoids.

What are you doing here with him, Sol, when you meant to stay away? Yet something about Oskar draws her inexorably closer. She can't fight the pull, can't seem to avoid or resist him.

Oskar explains what little archaeologists have gleaned from the petroglyphs. "If the artist rendered these drawings accurately, Martians looked generally like us, though longer-limbed, as you can see."

"That seems so unlikely, given the scope of the universe."

"You may well be correct, but many scientists support an 'ancient astronaut theory,' the idea that advanced aliens visited Earth millions of years ago. Perhaps Martians interbred with hominids before departing."

"Without leaving a trace behind?"

Oskar shrugs. "Our home planet is young in the vastness of the universe. We've proof now that we aren't alone." He nods at the drawings. "It's plausible that much older sentient life might have developed technology beyond our imaginations, and if they could do that, surely they could cover up any traces of themselves when they abandoned Earth. Look at how well the Martians hid their wormhole."

Sol considers this, then points to a dragon. "What are these?"

He holds the lantern high. "We can't say. Could be real creatures that used to exist in the canals on the surface, or the drawings might be symbolic. Who knows."

"Being an archaeologist must be frustrating. So many fascinating hints of past civilizations, yet no way to prove anything."

"It's challenging, that's true, but exciting as well. Come along, and I'll show you something else."

He offers his hand. She slips her palm into his larger one. He pulls her around a bend and through several more turns. Fallen rock impedes their progress, and she's sure no tourist ever sees *these* Martian passageways. The tunnel ends in a pile of rubble, past which is a sheet of some pale metal filled with lines that run top to bottom and look a bit like hieroglyphics. Oskar drops her hand and gestures. "Go ahead. Touch it."

Sol looks toward a small sign someone tacked to the wall. *Warning. Do not touch. You are in a restricted area.* Yet he nods encouragement, so she reaches out. The metal warms her fingertips like it's lit from within. The glyphs light up when she brushes her skin against them. She gasps and pulls back. "What did I do?"

"I've no idea." He grins. "We conjecture that this panel is a sort of supercomputer, and that when it was damaged by rockfall, the cloaking device hiding the ARH quit working. I've laid hands on every inch of this thing, and nothing ever happens except the glow you just experienced. It'll go away in a few seconds."

She's awestruck to stand before something so ancient, so beyond anything she's known. If not for the Martians, or the earthquake, or this strange device standing before her, *she wouldn't be here now*. She wouldn't have gotten close to Anton and wouldn't have met Oskar.

Sol draws a shuddery breath, and he steps closer. "I know," he says solemnly even though she didn't speak. His fingers inch toward her. When she doesn't draw away, he slides his hand around hers—gently—like she's a wild animal he doesn't wish to frighten. But in this dark, foreign place, withdrawing doesn't occur to her. Sol's entered a different reality, an alternate universe in which there is no Anton, no danger, no survivor's guilt or need for retribution. Only one lonely woman and one lonely man.

Sol and Oskar.

She turns into his arms before she can convince herself not to. Sol looks up into his shadowed face. He smells vaguely of soap and something undefinable, something uniquely Oskar. He's holding his breath, standing still as a block of marble. She should back off. She …

Then he's kissing her. Not a shy brush of lips, either, but the kiss of a man who knows what he's doing even if he claims to be rusty. His hand drops hers and moves around her back, urging her closer. His body warms and envelopes, makes her forget everything.

Until a groaning, rumbling sound startles them both. Fear shatters the moment, and she jumps back and looks about. "What's that? Is the tunnel about to come down on top of us?"

Oskar blinks like he's emerging from a dream, then gathers himself. "No. These passages have been cleared by multiple engineers. They're just the start of a huge city we've only begun to excavate. The earthquake that revealed the ARH also blocked ancient corridors with tons of rock. X-ray machines have picked up traces of the Martian metropolis, though. These tunnels often speak. No one is quite sure why. It could be reverberations from deeper inside the mountain's roots."

"I don't like it. Sounds like Arsia Mons isn't happy we're here. Like a bad omen."

A smile touches his lips. "I didn't think you'd be superstitious."

"Any sane person would be worried to hear that sound while trapped beneath a mountain."

"You aren't trapped. Come. I'll take you back up."

He holds out a hand, yet she hesitates. If she touches him again, will he propel her back into his arms? Will she have the strength to resist?

There's no fire in Oskar's eyes, only concern. She allows him to lead her back to relative safety—if there is safety to be found anywhere in the world.

27

Clera

In the bunk cavern, Clera settles on her cot. Sol went off to explore the city after they ate, but a pressing weight propelled Clera back to the quiet, empty sleeping room. She examines her feelings and admits Zavi is causing her depression. Or rather the *lack* of Zavi. Maybe it's time to face facts, to read the message he sent before the celebration, to get the heartache headed her way over with.

She finds the old message and opens it.

Clera, I'm so sorry I haven't been in contact. Despite all the preventative meds and vitamins they give us, somehow I managed to contract a flu virus. The doc has me quarantined. They're very picky about spreading contagion in *Calliope*'s closed environment. At first, I was feeling too sick to message anyone. Once I got better, I worried you'd think I was making excuses, that I was the close-minded kind of person who wouldn't accept you and all you've done or had to do.

You should know it wasn't that at all. Well, not once the first shock of what you told me about stealing a shuttle wore off, anyway. Please believe this is the truth. I want to see you as soon as I'm released from "berth jail."

Several days later, he added another note to the thread.

Since you haven't replied, I'm guessing you don't believe my sickness excuse. I don't know what more I can say. I'll be at the Biosphere celebration and wait for you in the orchard. Look for a small fountain with a Greek statue in the center. It's not Persephone, just the best I can do.

Clera sits up on her cot. He waited for her, and she never showed, all because she was too cowardly to open a stupid Skinpad message. Sunshine breaks through the clouds. She wants to pump the air or high-five someone. Zavi knows everything, yet he still wants her. The reference to Persephone proves it, right? That was the statue on the arboretum grounds in New Chicago and the first place they kissed. The first time she knew he might return her feelings.

What must he think of her now? She dashes off a message and hits *Send*.

His reply appears five agonizing minutes later. He can't meet up with her in the underground city because he's still aboard *Calliope*. He got behind with work when he was sick and is spending this week catching up at his office.

Clera gathers her belongings and tucks them into her bag. She straightens the cot, sends Sol a quick, somewhat cryptic message explaining her absence, then heads toward the transport hub.

It takes several tries to find the correct person to book her on a shuttle heading up to the starship. *Calliope*'s passengers aren't returning early, so finding a ride is next to impossible. Eventually, a helpful official convinces the captain of an asteroid mining vessel to make a quick stop in *Calliope*'s main hangar before shipping out. She breathes a sigh of relief.

The official settles her on a bench near his kiosk with a cup of coffee—thick, strong, and foreign tasting. He contacts *Calliope*'s bridge to alert them to the unexpected arrival. She waits nervously, tempted to update Zavi but then deciding to surprise him. She tamps down self-doubt. *When has being shy ever gotten you anywhere, Clera Diaz? Stiffen your backbone. What's the worst that can happen? He'll reject you for real this time?*

The hard bench presses against her bottom. Clera ignores the discomfort and watches utility vehicles loaded with goods and people come and go. Crates and bundles strapped with nylon cords await transport out of the airlock and onto ships. A motley array of people dressed in robes, embroidered saris, dusty uniforms, and even jeans and cowboy hats stir up red cave dust beneath the thick-treaded tires of their UTV's. Every one of them is here because they reached for something. Dared to believe in their dreams. *I can do that, too.*

A voice in her head reminds her, *You already have.*

Finally, a man in khaki trousers with a dented felt hat tied beneath his chin speaks to the entry official, then approaches Clera. "You the girl, then? Come on. They're waiting outside. Got your breathing apparatus and suit, have you now?" His accent is Australian.

Clera holds up a helmet, then pulls her heavy spacesuit from her pack. After she slips it on, the captain checks her over and adjusts her seal. He dons his own suit, then leads her through the airlock and up to the surface. A few shuttles rest between shallow hills and jumbled stone. Far off, the domes of the first colony, Mars One, bulge like turtles' backs. A thin layer of dust coats everything. The stark landscape is comprised of reddish earth, rocks, and faint tire tracks that fade in the distance.

It's only a short walk to the shuttle. The captain grabs her arm and pulls her along, mumbling something she can't make out. She probably doesn't want to know what he said.

The mining shuttle is a far cry from NASA's state-of-the-art vessels. Metal benches and exposed wiring don't say much for the company's decorating tastes. She straps in between two anonymous miners who slide apart to make room. A bumpy takeoff has her clutching the seat, but a short time later, the mining shuttle glides into *Calliope*'s hangar, and Clera's shoulders relax.

She's not sorry to leave Mars early. She longs for the Biosphere's greenery, the rustle of living plants, and Zavi. As quickly as she can, she changes into her blue jumpsuit, stores the heavy one away on the *Blue Goose*, and heads to his office. She checks the time. Four o'clock in the afternoon.

Zavi calls, "Come," when she knocks but doesn't look up when she enters, only says, "Just a minute, Barak."

"I'm not Barak."

His head jerks up, the surprise on his face making her smile. "Clera." He pushes a data pad away. Doubt and indecision war on his face.

"You're wondering why I'm not on Mars."

"Yes. I didn't know passengers were allowed to return early even if they wanted to."

She shrugs. "I didn't ask, just hitched a ride with a mining vessel. *Calliope* didn't refuse the landing."

The corners of his mouth tip up. "Just hitched a ride, huh? You sound like a professional space traveler. And why would you want to return early when you had a chance to escape this boat for a whole week?"

"It's not obvious?"

A frown knits his forehead. "I'm just not sure if you've come back to yell at me for being an idiot or to kiss me. Or maybe something in between."

She lets him wonder. He deserves to after what he's put her through—though that's not fair. He *was* sick. "Are you finished for the day?"

"I am now." He comes around the desk. "Would you like to see my berth?"

"You saw mine." She shrugs nonchalantly. Inside, though, her heart picks up speed.

They walk out together.

Zavi's shuttle looks unlived in. Despite its modern, sleek design, complete with plush carpets, lightweight faux-stone counters, a multi-screen video set-up, and an AI system that responds to his every whim, the place has no personality. "Brighten," Zavi calls as they enter, and lights flare. "After work," he calls again, and soft classical music wafts from speakers while a whiff of lavender and rosemary join the oxygen flow whooshing through the vents.

Clera runs her hand along a leather sofa. "This place is nothing like your bungalow. You haven't decorated."

He glances around as though seeing the shuttle's interior for the first time. "No, I guess not. Didn't seem important since I'll be gone soon."

"At this point you will," she agrees, leaving unsaid that wasn't the case when *Calliope* launched. A fancy camera sits in a holder on the coffee table. The main vid screen shows a frozen scene from the Biosphere party—a group raising cups while dancers whirl in the background. "What's that?"

"Oh, an officer I knew from Earth loaned me his camera. He thought I'd enjoy seeing all the pictures he took at the Mars landing celebration. Sees himself as a semi-pro photographer. I think there might be one of me in there hunched in the orchard looking glum." He gestures to the couch. "Want to take a look?"

She nods and sits, wondering if she only came here to admire a bunch of strangers at a party she doesn't care to remember. Zavi sinks down beside her, not far off but not so close they touch. He picks up the wirelessly connected camera and clicks a forward button, then groans when a photo of himself does come up. He sits in shadow under the spreading leaves of a fruit tree. A fountain bubbles nearby. "I seriously didn't mean for you to see that." He hurries past the shot.

Several slides later, the head Steward appears, dancing on a table with a group of young women. "Wait. Stop right there." Clera touches Zavi's wrist.

He looks at her hand, and she hastily withdraws. "That's Juke. See?" She points to the left of the Steward. "He's the one who hacked our way aboard the ship and got me a Skinpad. There, by the bar." Accidentally included in the photo, Anvil arm-wrestles with someone Clera doesn't recognize while Juke looks on.

"He seems like he's having fun," Zavi remarks.

Clera wishes she hadn't reminded him of how she arrived on *Calliope*. "Wait!" She stops Zavi before he can press *Forward*. "What's that thing on the dark-haired man's bicep? Can you zoom in?"

Zavi fiddles with the camera, and the arm-wrestling figures lurch toward them.

"There. He's got a tattoo of a sphere bisected by a spear. Normally, it would be hidden, but he's pulled his sleeve way up to show off his muscles."

"You know the mark?" Zavi looks toward her with a frown.

"Yes. It's the Earther emblem. Don't you recognize it?"

"All too well. Similar signs were spraypainted all over the wrecked air rail cars that killed my parents."

"Oh." They fall silent. Clera's thoughts snowball. Could there be Earthers aboard *Calliope*? But why? And does Juke know?

Finally, Zavi says, "About a fourth of the colonists came to the starship via lottery. I suppose some ex-Earther could have won a berth. That tattoo isn't in an obvious spot. I wouldn't think he'd want to be caught with it, though. He probably forgot he even had it."

"You'd think an ex-Earther might have had the tattoo removed. Especially since such procedures are common here. Sol had a scar done, and you can't tell she ever had one."

"Like I said, maybe he forgot. And he didn't want to admit to some doctor aboard ship that he'd been in a cult. Not that they could kick him off … though he could have been left stranded on Mars."

"Right." *Nothing else makes sense.* Calliope *is the last place an Earther would show up.*

Zavi flips the camera off and sets it back on the table. "I didn't invite you here to look at Zed's photos." He smiles apologetically.

"Why did you, then?"

He ponders this for a long time. "I wanted you alone where no one could interrupt us. We can talk here. We can do whatever we want."

The first tingle of desire races up her spine. If she moves the tiniest bit toward him, will he draw her into his arms? "The timing has never been right for us, has it? When I first met you, I had secrets, and I thought if you knew I was a low class Slummer, you'd reject me. Then, just when I was coming around to realize you weren't like that, your grandfather insisted you take the director job on *Calliope*. By the time we left Earth, I had *new* secrets, and now—"

"Everything's out in the open. Right?"

"And you aren't judging me?"

"No."

"Or turning me in?"

"Absolutely not."

"So where do we go from here?"

He inches closer. "I'm tired of carrying on like you're my little sister. Like it's okay to give you a job, to try to protect you from women like Kris, but I don't get to go further. I'm tired of being a gentleman."

A grin tickles the corner of her mouth. Every cell in her body vibrates. "Is that what you thought you were doing? It seemed more like torturing me."

"It did?" He cocks his head. "That's the last thing I want to do." Another inch closer, and his knee brushes hers. "Forgive me?"

"If you forgive me."

"For what?" He takes her hand and brushes the back with his lips.

"For ... for ..." Her brain can't function while his mouth feathers her skin with kisses.

"Trying to reach for something better?" he finishes for her. "If you hadn't, we wouldn't be here together."

"I want ... I want so much ..."

"Hmm?" His lips move to press against the inside of her wrist, then climb her inner arm.

"For you to really see me. To bare everything. No secrets. Nothing between us."

His eyes dart to her face. "Do you mean that figuratively or literally?"

"Both, I suppose." Her cheeks flame.

"Maybe you want me to 'bare' myself first?" He grins, then drops her arm and in a single, smooth motion, shimmies out of his suit. Golden hairs dust his chest. Briefs sit low on his hips. "Let me help with yours."

"Oh!" Before she realizes what's happening, he's peeled the top of the jumpsuit down to her waist, trapping her arms inside the sleeves. He leans in and kisses her mouth. She can't embrace him, only turn her face up and accept what he offers.

"Why didn't we do this before?" he murmurs against her cheek.

"Because you were leaving."

"And you had secrets."

"Promise me you won't abandon me again."

"Promise you'll tell me everything."

"I will, even if you wish I hadn't. Elio says I can be a little bossy, just so you know."

He nibbles at her ear before responding. "Feel free to order me around. I've missed having someone do that in my life. Well, Grandfather was good at it, but he doesn't count." Zavi leans back and looks at her.

She falls into his blue irises like a person about to drown but not caring. His eyes have mesmerized her since that first encounter in the Boba Tea Cafe. It's hard to think while Zavi stares at her with a confusing mix of gentleness and passion. She finally blurts, "I love you."

"I love you, too." He says it without hesitation.

It's a miracle she doesn't question. Clera wrangles her arms from the clinging suit and wraps them around Zavi's neck. His skin warms her from head to toe. His arms encircle her waist and draw her so close it feels like they're one person. She kisses his neck, his collarbone, his chin, before he captures her mouth.

It's hard if not impossible to make love in zero-g, but somehow, they manage. Later, as she curls against his side, tucked beneath covers and secured by the bunk harness, Clera wonders at how life can change in an instant. Every decision she's made has brought her to this moment, and if she had to decide again, she'd do nothing differently—except, well, check her messages more promptly. Peace settles over her. Wrapped in Zavi's arms, she feels invincible. He's drifted asleep, chest rising and falling against her breasts. She fights unconsciousness to savor this moment. No matter what comes next, they'll face it together.

Day 40

Thank the gods—I am not the only animal trapped on this lonely planet (though I may be the only sentient one). I suspect that most of Vishnu's fauna lives in its vast oceans, where diving deep below the surface may provide escape from the deadly doomscap fungi.

Yet the stalwart rock beetles manage to survive on land, as do I. They are tricky to trap, as they disappear under rocks along the cliffs if I can't surprise them. It took much patience to harvest enough for a hearty meal. (Ah, protein, how I've missed you.) I never thought the sight of a dead bug on my dinner plate would make me salivate, but there it is. I hate to kill them, as we are compatriots in this desolate place. When I'm not ravenous, I talk to them, just as I speak to the sun spinners (the palm-sized silver fish that hide in the kelp forests).

Am I going crazy?

-N.J.

28

Niklas

Nik strips to his briefs and wades into the surf. Cool water washes over his skin, removing sweat and grime. He walks in deeper and dunks his head. If only the waves could wash away memory as easily as dirt. The dead faces of his team push into his thoughts, their mouths open in silent screams, their pallid faces the stuff of nightmares.

He dives under the surface and blinks at the world beneath. Sand merges with a kelp forest. Fronds wave in the currents, but no other life presents itself. He swims toward the cliffs, marveling at the vivid green seas. NASA's scientists theorize the color comes from microscopic phytoplankton. Nik doesn't want to think about why this planet is lovely, just drown in that beauty and let it distract him from Vishnu's darker side.

Diving down again, he kicks toward a cluster of boulders mired in sea mud. The kelp gives way to seagrass meadows, and Nik half-expects to see a turtle basking there, its patterned shell lit by undulating light from above. Instead, a narrow face framed by green and blue tentacles materializes near the underwater rock wall to his right. He flinches, backpaddles, and rubs his eyes. When he looks again, the face has gone.

I must be hallucinating. Nik fights for calm and swims up to the surface. He's comfortable in oceans and spent much of his childhood swimming in them with Zavi during summer vacations. Yet that face, imagined or not, has spooked him. He treads water and looks about but sees only himself and the endless waves. Something brushes his legs. He flinches again, ducks under. Nothing. He sidestrokes along the cliffs, sure he's going crazy.

Something tickles his foot. Fighting panic, he sucks in a breath and dives straight down a good ten feet, rights himself, and squints into the emerald murk. Left, right, then up toward the surface.

A sinuous body hangs above him: limbless, thick as three men, with a long snout and a mane of tentacles in shades of blue and green. They wave in the currents while bioluminescent lights blink and chase each other beneath the skin of a bony face. Helv! He frantically kicks away. The beast isn't coming for him, though, just hanging there. In another heartbeat, with a powerful flick of a finncd tail, it vanishes.

Niklas propels himself away from the last place the monster appeared. Alarm thrums in his chest. He breaks the surface next to the cliffs and grabs at the vertical rock wall. He'd scramble up it if this were possible. His hand scrapes along slick, algae-covered stone, then fumbles across an opening. Rough edges bite into his palm. He gasps and twists, treading water. Blood seeps from a shallow cut and swirls into the sea. *Great. Just what I need. To draw in every predator around with my blood scent.*

Water swirls past him into the cave he's discovered. He allows the surf to push him under an arch of slate gray rock. The creature that frightened him is reminiscent of some dragon out of a dark childhood fairy tale. *Act like a biologist, not a scared kid,* he chides himself as he washes forward with the next wave. A cavern roof shutters daylight, and arched walls rise on both sides of him. Two more strokes, and he bangs his knee on something solid. Waves chunk against rock, their sounds magnified. Nik feels for solid ground and hauls himself out of the sea.

He moves to the back of the cavern and sits shivering on a cold, wet ledge. The cave's entrance is a reassuring circle of sunlight. A breeze wafts against his face. He taps a light on his Skinpad, turns, and raises his arm. The light illuminates the cave's walls. Someone has painted drawings onto the rock with red pigment. Forgetting his throbbing hand, Nik jumps up. The top of his head brushes the ceiling. He walks close to the pictures and examines them.

A shiver runs down his spine that has nothing to do with the coolness of the cave. He recognizes the creature in the petroglyphs. It's a Chinese dragon. Long, undulating, with a tentacle-wreathed face. He's seen similar designs on Martian artifacts, and he realizes his monster wasn't some hallucination. Who could have drawn such a thing, and when? His team has detected no sign of sentient life forms on Vishnu, but they haven't explored the sea. Besides, this art could be thousands of years old. There's no way to test the petroglyphs with the equipment he has.

Something clanks when he shifts his feet. He shines the light down on a metal canteen. A messenger bag sits next to it. Heart in his throat, he kneels and opens the bag. A few wrappers fall out. The language on them looks familiar, yet it's not Swedish, English or French, the three tongues he's familiar with. He frowns and shakes the bag. Nothing else emerges. No identifying marks adorn the outside. He's certain of only one thing—the messenger bag, wrappers, and canteen don't belong on Vishnu. They're definitely from Earth.

He slumps next to the bag and rests his head against the stone behind him. For the first time, he pays attention to the pulsing pain in his palm. The Skinpad's glow illuminates the shallow cut. It's already stopped bleeding. The surrounding skin remains puffy and red, though, and he remembers the algae. Maybe he's having an allergic reaction. Or worse, some toxin has worked its way inside him.

Suddenly, Niklas feels very tired. In the movies, it's falling asleep that kills you. Or maybe that's just for freezing to death? Or concussions? He shakes his groggy head, but the world tilts and his stomach roils, so he stops. If he lies down for a few minutes, he'll be fine. Then he'll brave the water again and swim back to shore.

Nik drifts onto his side and rests his head on the bag, which smells faintly of flowers. *Roses*, he thinks. Water burbles where the cavern floor gives way to the sea. There's a soft swish. The sound of pattering water droplets. He's alone, and then he's not. Someone hunches beside him. His light reveals a thin face, wavy, shoulder-length hair dark with wetness, deep-set eyes, a pert nose, and a serious mouth.

She's human.

The girl speaks, yet his brain can't process the words. He tries to answer but only grunts. His tongue lies thick in his mouth, and his body feels impossibly heavy. He groans in frustration and manages to raise his hurt hand. It wavers before him, casting shadows on the wall. "Monster. Poison." Did he speak? Before he can answer himself, he drifts into unconsciousness.

29

Solast

Sol leaves Mars on a special transport less than twenty-four hours after Clera to start her new work assignment. Email directions lead her to a portal on Red Deck marked *Maintenance*. She scans her Skinpad, and the door slides open. As soon as she's through, it whisks shut behind her. She's in a sort of locker room. To the right, an opening leads into chemical showers and a head. Lockers and benches fill the space before her. Gas masks are clipped to a rack, and cleaning supplies reside in a clear plastic cabinet. A narrow corridor leads onward into the bowels of the ship.

Anton steps out of the corridor and stands before her, arms crossed. Brown work coveralls protect his navy spacesuit. "You're on time," he says, nodding approval.

Coldness creeps over every inch of Sol's body. This is the moment she's been waiting for. Finally, after years of tracking him, she has Anton alone. The knockout gun is back on the *Goose,* though. She couldn't figure out how to hide it in her pocketless jumpsuit. She eyes the tall, muscular man before her. He's getting older now, but he works out, and she remembers well the painful lessons he inflicted on her all those years ago. Anton trained her to fight. She knows martial arts, yet so does he.

It's best to say nothing. If she speaks, she'll give away her loathing.

Anton's lip curls. "Hanna Jones." The curl spreads into a wide grin. "From New Chicago."

"What of it?" She juts her chin. Why doesn't he get on with his stupid training?

He scratches his jaw. "But is she really from New Chicago? Or from a commune in the Barrens? Was she always Hanna, or was she Solast, a name she chose herself on her twelfth birthday?"

Fec. He knows who she is. He *does* remember. She backs away and comes up short against the wall.

He rubs his shoulder. "The old wound you gave me still aches, you know? I didn't think you'd survive all alone in the wilds. Sent men to find you, but they never could. Guess you've risen from the dead, Sol Bahri. Why do you really want to work on my crew?"

Her heart might explode from beating so hard. It's useless to lie—at least about who she is. Is this some cat and mouse game before he kills her? Does he even *want* to murder her? She wounded him, true, but that was over a decade ago, and she was just a kid. "Everything I said about why I want to change jobs was correct." She keeps her gaze steady on his face. "But why are you here, *Mons Vega*? I thought you hated all technology. 'Only by surrendering to the earth will we reclaim it. The earth belongs to the earth,' and all that."

"So you remember my teachings, little one. Very good." He takes a step closer.

"I recall *everything.*"

"Is revenge your aim, then?" He cocks his head. "You know your father gave me no choice that day. He taunted me. Defied me. Made me look weak. If I hadn't punished him, no other member of my flock would have listened to me ever again."

Sol waits until she's pretty sure her voice won't shake. Then she says carefully, "I wanted revenge, but that was a long time ago. Now I just want—"

"What do you want?"

"To survive. To make it to Vishnu and start over."

"Maybe that's what I want, too."

She gathers her courage. "I thought the leader of the Earthers would desire the opposite. Wasn't your group against colonization? Didn't you accuse the rest of us of abandoning Earth?"

"Yes." He falls silent, face unreadable.

Now, Sol. Jump him while he's thinking this over. She can't make herself move.

"Do you believe people can change, little one?"

She doesn't think he's changed, yet she offers a stiff nod.

"Perhaps all I want is a chance to start fresh, also."

She doesn't respond.

"Hmm." He turns and paces a few steps, then whirls back to her. "I can't have someone working for me who might try to stab me in the back one day."

"If you don't trust me, then get me reassigned."

"Here's the thing." He resumes walking, back toward her as though he's confident she won't attack. Suddenly, he stops. One minute he's ten paces away. The next he's right next to her, and before she can react, one hand wraps around her throat, pressed against her windpipe like a too-tight choker. She can still breathe, still gasp out words if required. Yet she can't shift that steel vise.

Panic rises in her throat while Anton continues reasonably, "I really do need another crew member. Otherwise, the rest of us have to take up the slack. It's not long before we reach Vishnu, but still. I'd like to keep you on.

I'd like to not have to hurt you when you decide one day that retribution is more important than living." He leans so close his breath blasts her face. "You do understand that I'll kill you if you attack me, right? It's nothing personal. Let's just say I value my life as much as you do yours."

"And what about your ideals? Do you still value those?" she croaks.

He only shrugs. "People change. Look at yourself. No longer a scared little girl. You've somehow managed to get a ticket to Vishnu and erase that scar I gave you. Maybe I've changed, too. It's possible, yes?"

She holds herself very still. "Yes," she concedes.

He lets her go and steps back, watching her, perhaps waiting for a sign she doesn't believe him. She gives none.

Finally, he nods. "Very well. Sol, or Hanna, or whatever name you want to call yourself now, I'm sending an app link to your Skinpad. On it is your schedule, your task list, and a booklet of safety rules and regulations you must read in order to work for Life Support and Maintenance. Also, there's a map of the parts of this boat no one ever sees. Most of these colonists work in the organs of the body, but we Venters work in the bones, the arteries, the muscles. We make everything run. Come along, and I'll show you just what you've gotten yourself into." He turns, then pauses and shoots over his shoulder, "And I'm just Anton here, not Mons Vega. If that name ever passes your lips, I *will* have to kill you."

That she believes, and the words send ice through her veins. She shakes them off and follows him to a locker.

"Open it with your Skinpad," he orders. After she complies, Anton adds, "Don't forget which is yours. Now suit up." Inside is a baggy brown coverall, none too clean. She slips it on. They continue down the hallway. It's the perfect chance to jump him from behind, but she doesn't. He's on to her, and he wouldn't turn his back unless he felt confident she couldn't best him. Her heart shrivels into a wrinkled raisin. She's failed.

No. It's best this way. Remember how you were going to find out what he's up to before you kill him? It's not all about you and your revenge. It's about every life on this ship and the man who has vowed to bring down the NASA space program. Figure out his plan. Get Juke to help. Revenge can wait.

⚬

During the twenty-four hours, Sol discovers the inner *Calliope*, the spaces between walls and above ceiling panels where, like Anton says, the real ship exists. It's not pretty or comfortable. She climbs through ducts, learns how to use her map, practices cleaning air scrubbers and understanding what a malfunction looks like. Half this job is just roaming the innards of the ship, checking to see that everything runs smoothly. Bots can be trusted for some jobs, but Command likes having human eyes on things such as breathable air and a climate that won't freeze them all as they sleep.

Sol misses the clinic but doesn't mind her job as much as she thought she would. She's not claustrophobic. It's almost a relief that Anton knows who she is. If she can block out the memory of his hand to her throat, she might stay strong. She doesn't have to hide her identity anymore, just her intentions, and she gets to roam freely through the parts of the ship no one sees. The work is independent, and though it's cramped and often dirty, she's used to dirt.

Sol segments her brain. A big part for her new job. Another part to plan how to discover Anton's intent. Her time at the clinic is a bittersweet, walled-off portion, the confrontation with Anton that first day a dark place she doesn't venture.

In some areas, screens allow Sol to peer below into corridors where people hurry from place to place. She even spies into offices. On her second day of work, when the colonists have returned from Mars and departure is imminent, Sol looks through the slats of a vent and sees Oskar.

He's in his office, seated at a desk and bent over a Martian artifact. He tinkers with something on the hand-sized white metal box, rubs at the surface with big, gentle fingers, then studies it. Sol crouches on hands and knees to watch. The last she saw of him was on Mars, and she isn't sure where they stand. He seemed disappointed in her decision to leave the clinic, not to mention confused. He's no dummy. Her actions looked suspicious, and he must know she's hiding something. But he kissed her anyway.

Something expands inside her chest. Though it feels wrong, Sol continues to watch Oskar work. His motions are delicate, controlled, patient. Just like him. Well, not delicate. She clamps down on a giggle. A giggle! That's not like her at all. What's wrong with her?

Sol's thoughts turn unbidden to Anton, and the smile falls away. She can't bear to think he might sabotage the ship. That Oskar's life could be snuffed out. Wouldn't hurting *Calliope* risk Anton's own existence? This part doesn't make sense, and she needs to figure it out quickly. In hours they'll be through the ARH. If he's planning something, it's going to happen soon.

It was a mistake to allow her thoughts to veer toward her nemesis. She feels his hand on her neck, the closing of her airway, the anticipation of pain. Yet it's not that which makes her press against the passage wall and put her face in her hands. It's the feeling of helplessness and defeat. Her father's death passes before her eyes, and tears well like they haven't since she was seventeen. That Oskar doesn't know she's just above him spying somehow increases the despair and loneliness.

Eventually, she rubs at her damp cheeks. The crying fit has left her tired but purged. She feels ready to carry on.

First order of business: Sol needs to speak with Juke.

⸺◈⸺

That night she finds an opportunity when the bulk of *Calliope*'s colonists begin shuttling back to the ship. Too often anymore, the young hacker vanishes from the *Goose*, but tonight she gets lucky. She's tossing and turning in her bunk when footsteps echo down the hallway. Sol hopes it's Juke, slides into her grav boots, and goes to find him.

She taps on Juke's door, then enters without waiting for permission. He sits on his bunk, about to remove his boots and strap in. His head jerks up. "Hey, ever heard of knocking?"

"I did knock." Sol clomps to the only chair in the room and settles. "We should talk."

He sighs. "Can't this wait? It's the middle of the night, and I have an early shift."

"I'm on your crew. We both have an early shift."

"Even more reason why we should get some shut-eye." He tries to grin, but his eyes are tired, the attempt halfhearted.

"Did you go to an Earther meeting yet? With Anvil?"

"Yes. Down on Mars." He bites his lip and looks away thoughtfully. Maybe he's trying to decide how much to tell her.

"Well?"

"What do you expect? That I'd record everything they said, and we'd go straight to Command with it? I'm not that brave, girl. These people are paranoid fanatics. Did you know they started off by reciting this scary pledge to destroy all technology and 'return the earth to the earth'? This while they're traveling on a feccing spaceship to colonize a new planet. What are they thinking?"

"Maybe that they aren't going to Vishnu. Perhaps that they'll take over the ship and turn back. Or commit mass suicide. I don't know."

Juke's eyes widen. "Anvil wouldn't do that." He folds his hands between his legs and stares at them. Sol waits patiently. Juke might be young, but he's smart. She lets him think. Finally, he mutters, "Not everyone at the meeting was part of our crew. There were a few red wristbands, even one white. The Earthers might know enough to steer the ship. I mean, all they'd really have to do is tell Matilda. She controls a lot of the bridge, anyway."

Sol reels from the knowledge that someone in Command is an Earther. Their infiltration goes deeper than she imagined. She prods, "After the opening, what did they discuss? Did they say anything about sabotaging the ship?"

He snorts. "I'm lucky they even let me stay. Anvil got some pretty vile looks from a few of them, but then Anton glared at each scowling person, and he didn't even have to say anything. They just went quiet."

"Why *did* he let you stay?" Fear tightens Sol's belly. Not for herself but for Juke. Something niggles in the back of her head. She rubs her crucifix and adds, "I don't know if it's a good idea for you to go to another meeting."

"Hells, this after you begged me to attend? No. You don't get to tell me what to do. You're not my big sister or my mom. And now I'm intrigued. If Anvil's gotten himself wrapped up in something dangerous, I have to help him get out."

The chill in her bones deepens. "There *is* no getting out of the Earther cult."

"You did it."

Sol sits back, his words like a flung dagger. She shuts her eyes, then opens them. "I barely escaped with my life. I was lucky, and I had thousands of acres of wilderness to hide in after I left the commune. Besides,

Anton wasn't as powerful then. And we're on a starship, if you haven't noticed. *There's nowhere to go.*"

"So I might as well keep going to meetings. I mean, won't it appear more suspicious if I only attend one time? Like I was just spying on them, or I'm not serious, just some scrull who might go off and blab to someone."

His words hit her like a freezing wind. "I didn't think of that. Fec all! I shouldn't have involved you."

He reaches out and pats her knee. "Too late for recriminations, darling. What's done is done. At least this intrigue you've pulled me into provides a distraction from my boring existence. My thanks for that."

She half-listens, busy thinking. Time's ticking, and they need answers before Juke gets himself any more entangled in the spider's web. "Can you find out which berth belongs to Anton?"

He emits a low whistle. "Are you saying you want me to hack Matilda's mainframe?"

"Yes, but only if there's no chance you'll be caught. I mean, you've done it before."

A slow grin transforms his face. "I got us here without the clinks knocking at our door, didn't I?"

She takes a deep breath and tries to smile back. "You did. So?"

"Easy peasy. Just let me grab a little shut eye first, if you don't mind?"

30

Clera

Clera stays with Zavi for the next few days. With most colonists still on Mars, it's enjoyable to roam the empty ship. She volunteers time in the greenhouse, strolls along Biosphere paths with Zavi, and straps into his bed every night. They discover how to make nil gravity work in their favor, and she asks herself why they waited so long for intimacy.

Zavi's experienced, and she's naive, but he meets every blush with a kiss, every wide-eyed discovery with a pleased smile. He makes her feel like the most beautiful woman aboard *Calliope*, and she makes him feel … what? One night, as they spoon beneath the covers, he whispers into her ear, "Please never leave me."

She clutches his hand to her breast. "Not if I can help it." She can't promise more—not with their future so uncertain and an unknown planet ahead. They know so little of Vishnu's dangers. The probes only told them so much, and even the plants they've engineered to mimic Vishnu's flora might vary from the real thing.

As though reading her thoughts, Zavi murmurs, "Everything will be okay, Clera. We'll make a home on the green planet, a life together. I've been alone too long. Let me believe in that dream."

"It's not a dream." She tightens her grip, then brushes her lips against his knuckles. "We'll make it happen."

But as his breath deepens and he sighs in slumber, she remains awake. Something's bothering her. She thinks back on the photos Zavi's friend took and zooms in on the one of Anvil arm wrestling. Clera disentangles herself from Zavi and taps her Skinpad. Keeping the screen light on low, she opens a search box, looks up "Earthers," and begins to read.

The Earther cult's origins date back to approximately 2059, when a commune leader in the Barrens named Anton Cheverra began a movement, the goal of which was to save Earth from human-caused destruction and reverse climate change. He decried technology as the root of the planet's problems and promoted "clean living" outside large cities.

By 2069, his organization had spread to countries beyond the United States, and the group was classified as a "terrorist organization" by the FBI and Interpol. At an unknown date, Cheverra moved his base to New Chicago, took the alias "Mons Vega," and published a manifesto promoting his ideology. His frequent rallies are hot points for violence and arrests, yet the cult leader always slips away unscathed. The emblem of the Earthers is a circle within a circle, bisected by a spear. Like the man himself, mystery shrouds his logo and his organization.

Clera scrolls to a link on Anton Cheverra's name and finds a brief biography.

Anton Cheverra, 2018 - , was born to a nightclub singer and the infamous drug lord, Guido Cheverra a.k.a. "The Chemist," in Mexico City, Mexico. His mother and younger brother died in a bombing perpetrated by rival drug lords when he was ten. Shortly after, police captured his father, who was given a life sentence on the notorious island prison of Mala Van.

After that, Cheverra may have been taken in by relatives, or he may have lived on the streets. Little is known about his remaining childhood. He resurfaced in New Mexico ten years later and was briefly detained on suspicion of narcotics manufacture. The charges were later dropped, and he disappeared from the public eye until rumors attached his name to a movement called "Earthers," which took hold in ungoverned areas outside New Chicago. In 2071, the Earthers were classified as a cult. Their leader, the enigmatic Mons Vega, continued to slip through the authorities' fingers. Cheverra has no criminal record, though ...

Clera skips the rest, her attention caught by a recent photo of Anton Cheverra filling the bottom of the screen. She looks closely and feels a chill of recognition. She's good with faces and sure she's seen this one before. But where? Clera sifts through her memories, and there he is, leaving one of *Calliope*'s workout rooms with two companions, a bag hung from one shoulder.

She'd passed him on the path by the apple orchards more than once as she walked to work. Why had he caught her attention? She thinks it was the glance he gave her, dark eyes lingering a second too long. His features might be nondescript, yet that look implied an unconscious charisma, a natural confidence, something indefinable that attracted her notice.

Of all the people to book a berth on *Calliope*, why Anton Cheverra? He must have joined the colonists using a fake surname, or he wouldn't have been allowed to embark. Why would someone so against technology and abandoning Earth *want* to leave it?

She's safe in Zavi's bed, his body reassuringly warm beside her, but cold creeps over her. Sol visits the gym religiously. Maybe she's met this Cheverra guy. It's time they talked.

•

Clera has to wait until the colonists re-board *Calliope* and the ship pulls away from the space station, headed toward the ARH, before she finds the chance. She finally catches Sol leaving Mila's cabin. "How is your patient?"

Sol looks distracted, harried even, yet she answers in a normal voice, "Scheduled to deliver on Vishnu. No early pains, and the baby kicks like a fighter."

"Sounds like my brother's child." Clera smiles around the weirdness of that. Elio will always be her little brother, not a father. The sense she's losing him has become familiar. She shakes it off. "Can we talk? Alone?"

Sol fingers her hidden crucifix. It's a tell—a sign of worry, and something Sol's done more often lately. But she nods, and they slip into her cabin. Once the door shuts, Clera eyes her critically. Are the dark circles under Sol's eyes new? Did she wear that tiny, permanent frown when she worked in the clinic? "You're missing your old job," she surmises as they face each other.

Sol's arm drops. "What do you mean? I still have a patient."

"You know what I'm talking about."

She shrugs. "The new work's okay. I'm learning a lot about *Calliope* I didn't know before."

"I've been learning some things, too, and they worry me." Clera lays out what she's discovered about the Earther leader. Sol's mouth tightens when she brings up the bio picture on her Skinpad. "Well, does he look familiar?"

Sol barely glances at the photo and sighs heavily. "It's time you knew some things. You'd better sit down for this."

An hour later, Sol has stuffed Clera's mind with new information, laid every secret out in the open. Clera understands better why Sol was so angry when they first met. Their stowaway believed they'd stolen not just her shuttle but her chance for revenge.

Sol asks, "Well, does all this change your opinion of me?" She stares at her feet.

"Of course!"

Dismay flashes across Sol's face before she quickly smooths her features.

"I think you're the bravest person I know. And the most self-sacrificing."

"But I was only going after Anton to fulfill my own need for justice. Not to help you. In fact, I could have gotten you into a lot of trouble."

"Maybe at the start. Not now. You said you're working on Anton's crew to spy on him, right? To find out why he's really here so we can stop him."

"We?" Sol shakes her head. "No. I've already involved Juke way too much. I can't let anyone else help me. You don't know this guy. He's very smart and very tricky. I thought I'd stayed a step ahead of him, and then he gets me alone in the maintenance room and tells me he knows exactly who I am and what I'm up to."

"But he didn't kill you."

"I don't know his game, only that there is one. And now I've gotten Juke into this mess. He's decided to sink his teeth in and play detective. He's convinced himself he can save Anvil. I'm careful. I've had to be. Juke is a rich kid raised on steak and champagne. He has no idea what he's involved in, and it's my fault."

Clera bites the inside of her cheek. Silence stretches between them while she considers. "I think it's time to gather the whole crew and make sure everybody knows what we do. You don't have to go this alone. We're a family, and the *Goose* is our home, at least for the moment."

Sol opens her mouth, then snaps it shut. Something shimmers suspiciously in her umber eyes. "Let Juke and me try to find out a little more before you talk to Elio and Mila."

"How long?"

She hesitates. "Another day."

"You aren't planning anything illegal or dangerous, right?"

"Are you looking for reassurance?" Sol raises an eyebrow.

Clera realizes that she is and that it's hypocritical to demand Sol and Juke play by the rules she herself has broken. She smiles ruefully. "Maybe? Just try to be careful, okay?"

"I always am."

31

Solast

Juke calls in sick the next day, but he keeps in contact with Sol while she works cleaning air scrubbers. The scrubbers must be constantly freed from coatings of mold and dust, and the crews keep supplies for this tucked into storage boxes next to each scrubber. *Couldn't bots do this job?* she fumes. Maybe the task is designed simply to keep poor lottery-winner scrulls busy. She pulls a bristled brush from storage and sets to work, grumpy that some Venters use the small cabinets as their own personal trash cans. She gets that there aren't recycle bins up here, but really?

By noon, Juke's found Anton's berth and hacked the entry code. On a private chat, they discuss when to search his shuttle and decide it better be today. Anton shares Sol's shift, yet she knows his pattern of visiting the gym after work.

Is there enough time? She messages.

Depends on what we find.

Sol calculates how long a search could take. **Can you tell if Anton shares his shuttle with others?**

Creek and Jersey.

She's encountered them in the locker room. Workout buddies. **It's unlikely Anton will leave evidence of his plans lying around. You might have to hack into a tablet. How long?**

Some people don't even protect their devices. But assuming he's as smart as you think, I'll need ten minutes. Maybe it would be better to steal his computer.

Sol bites her lip. **No. We can't leave any indication we were there. An hour is all we can spare, and if we run out of time, we'll have to get out anyway.**

You're the boss, girl.

Stop calling me that. I'm a grown woman.

Not old enough to be my mother.

She smiles and signs off.

Sol wishes she could find masks and latex gloves to hide their identities during the break in, but the second-hand clothing shop on Blue Deck doesn't carry such items. Hauling space helmets along seems unwieldy and might draw attention. She stuffed wipes into her messenger bag, and they'll have to do. Hopefully, Anton hasn't installed hidden cameras, though she puts nothing past him.

Anton is already doffing his work coverall when she hits the locker room after shift. His eyes flicker over her, then away, a secret smile curving his lips. He wants her to see it. Part of his game. The smile could mean everything or nothing. She stays away from him, even conversing with Anvil to avoid his loathsome presence.

"How's Juke doing?" Anvil asks her. He sits on a bench next to her storage locker and bends to tug coverall pant legs over his grav boots.

"Had a fever this morning." Sol shrugs. "I haven't spoken to him since. With all the drugs they feed us here, he can't be too sick, though. Right?"

"Maybe I'll go find him after I change." Anvil frees one leg and starts on the other.

Fear rises in her throat, but she resists the urge to swallow it back. Aware Anton might be listening, she forces nonchalance into her voice.

"Better text him first. In fact, better text Clera. She's in charge on my shuttle, and she doesn't like visitors, as you know. Bit of a recluse, like me."

"Bit of a Nazi, you mean." Anvil smirks. "I guess I'll message Juke and tell him to meet at my berth if he's up to it."

Sol sighs inwardly. "Good idea. Not sure he'll feel well enough to see anyone this soon, though." She gathers her bag and turns to leave, Anton and his goons just ahead of her. She follows them to make sure they head toward the Biosphere and the workout rooms before she does a U-turn and increases her pace.

Juke waits impatiently near Anton's portal. They exchange tight smiles. "Expect a message from Anvil asking if you want to meet up," Sol says. "And the answer is no. You still have a fever."

He tilts his head curiously but asks no questions. He's all business as they check the corridor for colonists. Then Juke scans the entry code with his Skinpad. The red light turns green, and they slip inside. Metal stairs lead to the shuttle's hatch. No one locks these, as berth doors offer more than enough security. Still, relief floods her when Juke presses the enter pad and the door slides aside.

"Hello?" he calls before Sol can shush him. He returns her scowl with a goofy grin. "Best to know up front if someone is here, right?"

"Keep your voice down." She moves past the air lock and into a narrow hallway, Juke following. The shuttle's design is much like the *Blue Goose*'s, with cabins beyond a commons area and down another corridor. She's wondering which belongs to Anton when Juke interrupts with a low whistle.

He nods to a table next to the couch, where a tablet charges on its magnetic pad. "Should we perhaps start with that?"

"Don't get cocky," she warns, reversing direction and joining him on the sofa. While Juke retrieves the tablet and fiddles with it, she scans the room for signs of cameras or recording devices. Seeing none, she takes in other items: an expensive vid system with giant speakers attached to a wall, a set of three waterfall photos printed on acrylic panels, a large crate secured to the floor next to the exit hatch.

Why is that there? She walks over and lifts an unlocked lid. Inside sits a jumble of gas masks, go-bags filled with water and energy bars, and toiletry kits. Not a good sign. She removes the contents, feels along the crate's bottom, discovers a hidden latch, and pulls it up. The false bottom reveals stun grenades and three PulseLock guns, the only weapons small enough to fit in such a shallow space.

"I'm in," Juke breathes.

She replaces the contents of the crate, drops the lid, wipes away fingerprints, and puts the used cloth in her bag. She sinks down next to Juke and leans close when he pulls up what appear to be Anton's personal files. Excitement shivers through her.

They spend the next half hour wading through endless documents: bills, receipts, self-important writings, and photos of various Earther events. Finally, hidden within a folder stashed inside another folder labeled "Birthday," an oddly named file appears. EREBUS. "What's that?" she whispers.

"Let's find out." Juke tries to open the file, but it's encrypted. His frown deepens into a scowl. He taps, thinks, taps again. "This is some heavy encoding. If the file is just some trumped up bio, why encrypt it so heavily? There's more inside it than a birthday list and a spreadsheet of guest addresses."

"We're running out of time." Sol checks the clock on her Skinpad.

"Hang on. One more thing I can try." A pause. "Nope. I can't believe this."

"I thought you could hack anything."

"You want to give it a go?" He narrows his eyes at her, but she only glares back. He says, "I don't know what else to do."

"Fine." She hands him a wipe. "Leave no trace of yourself. We have ten minutes. I'm checking the cabins."

One thing about life in nil gravity—no one leaves possessions lying around. The shuttle cabins sparkle like unlived-in storage units filled with extra suits, shower bags, and little else.

Juke calls, "Time to go." Tension raises his baritone into a tenor.

He didn't add *girl*, *darling*, or any other cringe-worthy nickname. She joins him, double checks the area, and they hurry out. They hustle around a few corners before they stop to heave simultaneous breaths.

"Fec," Sol mutters.

"Double fec," Juke agrees.

"At least we have a name."

Juke grunts. His fingers fly over his Skinpad. "'Erebus,'" he reads in a low voice. "'A primordial being in Greek mythology who represents darkness. He is the son of Chaos and in charge of a dark region of the Underworld.' Well, that doesn't sound good."

Sol grimaces. "Games upon games. Mons Vega envisions himself as some kind of God. He probably thinks *he's* Erebus."

"Maybe the name doesn't refer to a person but to a thing or an event."

"How in the seven hells will we figure it out?"

"I don't know, but it's time to bring the whole crew in on this. Let's go home."

She heads down the corridor. Juke jogs a few steps to catch up. She notices him looking at her with a bemused expression. "What?"

"You called the *Blue Goose* 'home.' That's awfully *domestic* of you. Maybe our little family is growing on you."

"Piss off," she grumbles. He only laughs.

They gather the others in a deserted lounge area on Blue Deck filled with circular tables. Vid walls show various sporting events from Earth—already played games set on mute with subtitles. From a food kiosk, they order freeze-dried dinners and tea pouches with straws. Mila's heavy stomach brushes the table edge as she slides into a chair. Before long, she won't fit in these bolted-down seats.

Elio hovers nearby like an eagle guarding his nest. Good for him. Mila will need that support when she gives birth in some camp on a foreign world. *If we make it that far.* Zavi—*It must be him, right?*—tucks in beside Clera and takes her hand. *So that's how it is.* He's not part of their crew, but Sol lets this pass. Clera's probably told him everything by now, in which case he might as well know about Anton. Hells. Maybe he can even help.

She clears her throat and makes eye contact with Clera, who introduces Zavi to everyone except Elio, who already knows him.

It's a weird feeling, this being-in-charge business. Sol doesn't like it. She begins, "Juke and I need to catch the rest of you up on a few things." Conscious of the occasional passersby, she speaks in low tones, but no one gives them a second glance. She tells them everything. How her father died. How she knows Anton. What she and Juke found in his berth.

Mila moves restlessly on the hard seat, face darkening, while Elio's eyebrows hitch higher and higher until they almost disappear beneath his hairline. When Sol finishes, his breath whooshes out. "Are Mila and I the last to know all this?"

Juke says, "Who knew what and when they knew it doesn't matter at this point. All that does is figuring out what 'Erebus' means, preferably before whatever plot that fanatic is hatching blows up in our faces."

Sol grips the table's edge. "I figure if the Earthers aim to unleash some catastrophe, there's a good chance it'll happen just before we pass through the wormhole or just after."

Elio's gaze sweeps over them. "Tomorrow is the big day. That doesn't leave much time."

Clera claps her hands. "Right. We need to get busy brainstorming. Dig deeper online. See if we can formulate some ideas on how to crack the mystery of Erebus."

"It sounds impossible." Mila rubs her stomach with one hand and sips tea with the other. The food packages sit mostly forgotten.

Zavi breaks in, "Sure you don't want to go to Command with this? They have more resources."

Sol replies, "But what do we have as proof? Just a suspicion based in big part on my own dealings with Anton in the past. We can't tell anyone about me, or they might discover I didn't win some lottery, and neither did anyone else on the *Goose*. If some officious person starts checking our backgrounds, what will he find?"

"A big, empty zero," Juke supplies. "I didn't have time to create elaborate stories for us."

Zavi falls quiet, his thumb absently kneading the back of Clera's hand. Sol's chest constricts. Oskar should be here, too. *Why not warn him? Include him?* She answers herself, *Because Zavi and Clera are obviously together, obviously have a relationship—but what are you and Oskar to each other?* She can't answer that question.

Clera folds her arms. "Any other suggestions?" When everyone stares glumly at her, she sighs. "Maybe something will come to us in the next twenty-four hours. If not ..." She lets that hang.

In her head, Sol finishes the sentence ... *we'll be well and truly screwed.*

32

Clera

Gloom and foreboding hang over the *Blue Goose*. Clera almost wishes the storm would break and damn the consequences. Thinking about a possible Earther attack makes her head throb. Back in New Chicago, she'd seen news vids of riots and bombings attributed to the cult. Maybe some Earthers tired of the fight and wanted a fresh start somewhere else. Sol doesn't believe that, though, so neither will Clera. Her friend has survived because she knows things. She understands how the world works.

It's Clera's day off, and she spends it on the feeds, in chat rooms, delving into databases, finding every Earther article she can. Nothing helps. Eyes itchy from strain, she finally switches off her Skinpad screen and rolls her sleeve down. No more.

She's been in the *Goose* alone all day. It's time to get out, take a walk. Juke's shift is almost over. Maybe she'll find him and see if he's discovered how to penetrate that encrypted file. Is it the answer or just another rabbit hole? An image of the ARH appears in her mind—a ring suspended in a vacuum, eerie lights flashing indecipherable patterns. Soon, they're scheduled to pass through it. Matilda keeps blasting reminders that curfew starts an hour before entry. There shouldn't be turbulence, but no one really knows what to expect since *Loki* and *Lycka* went silent after they blipped out of known space.

Pioneers I and *II* came back from the other side, though. Clera finds this reassuring. *Pioneer III*, the last probe NASA sent through the wormhole, was supposed to land on Vishnu instead of sending disposable drones surface-side to collect and examine samples, then wirelessly transmit data. Like *Loki* and *Lycka*, it blipped out. What if Vishnu isn't the Goldilocks planet everyone imagined but a vicious place full of monsters?

She follows *Calliope*'s corridors to Red Deck, fingers rubbing her temples. *You're only thinking like this because you're tired and disappointed and worried. Take a break. Talk to Juke. Have faith that everything will work out.* When she reaches the maintenance entry, she waits in an alcove across the hallway. Occasionally, people stroll past, a few chattering excitedly about navigating the wormhole. Others hurry along without meeting her eye. Maybe their heads pound, too. She thinks of Zavi, still at his lab to finish experiments while he can.

Clera checks the time just as Venters begin to emerge from the portal. She only recognizes Anvil, who doesn't notice her as he trails several women down the hallway. Another ten minutes passes. Anton leaves, surrounded by tall men with gym bags, and the hallway grows quiet. Did she miss Juke somehow? Or maybe he left early? If so, he didn't go home. And where is Sol? Maybe she's dawdling to avoid running into Anton.

Clera steps from the alcove just as a bald man exits the maintenance portal. He fists his hands and strolls off. She dashes forward to catch the door before it closes and slips in. Clera glances around a space that reminds her of gym changing rooms from high school. It doesn't smell much better, either, and she wrinkles her nose.

Even though she watched Anton depart, the hairs on her neck rise. Something doesn't feel right. She wanders down the narrow corridor that ends at a metal ladder leading up to a trapdoor. *No thank you.* Backtracking, she turns into the head. To her right is a small cubical with a vacuum toilet, and to her left, a door with the words "chemical shower" printed on it.

She opens that door and freezes.

Juke sways before her like he hears music she cannot. He's still dressed, and his grav boots hold him to the magnetized floor.

In gravity, things would have been different. Juke would have been splayed on tiles stained with blood. Here, nil grav traps him upright. Blood droplets float from the wound in his chest. He's dead. Surely, he's dead. Yet his lips form words. Clera makes her leaden feet move. She catches the syllables that fall from his mouth: "Erebus … unleashed."

"Wh …what?"

His eyes lose focus. His mouth droops open like he's surprised to find death waiting for him.

Clera taps a quick message to Sol with shaking fingers. She wipes a gobbet of blood from her cheek, then checks Juke's wrist for a pulse. Even though she knows he's gone, Clera feels for a heartbeat with her fingertips. Nothing.

She's reminded of another death in the foyer of the abandoned building where Elio and she were squatters. The dead man that time was a drug runner. "Oh, Juke!" she groans. *What will I tell Elio?* Tears spring to her eyes, but she blinks them away. Such a wasted death! Did Juke pry too deeply? Discover too much? He'd certainly found something, or he wouldn't have uttered those final words to her: *Erebus unleashed*. Words meant to convey something important.

Sol! Maybe she's been killed, too. Clera glances at her Skinpad. No reply. She backs out of the shower room and bumps into something solid. A cry escapes her. She whirls around, ready for a fight. It's only Sol.

"Thank the gods!" Clera gasps and embraces her friend.

Sol stiffens as she looks past Clera. "Fec!"

Clera lets her go. "I'm just so relieved it was you who walked through that door and not a killer."

Sol brushes past Clera and checks Juke's pulse just like Clera had, then shakes her head. "Stupid, stupid, boy," she rages. "I can't believe he's gone."

"Where have you been? I watched everyone leave except you and Juke, so I got worried and snuck inside."

Sol turns away from his body. "I always wait a good ten minutes after shift ends to avoid the others. Did you see Anton leave?"

"Yes, with his sidekicks. I'm pretty sure you were the last one here."

"Except for him." Sol stares at Juke. Lines tighten around her mouth. "I shouldn't have involved him in this. It's my fault."

"No blame. Only his murderer deserves it, not us."

She draws a shuddery breath. "I want to lay him down, but we can't, can we. This fell ship!" She closes her eyes.

It's the most emotion Clera's seen from her, and she understands that under Sol's anger lurks grief. Her fury is sadness in disguise. "I'll miss him, too," she whispers.

Though Sol's eyes remain on Juke, her fingers fumble for Clera's hand. Clera latches on, and they stand linked together, heads bowed. Clera doesn't know what you say when someone dies, yet she offers up a silent prayer. Maybe Sol's doing the same. After a few moments, Clera ventures, "We have to call Security. Or a medic. Or someone. We can't just leave him here."

Sol nods. She releases Clera and pulls her sleeve back. "We can send an anonymous tip on the emergency department's app, but we shouldn't be here when they arrive."

"Agreed. Do it."

They wait in a lounge area down the hall while medics use special codes to enter the maintenance room. A short time later, the emergency responders reemerge with a bagged body floating on a medi-board. "Well, that's that." Sol sniffs.

"We should go." Clera wants to offer comforting words, yet none come. She can't change what happened or force Sol not to feel guilty. Worst of all, Juke died for nothing. They aren't any closer to solving the mystery of Erebus than they were yesterday, and they've lost their most brilliant, youngest crew member. An ache builds in her chest. She rubs her hand over it.

Sol stops worrying her crucifix when Clera catches her eye. They share a look, silent understanding passing between them. A bond formed by sorrow. Clera holds out a hand, and Sol takes it. Side by side, they head back to the *Goose*.

———◇———

Elio takes the news hard. "He went off on his own, didn't he." His fist slams down on the dinner table. Mila stands behind him, one hand on his shoulder. Tears cling to her cheeks, and Clera remembers that the mechanic has known Juke longer than the rest of them.

"Where did they take him?" Elio asks through clenched teeth. This is the old Elio—the brother who might go off like a rocket in times of stress.

Clera looks to Sol, who checks on her Skinpad. "This says that bodies are stored in a cold freezer connected to the field hospital on Red Deck until a funeral can be held. Then the bodies are ejected into space."

"Like a maritime burial," Clera murmurs. "Probably some official will arrive after curfew ends and we're through the ARH to help arrange things. Then we can see Juke off in the style he would have wanted."

"He would have *wanted* not to die," Elio seethes.

"I think ..." Clera swallows and makes her voice firm. "I think Juke went off on his own, maybe spoke to someone who wasn't as trustworthy as he assumed."

"Like his boyfriend?" Sol sends her a sharp glance.

"Maybe."

"If we'd been seen in Anton's shuttle by some hidden security system, I'd probably be dead, too," Sol adds flatly.

"Unless Anton is letting you stew for a bit first," Mila puts in. "Is sadism his style?"

Clera jumps into the conversation before Sol can answer. "No, I'm pretty sure Juke found out something more on his own. Maybe what Erebus is or what was in that file. As he was dying, he managed to tell me something." She closes her eyes against the memories of blood, Juke's ashen face, and the two final words he pushed from his throat.

"Well, tell us," Elio commands. His knuckles show as white as Juke's pallid skin.

"Erebus ... unleashed."

Silence descends over the dinner table.

"That's all?" Elio finally asks.

Clera replies, "Maybe he would have said more, but there was no time. I didn't arrive until the last seconds of his life."

"Couldn't you have done something?" Elio's eyes flash to Sol. "Or you. You're a nurse, right, even if you don't wear the uniform?"

"He was already dead when I got there." Regret taints Sol's words.

"So." Clera sighs with her whole being. "We knew this would be dangerous. Juke gave us a last gift, and we have to figure out what it means."

"Erebus unleashed," Mila repeats. "Is there anything online about that phrase?"

Sol's already looking. She shakes her head. "Nothing."

Clera says, "The words imply that Erebus is a weapon, or perhaps a plan, and it's going to be unleashed on the colonists soon. Maybe as we travel through the ARH." She looks at the time. "In half an hour."

Elio lurches to his feet. "Juke promised he'd play us some of that Chicago music he's named for as we go through. I say we find some. We can't bring him back, but we can give him a tribute."

"Great idea." Mila pats his shoulder and turns. "Let's get something set up on the speaker system."

Sol tells Clera, "I'll be in my cabin." Her face closes tight. She won't show grief. Not in front of others, and Clera understands this, but *she* can't be alone right now. Juke's absence is a black hole. At least Mila and Elio fill a bit of that space as they search online for the retro music called "Chicago Juke."

Clera sinks onto the couch and messages Zavi to tell him Juke was killed. She wishes he was here despite Matilda's orders that passengers remain in their assigned berths. A request for a video chat dings on her arm. She accepts, and Zavi's face materializes.

"How are you doing?" he asks.

She wishes he'd break the rules and join her. "It's silly we're confined to our own berths."

"We don't have a clue what will happen during the trip through the wormhole. I guess Command wants to know everyone's location if something goes wrong."

"Right." Clera tells him the details of how she found Juke. He asks her the same questions she's asked herself. The ones with no answers. They fall silent for a long pause.

Finally, Zavi leans forward, the planes of his face etched in detail on the screen. "If anything *does* go wrong, I want you to know—" He groans and closes his eyes for a moment. "Gods! Juke dying brings home how little time we could have and not even know it. Clera ..." He stares hard at her. "I love you. I have since I first met you at the Boba Tea Cafe, though I didn't know it until later. If something happens ..."

"I love you, too," Clera tells him. "And nothing will happen. We'll be through in minutes, and I'll be at your shuttle seconds after that."

"Only if you teleport," he laughs.

"Be safe." She touches his face on the screen.

His hand comes up in response. "You, too."

Matilda's reminder filters through the ceiling speaker. "All colonists must remain in their shuttles until the all-clear. It is recommended that you strap in. There is no way to predict if the ride will be bumpy. *Bon voyage* and safe travels to us all."

Zavi signs off.

Elio says, "Fec that! I just got this music connected to the speakers, and I'm not going to listen tied to a chair. I'm going to *dance*. We all owe Juke that much at least."

Mila looks around. "Where's Sol? Should we get her?"

Clera shakes her head. "I think she blames herself for what happened to Juke. She'll come out of her cabin when she's ready."

Elio starts the music. Energetic, electronic beats blast from the speakers. Low bass notes vibrate, and syncopated rhythms make Clera want to move in time. Elio's head bobs, and he smiles through shining eyes. "Now this is bril!" He grabs Mila and pulls her close as he gyrates. She laughs through a sob and lets him lead. If Zavi were here, Clera would dance, too. But he's not, so she sits on the couch and wishes she could see out a viewport.

What's happening outside *Calliope*? Will the ship really go down some "rabbit hole"? Maybe be torn apart? The probes survived, but they're a lot smaller. Assuming the ship successfully navigates the space between solar systems, what will the stars look like past the ring? Unnamed constellations await, asteroid belts, nebulas—and the green planet of Vishnu.

Moments pass. Elio and Mila still sway in each other's arms, breathless and tear-streaked. Clera shifts nervously. She pictures Zavi's eyes and presses her hands between her legs to stop their shaking. The starship shivers, too. Seconds later, a male voice breaks the silence on the com. "This is Captain Holso. Congratulations, colonists! We are through the wormhole. You may unharness and leave your cabins. I recommend finding the closest viewing port. There is quite a lot to see outside."

— ◆ —

Day 96

Good news. I found fresh water today, located up an offshoot of the main trail where it climbs the cliffs. All my scans test negative for bacteria and toxins. I've been sipping a little more from the spring every day with no ill effects. Physically, I feel great. Better than great. The water tastes sweet. Could it contain nutrients unique to Vishnu which bolster constitution? No longer will I need to add water purification tablets to my collection jugs.

I wish I could present such a rosy picture regarding my mental health. I talk to the beetles before I kill them. What I wouldn't give to see another human face.

-N.J.

33

Niklas

Nightmares of dragons in murky underwater caverns haunt Niklas' dreams. Monsters vanish, reappear, vanish again. They stare him in the eye, blink out, then materialize, open jaws ready to bite. Part of him thinks, *Wake up! You must wake up!* But invisible bonds hold him to the clammy floor, remind him he's not in his camping cot or his berth aboard *Lycka*. This is some other world—a harsh, dangerous place his field training failed to prepare him for.

Pain lifts him from dreams before he sinks again. He awakens a second time, sure his hand's been severed. Yet when his eyes flicker open, he sees it resting atop his chest, bloated and red. Sometimes he wishes it would disappear and take this misery with it. White-hot daggers spread up his arm. Better to sleep. Drift into blessed oblivion even though dragons await him there.

Niklas wavers between pain and its absence, restless waking and tormented sleep. Always the shards jab at his hand, his arm, his shoulder.

Eventually, a rustling sound penetrates this torture. His eyes crack open to see a young woman kneeling before him. She *can't* be here. The odds are a billion to one. Everyone on *Lycka* died, right? That leaves *Loki*, the missing starship. Yet how could a solitary human girl end up in this cave? It doesn't make sense. Perhaps she's a delusion like the dragons.

Something emits loud groans. With a start, Nik realizes it's himself and bites back the humiliating sound. The girl—no, woman—doesn't seem to notice. She's busy spreading paste on a piece of white cloth. He studies her beneath half-closed lashes. It's hard to say how old she is. Her petite frame suggests youth, but that thin, serious face ages her. She's not exactly pretty, yet there's a delicate, porcelain doll aspect to her cream-toned skin and long-lashed gray eyes that attract his notice.

Nik's left a long line of disappointed and sometimes furious women in his wake over the years. He could hardly help it. Born to privilege, blessed with good looks and a playful, open personality, women came to him without asking, and he couldn't resist them. He had no reason to, really. Niklas had taken for granted so many things—his family's money, their love, his capacity to draw others to him. Back in Sweden he'd been a king who thought nothing could dethrone him.

Stupid. So stupid. Maybe he deserves this illness. No one gets to live their whole life beneath a lucky star. He's being tested and failing.

These thoughts seem coherent, so surely he's better. Has the girl been tending to him ever since he passed out? Healing him? "What's your name?" he croaks.

Her head whips up, gaze steady. After a moment, she replies, "Alice."

"Like Alice's rabbit hole," he murmurs, eyes wandering away. "The ARH." A laugh escapes, followed by a burst of pain. He clenches his eyes shut and grinds his teeth.

"Hush," Alice scolds in a voice like clear bells ringing.

He'd like to hear her sing. Maybe an old ABBA song or something even farther back. "I'm not ... myself."

"No." Laughter chuffs from her. "You cut your hand on the stones, then brushed the open wound against the *brella*. It's very toxic, but I have the cure. You'll be fine soon."

"You speak English."

"I thought it might be a language we both share."

"How? Why?"

She moves the cloth covered in green goo to his injured hand and secures it across his palm. Coolness soothes inflamed skin, and the pain eases.

"Thank you."

She nods, then rummages in a pocket and pulls forth a clear bulb with a needle protruding from it. She taps the bulb twice, then grasps his arm. "This will help you rest. You need to rest."

"Wait—" He's too late. The drug works quickly. One prick, and a veil falls across his mind. He tries to fight the sedative, but blackness descends.

Niklas drifts in and out of sleep in the following few hours. Once, he emerges from a dream to find Alice speaking to a dragon at the water's edge. In the dim, wavering light, he watches luminescence flash across the monster's snout. Alice's necklace of transparent beads pulses in response, a morse code of communication. *No*, he thinks. *I haven't woken. This is still part of the dream*. And he falls back into deep slumber.

Sometime later, he feels Alice's presence like breath wafting his skin. His crusty eyes crack open. Alice says in her bell-like voice, "I have to go. I'm sorry. They're calling me. If I can't get back to the cave in time, you must do what I say." Her fingers dig into his shoulder. "You can't leave this place until after the rain. Only several hours later is land safe. Do you hear? Beware the rains."

Her grip makes him wince. He nods just so she'll loosen her hold.

"I'm sorry," she says again, regret in her voice. "They won't let me stay."

He wants to ask, *Why do you sound sad? Where do you come from? How do you know the dragons?* But she drugs him again, and he passes out.

The next time Niklas awakens, his mind is clear. He thinks back and decides Alice's talk of dangerous rain was a vivid dream, just like her. He sits up and peers out the tunnel's mouth into a circle of teal-colored sky. There are no clouds, no rain misting beyond the opening. He spots the discarded messenger bag, canteen, and wrappers. At least some of his memories are real.

He remembers his hand and glances down, thinking the injury part of his nightmare. A damp cloth tied about his palm refutes this. He flexes experimentally. The joints feel stiff, but no pain shoots into his arm. Gingerly, he removes the bandage and shines the light of his Skinpad across his skin. There's no cut, no redness or swelling, not even a faint pink line. His life has been saved by a dream girl named Alice.

Not a dream girl. Real. Does that mean water dragons are real, too?

Niklas shakes his head and climbs stiffly to his feet. His stomach grumbles. He takes a step but stops when his toes hit something hard. He bends and retrieves a bowl similar to a mollusk shell, filled with what looks like a mixture of seaweed and curled pink shrimp. He pinches a bit between his fingers and tastes it. Some tangy sauce coats the dish, and it's surprisingly good. He eats hungrily, feeling strength rush back into his limbs. Placing the bowl on the cave floor again, he shivers.

Time to get back to camp. Who knows what Adrian and Dana must be thinking of his disappearance. How long has it been? Days, maybe. Helv. If that's the case, they'll be frantic. He walks to the water's edge and dips a foot in. Not too cold. The light of Kali will feel good on his sun-deprived skin.

Yet he hesitates and looks back. He should find Alice and thank her for healing him. He has so many questions for her. Nik's thoughts turn to the water dragon. It's an appropriate name for the creature from his dreams that made him panic and cut his hand. If not for Alice, he might have died from the algae's toxin. The *brella*, she called it.

Remembering the monster under the water, with its huge snout, flaring nostrils, and vibrant mane of tentacles, Nik hesitates at the cave lip. Water sloshes over his feet. He's never been afraid of what lurks beneath, but it was always a stray jellyfish or eel. Here on Vishnu, anything could be waiting down there.

You can't start fearing every shadow, Nik. That's no way to start life on a new planet. There's nothing for it. You have to swim out of here and rejoin what's left of your crew. He draws a breath and dives. Water bubbles over him, waves cradle him, and he propels himself into the open. A current tries to push him back, but even in his weakened state, it's no match for his muscles. He kicks upward from the shallow dive, bursts above the surface, and turns his face skyward to bathe in the sun's warmth.

The cloudless skies remind him of summers in Greece. Faint alien rings recall how far he's come from Earth, though. He turns toward shore and strokes. As he nears the beach, a chemical smell like ammonia stings his nostrils. Treading water, Niklas squints at the plant-life bordering the sand. Something looks different. He swims closer and realizes giant mushrooms sprouted while he was away. They extend right down to the beach. Inland, spores drift and settle in white clouds of dandelion fluff. Fog wreathes far-off hilltops, and he realizes a rainstorm recently came and went.

Beware the rain. Alice's warning. Was she telling him about the rain itself or about the huge fungi that have spontaneously burst through the earth? He treads water, thinking. Does that foul odor emanate from those plants and their spores? Fear for Adrian and Dana raises goosebumps. He's anxious to find them, but he'll wait until the dandelion puffs settle. They don't seem to hurt the waxy-leafed foliage, at least. Maybe those thick-coated leaves have developed *in response* to the spores. Could they be toxic, just like the cave algae? He won't do his crewmates any good if he returns to camp only to succumb to the foulness in the air. Niklas can tread water for hours if he has to.

Before long, the fungi shrivel beneath a midday sun, and the spores vanish so quickly he watches it happen in open-mouthed amazement. The six-foot tall mushrooms, gray mottled with blue smudges, shrink quivering into the earth until no trace remains.

Nik swims until his feet brush sandy shallows. He sloshes out of the sea, heart hammering, and looks for signs of life at his camp. There are none. He calls out. No one answers. He calls again. A breeze full of secrets ruffles his hair. Foreboding haunts every footstep he takes toward the team's olive-green tents near the shrubbery.

As he draws close, he notices eruptions of dirt and cracked ground. It reminds him of the place in the forest where they found the deceased scouting party. His crewmates didn't know about the rain or the mushrooms and spores. They'd had no Alice to warn them. What had killed them? Poisonous droplets? Some alien venom seeping into the air from the fungi? He'll need to run tests, but test what? Until the next storm, he's stuck.

Niklas finds his friends' bodies near the cooking fire and supply crates. Their faces are death masks of pain. Adrian fell backward, hands frozen into claws on his chest. Dana lies on her side, facing the water as though searching for him. Her mouth is parted, her body curled around itself like a snail's shell.

Niklas holds back tears with difficulty. He paces until he doesn't feel like he'll break in two. Once numbness overpowers pain, he builds a fire and sends Adrian and Dana up to the heavens in a cloud of smoke.

Sparks fly around him like fireflies. The last of the fire starter logs burns long and hard, erasing his friends' existence with a thoroughness he envies.

To be the only one left, the last survivor of *Lycka*, feels like starring in a one-man apocalypse movie.

He doesn't know how to pilot a shuttle. Adrian did, as did Ben, the party's other security member. If things had gone as planned, more exploration teams from *Lycka* would have joined theirs and started building a colony. They'd have sent long-range reconnaissance parties to search for signs of *Loki*. They'd have named the plants, the communities, the trails they made. They'd have created a home.

Now, though? He doesn't want this place. Not without the others.

A ghost invades his thoughts—pale, sharp-faced, with the voice of an angel. Who was she, and why had she left him? *They won't let me stay*, Alice told him during his dream-fever. Were there others like her, or did "they" mean the water dragons? If so, sentient beings exist on Vishnu. He doesn't know how to feel about that possibility, but it doesn't decrease his fear of the water.

Niklas' thoughts turn to his cousin. It will be months before *Calliope* reaches Mars. Even if the ship navigates the ARH successfully, the colonists may have to deal with another sabotage. How large is the group of murderers that slaughtered almost everyone on *Lycka*? And how did they sneak their poison past the inspectors?

Nik dreads the thought of being alone long enough for Zavi to find him. He's never been solitary, always had plenty of friends and family about. *Stay busy. That's how you'll survive this. Set yourself tasks, run experiments, and message Zavi a record of everything you discover. Eventually, he'll see it.*

At least Niklas' team managed to retrieve enough supplies to keep him alive until he can figure out how to make use of the flora on Vishnu. Zavi probably knows such things already since his job is to study plant samples and data from the *Pioneer* probes. Nik is the biologist, and his specialty is animal life forms. But he can teach himself other areas of study and document experiments he runs. Maybe, if he stays busy enough, he won't go mad.

Perhaps Alice will return some day. That hope keeps him from despair as his days alone on Vishnu multiply. When clouds gather, Niklas retreats inside the shuttle on the beach. Sometimes after a storm, he dons his heavy suit and helmet and ventures out to gather spores or rain droplets cupped on broad-leafed branches. He even manages to cut a chunk of flesh from the doomscap fungi before it retreats below ground.

Time passes. Before long the skies clear, the storms don't come, and he knows the rainy season on Vishnu has passed.

He notes everything and sends it on to his missing cousin. He keeps a calendar, marks off each day like a prisoner trapped in a cell. Alice doesn't appear. Nik talks to himself, lets his hair and beard grow. Goes native.

34

Solast

Sol stares at her cabin's blank walls and replays finding Clera and Juke in the shower room. One dead, the other shell-shocked. She's to blame, and the worst isn't over. They made it through the ARH without incident, but something big is coming. She feels it like spiders crawling under her skin.

Music wafts toward her down the hallway. How can the others stand to listen to it? Do they grieve by dancing? That's the last thing she wants to do. Oskar's presence would soothe her. Sol could go find him, yet she doesn't. She's out of time. Ready or not, her only choice is to confront Anton. She grabs her bag, tucks the knockout gun inside, and sneaks away from the *Goose*. No one seems to notice her departure.

Berth 113 either has a new door code, or Juke reversed her access to the old one. Knocking and shouting have no effect, and she finally gives up. Sol checks the workout rooms and Smoke and Ashes to no avail, then heads to the maintenance room. Everyone aboard *Calliope* is celebrating. It's an unofficial holiday until Matilda tells them otherwise. The locker room feels deserted. She walks down the corridor toward the steel ladder, then back past the head, but no one appears. If Anton's up in the ducts, she'll never find him.

The urgency pulsing through her veins dissipates, leaving her exhausted. She turns to go but stops, facing the lockers. Something looks different.

It dawns on her that the rows of gas masks they use for contingencies are mostly gone. Why?

The answer hits her like a steel girder. Anton and his Earther friends needed them. She leaps to the next conclusion, that Erebus must be some sort of lethal gas. Feccing hells! How will they release it, and when? Panic worms up her insides. She worked yesterday and didn't notice anything missing from the cabinet, and she would have, right? The truth is chilling and unstoppable. Somewhere on this ship, Erebus is about to be unleashed.

Sol takes the remaining two masks from the cabinet, messages Clera a warning, and leaves to find Oskar.

She rushes down hallways filled with milling people. They talk excitedly or gather in lounge areas where huge screens broadcast shots of the new solar system. *Lycka* appears in one, distant but recognizable, lights gleaming as she circles Vishnu's blueish-green orb. The sight distracts Sol for only a second before she shakes her head and barrels on toward Oskar's office. But wait a minute. He won't be working. He's probably at a viewport. *Message him, idiot. He's not Anton. You have his private chat number, and it'll be faster.*

Sol makes herself slow down, take a breath, and roll up her sleeve to type—awkward with gas masks hanging from her arm. A few people give her funny looks. She doesn't care. They may all be dead soon if she doesn't figure this out. Sol's about to type a message when a familiar voice calls out to her.

Oskar emerges from an offshoot corridor that leads into the research department. "I was just coming to find you."

Sol runs to him, too terrified to feel relief. She grabs his arm and pulls him back down the hallway. He doesn't resist, but his eyebrows rise as he sees what she carries.

"We're in danger." She spills out her theory about Erebus and hands him a mask.

He holds it in his hands, a bemused expression on his face. Gods. He doesn't even know about Juke's murder or how they broke into Anton's shuttle. Now there's no time to explain.

"Well?" Sol says.

"It's a lot to take in."

"Hurry up and do it, will you? We've got to find the others."

"Did you warn them on your Skinpad?"

"I told Clera to get back to the *Goose* as quick as she can, find masks, and tell the others. They might already be there. The crew was still in the shuttle when I left. I don't know."

"I need to alert my department." He shoots off a message, then looks up. "And we need to warn Command."

"They won't believe us." Sol grabs Oskar's arm.

"They'll believe me, especially if I go in person."

"Don't, Oskar."

"No need for both of us to waste time on the bridge." His eyes soften, and he cups her cheek in his big hand. "You do what you need to. Take care of your crew, and I'll be at your berth before you know it."

Matilda's placid voice breaks in, "Attention, passengers. Life Support has detected a foreign substance in the air. As a precaution, please don gas masks, making sure to seal them tightly between skin and polymer rubber. There is no need to panic. This is ..." The voice cuts out.

Sol gestures to the mask she gave him. "Put it on."

"Go," he tells her. Then he does what she says.

She stands transfixed. Undecided.

Sol follows Oskar into the main corridor, fitting her own mask over her face. Passengers fill the hallway. They murmur to each other or frown in confusion. More spill from side hallways and viewing areas. The crowds close in around her, and she loses Oskar in the mob. She yells, "Oskar, wait!" but the mask muffles her words.

She only knows one thing for certain. They can't be separated. She pushes down the corridor and catches a glimpse of Oskar's tall frame before a new group breaks into the milling colonists ahead of her. People aren't talking anymore. They stumble, gasp, and clutch at each other. Sol sucks in filtered air and checks her seal. Someone grabs at her arm. She backs away. People cry out, then slump, fall into each other, grow still.

Sol moves forward, but Oskar has vanished.

35

Clera

The electronic rhythms of Chicago Juke fade. Holding hands, Elio and Mila retreat into their cabin. Clera heard Sol sneak out the main hatch moments before. She wanted to follow, but her crewmate's back was an iron rod, her face a closed door.

Clera wants to see Zavi. She hurries to her cabin and dabs blush on her cheeks, a touch of mascara on her lashes. She arranges her long hair in a messy bun, not sure if she's done it right and wishing she had a hand mirror to see the back. She also wishes she had real clothes instead of her jumpsuit, but it's comfortable, at least.

As she's leaving the *Goose*, her message alert pings. It's Sol. Clera halts just outside the berth to read.

Erebus is being unleashed. It's a poison in the air. Find a gas mask. I don't know how they're doing it. Tell the others.

Later, Clera realizes she should have turned back and rummaged for gas masks in the *Goose*'s engineering room where she found suits and boots, but all she can think of is Zavi. She messages him, Elio, and Mila, then runs for his berth, praying he's still there. People give her strange looks and move aside with annoyed frowns. Suddenly, Zavi's among them. Two masks dangle from his fingers, and he looks as panicked as she feels.

They brake just before colliding. Zavi pants, "My cousin Niklas. He was on *Lycka*. I lost contact with him once his ship went through the wormhole, but all his messages came up once we passed through. He says *Lycka* was hit with a poison gas ..."

Matilda interrupts, "Attention, passengers. Life Support has detected a foreign substance in the air. As a precaution, please don gas masks, making sure to seal them tightly between skin and polymer rubber. There is no need to panic ..."

Zavi grabs her arm and propels her back the way she came. "I already messaged Barak and Stark. We've got to get to the *Goose*. Are the others there?"

"Elio and Mila are. Sol left. She just sent me a message. I don't know how she found out, but she says Erebus is a toxin transmitted through the air, and we're in imminent danger from it."

"Right." He barely glances at her. "Five minutes ago, I read Nik's warning about what happened after they entered Vishnu's orbit. Most of the people on *Lycka* are dead. Killed by some poison in the air." He hands her a mask, and they tug them on as they hurry toward Berth 235.

"There were Earthers aboard *Lycka* who sabotaged the ship?" Clera yells past her face shield. They dodge a cluster of panicked Blue Deckers, and the berth comes into view.

"Nik was on the planet with the first exploratory shuttle. I haven't had time to read most of his emails. There are a lot."

The colonists closest to them start to cough and clutch their necks. Clera scans her code, and Zavi draws her through the portal. It slides shut, and the chaos behind them ebbs.

"Those poor people! Isn't there anything we can do?" Clera stares at the door, still seeing the wide-eyed colonists beyond it.

Zavi hesitates, then shakes his head. "It's already begun. There's no time to find them all masks." He grabs her hand. "I don't want to leave them, either, but we failed. We didn't figure things out in time." His mouth forms an angry line past the glare of the mask.

"Oh, fec." She never swears, but now seems like a good time to start.

Once they enter the *Blue Goose*, Clera calls for her brother. Her shoulders slump in relief when he answers somewhere down the hallway. Thank the stars he and Mila didn't follow her out. She sends Sol a message. **Zavi, me, Elio, and Mila are in the *Goose*. Where are you?**

No answer comes.

Clera runs through the shuttle. She bumps into Elio and Mila looking disheveled and fumbling to put on masks. She leads the way back into the commons, where they find Zavi waiting. Clera shares Sol's warning, and Zavi adds, "My cousin was on *Lycka*. His messages finally came through. Gas killed almost everyone aboard."

"I'll send that on to my superiors," Elio mumbles past the heavy faceplate. He opens a chat on his Skinpad.

Clera's brain runs at full tilt. What else can they do to survive this? "Should we evacuate the ship? Try to get to the escape pods?"

Zavi shakes his head. "They're clear up on Red Deck, and I don't know how much time we have. You saw those people in the corridor. It's already starting."

Elio clears his throat. "Excuse me. Pilot standing right here. *In* a shuttle."

"Are we allowed to disconnect from *Calliope* and launch? Do we even know how? And does the *Goose* have any solar power left after sitting in a berth so long?" Clera asks.

Elio replies, "The shuttle's power is stored in batteries that drain over time, but the power's meant to last through months or even years in space.

That's what the display sign at the aerospace museum said, anyway. And luckily, I've covered how to disconnect from the starship in my security classes. It was part of our emergency protocol training in case *Calliope* was ever compromised. There's a hidden panel just inside our berth that should let me manually override the life support systems which connect us to the main ship. I can also manually release the clamps holding us in place."

"Sounds like a plan." Clera sighs. "Go!"

Elio tightens his mask and races for the hatch.

Her panic recedes now they're doing something. Or Elio is, at least. But where has Sol disappeared to, and why hasn't she messaged back? Clera tries again to contact her, telling her to return immediately, that they're heading for Vishnu on the *Goose*. No reply.

Mila paces for about five seconds, then starts toward the exit. "Fec this waiting around while Elio does all the work." Clera follows her and watches from the exit hatch while she makes her way down the rolling stairway.

Clera returns to Zavi. She takes his hand. His touch loosens terror's hold, especially when he pulls her to him and rests his chin on her head. Only minutes ago, she was worried about her hair while Sol was—what? Getting herself killed maybe? How did she find out about this gas, and what price has she paid for that knowledge?

Clang. The *Blue Goose* shivers. Zavi's head jerks, his body tensing.

Clera says, "It's just Elio. He must have managed to sever our connection with *Calliope*."

Zavi nods but remains stiff, and she pulls away. After another minute, the tromp of feet sound on the stairs, and Elio and Mila bustle inside. Elio speaks something unintelligible into his mask, eyes wild. Clera shakes her head and points to her ears.

Mila lays a hand on his arm. Elio looks down like he doesn't recognize her touch, then he takes a huge breath and expels it. He yells to make himself heard, "I had Mila take a peek into the corridor. People are dropping. Well, not exactly dropping because of zero gravity, but they're unconscious. Like … everybody."

Mila's hand falls to her side. "No one had a gas mask on yet."

"What else did you see?" Clera asks. Bands tighten around her chest, yet she holds on to calm. No time for panic attacks.

"People leaning against walls, or slumped over each other, or just wavering like ghosts, stuck in their boots. Red faces. Expressions of … I don't know … intense pain."

"A neurotoxin," Zavi elaborates. "Sounds the same as what my cousin described happened on *Lycka*."

Elio tells them, "We can launch any time, and the sooner the better. There's nothing we can do to help those people."

"But what about Sol?" Clera gasps. "We can't just leave her!"

"Where is she?" Mila asks. "Has she answered your last message?"

Clera shakes her head. Tears spring to her eyes.

Zavi takes her arm. "She might be dead."

"She wouldn't leave us," Clera whispers. The others can't hear her low-spoken words. She drops her head to her chest. *Would* Sol have deserted them? Maybe seven months ago, but not now. Not unless she knew all hope was lost. And it is, isn't it? Sol hasn't answered, which probably means … She cuts off the thought and faces the others. They look to her as though for permission.

That's right. I'm the captain. And Earthers could be here any time to finish us off. She juts her chin, grits her teeth, then says to Elio, "Do it."

36

Solast

Sol will find Oskar again if she just keeps heading toward the lifts. He has the gas mask, so he'll be fine. Her Skinpad pings. She ignores it and focuses on wading through the mass of bodies obstructing her way.

Panic is its own kind of poison. People reach for her, yet she can't help them, can't stop them from toppling into her, hands clutched to throats, faces like ripe plums, terror reflected in the whites of their eyes. A few cling to her, and she's forced to pause, brush them off, then watch helplessly as they fall unconscious.

She trips over a body, collides into another. Sol wishes the gas mask covered her ears, too. Cries, sobs, moans, and choking sounds echo down the corridor. She adds her own cry of "Oskar!" but the mask muffles her voice. How dare he leave her! How dare he try to play the hero and save everyone when it's obviously hopeless. The toxin is all around. She can only hope that a few people found gas masks in time. That's unlikely, though. They might *have* masks aboard their shuttles, but they'd have to hunt for them. Plus, most people left their berths to view the new Kali System.

The colonists don't clutch at her now, and if there weren't so many bodies, she might catch up with Oskar. *There!* She spots him, almost at the lift that leads to the bridge. When she blinks, he's gone. A commotion erupts in a side passage. Feet tramp toward her. Instinctively, Sol ducks into an alcove meant for viewing outer space. Vishnu floats by, fringed with handfuls of alien rings. Not one but a *dozen*.

A group of people erupt into the main corridor. Distracted, Sol turns toward them and presses into the darkest corner of the view space. These colonists aren't panicked, nor are they in pain. Each wears a face mask just like her own. She recognizes them all—Jersey and Creek, JoJo, R.B., Orion, Muff, Anvil—with Anton at their head. They aren't looking her way but toward the lifts. The way Oskar went.

Sol finally glances down at her Skinpad. Clera's messages come up, first the one asking where she is, then another that reads, **We can't wait. If you're still alive, get to an escape pod. Zavi says they'll be programmed to land near *Lycka*'s camp. I'm sorry.**

Fec all! They've deserted her. Every one of them. Even Oskar. *Just like always*, a snide voice whispers in her head. *First your mother and baby sister, then your father and everyone at the commune who might have joined you in attacking Anton or come to find you afterward. In the end, you're left alone again.* Sol *should have been* Sole. *More fitting. Not the sun but a single star in a vast universe of silence.*

She pinches her arm. *Snap out of it. No time for wallowing*. Not when she can warn Oskar. She taps a quick message to him, then another when Anton and his crew board the lift. The UP arrow glows green.

He types back, **I'm on the bridge. Don't follow the Earthers. Too dangerous. If you can't get back to your shuttle, take an escape pod down to the surface. There are more escape pods for officers up here. I'll be fine.**

Of course you will, she thinks. *It's me who's a mess.* She clenches her jaw, rubs her crucifix for luck, and finds her way around the dying. Their cries of distress have diminished to moans if they haven't already gone quiet. Eyes stare blankly out of discolored faces. "I'm sorry," she murmurs again and again. They can't hear her, though. Resolute, she moves on, careful not to trip on sprawled limbs, wondering if a lift might descend with Anton inside. Fitting, somehow, for them to meet across a sea of the dying.

But she makes it to the pods, which line the hull. Numbers mark each closet-like enclosure. She enters the first she comes to, and Matilda's voice flows over her, "Welcome, traveler. Do you mean to eject from the ship? This escape vehicle is designed to carry you through an atmosphere and safely deposit you on a planet's surface. Is this your desire?"

"Yes," she breathes.

"Is this your desire?"

Realizing the AI can't hear her, she shouts, "Yes!" but immediately second-guesses her decision. What is she thinking? Oskar could be in the clutches of the fanatic, murderous Earthers by now. He's no fighter. She's got to get to him, to do what she can to save him.

Matilda tells her, "Please open the pod door and take a seat. You have two minutes to strap in securely and select a pre-plotted destination on Vishnu." The entry behind her clunks, a red "Door secured" sign lighting up. She tries the portal anyway before realizing she's already in pre-launch. There's no going back. Still, she bangs hard against the thick metal.

Matilda drones on, "One minute, thirty seconds to launch. Choose a destination on Vishnu, or one will be provided for you."

Sol turns in defeat, opens the door to the egg-like pod, and straps into a massively cushioned reclining seat. Before her, a screen lights up. "One minute to launch. Please select a destination."

She touches the screen. The pre-programmed choices are exactly one—the location that top astrophysicists from Europe and the U.S. decided on when planning their colonies. It's a place called Landing Bay, a beach in the planet's midsection according to the brief description following the title. Sol selects the route, her door locks, and Matilda says, "Safe journey, traveler."

The pod tilts until she's looking down a long tube. She grips the harness and closes her eyes. The last thirty seconds take ten years. Sol tries to picture Oskar's face but fails. She sees only her father, his blood soaking the earth, his eyes staring into hers for the last time before life leaves them.

Lights outside her capsule turn green, and the pod drops. Sol yells in panic, then clamps her lips together. She surges forward like an embryo thrust violently out of a black womb.

Vishnu grows rapidly, the pod's momentum increasing as it approaches atmosphere. Gone is the lulling AI voice. Sol's left with her own thoughts and a silent scream. When the vehicle hits atmo, flames erupt through the round, radiation-and-heat-proof glass window. Her seat shakes, and Sol remembers the last time she pierced an atmosphere. Then, though she hadn't known it, she'd been leaving a planet. The shock of the transition into outer space had disoriented and terrified her.

Now, the inferno outside magnifies that terror. Is it growing hotter in the egg? Will she boil inside her shell? But then the pod bursts past hell into a clear sky. It adjusts course. Far below, an emerald sea stretches toward the horizon. To Sol's left, sand and a foliage-covered, craggy landscape slide into view. The capsule hurtles down on a collision course for the ground.

Seconds later, there's a jolt, a sound like cracking whips, and words light up the screen. **Parachute engaged. Landing in approximately thirty seconds. Door will open automatically upon touchdown. If a water landing, floats will deploy.**

Water landing? Sol stares out the window and watches a variegated blur take on definition: white-capped waves, a cream-colored strip of beach, jagged gray cliffs, and stocky trees with thick, palm-sized leaves. A wind gust rocks the pod, nudging it away from the sea. She can't see her parachute, just a bit of cord. Another gust, and the pod sways. Will she land on the beach or in the sea?

Suddenly, a deep green forest crowds out all other views, rushing toward her. The capsule breaks branches as it crashes downward but slows with each new collision. Finally, the egg comes to rest in a mass of ferns. Her pod hasn't been cracked, boiled, or even poached. It perches on a nest of fractured greenery. Above, the parachute ripples.

Sol lies on her back, facing the sky, and from that perspective, she watches the blue and yellow sail settle twenty feet above her atop a canopy of broken foliage.

The pod's door clicks, and light illuminates the interior. The screen flashes, **Welcome to Landing Beach**. But there is no sand, no ocean.

Just a forest of alien plants.

37

Solast

Sol wills her rapid heartbeat to slow. She strips off the gas mask and presses back against the cushions. Adrenaline drains from her limbs. She stares outside, giving herself time to recover. Palm-like, waxy fronds shiver in a breeze, and a pinhead-sized ring pocks the greenish sky. Probably not the wormhole *Calliope* came through because *there are more than one.* She'd barely digested this fact while hiding in the viewing alcove with Earthers close by. Now it explodes everything she thought she knew about Vishnu, Martians, and life outside her solar system.

Enough time to ruminate later. Sol studies her fingers and finds them almost steady, so she sends Oskar and Clera the message that she's gone off course and landed in the jungle. Or forest. Whatever. No one answers. Are they all dead? Did the Earthers find Oskar and do what the neurotoxin couldn't? She imagines him with his carotid artery cut like her father. Or a stab wound through the heart like Juke. Despair wells up, so she summons anger, the old friend that's kept her fighting all these years.

Oskar left me. I guess warning Command was more important than making sure I survived.

Another voice intrudes. *Maybe Oskar knew how self-sufficient and capable you were. Or he wanted you to evacuate while you could, not risk running into Anton as you wandered around the bridge.* She shakes off the voice of reason. Rationalizing will only weaken her will. *Anger* keeps her from fragmenting into a million pieces. *I thought I could be some kind of savior instead of the failure I really am. In the end, I couldn't even save myself.*

What will she do now? She has no navigation equipment, no supplies, not even water. Wild animals might be prowling outside, and if they aren't, why not? How can she live on a planet where nothing else survives? Scientists desperate to give humanity hope have probably misled them all.

Her thoughts turn to Anton. How did he sneak that poison aboard? More importantly, what's his plan now? As far as she knows, the Earthers aboard ship only number a dozen at most. They were headed to the bridge, which might mean they plan to take command of *Calliope.* Can they fly her? Perhaps they won't need to in any real sense. They'll program a course, then sit back and allow Matilda to drive.

She imagines how Earth's news feeds will react upon hearing that *Calliope*'s mission was a bust. The Earthers still there will say, *See, we told you so. Wasting money on space programs will only hurt you. Those colonists got what they deserved for abandoning our planet.* And lots of people will believe them. The U.S. government is so closely tied to *Calliope*'s fate that it could collapse under the public pressure. Riots. Demonstrations. Bombings. Sol imagines them all.

She unbuckles her harness and tries the door. It opens easily. *Focus on what you can fix, not on* Calliope *or Earth. Not even on Oskar and the others.* She slides out of the pod into a pile of broken branches and ferns, leans against the smooth egg for a moment, then pushes upright. Flowers perfume the air though she doesn't see any. Quiet blankets the forest. No birds chirp. No insects buzz. At least a faint breeze rustles leaves in the canopy above.

She doesn't remember ever being so utterly alone. What happened to those left on *Calliope*? Kind Dr. Chandra. Sadiki. Nora. And more than a thousand others who didn't deserve to die.

Moving away from the pod, Sol turns in a circle and searches for a landmark to point her toward the beach. Towering trees block the view. She'd try climbing one, but the smooth red trunks offer no branches for handholds. She could remove her heavy grav boots and attempt to scramble up in socks or barefoot. Sol runs a hand down the bark. No. Won't work. She's no monkey. Better to make an educated guess and set off before the sun goes down.

Kali hovers overhead like an angry red eye—larger than Earth's sun and still visible above the treetops, so dusk must still be a few hours off. Sol searches her memory for what she's learned of Vishnu. Days and nights will be similar to Earth's, the atmosphere close enough she won't notice much difference, and gravity a shade less of a drag on her body. She tests this theory by taking a few steps away from the capsule and finds movement easy even in her boots.

That brief pleasure evaporates soon after she sets off. Her feet crunch loudly on long-dead, decaying plant life, and the forest's strange, reproachful silence pushes back against her intrusion. That feeling of abandonment returns. Her throat dries, and sweat rings form under her arms. She feels like she's walking in circles. All the trees and shrubs look the same. Maybe she'll wander until she drops from exhaustion, she'll die of dehydration, and no one will ever know what happened to her.

Sol stops. She squats against one of the thickest palm trees, forearms resting on her knees. She folds her hands and sets her slick forehead on them. Water and food would be nice. Also, someone to acknowledge she exists on this empty planet. What's the use of walking without direction?

Maybe she deserves this. She failed to uncover Anton's plot in time, just like she failed to save her father.

This time anger doesn't save her, and the stubbornness that's kept her alive so long deserts her. It belonged to someone else in another life. Thirst saps her energy. She's an empty husk, a piece of discarded refuge, an insignificant speck in a vast universe. There are no tears for what she feels. She's beyond them.

Sol wants to lie down and sleep. She can't say why she doesn't do it, or why her father's face suddenly swims before her eyes—the Ridge Bahri that was. A laughing, big-hearted rock of a man in an unreliable and often scary world. Longing for her father stronger than she's felt for many years stabs into her chest. If he could see her giving up, how disappointed he'd be! He'd frown at her, lips pursed, not saying anything because he never had to. That look had always been enough to pick her up and stiffen her spine against whatever challenge awaited.

Remembering her father makes her sit up, draw a breath, then lurch to her feet. She's not going to die here in some nameless forest. If she perishes, she'll do it on her feet, fighting back against a world that never did her any favors.

Weariness falls away, and fresh energy rushes through her. *Be the person Father raised you to be. Don't give in to despair. Don't let the past consume you. You are more than your tragedies, more than your revenge. If there's any hope for a future, you have to go find it. And if you must face that future alone, so be it.*

Sol's Skinpad pings, and she looks at the message. It's from Oskar. **I'm down. I had to hide from the Earthers for a bit but eventually made it to an escape pod. Tell me where you are.**

38

Clera

Elio sets the shuttle down on the beach not far from another spacecraft. It must belong to Niklas' *Lycka* crew. Clera and the others spent the short flight listening to Zavi read his cousin's many messages. They learned more of the Swedish starship's fate ... and the fate of Zavi's cousin. At Niklas' tale of giant mushrooms exploding after rainstorms, Zavi had frowned. "The plant data from the probes never mentioned fungi," he muttered.

Nik had described in stark detail how his last two crewmates died. After that, there was no more talk of catastrophic rain, and his texts became more like journal entries—descriptions of days filled with experiments, documentation, foraging, and chopping trails through thick brush. He spoke of naming his finds, of the dry season, of discovering a spring near the cliffs where water tasted like honey.

But gloom pervaded most of the entries. Zavi had described his cousin as a light-hearted prankster, yet Clera didn't hear that in the messages. Instead, they increasingly hinted at despair and loneliness. She watched the lines on Zavi's forehead deepen with each new entry.

As Elio entered atmo and located the beach on the *Goose*'s navigation panel, she remarked, "Those messages are months old. Who knows how Niklas is doing now."

"I've only gotten through half of them," Zavi returned glumly. "I hope he's okay." His hand balled beside hers. She covered it with her own but didn't otherwise try to comfort him. What could she say?

⚬

After the shuttle settles in a cloud of fine grit, Zavi bounds for the door. By the time the stairs roll out, Clera has joined him. "Zavi—"

"I need to find Nik. I sent him a message that we're through the wormhole, but he hasn't replied yet."

Unsure what she was going to say, she follows him down to the beach. They didn't hear all the messages, and she doesn't know if Niklas still lives. Clera wants to protect Zavi from whatever horrible truth lies in wait but knows she can't, so she trails him in silence.

The camp looks neat but lived in: still-smoking ashes in a firepit, a camp stove, several tents, rain covers ruffling in the costal breeze. She glances toward a wide green sea and catches her breath. It reminds her of translucent stained glass, except it's not static but rippling in constant motion. Foam fringes the border between water and sand, swags of white that push and pull. There should be seagulls and long-legged sandpipers chasing the tide, yet the scene is strangely empty.

Zavi calls out, "Niklas? Are you here?"

If he'd seen them land, he'd surely have come running.

The others clamber down the stairs and join them at the beach.

Clera says, "Your cousin could be out scouting. You can't expect him to stay at Landing Bay all the time."

"Right." Zavi sighs. "We should at least check to be sure, though." He heads toward the other shuttle.

Mila arches her back, a pose which exaggerates her growing stomach. "Wow! I've never seen the sea except in vids. The real thing is different." Her nose twitches. "Doesn't smell like dead fish. More like—I don't know—brine?"

Elio leans down and speaks against her belly, "This is your new home, baby boy."

Mila says, "Girl, you mean. Come on. I want to walk down the beach. We need a distraction from ..." She trails off, shadows momentarily transforming her face.

Clera isn't sure they should venture away from the shuttle. There could be hidden dangers the classes on *Calliope* didn't prepare them for. Case in point—giant fungi that emit poisonous spores. "Be careful!" she calls. "Maybe you should ..." Her voice trails off. They won't listen anyway. She isn't even sure she's the captain on Vishnu, at least not until they have to make hard decisions about what to do next.

By the time she reaches the other shuttle, Zavi has reappeared through the hatch. He calls down, "Nik isn't here, but the ship looks lived in."

"I'll check the tents." She heads toward one and unties a flap. Inside are bundled bedrolls, a flattened air mattress, pillows. The other five tents contain similar items. Clothing and blankets in plastic crates also fill a few.

She and Zavi meet by the firepit, where the scouting crew from *Lycka* arranged fallen tree trunks to provide seating. A foldable writing table and cloth chair sit nearby. Vials, pipets, slides, and other scientific equipment lie neatly in a large trunk, the interior of which unfolds into shelving and small compartments.

"The tents haven't been occupied for a long time." Clera rubs a toe in the sandy dirt, then stares toward the fringe of trees and shrubs further up the beach. A path disappears into a maze of thorny branches. "Your cousin wrote that after a rain, giant mushrooms erupted from the earth and spread spores everywhere. But the tents are intact, and the forest seems healthy."

"These are military grade tents made to withstand violent conditions. I think they coat them with a resin to preserve the fabric beneath. As for the flora, I've wondered why so many of the plants I've been studying have thick, waxy leaves. It could be a defense against the spores if I had to guess."

"And the lack of animals could also be explained by the spores?" She shivers, imagining her old cat, Duro, caught in a storm of toxic drift. She lost him just before they stole the shuttle, and he wasn't hers for long, yet his absence still stings. She shakes off the memory. "What about birds? Couldn't they fly away?"

Zavi stands beside her. They look toward the gray cliffs that intersect the shoreline to their right. He places an arm around her waist. "I don't know. It's quite possible that birds never evolved on this planet. To find carbon-based lifeforms at all on an alien world is miraculous. Look how similar those trees are to Earth trees. It makes you wonder if there's some higher being up there giving order to the universe."

"That sounds like something a priest would say," she teases.

He shrugs. "I like to think life isn't just some random set of occurrences. There's comfort in that."

Clera turns into his body and wraps her arms around him. She resolves not to think about all those poor people up on *Calliope*. Maya and Lin. Barak and Stark. Sol! Clera gasps and checks her Skinpad. Niklas' messages distracted her from checking earlier.

I got away from the ship but landed off course in the jungle ... or forest. Don't know directions. Will take a guess and try to find the beach.

Thank the stars. Clera writes her back that they're coming to find her, then shares Sol's message with Zavi. "We need to send out a search party."

"Except we've no idea of direction." Zavi frowns. "The escape pod should have landed near the bay. Maybe Elio and Mila will find Sol on their walk. Try messaging her again, and I'll message Nik."

Clera knows he's right, but their texts are met with silence. "I wonder if our apps are working the same here on Vishnu. Could there be a delay?"

Zavi shakes his head. "Who knows. I guess we can try again in a bit."

Her thoughts briefly return to her coworkers in the Biosphere. They're gone forever, unlike Sol. Clera will mourn them when the pain of loss isn't so fresh. At least she survived, and so did Zavi. Sol did, too, surely. There's no one more capable, which is a small comfort.

Clera soaks up Zavi's nearness. Without him, everything would be so much harder to endure.

"What?" A bemused half-grin softens his mouth.

"I think I can face whatever comes if we're together."

His hands cup her skull. He kisses her gently. "With you beside me, this new world feels like it could be home."

She smiles and pulls back, cheeks hot with the guilty pleasure of his words. "We should rummage up a meal to surprise Niklas and Sol with. If they don't show up soon, we can go up that trail over there to search." She points.

"Maybe I'll find a flare in Niklas' shuttle. Might be quicker. If she's lost, she'll hopefully see it and figure out where we are."

A search of the shuttle doesn't reveal a flare, but they do discover a lot of dried kelp hanging from lines strung across one of the empty cabins. The tiny kitchen's cold storage reveals several containers of what look like dead beetles and a bowl of chopped, thorny leaves and luminescent flowers. "Is Niklas a good cook?" Clera holds up the container of beetles doubtfully. At least they're proof that animal life does exist on the green planet.

"Definitely not. He never had to learn. His family employed a chef." Zavi takes the beetles and makes a face. "I guess we'll have to trust him on this. At least he's getting his protein. And by the looks of that salad, he's still alive. It's fresh."

By the time they've set food on the worktable outside, the overlarge sun has passed its zenith, and Elio and Mila appear far down the beach, headed their way. Clera stares up at the clusters of alien rings flanking Kali. She noticed them before but only now takes in their significance.

Zavi remarks, "I think our Martians might be more accurately called 'Vishnuians.' They must have set out for many different systems, not just the Milky Way. I wonder why? What made them leave this place?"

"The rains, maybe?"

"Their technology was so incredibly advanced that they should have been able to find a solution to that problem."

Elio calls out, "Hey, did you find your cousin?"

He tows Mila along behind him. Her cheeks are red apples, and a sheen of sweat glosses her skin. Clera offers her the folding chair, and she sinks down with a sigh. "Not used to real walking," she huffs.

"Are you all right?" Clera can't imagine having to deliver a premature baby without Sol here to help. "You didn't see Sol wandering along the beach, I guess? Where could she be?"

Mila answers, "Did she make it down? No baby yet, but I'm going to need her soon. I hope she's safe."

Clera shares Sol's message. It was sent over an hour ago.

"Well, fec all," Mila huffs. "How are we going to find her?"

"Let's eat a quick meal," Zavi suggests. "After that, you can stay here while Elio, Clera, and I go up that trail and start calling. Hopefully, we'll find Sol before dark. Maybe Niklas, too."

"I'm not staying alone." Mila folds her arms.

Clera says, "None of us should be alone. I'll wait here with Mila."

"Bonding time, brother." Elio grins at Zavi, who offers him a curled-up beetle.

Just then thunder rumbles. Sometime in the last few minutes, a storm has moved in. The sea roils in murky shades of jade. A cloud bank covers the sky, and Kali hides behind it.

"Oh, no," Zavi breathes. "None of us are going to be doing any searching. Remember what Nik said about rain?"

Clera goes cold. "The mushrooms. Everybody, gather up the food. We need to be ready to bolt inside Nik's shuttle if rain starts falling." She's their captain again, and they rush to comply. She casts a worried glance toward the forest before she joins them. Sol's somewhere out there, and she doesn't know about the rains. Clera dashes off a quick warning message.

Damn it all. She should have done it before.

39

Solast

Tell me where you are, Oskar demands.

In a very tall stand of palms, Sol replies. **Best I can give you.**

I see them. Stay there. I'm coming.

Sol blinks back tears. *I'm coming.* The words light a fire in her heart. She's not alone, after all, though she's got no idea how Oskar can differentiate her group of trees from any other group. Except they *are* very tall.

She believes in him, though she's still fuming over his desertion on *Calliope.*

Sol leans against the red bark, lets her hot skin cool, and watches the brush. Sooner than expected, Oskar pops out of a stand of ferns. He sees her and jogs over with relief on his face. He reaches for her, then hesitates.

Part of her wants to hug him. The other part wants to hit him. When he left her aboard the ship, he only meant to help others. Her mind knows this, but her heart?

"Sol?"

"I'm here."

"Are you hurt? Have some water." He holds out a canteen.

"Where did you get that?"

"The escape pods have compartments filled with basic first aid, food, and water. Not much. Just a few energy bars. Here." He hands her the bottle and a foil package.

She drains the water, then rips open the energy bar and bites into it.

One side of his mouth tips up. "I take it you didn't find the compartment."

She chews and swallows. "No."

"Better?" He takes back the canteen.

"Yes."

"Sol, I—" His gaze falters. "I shouldn't have left you. When I set off down that hallway, I thought you would be safer getting back to your shuttle. But after a few steps, I realized I didn't want to leave you. By the time I turned back, the crowd had gotten between us, and I couldn't see you. I had to make a choice. Get to Command or go look for you. I knew you'd be fine without me, so I left." He frowns, then searches her face. "Did I make the wrong decision?"

What would she have done in his place? Probably the same thing, so why does his admission hurt? She's let him squeeze through cracks in her heart without even realizing it, and she doesn't like the power it gives him. Still, she's so *feccing* glad he's here. Her bitterness washes away. She throws her arms around Oskar's neck and hugs him tight. His shoulders drop, and he burrows his face in her neck, murmuring, "I'm so relieved you're all right."

Thunder rumbles. They break apart to stare at the sky, where a huddle of slate gray, ominous looking clouds have gathered.

"I hope those branches will keep us dry." Oskar eyes the waving palm fronds doubtfully.

"How did you find me, anyway?"

"I happened to be on a slight rise when you messaged me and was able to look out over the brush. The trees you described were evident—the biggest things around, so I set off toward them."

"Thank you." She wishes the thunder hadn't made them jump apart.

Oskar bends his head, pauses for an excruciating moment, then touches his lips to hers. Despite his hesitation, the kiss feels like a promise. Something sweet uncoils in her belly. She presses closer and tilts her head so their lips mesh like interlocking gears, perfectly matched. His hands rest on her hips, then slide up, the kiss deepening, and she forgets all that happened on *Calliope* ...

Until a man bursts through a stand of thorny bushes and yells at them, "What in helv do you think you're doing? We've got to get back to the beach! Immediately!"

Day 191

Palmeria is my name for the prolific trees with reddish bark and dark green, wax-coated fronds. They look like they belong in a jungle (as do the shield ferns), yet the surrounding woodland contains more characteristics of a forest—albeit a temperate one. The trees provide welcome shade, but I've not found another use for them. Climbing earned me scraped shins and a sore back when I fell after managing only a ten-foot shimmy up the smooth trunk. I'm almost glad no one was there to see my clumsy attempt. No. Scratch that. If anyone at all had shown up at Landing Bay—even my worst enemy—I'd have run toward them and kissed their feet.

Yes, that's how desperate I've become.

-N.J.

40

Niklas

Day 191. Nik scrawls a handwritten note in his journal. He's given up technology unless he needs it for experiments. His mother gave him a set of leatherbound journals with his name embossed on the covers when he departed for *Lycka*. He'd labeled them a sentimental, impractical gift and tossed them in the bottom of his suitcase, yet now he wonders. Technology can fizzle out or be hacked, but the journals unearthed from his luggage look as pristine as the day she presented them to him.

He found her name inside a front cover along with a quote: *Sometimes letting go is how we save ourselves. - Helen Johanssen.* He's fairly sure she was talking about his imminent departure. Did she think he needed saving? Or had she been referring to herself? Perhaps hinting that she needed to let him go, needed to sacrifice her happiness for his. Knowing he might not return, she'd released him like someone opening a bird cage. Letting him fly because she sensed he needed to.

Niklas had found the journals just after his world collapsed, on that fateful day the ocean spit him back on shore, only to discover spores had killed his last two companions. Now the mounds of disturbed earth make sense. He's solved one of Vishnu's mysteries, yet this world holds many more. He's done his best to uncover them during his months alone. At first, he watched the skies with paranoid dedication, but gradually he's come to believe his crew landed at the end of the rainy season. How long the dry one will last is anyone's guess.

Of late, more clouds scud across the sky. They've begun to build but haven't broken. He's moved most of his possessions back into the shuttle. With its stainless steel hull, it has to be safer than the tents.

Niklas skims a thumb across his mother's name. The warm leather against his palm offers comfort. He remembers Zavi, speeding across the heavens to reach him, and this provides solace, too, though it's mixed with worry. If Earthers penetrated *Lycka* and her defenses, what of *Calliope*? His Skinpad messages may never reach his cousin, yet Nik keeps sending them. *Please get here safe, and let it be before the rains.*

Sometimes he thinks about the girl-woman from the cave. Sometimes he wonders if all of it—the messenger bag, canteen, wrappers, poisoned wound—might have been a dream. He wants to swim into the sea and find out if Alice is real, but the memory of the monster with iridescent skin and tentacles holds him back. Was *that* a dream? Or maybe a hallucination? He didn't used to fear water. He fears it now, though.

Nik makes notes on the new food source he's testing, then closes the journal and fastens the clasp. He chooses the largest sea beetle from his plate, tries to imagine it's a French fry, and pops it into his mouth. Beetles were the first animal life on Vishnu he discovered. Their hard, domed shells defend against the mushroom spores, but if you cook them in oil, they turn brittle and crunchy. With a little salt, they aren't bad.

He's found fish among the kelp forest offshore, too, yet he doesn't swim past where the sandy bottom drops into a deep undersea canyon. Any water over his head feels too far out, too close to the place dragons lurk. These fish are palm-sized and silver, hard to catch, but he's making a net from moss and hopes for success soon.

Nik closes the chest that contains the fold-out shelves and compartments of his work station. He carries the journal up the stairs to the shuttle and leaves it on his bed. He worked all morning and part of the afternoon testing flora. It's time he cut more trails through the forest. Every day he explores a bit further, always hoping to find a trace of the colonists from *Loki* or the missing U.S. probe, *Pioneer III.* So far, he's been disappointed.

The main trail leads to his most important find—a freshwater spring on the cliffs that's safe for drinking. He fills his canteen there before hiking inland, a hand-carved staff in one hand, his machete in the other. Primitive as a caveman, and almost as wild-looking. His hair has grown past his shoulders, wavy and sun-bleached, the matching beard full and dark. Why bother shaving or trimming? No one will see … maybe ever again.

He herds his negative thoughts into a dark corner. Being marooned on Vishnu has brought forth what turns out to be his greatest fear: solitude. Well, that and water dragons. Their potential existence has kept him from looking for Alice. Maybe she isn't real, anyway. Recalling her pale, serious face keeps him from going crazy, though, so why not believe in her?

Niklas reaches a clearing of shield ferns. Like so much of the flora in this area, they've developed a tough outer layer to their pale green leaves. If he soaks them overnight in water, they become tender enough to chew. With beetles crushed and sprinkled on top, plus a touch of his precious vinegar store, he eats well enough.

Nik has begun hacking a new path toward a stand of palmeria, the trees with reddish bark and dark green, wavy fronds. They look like they belong in a tropical rainforest.

He flexes his muscles and gathers his strength to chop at a swath of thorny shield bark. His machete bot malfunctioned last month, but it's still useful as a manual tool. The shrubs grow higher than his head, and he's carving a tunnel through them as the straightest path to the palmeria. The task is brutal, though. He returns to camp every day with scraped arms and burning muscles. On the other hand, the branches—sans thorns—store a liquid sweet with nutrients. Chopped into small bites, the plant adds variety to his salads.

Deep inside the dim, cool tunnel, Nik pauses to wipe his brow. A faint whining sound penetrates the thicket, sounding almost like an engine. He listens hard, then walks into the sunlight and listens again. Nothing. He studies the sky and doesn't like the look of the clouds, but the first storm of the season won't arrive for a bit, so he reenters his green tunnel and takes up the machete. Several hours later, arms numb with effort, he finally breaks through the far side.

Nik waves the machete and whoops. His voice sounds so hoarse he barely recognizes it. The palmeria loom close now. A strong breeze ruffles their tops, and he wonders if he should head back. Something shiny streaking through the sky catches his eye. A falling star? Except it's growing bigger, not disintegrating. A parachute explodes from the round bit of metal. The capsule jerks upward, then floats lazily down into a far-off stand of trees.

Niklas rubs at his eyes, hardly daring to believe. He sets off running in the direction of—he realizes with surging hope—an escape pod. It has to be *Calliope*'s. Why someone ejected from the ship doesn't cross his mind. He's too busy absorbing the fact that a person besides himself exists on this godforsaken planet. Ferns and toxifera vines try to trip him. Less poisonous vines dangle from the squat waxleaf oak, which he named for the shape of its golden leaves. By the time he finds the capsule, the door hangs open, and the occupant has gone, but he hears a voice, so he follows a trail of broken twigs and trampled plants into the forest.

Just then, thunder growls. Helv! He's forgotten about the storm. *The storm!* And whoever just landed has no idea of the mortal danger they're in. A burst of speed propels him into the palmeria grove. Two figures stand close together among the trunks. As he bursts through a clump of ferns, Nik yells at them to get to the beach.

The tall woman and lean, brown-haired man turn to gape at him. "Who are you?" the woman asks. She's striking, with short brunette hair and almond-shaped eyes.

Her companion steps toward him. "We'd be glad to go to the beach, friend, if we could find it."

Niklas pulls up, panting. He must look like a madman, waving his staff with one hand and the machete with the other. Finally, he manages, "I'm from *Lycka*. And it's going to rain. You don't want to be out here when that happens. Follow me."

Thunder rumbles again to emphasize his point. The two look at each other and nod. "Lead the way," the man says.

Nik hustles them toward his manmade tunnel, speaking while they jog. "My name's Niklas Johanssen. I was in the first scouting party from *Lycka*. The rest of my team got caught in the rains. I'm the only one left."

The woman looks sharply at him. "Are the rains toxic? Acid? No one told us about that." She's panting a little but trying to hide it.

"No." Nik darts beneath protective thorns and hurries into the tunnel. He shouts over his shoulder, "It's what the rain makes spring from the ground. Giant fungi that shoot out toxic spores. They don't harm the planet but kill humans in about five minutes."

The woman glances at her companion, mouth a thin line.

"Out of the frying pan and into the fire," he says mildly.

Nik wants to ask what he means by that and why they used escape pods, but it's hard to talk in the narrow space. They travel single file until a pinprick of light indicates the end of the thorny shield bark. Nik hurries forward and pokes his head into the open to check the sky. They aren't far from the beach. There's time if they hurry. Maybe they should wait inside the tunnel, though.

The man edges up beside him and offers his hand. "I'm Oskar, and this is Sol." He nods over his shoulder.

Nik accepts the handshake. Gods, it feels good to touch another person. He doesn't want to let go, but he releases his grip, then nods toward Sol. He's about to ask if they're from *Calliope* when a growl of thunder distracts him. "The storm is close," Nik tells them. "We might want to wait it out in the tunnel." He points toward the clouds with the machete.

Sol speaks up. "My friends landed a shuttle on the beach. They may not know about the rains or the spores. We have to get there and warn them."

Well, that changes things. Nik gives the sky one last glance. "Then we'd better run."

Thunder cracks, almost above them now. They set off along the trail. The first drops fall as they reach the spring near the cliff tops. Niklas hopes mushrooms won't erupt until the shower finishes, but he isn't sure. He's only seen the phenomenon a few times. Rain plashes off leaves and makes divots in the dry soil at their feet. They hurry down a switchback trail. It levels out, and Nik spots a sandy stripe. Moments later, they burst onto the beach. Niklas skids to a stop. He takes in the second shuttle near his own, then the four people whirling to face him as he shouts, "Get into my shuttle!"

Silence descends, then abruptly shatters as a squat woman with dark braids yells back, "We know!"

Someone else calls, "Niklas?"

"Zavi?"

Joy and terror mix in Nik's chest. "Go!" He jabs his staff at the shuttle, then rushes toward his cousin, the others on his heels. A caramel-haired girl pulls on Zavi's arm and points. The other two—a young, dark-haired guy and the short, overweight woman—are already jogging toward the stairway. The rain, which had moments ago been a pleasant kiss of coolness upon his skin, starts a tap dance that spurs him onward.

They clatter into the ship, first Zavi's group, then Sol and Oskar a short time later, and finally, Niklas. He closes the hatch, drops his staff and machete, and puts his hands on his knees. He gasps, speechless, trying to process that *Zavi is here.*

Nik hears mumbles. Footsteps. Rustling. Wonderfully human noises. Then a hand pulls him upright, and Zavi peers into his dripping face. "Is that you, cousin?"

Zavi looks the same, his mild, gentle features punctuated by blue eyes a shade more vivid than Nik's. Someone laughs. Niklas realizes the sound bubbles from his own throat. He can't stop himself—doesn't want to though he must sound deranged. Zavi pulls him into a hug, and they cling together, just like when they were boys reuniting for summer break.

Tears prick Nik's eyes. He blinks, pulls away, and makes a show of wiping wet hair from his face to hide his out-of-control emotions. "I've never been so glad to see anyone, little cuz." He grips Zavi's upper arms. "Didn't I tell you we'd be together again? Didn't I?"

Zavi grins. "I probably should have listened to you. I've been meaning to say sorry for being so non-supportive when you first told me you were headed to Vishnu."

"Well, maybe you were right to be critical. Things haven't turned out well so far." He's about to ask for Zavi's story when the caramel-haired girl turns toward a window and gasps.

Everyone crowds into the narrow space behind her, trying to see. Niklas listens for the rain, but it's already stopped pinging against the outer hull. It dribbles into silence, and Nik knows what's happening.

The girl squeaks, "The ground near the tree line is erupting! Look!" And a few seconds later, "It's the giant mushrooms! How can they grow so fast? See the clouds of spores?"

The short woman nudges her aside. "Give the rest of us the chance to see!"

While the two women share the view from the exit hatch porthole, the others rush to the cabins so they can look out. All but Niklas. He doesn't want to see or remember, so he wanders into the commons area and sinks down on the couch. Cushions cradle his exhausted body, and he rests his head back. It takes all his concentration to blot out the dead, contorted bodies of his friends.

Eventually, the others trickle into the room. Niklas scoots over so Zavi and Clera can share his couch. Zavi takes her hand. Clera frowns at the floor, but she squeezes her fingers tight around his cousin's. *So that's how it is.* Another thing he's lost—the comfort of a woman.

The others remain silent, absorbing the shock of the fungi eruption. How violently the mushrooms break through the ground, and how quickly they slither back inside, leaving only mounds to mark their passing. Finally, Zavi says, "On Earth, my mother had a garden. When she watered too much or there was a lot of rain, I'd go out to look for carrots or new flowers, and I'd see white clusters of mushrooms where there was nothing the day before. Then the sun would heat up, and I'd return to find the fungi had vanished."

Clera remarks, "Maybe the rules for plants aren't so different here. Only these are monster-sized."

"And deadly," the dark-haired man adds.

Zavi glances sideways at Niklas and says, "I can't believe we've found you, Nik. I finally got your many messages, though I've only read half. Still, everybody here knows most of your story, but you don't know ours."

"Maybe start with your names," Nik suggests with a tired smile.

Zavi introduces everyone except Oskar. "Aren't you in the archeology department? I think we've met, actually, but I don't remember ..."

The man intercedes, "Oskar Lehmann, specialist on ancient Martian artifacts. I conducted several classes aboard ship and acted as a consultant." He grimaces. "I'm not much for social interactions. I stayed in my office a lot, so it's not surprising you don't remember me."

Clera cries, "I do! Sol and I were at that first class you did. On the ancient ruins of Mars."

Sol clears her throat. "Oskar is a friend of mine. We escaped *Calliope* in separate pods. Niklas found us in the forest."

"Better tell your whole story," Mila suggests.

"Right," Sol begins. She and Oskar take turns. Nik watches how they interact and feels a pang of jealousy. Elio and Mila also appear to be a couple, which leaves Niklas the odd man out. Novel, but a lot better than being alone. He can hardly believe he's stuffed all these people into his shuttle. Their heat, their breath, their *aliveness* fills his heart with joy.

Sol and Oskar finish their account, and Nik's attention turns to the others. When Mila shifts in her seat, his gaze sharpens. She's not overweight. Her belly is a hard beach ball, and her enlarged breasts spill over the spacesuit's neckline. He knows he's staring yet can't seem to stop.

"What?" She glares at him, then adds a second later, "Yes, I'm pregnant. Yes, Elio's the father. And no, I'm not going to explain how I got that way." Her chin juts. "I'm due in a couple of months, Sol says."

"I'm a medic," the tall woman murmurs in explanation.

Niklas hardly hears her. His lips move silently. Eventually, words emerge. "There's a baby? But—" He remembers how she said no questions and falls silent.

"Do you want proof?" Mila beckons. "Come over here and feel him for yourself. He's holding a one-man dance contest right now."

"Can I?" An incredulous grin breaks across Nik's face. His facial muscles twinge from the unaccustomed effort.

Mila's combative stance softens. She nods.

He covers the distance in two steps, kneels at her feet, and places a hesitant hand on her stomach. It's too personal. They've only just met. But again, he can't seem to resist. There's a ripple beneath his fingers. If possible, his smile widens. "I can't believe it."

Without warning, a sob rises in his throat and spills out before he can stop it. He covers his face, wishing he were anywhere else, unable to stem the flood of tears. A fountain leaps from his eyes and falls between his fingers. His shoulders heave.

No one says a word. Eventually, a hand falls on his shoulder. "Nik, it's all right." Zavi's voice.

Niklas sniffs and swipes the back of a hand across his cheeks. "I know that."

Elio murmurs, "So those were happy sobs?"

"Of course they were." Mila ruffles his hair, which makes it stand further on end. "Who wouldn't be deliriously happy to welcome Vishnu's first human baby onto the planet?"

A picture of Alice, the ghost girl, rises in Niklas' mind. He shoves it aside, stumbles up, and returns to his seat. Clera shoots him a sympathetic smile and claps her hands together. "Well, let's get the rest of our stories out of the way, shall we?"

And they fill him in.

41

Clera

Clera describes the attack on *Calliope*: her confusion, panic, then relief when she saw Zavi running to meet her. She concludes with the awful decision to leave without Sol. Clera glances at her friend. "I'm sorry we didn't wait for you. We *could* have, I think. But we didn't know that at the time."

Sol flicks the apology away with a shake of her head. "It's fine. Besides, the escape pods were closer to me than our shuttle."

"So were the Earthers," Clera mutters.

"Oskar was in the most danger from them." Sol looks toward him with a mix of emotions Clera can't read.

She shoots Dr. Lehmann a curious glance. How did Sol develop a relationship with the professor without anyone knowing? Clera thought they'd moved past the point of secrets, but she didn't see this coming.

Niklas breaks in, "So, you're saying that everyone aboard *Calliope* is dead except for a handful of these Earther people?"

"Closer to a dozen of the Earthers, far as I could see," Oskar corrects him.

Nik continues, "When we returned to *Lycka*, we saw no one alive. The ship was orbiting Vishnu on autopilot. I have no idea if the escape pods had launched. Assuming Earthers were responsible for that attack, which seems likely given the similarity of sabotage methods, what happened to *those* saboteurs?"

No one answers. Finally, Clera asks, "You're sure no one survived up there?"

"We weren't searching for survivors, but *Lycka*'s AI indicated that my team were the only ones left." Nik thinks. "If the AI was wrong and there were Earthers with gas masks aboard, why would they just hang out after the attack? Wouldn't they—I don't know—turn the ship around and head home? Assuming they knew how."

Elio says, "It's not as hard as you might think to navigate a starship. The AI does the heavy-lifting, especially if your route is already programmed, which it might have been."

Clera tries to veer the conversation back on course. "What about *Calliope*? What are we going to do? We can't just leave the Earthers up there, can we? What if they decide to come here? We won't be safe."

"That's right," Sol agrees. "They have to be dealt with." Her hand moves to her crucifix, a sure sign she's anxious.

Zavi says, "It would be helpful to know how the Earthers spread a neurotoxin through the vents, what it was, how long it lasts. That kind of thing."

Niklas breaks in. "If they used the same toxin that killed people on *Lycka*, I can tell you that. I collected a sample." He pulls something up on his Skinpad. "I was able to obtain answers from downloaded databases on my science vessel." He summarizes the information he collected on Soporon-D, then adds, "There is no known antidote for this toxin. Signs of poisoning include muscle weakness, paralysis, nerve pain, respiratory impairment, and confusion. Death typically occurs within a few minutes. Sound familiar?"

They all nod.

Sol speaks up. "I think I might know how they dispersed it. I wasn't sure before, but hearing your description gives me a strong theory. By the way, the Earthers don't call it Soporon-D. They have a code name. Erebus. I believe Juke somehow discovered what Erebus was, and the cult killed him for it."

"Juke?" Nik asks.

Clera explains what happened to their flashy friend, then draws a shaky breath and turns to Sol. "Tell us your theory."

"Niklas, you said Erebus is a crystal in its inert form, right?"

He tips his head.

"Well, the Earthers were also Venters aboard *Calliope*. At least most of them. That was the name for colonists working in Life Support and Maintenance. Our job was to crawl through ducts, check and double check that everything was working correctly, and also clean the air scrubbers behind the screens."

Clera sees where this is going. "So, you're saying that they snuck crystals aboard and placed them in the vents?"

Mila says, "I thought the luggage would be carefully checked to keep anything suspicious like that from getting aboard."

"They did check," Zavi affirms, lines forming between his brows. "But crystals are small. They could be hidden inside something else, disguised as something innocuous."

"Right." Sol takes back control of the conversation. "The last thing Juke said was 'Erebus unleashed.' That was only a short time before people started dropping. I think the Venters hid their packets of the toxin in these storage compartments located next to most of the scrubbers."

"Storage compartments?" Clera echoes. "Why would there be storage ..."

age ..."

Sol interrupts, "It's a pain to carry around cleaning supplies in the ducts, so *Calliope* stocked brushes, disinfectant, and abrasives in the compartments. But you could also hide a packet of something in the bottom of those compartments. I found someone's trash stuffed down there a few times."

Elio breaks in excitedly, "So they put on gas masks, go into the ducts, and open the packets near screens. The crystals dissolve when they hit the air, and the air handlers push the gas into the hallways. We'd just been released from curfew, and everybody was in the main corridors so they could catch their first glimpse of Vishnu."

"That's right," Sol nods. "When I returned to the maintenance locker room looking for Anton, I noticed most of the masks were missing. It's what tipped me off that the sabotage had begun. Erebus was unleashed."

"Who's Anton?" Niklas asks. "And I thought you were a medic, Sol?"

Sol's face remains carefully blank. "I *am* a medic. I only took the transfer into Life Support and Maintenance to get close to Anton. And he's someone who must be destroyed." Her words grow clipped. "I used to think killing him no matter the cost was my purpose. That was before I had friends." Color rises to her cheeks. "It took me a while, but I finally realized saving the people on *Calliope* was more important than my personal vendetta. Yet I failed at both."

Clera breaks in, "No. You didn't fail. You warned us, and Nik warned us, and we're all alive. Not everyone died." She pauses to let this sink in. Sol meets her eyes, and they share a look. Clera takes her friend's silence as grudging acknowledgement.

"We aren't done. I've still got time to complete what I started." Sol stands, arms crossed, and begins to pace.

Oskar speaks. "I don't understand why you hate this Anton fellow so much."

She comes to a halt and faces him. Her eyes flicker. Finally, she blurts, "He was head of my commune in the Barrens, back before he became Mons Vega and expanded his movement. When my father stood against him, he cut Father's throat. I ran."

"Sol." There's pity in Oskar's tone.

She lifts her chin and doesn't waver. "I've sworn to kill Anton. It's been my only goal for eleven years, and it's still my goal. He has to be stopped before even more people die."

Oskar's voice rumbles out, soft yet certain. "We have time. You aren't alone anymore." He hesitates, then rises and goes to her. He places a hand on her arm, and she lets it rest there.

"So." Clera's eyes slide over each of them in turn. "The question is, what are we going to do?"

Niklas replies, "If you're headed back to *Calliope*, my shuttle won't get you there. It's about out of fuel. We were in a hurry and might have forgotten to stock up. Sorry. No one was thinking straight."

"That's not a problem." Mila smooths her hands over her belly. "We've got the *Goose*."

At Niklas' puzzled look, Clera explains, "The *Blue Goose*. Our ship. Sol named her."

Elio adds, "Her solar panels will give us all the boost we need to break atmo, even with this rain." He glances out a viewport. "Plus, I think the sun's back out."

Niklas warns, "The rains are just starting. The storms will get worse, longer and more intense until the monsoons break in about five months. Of course, this is somewhat conjecture on my part. I've not lived through an entire season yet."

"Let's deal with one problem at a time," Clera tells them all. "But first, I'm hungry."

"Oh, no. Not more beetles." Elio pretends to retch.

"Hey, don't knock them until you haven't had protein for a month." Nik heads to the kitchen area. "I can crush them to bits if you like, then sprinkle them on salad. You'll never know what you're eating."

"Oh, yes, I will." Elio rises. "But I'll take you up on that anyway."

He and Niklas put salads together and toss them with vinaigrette while Mila offers unheeded tips. Clera watches from the couch and takes in how they've come together like a family. A flash of happiness drowns out worry, fear, and doubt. Her old friend panic seems to be sleeping. For now, she's simply enjoying this moment of peace.

42

Solast

Sol does a mental tally. Seven good guys against close to a dozen sociopathic killers. The math stinks. She's trained in martial arts but out of practice. Elio's had some military training. Niklas looks like he could pack a punch. Same for Oskar and Zavi. Clera's no fighter, and Mila shouldn't even be on this mission yet refuses to stay behind. Sol can't blame her.

She rubs her temples and sighs. At least they have weapons. Niklas' scouting party came armed with PulseLock guns—good at close range. Sol would rather fight at a distance, though, and pick off the enemy one by one. It's unfortunate that *Calliope*'s policy was no onboard lasers or bullets. Too dangerous. What a joke, since packets of crystals have killed most of the people aboard anyway.

They didn't damage the ship, though. That irony is not lost on her.

"Sol?" Clera calls from up the beach.

Sol ventured to the sea hoping to calm her nerves, but the surf's ebb and flow only reminded her of Anton's dogged, patient planning—like water breaking down stone. She ignores Clera, sighs, and hurls a pebble into the waves. Father taught her to skip rocks, but she needs a glassy lake for that. She wishes he were here. Maybe he'd know the right course of action.

She and the others plotted and planned late into last night, yet Sol's not satisfied. Too much can go wrong. Maybe Anton and his followers will stay together on the bridge as Sol's plan assumes, but maybe they won't. Maybe her crew will pull their weight instead of becoming liabilities, but maybe they won't.

Clera comes up beside her. "Niklas thinks we're ready."

Sol turns to study her. She's braided her hair to keep it from flying around—small difference that will make in a fight. Determined eyes stare out of a pale face. If something happens to Clera or to any of them, Sol will blame herself. "It's a bad idea for all of us to go."

"Like you said before."

"Elio, Niklas, and I would work best."

"Nevertheless, we all have a right to be there and try to save *Calliope*. To defend ourselves."

Sol knew this would be Clera's answer, but she had to give it one last try. They stare at each other like combatants. "Your stubbornness will get you killed."

"So might yours."

"It's my life to lose. I don't want to have to worry about the rest of you, to have you on my conscience."

"We feel the same about you. About each other. I think Elio and Mila had their first serious argument last night." She smiles.

"Well, Elio might be smarter than the rest of you."

That makes Clera laugh. "He'd be glad to hear that. Our parents tended to call him 'reckless' and 'impetuous.'"

"I can't convince you to change your mind?"

"Don't even try." Clera beckons. "Come on. Your professor is waiting for you."

Sol kicks at the sand, then mumbles, "Oskar is not 'my professor.'"

Clera glances sideways at her. "Sure seems like it. I see how he looks at you."

Sol's traitorous cheeks heat.

"I don't know how you managed to carry on a relationship with him and keep it a secret. Well done."

Sol shrugs and mutters, "I'm not clear how that happened myself. Not sure what we have, either, so no labels. He *did* desert me just before I found an escape pod."

"I thought it was more that you were separated."

"He insisted he had to go warn Command that a toxin was loose, but it was way too late for that. He told me to get back to the *Goose*."

"Pretty selfless move, though."

Sol shrugs again. They've reached the shuttle, yet she hesitates at the bottom of the steps. Breath hisses through her teeth. She stares up, remembers how she found this ship, how it became her home and her solace. Now, it might be flying them all to their deaths. "Have we planned everything out well enough? Things are happening so fast."

Clera pauses. "Aren't you the one who said time was of the essence? That we had to get to Anton before he could come down to Vishnu or fly back through the wormhole—or do whatever deranged thing he's planning next?"

"Yes. But what if Elio's wrong about making it into the hangar unnoticed?"

"He knows how to scramble our signature thanks to his Security and Defense training. We'll just have to hope no one is looking out the window."

"You sound flippant. This is serious." Sol scowls.

"I don't mean to be. But my whole life, I've tried to avoid trouble and confrontation, and it got me nowhere. Eventually, you have to take risks.

No one gets a free pass. Now come on. They're waiting." Clera starts up the stairs.

"Aye aye, Captain." Sol salutes her retreating back and follows.

Everyone is buckled into seats on the bridge or harnessed to the wall railings, dressed in spacesuits, gas masks at the ready. A crate of PulseLock guns is secured next to the exit hatch. They're the best protection but won't be enough. Surprise is a better defense. Yet when has Sol ever been a step ahead of Anton? Why will this time be any different?

"Hey. Saved you a spot." Oskar points to the empty harness beside him.

Sol takes the equipment he hands her, climbs into her spacesuit, and straps in.

"You all right?" His brown eyes search hers, far too perceptive.

She hates that he's here, that all of them are. Anton should be hers alone to destroy. Juke already died. Who will be next? She hides her thoughts and manages a wavering smile. "I'll be fine when this is over."

Elio calls back to them, "Is everyone accounted for?" Mila sits nearby in the co-pilot's chair. *Juke's old place*, Sol remembers.

Clera answers in the affirmative, and he brings the *Goose* online and plugs in their destination.

Elio tells them, "*Calliope* is on our radar, still in orbit and about where I calculated she'd be at this time." He heaves a sigh, but Sol senses barely tethered excitement in his voice. "Here we go!"

The *Goose* uses converted solar to fire up thrusters and takes off at a steep incline. Sol grips her straps and recalls the last time she left the ground in this ship. She'd been terrified and confused. Then came rage and despair. She thought she'd lost her chance with Anton. This time is different yet just as terrifying. The shaking as they burst through atmo scares her, but what might come next frightens her more. She crosses her fingers and closes her eyes.

Oskar's hand finds hers, and she lets his touch soothe her nerves. For now. Once they reach *Calliope*, she's got to be *his* rock, the person in charge of this mission. That was the deal and the only reason she agreed to their plan. The *Goose* enters the black, and a hush falls over everyone. Sol's anxiety quiets, and she blinks her eyes open. Stars wink on. Close by, a ring that might be their ARH or possibly a different alien-made wormhole flashes lights in random patterns. Oskar's hand presses hers, then withdraws. She misses his warmth.

Elio reports through his mic, "We should see *Calliope* soon. We're on course to intercept in about twenty minutes."

"And you scrambled our signal?" Niklas inquires casually.

"Yep." Elio leans forward and stares out the viewscreen. "Do any of you see those dots?"

Zavi replies, "They look like ..."

"... bodies," Mila finishes. "And some other junk."

"Why?" Clera breathes.

Niklas grinds out, "They've vented the ship like we did with *Lycka*. It's a quick way to get rid of the gas, though *Calliope* needs time to replenish its oxygen-nitrogen mix afterward. The vacuum of space sucks out anything not nailed down or blocked by walls."

"Those people were already dead, though. Right?" Clera ventures.

"Yes, most of them anyway," Sol reassures her. "They were likely the colonists in the main hallways near an outside hatch. There will still be plenty of bodies left to stumble over when we get into the ship." She recalls her clinic friends, and her heart grows heavy.

"Will the air be breathable at this point?" Niklas asks.

"Hard to say," Elio replies. "Depends on when they vented." He sounds less excited now, and Sol wonders if some of the dead drifting through space might have been pilots Elio trained with.

Zavi says, "Nik and I have scanners to check the air quality once we land."

Sol reaches for her gas mask. "We should mask up anyway, just in case. If there's a welcoming party, we won't have time for scientific calculations." She fits the device over her face and presses it tight against her cheekbones. The rubber and plastic let her distance herself from the others. She needs that.

Calliope appears and grows swiftly into an elongated capsule with a bulbous, rotating tail. The others reach for masks. Soon lights along the bridge become viewports. No one greets them with a barrage of laser fire. Maybe Elio was right. They're almost invisible. They'll have surprise on their side.

The hangar becomes a gaping maw, and Elio takes over from the AI, directing the ship into the gap, thrusters reversed, so she glides in and sighs to a stop at the closest docking port. Clamps engage automatically, tethering the *Goose* to the floor.

Sol unclips, jumps up, and tries to run forward, remembering too late she's back in zero-g, her boots secured to the floor. There can be no fast movements, only clunky lumbering. She makes it to the panoramic windows while the others unstrap and gather weapons. Shuttles sit clamped to docking ports, but no people scurry about. An air of disuse and neglect permeates the hangar bay.

"It's eerie," Clera breathes beside her.

Sol ignores her and barks at Elio, "Check outside."

He seems to understand. "On it." He works his control panel. The rest of them wait tensely, eyes jumping between the windows and his screen. "The *Goose* isn't picking up any life readings nearby."

Sol's shoulders relax a little. "Next step. Roll down the walkway."

She's first out the door, Elio and Niklas just behind her. Near the bottom of the stairs, she realizes she's missing something ... her PulseLock gun. How stupid can she be! She steps off the last stair, saying to Elio who's just behind, "Go secure the bay. I need something on the *Goose*. I'll be right back." She doesn't want to say what she's forgotten, but Elio's eyes drop to her empty utility belt, and he raises an eyebrow.

He leads the others into the bay. Oskar hesitates before he passes her. "Are you okay?"

"Fine." She makes herself smile. "Go ahead. I'll be right there."

She clambers back up the stairs and slips inside. *You have to be smarter than this, Sol. Quit worrying so much about the others and focus on the mission. Some mistakes you can't come back from.* She collects her weapon and returns to the stairway. She starts down, then stops. Something isn't right. Yet the bay appears just as she left it.

The answer comes too late. Several of her crewmates exclaim, their cries loud in her open comm. Sol's eyes jerk up. The crew remains grouped together but has stopped moving across the hangar floor toward an airlock. The space around them shivers like a mirage on a rainswept road. A frisson of blue energy has surged up in a square around them. At each corner rests a cube. Sol recognizes the cubes from the Biosphere, gray like the floor and barely noticeable—portable energy field fences the botanists use to protect plants.

In one of the first colonist lectures, Command warned people to leave the energy fields alone, that touching one would deliver a shock powerful enough to knock you out. The transition tube into the Biosphere had flashed similar warnings on its vid panels. She reaches the hangar floor and stands uncertainly in the shadows next to the *Goose*. Part of her wants to rush to her friends and power down the cubes. Another part realizes someone must have set a trap activated by remote control.

Anton knows they're here. He's probably in the airlock with his people, watching through its small window. Sol's team fell for his trick so easily. Still, she might have time to reach them. Even as she thinks this, the airlock opens, and a group of Earthers armed with PulseLock guns and wearing spacesuits and helmets emerge.

Sol ducks beneath the shuttle and stares. Horror stops her breath. She wants to *do* something, but getting captured won't help. Her friends turn toward the newcomers as Anton leads his crew into the bay. She knows him by the way he holds himself. He shouts for the intruders to stand down and drop their weapons or his people will increase the force field. Make it so hot they'll fry. Can he do that? She doesn't know. Zavi might, but he stays quiet.

Sol looks on, heart in her throat. Oskar discards his weapon last, and she's praying he won't defy Anton. In the end, he complies without a glance toward her. Anton signals one of his men to take down the field. Orion, she thinks. He pushes buttons on the black remote he holds. Then the Earthers prod Oskar and the others into the airlock.

Sol crouches near the *Goose*, frozen in place. She never imagined this. A million scenarios, but never that the others would be captured, leaving her alone. Her original plan was to come aboard with a small team, to pick off the Earthers one by one or maybe capture Anton and hold him as leverage. That plan wouldn't have worked, either. At least she's escaped the trap. For now.

What can she do? *Follow them, of course.* But if she tries, they might spot her and capture her, too. No. She has to be smart. Smarter than Anton, for once. How can she track the Earthers without being noticed? The answer is simple, and despite her terror, Sol smiles.

There's a chance to save her crew. Anton didn't space them right off, so maybe he's decided to interrogate them first. He'll know Sol escaped his poison. Somehow, she's sure of this. And she's also certain he wants her. The cat never gives up on the mouse until it has the creature between its teeth.

She goes back inside the *Goose* and makes her way to engineering, rummaging until she finds a toolbox with a set of screwdrivers. She isn't sure what size she needs, so she takes them all. When she slips into the airlock, it's empty. There's another glass window that looks into the hallway. She peers out while the room fills with breathable air. A green light flashes, and Matilda's voice announces that it's safe to remove her mask.

Sol keeps it on for now. She steps into a deserted hallway and finds a vent near her knees. She removes the vent cover, then crawls inside and pulls it back into place. The screen wants to dislodge without its screws, but she wedges a screwdriver between the scrubbers and the wall, holding it in place.

Sol sits back against the aluminum alloy ducting and wipes sweat from her face. She collects herself. Breathes. She feels safer now, yet she can't rest. Her friends might not have much time before Anton decides they aren't useful and disposes of them. She brings up the Venter map on her maintenance app, considers where to look first, and crawls forward.

43

Solast

Soon the small duct intersects with a larger one, and Sol's able to walk hunched over. She considers messaging her crew, then decides it's too risky. Their Skinpads might be monitored, and surprise is a weapon she needs. She heads for the brig on Red Deck since it's close and the likeliest place to take prisoners. Her polymer faceplate fogs, and her magnetic boots weigh every step on the metal walkway. Even though the ship should be pumping out new air, she isn't convinced it's safe to breathe yet.

Each time Sol passes a vent cover, she checks for signs of crystal residue. After the third failed sighting, it occurs to her that there won't be any residue, but there might be a discarded package. At the fourth opening, she finds an empty baggie wedged between the scrubber and metal cover. She doesn't touch it, just takes a few pictures with the simple camera that's part of her Skinpad.

She checks her map, moves on, and tries not to think about Juke, who hated this job as much as part of Sol liked it. Not the cleaning, but the clambering through secret passageways like a spider or a ghost. Soon she comes to the brig. There's a security checkpoint with an unguarded console. Her map shows a hallway leading to a line of cells, each equipped with an air vent. She finds her crew isolated from one another: Mila lying down on a cot, Elio pacing, Clera staring into space, Zavi bent over, head in hands, Niklas much the same. And Oskar.

She peers down through his cell's vent screen and remembers the last time she studied him unawares in his office. He paces, arms crossed, face drawn with worry. *For me,* she realizes with a jolt. She wants to call down to him but catches sight of a tiny camera in the corner. Of course, there will be security cams. She doubts the Earthers will take time to check them, yet if they do, she can't let them spot Oskar talking into the vent. It's possible Anton doesn't know she came aboard, and she needs that advantage.

Sol watches Oskar for another moment. Her chest pinches in a way that feels more like love than fear. More like hope than despair. She'll save him or die trying. Her need for retribution is an afterthought. Oskar drives the shadows back.

She can sit there watching him and wanting him, or she can act. So far, her friends look unharmed. What if Anton decides to interrogate his prisoners, though? She reverses direction and heads toward the bridge. Ten minutes later, she's looking down at consoles and screens and swivel chairs through various vents. Her heart leaps. The Earthers are there, masks hanging from utility belts, identities exposed. She recognizes the Venter crew and lets her gaze linger on Anvil. Anger ignites. *Did you kill Juke yourself, or did someone else do it?*

Two of the group wear white wristbands, another a red one. She recognizes none of these Earthers. The whites are explaining the workstations scattered across the bridge. She listens in and puts two and two together. *They must be planning to take* Calliope *back through the ARH and return to Earth, but then what?* Elio thought Matilda could do much of the navigating. Still, it'll be wise for this skeleton crew to have a basic sense of how the ship flies.

Sol scans the group, looking for Anton and not finding him. *Where is he?*

She quickly discards the idea of dropping down through a vent into the middle of the Earthers. True, their looks of astonishment would send vicious pleasure coursing through her, but only until they put guns against her skin and released disruptor pulses to fry her brain and stop her heart. No, she's got to pick her foes off one by one ... or kill the head of the snake. Without Anton, the others might not pose such a threat.

She wavers. Should she return to the brig for her friends? Then she remembers her stolen knockout gun, safe in her cabin aboard the *Goose*. *Strike two, idiot!* Sol shakes off self-recrimination and thinks hard. Eleven bad guys versus seven wanna-be heroes. Not great odds. She decides to look for Anton. He's probably alone, and maybe she can take him by surprise. If she captures him, she'll have a bargaining chip.

The Biosphere seems like a good place to search first. Sol climbs down a duct ladder leading to Blue Deck. Through vents at her feet, she glimpses bodies piled in corners. The Earthers have been cleaning up when not attending *How to Fly Starships for Dummies* class.

She moves from vent to vent, and the bar, Smoke and Ashes, appears below her—a dim rectangle of tables lit by recessed lights. One more vent, and there's Anton. He sits alone at the bar, a plastic, made-for-space bottle of real whiskey tucked under his arm. He unscrews the lid, tips the bottle against his lips, squeezes, and neatly sucks in a mouthful.

Sol stares down at his dark head and bulky shoulders. If only she could crash through the grate and land on him, push her PulseLock gun into his neck, and blast away until his neural pathways severed. But in zero-g, there will be no "crashing."

She heads to the next cover, which looks down into a kitchen area. It'll have to do. She frees a screen, grips the edge of the hole, and uses her arms to push her body through. She nudges the ceiling and drifts away from it. Her boots snap to the floor and anchor her.

Sol reaches for her gun and turns toward the door that leads behind the bar. She crouches, listening. Now what?

Anton sits facing her on the other side of the wall. He'll notice her the moment she walks through the entryway.

A voice drifts toward her from the bar. "I know you're in there. You might as well come out. Don't make me chase you down. You know you'll lose."

Fec all!

His voice makes her brain itch. Anger, fear, and pain fight for dominance. She pushes them aside, sucks in a breath, and walks through the portal. She finds herself in the narrow area behind the bar. Wipes, bottles of various liquids, a recycling bin, and stainless-steel refrigerators take up most of the space. Everything is battened down with little room to maneuver.

Anton sits a short distance from her. He tilts his head, the mockery of a smile spreading across his face. "Well, well. I guessed it would be you. I looked for your body as we cleaned up, but I never found you. Now I know why."

Sol stares back, mute. She can't very well pulse the feccing hell out of Anton from across a countertop. He'll see it coming and get out of the way—or pulse her first.

He doesn't seem to mind her silence, simply gestures toward the whiskey and says, "Why don't you join me for a drink. It's real Glenlivet, not that piss poor stuff they pawn off as alcohol up here. I've been saving it for just such a moment."

"I think I'll stay where I am." She hates his fake charm. His bland face. His smarmy voice.

"Suit yourself." He toasts her and drinks. "Want to explain how you escaped the gas?"

"Not really."

"Did that boy, Juke, tip you off? I thought we got to him before he had a chance. If we didn't, I've gotten careless."

"Did you kill him?"

Anton shrugs. "One life is worth very little in the whole scope of things. My life. Your life. Juke's. There are bigger issues at stake. The fate of Earth, for one."

"How does killing almost every colonist aboard *Calliope* serve that purpose? And what about *Lycka*? What about *Loki*? I don't get it." Her voice rises like a teakettle ready to blow. *Steady, Sol.*

"Ah, so you figured out what we did on *Lycka*? And on *Loki*? I have no idea what happened to that ship, by the way. There's been no word." He props his elbows on the counter's edge. "As for the other vessels, I believe you *do* understand. Come on, Solast. You tell me."

Coldness congeals in her belly. That's how he spoke to her when he trained her in martial arts. *Come on, little Sol. You tell me what you did wrong. Then try again.* She says coldly, "Killing the colonists sends a message that fleeing from a dying planet won't work. There's no choice but to stay and fix things or die trying."

He raises his bottle. "Exactly. Well done."

She grits her teeth. "Why are you going back? You'll be the most wanted man on the planet. There won't be anywhere you can hide."

"True, perhaps. But imagine this. My crew passes through the ring, skirts Mars, and eventually enters Earth's orbit. Because it's impossible to communicate past the ARH, no one back home knows what happened. They'll be unsuspecting when we set *Calliope* on a collision course with New Chicago, then bail out in escape pods. Can you imagine the explosion? It'll be better than President Bendurin's birthday fireworks. With any luck, no one will ever know what happened. We'll be 'dead' men, not 'wanted' men. Now that's a freeing thought." He takes another swig of whiskey. "Sure you don't care for some?"

"What about the colonists in the brig? What's your plan for them? For me?"

"You could join us, little Sol."

The old name makes her cringe. "Don't call me that."

"You didn't always hate me. We were almost friends once. You were my best pupil. My greatest success. If your father hadn't gone crazy and tried to kill me, who knows how far you'd have risen. You could have been my lieutenant and lived for a nobler goal than revenge."

"I don't call it noble to slaughter innocents," she replies flatly. *Keep him talking.* A crazy idea forms in her brain. Sol grips the ledge, then bends down. "Maybe I will have that drink, but I'm not sharing a bottle with you." Pretending to search for a cup, she unfastens her right boot. "Wait. That one's dirty." She frowns and unfastens the left. Her feet feel loose inside them. A gentle push, and she'll float right out.

Anton slides to the seat directly across from her, takes her covered glass, and awkwardly manages to transfer the Glenlivet into it, though a few amber drops float off into space. "*Salud,*" he says, and knocks his bottle against her cup.

Sol swallows a mouthful. It burns, and she chokes back a cough.

"I didn't take you for a sipper," Anton says.

"Are you kidding? I haven't had a real drink in years. I'm going to savor it."

"That's right. You were living on the street. How in all hells did you manage to hitch a ride on *Calliope*?"

"How did you?" she counters. Sol wiggles her toes, nudging her feet almost free of the boots.

"Credits. Lots of them. You, on the other hand, must have snuck aboard."

"I'm sorry now that I did. It was a stupid idea thinking I could get you alone and kill you." She hides the simmer of rage.

"How did you even know I was here? I used an alias. Kept the whole thing quiet."

Sol shrugs and tells the truth. "I overheard you making the deal in the back hall of Smoke and Blues." She glances around. "Looks a lot like this place. Gave me a clue I could find you here."

His eyes follow hers, then snap back. "One of my guys fixed it up special. I missed that bar, thought I could recreate it, but you can never go back."

"No, you can't."

Now, Sol. She thrusts against the floor with her legs. The movement hurtles her toward the ceiling. Her arms take the impact, and she pushes off again. Sol ping pongs straight at Anton's head. She lands on his back and grapples with him.

He jumps up and reaches for the weapon at his waist, but she's trapped his arms. Before he can free himself, her PulseLock gun drives into his neck.

The weapon makes a puffing noise when she pulls the trigger. Anton goes rigid, then jerks back to life. He fumbles for her. She pulses him again. And again. Each time, his body spasms and arcs before life returns. He tries to speak but can't process words. Not with electromagnetic disruptors cutting through his neural pathways. A strangled sound gushes out of Anton—half anguish, half fury.

He knocks his stool from its magnetic base, and it floats off to crash into a table. He backs away from the bar, bucking. She clings like a barnacle. Another squeeze of the trigger. Another muscle spasm. Anton's jerky movements propel him toward the floor, but his grav boots hold him upright.

Suddenly, the tension goes out of him. He quiets, and the acid tang of urine wafts toward her. He's unconscious.

It takes supreme control to pull her gun away from Anton's neck. Part of her wants to keep blasting until his heart stops. That was the plan, right? Was it a *good* plan, though? Anton will prove useful as leverage only if he's alive. Her friends are still prisoners, and she may need him.

She untangles her limbs from his body and keeps hold of him while she searches for cuffs on his utility belt. The Earthers all had them when they captured her friends, but Anton only watched as his minions led the *Goose*'s crew away. *Yes!* She clips the cuffs on his wrists and tightens them, then stands back, trembling. His slack face and parted lips enrage her anew—almost tip her over a line she doesn't want to cross. Not yet, anyway. Sol reaches for detachment. *Pretend he's a patient. A stranger.* She feels for a pulse.

It's there, though faint. He'll be out for a while. She could have killed him, yet she'd stopped herself. Sure, it was the practical thing. The rational thing. Maybe there's another reason she stopped herself, though. *You aren't a killer. You never were, just pretended you could be.*

What now? Her friends are still in the brig. Time's running out to save them. She needs to get back there before the Earthers do.

44

Solast

Sol leaves Anton and launches toward the bar. She works her way back to her boots and slips them on, too shocked to feel elation, too aware of danger for relief. She sucks down her whiskey, which is nothing like throwing back a shot on Earth. It helps her thoughts settle, though.

Anton will have to come with her. If she leaves him in the bar, some Earther might find him.

She returns to him and unfastens his grav boots. With a little prodding, he lifts free. Sol grabs his collar and tugs him after her. It's easy until she reaches the duct ladder that leads to Red Deck. Taking the lifts would have been simpler, but it's too dangerous. Where are the Earthers now? On Red Deck? The bridge? Torturing her friends in the brig? Sol longs to move faster, but pulling Anton along in tight quarters doesn't allow for speed.

At least this gives her time to plan. She decides to stop in the hangar bay and retrieve the force field fencing the Earthers left behind. Leaving Anton wedged at an intersection, Sol enters the airlock, then the bay. The cubes are still there.

Sol relaxes a bit. Her plan won't work without the containment field. She collects the cubes and returns to Anton. He's still passed out, but his pulse beats stronger. She releases his cuffs and brings his arms to his belly, then shackles him again. The cubes fit snugly beneath his biceps. *Thanks,*

Anton. Once again, she considers killing him. No. This plan is best. Later, they can hold a trial, perform an execution.

Sol drags Anton through the ducts by his collar while she reviews her idea. It will go sideways if the Earthers beat her to the brig. *If. If. If.* No sense worrying. She draws a calming breath and checks the duct map. Step by step, she heads toward the cells. When Sol reaches a vent above the bridge, she peers down. Listens. Shifts to another screen to look for movement below. She finds nothing. The Earthers have left.

Sol works her way to the brig's security station, half expecting to find Anton's people there, but it's quiet. She unscrews the vent cover and propels Anton and herself to the floor. The guard checkpoint contains a workstation and storage compartments which she missed earlier. Nothing else. Ten paces away sits the hallway leading to the cells.

Sol pushes Anton behind the workstation, secures him under the desk, and pries the force field boxes from his arms. She has no remote like her enemies used, so she studies the cubes. A button labeled SET somehow secures a box to the floor. Another labeled ON activates the field. She places them as far apart as she can, keeping one with her at the security station so she can stay hidden while she activates it.

Anton's crew must come here eventually. Should she check the cells? Alert the others? Gag Anton so he can't cry out if he awakens? Before she can do anything, voices erupt in the main corridor.

Sol ducks down and tries not to panic. A portal slides open, and the Earthers enter. She counts them. *Ten. And Anton makes eleven.* Maybe they were supposed to meet him here at a prearranged time. Her finger hovers over the ON button. *Wait for it.* The Earthers drift into the space between boxes. They talk among themselves, relaxed, oblivious to the force field cubes.

At least until JoJo calls out, "Hey, how did those get in here?"

Sol activates the field. A translucent blue wall of light jumps toward the ceiling. It ripples like water flowing uphill. For a second, Sol enjoys the Earthers' fear-filled exclamations. Then she springs up next to the workstation and calls, "Hello, there."

They don't hear her, so she raises her voice and tries again. One by one, the Earthers turn in her direction.

Something blurs in Sol's peripheral vision. *What the—.* A fist plows into her jaw. She hits the floor, left hip first, the gun trapped beneath, her left arm flung above her head. Before she can bounce up again, a boot presses against her midsection.

Her head swims until pain brings clarity rushing back. Daggers pound into her bruised jaw, and she tastes blood.

The other grav boot rests next to her head. Sol's gaze travels upward to meet Anvil's. Somehow, she didn't think he would be her attacker. *Juke's friend. The big, dumb boy toy.* She gropes for Anton's utility belt with her left hand. Fingers scrabble, and her palm settles on something hard.

Anvil says, "You. Juke's friend."

"Traitor," she spits back. *Keep him talking.* "You killed him."

"No." His eyes alight with rage, pain ... and guilt, maybe? "I liked him. Even when he snooped too hard and got caught, I stood up for him. Almost got nixed myself. Why did you make him spy on us?"

Sol forces words past her swelling mouth. "Why did you Earthers have to kill everyone? I thought you were all about *saving* the planet. Doesn't that include its citizens?" Her fingers encircle Anton's PulseLock gun and tug gently.

"Mons Vega says you sometimes have to do bad things for the greater good. When we go back, Earth will see running away is hopeless, and people will have to actually fix things like they should have a long time ago."

"He's tricking you, Anvil. Can't you feel it? Anton is crazy." She doesn't want to hurt him. *Even now.*

"He's not crazy! Everyone else is, including you! Why did you trap them? What's to gain? You don't even have Mons Vega penned behind that force field. Did you know that? He's too slippery, and he'll show up any minute. Then you'll be sorry."

Up to that moment, Sol wasn't sure Anton was truly hidden.

Anvil clenches his fists and glances at his corralled companions.

"Waste her!" someone yells from inside the barrier, and several others echo the sentiment.

But Anvil's no killer. Sol sees his indecision, watches his expression waver between scorn, bravado, and something deeper—a sorrow she recognizes. It's her own. She's carried it ever since her father died, and it keeps her from using the hidden PulseLock gun.

Until his boot digs into her ribs.

Sol twists and shoves the gun against Anvil's thigh. She squeezes the trigger. He goes rigid but doesn't let up, so she hits him with another pulse. And another. That does it. His eyes roll back, and he slumps. She slides away and staggers to her feet. Her cheek throbs. From inside the trap she set, the Venters hurl insults, but she barely hears them.

A workstation tablet lights up at her touch, and she locates the cells. Unsure which ones hold her crew, she opens them all. A menu choice called "Security Cameras" brings up black and white feeds of her friends' disbelieving faces as their doors buzz open. Moments later, they trickle into the security checkpoint. Clera spots Sol and cries her name.

Sol sees Oskar, and her heart flipflops. His eyes meet hers and flicker with relief. He edges around the force field's perimeter to reach her. "You found us. I was afraid you'd been taken." His knuckles brush her jaw. "You're hurt."

She winces. "Anvil clocked me. I thought I had them all inside the cubes, but I missed one."

Oskar's eyes drift down to the unconscious men at her feet. The corners of his lips rise. "Remind me not to get on your bad side."

She's too distracted to respond. "We need to get the Earthers into the cells. Let's start with these two." She nudges Anton with her foot. "He's bound, but Anvil isn't. He might wake up a *little* angry."

Sol endures the others' thanks, hugs, and questions while they fill empty cells with new prisoners. Clera located the crew's PulseLock guns in the storage compartments, and it was easy to herd their captives into detainment after that. No one seemed eager to experience a neural disruptor after they saw what Sol did to Anvil.

Back at the security station, Zavi gathers the force field cubes and raises an eyebrow at Sol. "And I thought these things were only good for protecting plants." He stores them in the compartment alongside more pulse guns and a first aid kit.

Oskar never leaves Sol's side. Part of her likes his closeness. Another part still isn't sure about him. The aftereffects of her adrenaline rush have left her exhausted, but the others have questions. She answers them all.

Finally, Clera says, "It's lucky you forgot your weapon aboard the *Blue Goose*. I hate to think—" She shakes her head and switches gears. "We should go back to the bridge and try to send a message to Earth. They might not get it right away, but there needs to be a record of what happened here."

Sol hears the unspoken words: *In case we don't survive to tell anyone. In case no one else ever ventures out here to find us.*

While Mila rests in one of the bridge's console chairs, Niklas, Oskar, and Zavi go in search of food and drink. Elio examines the pilot's control station, Clera watching over his shoulder. Sol sinks into a padded leather seat and leans her head back. What next? She has no answers. A picture of her father floats before her. *I kept my promise. Even though Anton lives, vengeance is ours, Father. You would have been proud of me.*

His voice drifts out of the past. *I was always proud of you, Sol.*

She's lived and breathed her need for revenge. It's been her sustenance, but her father is beyond caring. *He's dead. At peace. It's you who lives. You who still dreams of slit throats and blood soaking the earth. You who were left alone to survive in a world that didn't want you.* Now that world is gone. The green planet awaits beyond *Calliope*'s viewscreens.

If Sol's no longer an avenging angel, what is she? Maybe it's time to find out.

45

Clera

Elio looks up from the pilot's console and tells Clera, "Looks like the Earthers programmed a return route to Earth. At the moment, *Calliope* is set to maintain orbit, but they were ready to turn her around and head back through the wormhole."

She leans against the pilot's chair. "What did they hope to gain? They couldn't exactly hide aboard a giant starship."

Elio rubs his chin. "No, but they *could* set this ship on a collision course with some part of Earth they really hated … NASA headquarters maybe? Or the White House? Then use the remaining escape pods to bail out."

"You think that was their plan?"

He shrugs. "We'll have to question them. Maybe they'll tell us, and maybe they won't."

"We're *not* going to torture them."

Elio knocks her hands off his chair as he swivels to face her. "What do you think I am, sister? A monster?"

"Well, you *have* been trained by the Security forces." She studies his face, trying to remember the little boy, the reckless teenager, the brother who was her only anchor after their mama died. When had he become a man?

"I'm trained to defend myself. To fly shuttles. Navigate, okay? Geez."

"Okay." She grins. "You know I wasn't serious about the torture, right?"

"But what do we do now? We can't stay up here on *Calliope*. I don't want to fly back to Earth. Can we establish a colony all by ourselves? There were supposed to be thousands of us, and it'll be a long time before reinforcements arrive."

"Of course we can settle Vishnu. We've survived this long, right?" Clera ruffles his hair, then steps away before he can retaliate. "We have you. A Martian expert. A botanist and a biologist. A mechanic, a medic, and me." She winces. "Out of everyone, I'm the most useless."

"Not true." Elio frowns up at her. "You have enough heart for all of us. Mila and I wouldn't be here if not for you. You're cool under pressure, think things through, and know how to deal with people."

"The perfect leader, right?" she jokes.

"*Yes,*" he replies in perfect seriousness. "You're always selling your-self short."

"Well, I'm still learning how to stand up and fight. How to be brave like you."

Elio takes her hand. "You're the bravest person I know." He hesitates, then continues, "Mama would be proud of us. We're going to make it out here, and we'll build something better than we had on Earth. We won't take anything for granted."

She presses his hand before drawing back. Mila snores softly in a chair near the viewport. "Maybe you should go find your girlfriend a real place to sleep. There must be officers' quarters up here some-where."

Clera and Elio find the posh rooms reserved for top brass. Her skin prickles when she thinks of the dead men and women who occupied these cabins so recently. They find no bodies, but a lived-in aura permeates the officers' cabins, and she'll be happy to get back to Vishnu even if they have to sleep in tents.

They return to the bridge just as Niklas, Zavi, and Oskar return from foraging below deck, arms laden with food and water. They hold an impromptu feast in a conference room down the hall from the bridge, where Sol fields more questions.

"So Anton *did* plan to return to Earth." Clera shares a look with her brother. She imagines New Chicago burning. Much of it was already a crumbling junkpile. Anton would have made it an ash heap.

After they finish eating, she suggests feeding the prisoners and starts collecting food pouches. She leads the way to the brig with Sol beside her carting water. Zavi and Oskar insisted on coming along though two people would have been enough to perform this task. Clera doesn't mind. She likes this protective side of Zavi. He told her flat out she wasn't going anywhere near the Earthers without him. But there's no danger. She won't be opening cell doors, just sliding food and water through slots near the floor.

They pause inside the guard room that leads to the cells. A mix of emotions flicker across Sol's face: determination, resignation, and a strange eagerness. They pass the security workstation and head down a hallway to the first cell. Through the peephole, Clera sees a woman asleep on a cot. She locates a speaker box beside the door and says into the mic, "We have a meal for you. Hello in there?"

The Venter doesn't move. Sol bangs her PulseLock gun against the titanium door. Still nothing.

Clera turns away. "Something's wrong." A niggling premonition makes her shiver.

Sol peers into the cell for a long moment. When she backs away, she's pale, her mouth a thin line.

"What?" Oskar grips her arm while Zavi pushes forward to look in.

"They didn't have weapons on them when we locked them up, did they?" Sol asks.

"Of course not." Clera looks from her to the men, but both seem flummoxed.

Sol stabs the door release with an index finger. Before anyone can stop her, she steps into the cell and strides toward the cot. No hesitation. No caution.

Oskar hurries after. Clera starts to follow, but Zavi's hand clamps down on her elbow. "Wait."

Sol kneels next to the bunk and puts two fingers against the Earther's neck. No one breathes until she twists around and says in clipped tones, "This one's dead. I'm betting they all are."

Zavi's grip relaxes, and Clera rushes to Sol's side. Her friend pushes unsteadily to her feet. When Oskar reaches for her, a fierce look makes him back off. "I should have thought of this. Stupid. Stupid." She knocks a fist against her forehead.

"Tell us what you know." Zavi's mild tone makes her blink.

Sol points at the dead woman's arm, where a rolled-back sleeve reveals a Skinpad. "She had a suicide hack. I'm betting they all did."

"Explain." Clera avoids glancing at the Venter's bloodless face and staring eyes.

"It's a hidden code you can buy on the black market. Juke would have known. He'd have thought of this. If you want to kill yourself, you just open a hidden file on your pad and type in the code. The Skinpad sends electromagnetic overload through your system. It's a quick death."

"Why?" Clera stammers. She hadn't meant for anyone to die. She hadn't known what to do with their prisoners, but they'd have figured something out.

Sol ignores the question. She mutters, "We better check the rest of them," and hurries out of the cell. Clera rushes after her, the others close behind. They discover unresponsive bodies in every cell but one. Anton's.

They stare at him through the reinforced glass window of the door. He's sitting up, waiting for them, hands folded and expression distant.

His gaze shifts and sharpens when Sol opens the cell. Clera catches the glint of fanaticism there, the misguided fervor of a true believer. She chides herself for wanting to run away. He's no threat now, and it's Sol his attention centers on anyway. She strides into the cell.

"What are you doing?" Oskar rasps in alarm.

She spares him a brief glance. "It's all right. Keep your gun trained on him." She holds her own PulseLock tightly.

They follow her into the cell and form a half circle around Mons Vega, Prophet of the Earth. He smirks at Sol. The rest of them might as well be furniture. Clera sticks close to her friend and hopes she's not underestimating Anton Cheverra.

Sol says, "You made them kill themselves, didn't you." The monotone words belie a cold rage.

Anton shrugs. "They knew the risks when they joined my inner circle. If we were ever compromised, we'd use the kill switch. Better to self-destruct than have our plans revealed to the world."

"Then why didn't you punch *your* code?" Sol asks.

"I was waiting for you, little one."

"Don't call me that. I was never ... that."

"No?" Anton raises an eyebrow. "You were always my favorite pupil. Yet never a true Earther, I see now. Your father was, but not you. And he wavered. Lost the faith."

Sol replies with an evenness that sends chills down Clera's back. "I think trying to kill you was the least crazy thing he did after my mother died."

"Ridge certainly wasn't thinking about his only child when he attacked me," Anton counters.

If the words wound her, Sol keeps it hidden. "That's true. But I'm glad he did it. Or tried, at least. We should all have something bigger than ourselves to fight for. Something bigger than our families."

"What did you have?" Anton waves a dismissive hand. "This need for revenge that's fueled your life since you left the commune seems a paltry goal. I've been trying to save the Earth, but you? What larger calling have you followed? You can murder me." He nods toward her weapon. "Yet will that fill the hole in your chest? Your father will still be dead, little one." The endearment burns through the air like lightning.

Clera grits her teeth. Oskar looks grave, Zavi concerned.

Sol smiles. "You think I care about you? That I'm still the girl who ran from the commune, who hid in the Barrens and sought you for years in the capital? I'm not. I don't need to kill you anymore. Your death doesn't have to free me because I've already freed myself."

They stare at each other as if no one else exists. The moment expands into a universe of frigid silence. Anton's eyes widen like he's just realized something.

He scowls at Sol's words. His ego probably demands he be hated, feared, worshiped. He likely *wanted* Sol to seek revenge, to eventually find him so he could punish her just like he did her father. Only he'd draw it out, make her suffer. He can't now because Sol has changed. She's not a stowaway. She's a medic, a colonist, a part of something bigger than herself.

Anton reaches for his Skinpad, his sleeve already raised. His fingers touch his forearm.

"No!" Sol lunges toward him, but Oskar holds her back.

In seconds, Anton has completed the suicide code. He must have had the secret app open and ready, Clera realizes. Zavi's arm settles across her shoulder and draws her against his side. Anton goes rigid. A strange smile wreathes his face. Then his eyes roll up. He spasms briefly and slumps.

Oskar releases Sol, and she darts forward to kneel beside the Earther. Though he was a fanatic and a killer, she bows her head and weeps.

———◦———

Later, Clera finds Sol on the deserted bridge, staring out at Vishnu, hands behind her back. "Sol?"

"I'm fine. You can join me if you want."

Sol doesn't turn, but Clera senses a storm has passed and walks closer. They look out at their new home shoulder to shoulder. Clouds wrap the planet like wispy garlands. Emerald seas vie for dominance against the darker green forests and chalky plateaus.

Sol says, "You probably don't understand why I would cry for a man I hated."

"It's not my place to ask."

"I'm not crazy, if that's what you think."

"I don't."

"My feelings are ... complex. I guess I never really grieved for my father. Or not for long. Instead, I put all that sadness into a tight little package wrapped in fury. It was easier to feel mad than empty. The mad filled me up and helped me survive. But now …"

"When Anton died, it was like seeing the last bit of your father vanish forever."

"Yes." Sol sighs. She turns to look at Clera, eyes red-rimmed but smile radiant. "You *do* understand."

"Is it horrible that part of me rejoices the Earthers are gone? I didn't know what we were going to do with them. We couldn't trust them, and I didn't want to be looking over my shoulder if we let them go. I didn't want to keep them locked up forever, either."

Sol shrugs. "That's the life of a leader, I guess. You get to make the hard decisions."

Clera shakes her head. "I don't know why everyone keeps insisting I'm in charge."

"Maybe because the rest of us don't want to be. We'll help, though. You're good with people. A lot better than me. I'd elect you mayor of our new colony."

Clera laughs. "We're going to need a name for it." She turns her attention back to the green globe with its spangling of alien rings.

"Ask Niklas. He seems to have come up with quite a lot of ideas in the months he spent alone on Vishnu."

"He told you that?"

"No. I've barely spoken to him, but I caught a glance at one of his old-fashioned journals."

"Before long, we're going to know each other all too well, even without snooping in private journals." Clera releases her breath. "Can we do this? Make a life with just the seven of us? I mean, even if Earth sends more colonists, it'll be a while until they arrive. Other Earthers are out there.

Look at what happened to *Lycka*. We don't know the fate of those saboteurs. Maybe they're still around."

"First of all, there are about to be *eight* of us. And I'm not going to worry about the future. For the first time in a long time, I'm going to settle into the *now* and see how it feels to live without plans and plots chasing each other through my head."

Clera squeezes Sol's shoulder. They stand companionably at the viewport, their forms reflected in the glass like two ghosts. No, not ghosts. Determined pioneers. "I think that's a great idea."

Day 220

It's high time I put this into words, and let posterity forgive my delusion if that's what it was.

There's one alien life form I have not mentioned, though it's long been on my mind—the first I encountered on this beautiful, dangerous, mysterious planet.

I was swimming in the sea some months ago when I felt a brush against my leg. I turned and came face to face with a creature thick as three men, with a long snout, flared nostrils, and a mane of tentacles. These shimmered in every known shade of blue and green. Beneath the skin of that bony face, bioluminescent lights blinked in patterns akin to Morse Code. A finned tail acted as rudder to that long, sinuous body. The creature seemed able to appear and disappear at will. Due to this "magical" property, I've named it a water dragon. *Note: this animal bears a strong resemblance to pictures painted on Martian artifacts.

And yes, it's entirely possible that such alien works of art inspired this fever dream. Still, the possibility of dragons has kept me from swimming out past the shoals since that first encounter.

-N.J.

46

Niklas

It takes days to remove the remaining dead from *Calliope*'s hallways. Niklas and the others walk around tight-lipped and slump-shouldered. By the end, Niklas is numb to the lifeless bodies. He still feels a twinge watching them float into space, however. They're empty shells, but part of him wants to bury them, to exhaust himself with shovel and dirt, to show them they mattered.

The crew removes Juke from the morgue and sends him into the black accompanied by the beat-heavy music Elio calls Chicago Juke. A few of the crew weep, but Niklas didn't know Juke. He only cries when he and the others return to *Lycka* for more body disposals, and he discovers people he knew sprawled in hallways.

On *Lycka*, Elio stumbles upon a berth filled with dead Earthers. Unlike *Calliope*'s Earthers, this group had no intention of surviving their attack. They left a message looping across a vid screen followed by photos of icebergs breaking away from floes, forests burning, islands drowning, and towns turned to tinder by tornadoes. *You can't escape. Better to stay and fix your mess.* Over and over it played while the cult members activated suicide codes and martyred themselves.

On both starships, Clera takes charge of entering names of the dead into the logs. Elio converses with the AI they call Matilda to make sure the ship will maintain orbit until they next return from Vishnu. *Lycka's* auto-pilot proves more difficult to communicate with. She'll stay aloft for a time but eventually sink into the green planet's atmosphere and break apart. Is that what happened to *Loki*? No one knows.

Mila checks over *Calliope's* many systems. Though her expertise lies in mechanics, she seems to intuitively grasp much of the ship's workings. Zavi and Clera tend to plants in the Biosphere. Unlike *Lycka's* Biosphere, this one didn't vent. No sub-zero cold froze the orchards and gardens. Though automated systems water the plants and supply light, there's still much to do. Nik fills in where he can but feels like an outsider.

This new team of his will return to *Calliope* many times to transfer building materials and other supplies to the colony on Vishnu. They found a transport vessel secured in the hangar bay that's large enough for big loads. Hopefully, its fuel will hold out long enough to fly everything down to the landing beach.

Sol helps Clera and Mila while Oskar loads his research tools and artifacts from Mars onto the *Goose*. Everyone straightens lounge areas, eating spaces, hallways. Niklas takes care of the chickens. He writes in his journal and searches for his old sense of himself. He's not alone anymore, and that's something. Yet he's different—a new man in an old skin.

Being with others eases the mild depression he's suffered since his last crew succumbed to the spores. Clera puts him in charge of naming everything on Vishnu, though she didn't need to. He'd already named hundreds of new species during his months of isolation, but now the christenings become official. Sun spinners and rock beetles. Thorny shield bark, palmeria, and shield ferns. These are just a few of the names he chooses. Their colony will be called Landing Bay, its location situated above the beach on a wide shelf of rock along the limestone cliffs and near the spring.

There's a rocky path down to a shallow, clear pool separated from the sea by a spine of rock.

Niklas longs to swim again, to feel water caressing his skin, to lie on his back in the buoyant waves and stare up at a turquoise sky which feels like a dream. Then he remembers the water dragon. *That* name isn't official. He hasn't mentioned it to the others, still isn't sure it's real. Maybe nothing is. He has no scar from his cut. Perhaps he hallucinated his stay in the cave, his poisoning, even the woman named Alice.

Petite Alice. Fair Alice. Kind Alice.

She's not the type of woman he'd normally fantasize about, though in his younger days, he'd chase anything with a skirt. *Younger? You're only thirty-three. Hardly an old man.* Yet he feels immeasurably aged.

Nik shakes off the glum thoughts that sporadically overtake him. Zavi's here. He swore they'd be reunited, and they have been. Thoughts of his cousin propel him toward the Biosphere. Zavi's often there with Clera, but today Niklas finds him alone, picking apples from the first crop of a fast-grow variety.

Nik's heart lifts. He attempts to sneak up on Zavi but steps on a fallen twig.

"Hey, Cl—" Zavi breaks off when he sees Niklas. A broad grin breaks over his face.

Niklas grins back. "I thought maybe you were disappointed I wasn't your girlfriend."

Zavi holds the apple bin against his stomach. "I'll never be disappointed to see you, Nik. There was a time I was sure we'd never meet again."

"You should have listened to me, eh?" Niklas sweeps a hand through his overgrown hair.

Zavi looks him over. "You all right, cuz? You were here a long time by yourself. It must have been hard."

"Yeah." Niklas lets that hang. The single word speaks more than lengthy explanations.

Zavi sets the bin down and steps forward, head cocked to one side. "Everything's okay now, right? We're here, and we can build a new life together. Nothing will ever separate us again."

Faces of lost friends swim before Nik's eyes. He blinks them away and musters up another grin. "Maybe you'll name your first baby after me. Nik if it's a boy, Nikola for a girl."

"I'm not thinking about kids yet! I don't even have a place to live."

"Mila and Elio didn't seem too concerned about that detail."

"I don't believe they planned their baby. Anyway, it takes time for the anti-pregnancy meds to wear off." He shrugs. "Truthfully, children are the last thing on my mind right now, though maybe they shouldn't be. There are so few of us. Perhaps in another year more colonists will come, but we can't be sure. Depends on how things are going on Earth ... and if we can warn them about the Earthers."

"How is Grandfather?" A picture of the old man forms in Niklas' head—white-maned and fierce as a lion.

"He was fine last I spoke to him, though he was calling himself 'too old for this trip,' something I haven't heard before. I'll admit I'm worried about him. He had to coerce me into leaving on *Calliope* by telling me it's what Mother and Father would have wanted—to have someone aboard who'll make sure this planet's protected better than we protected Earth."

Nik squeezes his cousin's shoulder, thinking how much Zavi has changed. Niklas remembers him as a lithe, not terribly athletic boy who grew more frail after his accident. *Everyone changes.* "I'm glad you came."

"Me, too. And I thought I was leaving Clera, yet here she is." The smile returns, full of wonder, as though Zavi can't believe his good luck.

Nik's heart twinges. It used to be just them. Girls came and went, but *this* woman, Clera, is different. "That's a story I haven't heard yet. Plenty of time for it later, though. I'm happy for you, little cuz." He squeezes Zavi's shoulder again. "Or maybe *not* so little anymore."

"Bet I could take you down in a wrestling match, Nik. Not like when we were kids and I never stood a chance." He surveys his cousin. "You've still got muscles but no style. Look at that hair! And your beard! All the animal life on Vishnu could be hiding in that nest! We need to find you a woman to clean you up."

The teasing banter trickles into silence. Loud is the unspoken fact that there are no available women. Everyone but Niklas has paired off. He breaks eye contact with Zavi and picks up the apple bin.

Zavi clears his throat. "Hey, more people will come. It's just a matter of time."

"You're right." They fall into step together on the path. Above them, the fake blue sky casts no shadows. Nik considers his new life on Vishnu. He'll be the namer of things. A founding father. Yet will he ever be an actual one? For the first time in his life, he might want to be.

Like Zavi said, they've got plenty of time. He should be grateful for what he has. Stay busy. Try to forget about water dragons and girls with serious eyes.

47

Solast

Sol stands at the viewport and watches the last bodies float away from *Calliope*. They become dolls, then specks, then nothing. The Earthers killed so many. Still, she pities them. They were drawn into a cult by a charismatic man and consumed by the mistaken belief that the Earth could be saved through destruction. Anton was wrong. No planet and no person can find salvation that way. For her, letting go is hate's answer. It allows peace to take hold and paves the way for joy.

Maybe that tiny figure who just disappeared into the void was Anton. She spent so much time seeking vengeance, yet there's no satisfaction in it. Satisfaction comes from practicing medicine again and helping others. It took her too long to realize this. Now that she has, she's lighter inside. Still, something's been bothering her.

Sol searches herself for that needling thorn. *Oskar.* She took a cabin by herself and has been so busy and emotionally drained that they've barely talked. She's felt him watching her, though. Maybe he's remembering their kisses. She hopes he is, anyway. And she hopes he can forget how she blamed him for losing her in that hallway when the mob separated them and Oskar made the choice to try and save everyone.

She loves that he thought of the whole ship rather than just himself. Sol wants a man with enough room in his heart to encompass everyone.

Someone who considers others before his own happiness. When she first met Oskar, he was lost, like her. Together, they are found. Despite their disparate backgrounds, they understand each other.

Tomorrow, the crew returns to Vishnu for good. They'll be stuck in tents or the tiny cabins on the *Goose* until habitats are built. But for one more night, they'll enjoy the Command suites off the bridge with their plush beds, fancy decor, and state-of-the-art tech. Sol turns from the viewscreen and heads to the cabin Oskar claimed. She knocks on the door, and he opens it.

In another world, perhaps he'd have been out, or she'd have lost her nerve. Maybe he'd tell her he wasn't interested in her anymore. But she's in this one, and Oskar stands before her fresh from a shower. The towel he clutches at his waist tries to float up. Grav boots hold him to the floor. Damp, uncombed hair curls over his ears, and frosted gray hair spreads across his chest. His muscles are still defined, his shoulders broad enough to rest her head against. And he's tall enough to make her look up. She likes that feeling of looking up.

"Can I come in?" she asks.

He blinks in surprise to find her there. It's hard to tell if he's pleased. In his quiet way, he says nothing, simply opens the door further and lets her duck under his arm. "I'll go get a suit on," he calls from behind.

"It's fine." She turns and allows her eyes to rove over his tall frame. She almost loses her nerve, but in the end, holds firm. After all, she's come this far. "You don't need to get dressed."

They stare at each other for a long moment. Then he steps forward, releases the towel, and cups her face with callused fingers. His thumbs trace the tops of her cheekbones. "I thought maybe you didn't want me anymore. After I lost you during the attack ..." He closes his eyes and lets out a breath.

"Hey, it's okay. I'm here. You're here. We both survived." She hesitates, then plunges on, "And now I want to live."

Does he get her meaning? Understand the code words for things she isn't sure how to voice? Suddenly, he's kissing her, and it's clear he speaks her language. His lips fit to hers and move across them in a way that sends shivers down her spine. Sol steadies herself with hands on his shoulders. Oskar's arms slide around her back. He pauses to murmur, "Sol, I …"

But she interrupts, "I've never done this before." Heat flames across her cheeks. "Sex, I mean. I just thought you should know."

Surprise spreads across his face. Then a smile tugs at his lips.

Sol stiffens, wondering if he's about to mock her, yet she doesn't pull away.

"You want to … with me."

"Well, yes." She squirms with mortification and desire.

"It's been a long time, but I think I remember how."

"You're making fun of me."

"I would never do that. You might murder me in my bed."

"That's not what I want to do to you in bed."

"Oh?" A teasing eyebrow lifts. "Show me, then."

"I thought you were the one with all the experience," she grumbles.

When he doesn't reply, just stands so still he might be a statue, she hesitantly leans up to kiss him. At the last minute, she pecks his cheek instead of his lips, then trails breathless kisses down his neck. She nips him gently, and he laughs.

"You know more than you think, Solast Bahri." Oskar pulls her so close that every part of her touches every part of him. He finds her lips again and kisses her harder, letting her know he wants her, too. Those lips promise that everything will be alright. When it comes to *this*, at least, she can't do anything wrong.

Somehow, her boots come off. Somehow, her suit follows. The towel between them dislodges and floats away. Oskar frees his legs from his own boots, and together they float up, twined about each other like kites tangled in a windless sky, miraculously held aloft by faith, hope, and the promise of a new future.

48

Solast

Sol stands atop the cliff overlooking Landing Bay. She faces the Emerald Sea, which shimmers like white-edged green satin beneath the red sun. A bank of clouds builds on the horizon. The crew will have to take shelter before the rains come. In the last few months, they've become accustomed to that necessity. Rock is always safe from the mysterious mushroom eruptions, but the spores spare no one. Luckily, they only remain airborne for a few hours, then settle, shrivel, and die.

It's fascinating to watch a rain shower pound against shivering palmeria out the windows of her fabricated home. The storms never last long, and the fungi erupt soon after. They explode from the damp earth like huge gray worms and writhe upwards, spreading their caps, opening ventricles that emit deadly spores in fluffy white clouds. The spores spread across the forest but can't hurt the waxy leaves, thorny bushes, or tough bark. If she continues to watch, she'll see the sun come out. Its rays dry the rubbery mushroom stalks. They shrink, fold in on themselves, and vanish below ground, leaving only dirt mounds to remind everyone of their secret, venomous presence.

Vishnu is so beautiful yet so deadly. Vast, fascinating, and scary. Sol now understands why they haven't seen animals on land other than the beetles that scurry under rocks along the beach. Their hard shells seem to protect them from spores. Animals without such armor were eradicated long ago—if they ever existed here.

The oceans, however, probably hold an abundance of life they've yet to discover. The sun spinners make their homes in kelp forests, tricky to catch but good eating. And lately the colonists have seen dolphin-like creatures that leap above the waves, chasing cloud banks and each other until storms drive them into the depths. Niklas names them stormrunners. He's named everything so far. Well, except for Mila's baby, who was born just last week. That red-faced, screaming little girl came into the world in a feisty rush and bears Sol's given name, Anna. It was an easy birth. A good omen. A promising start to the life they hope to build here.

Sol turns toward Landing Bay and brushes hair from her face. It's grown too long and gets in her eyes, but Oskar likes it that way, and she's obliging him for now. She stares down at the colony, a huddle of white prefab homes circling a central square. At its heart are smoking bonfire coals and a ring of benches. Her friends bustle about like ants, each engaged in the tasks that make Landing Bay work. There's more to do than hours in the day. Sol likes it that way.

She's been helping Zavi test plants for medicinal uses. She treats small cuts, checks on Mila and the baby, and organizes the back room of her home, which she's filling with medical supplies as fast as the transport shuttle delivers them. Oskar's place sits adjacent to hers. He didn't press her to live with him, and she didn't ask him to move into her quarters. That doesn't mean they don't share beds. This thing between them feels like a shoot growing from rich soil, stronger every day—something that might bloom if she lets it. If she's brave.

The *Blue Goose* and Niklas' shuttle sit down on the beach alongside the larger transport ship. Past them, just visible, is Nik. She shades her eyes and watches him splash through the surf barefoot, then stop to look out across the waves. He does that often, yet when Zavi suggests they go for a swim, he always shakes his head.

What happened to *Lycka*'s biologist all those months he was alone? Niklas doesn't say much. Sol thinks his melancholy expression has something to do with water. She never learned to swim, but she'd like to. Maybe Oskar will teach her. He used to surf off the coast of California. She'd like to cook, too, and wander the forest searching for new medicinal plants. Something unlocked inside her once Anton died. All her dreams—even ones she didn't know she had—have spilled out like fruit from a cornucopia.

She barely recalls now how she raged when she first left Earth. That was some other Sol, a misguided version of herself. This new Sol is her own bright center, and what she'll become is up to her. Not Anton. Not even Oskar.

Epilogue
Alice

Alice kneels next to her messenger bag. She toys with the wrappers she left there, then stuffs them inside along with her canteen. She doesn't know why she never cleaned up. It felt like defiance at the time, but now it just feels—stupid. When the metal egg deposited her upon the ocean, and it swept her into the cave, she thought herself lost. She *was* lost—without her computer, her music, her puzzles, and her neat, austere cabin.

She'd sat on the slimy stones, shivering and tugging at her tangled hair—an anxious habit even before Vishnu. She'd eaten all her food in a voracious rush and scattered the wrappings. She'd pounded useless fists against the petroglyphs, screamed, stomped back and forth. She'd tried counting to calm herself, yet even that old trick couldn't comfort her.

Finally, she dipped a toe in the water but pulled back, afraid to swim out of the cave even though she knew how. She'd learned as a child in Norway. This ocean was different, though. Too green. And out here it smelled more of growing things than of brine. Who knew what might be lurking under the waves? So she paced, waited, grew hungrier and hungrier. Until, finally, her stomach conquered her mind.

The sea tried to push her back when she finally slipped into its arms, as though it wanted to protect her, perhaps. But maybe not. It didn't know her, and she didn't know it. She kicked hard, angry with herself and this situation. Eventually, her arms and legs overcame the unhelpful waves. She ducked underwater, swam past the cave's mouth, and surfaced in the open sea. She found herself alone, the only thing not made of liquid besides gray cliffs and a far-off shoreline.

The sky was a weird, blue-not-right color. Alien rings bracketed a sun too big and too red, and it felt wrong to be alone. Normally, she liked solitude—just not under these circumstances.

Alice shakes the memory loose with a toss of her head. She doesn't want to remember her past self. Maybe she isn't even Alice anymore. Not even human, but Vishnuan. *No.* Too hard to say, and she never liked that name. *Gaia* is a better title. Gaia was the Greek goddess of all life, just like this planet might be the genesis of all life. If she can believe the water dragons, anyway. They've never been off planet, never traveled through the dark vacuum of space. They told her the man she saved would not return, but *what did they know*?

He hasn't come back, though, has he? She's returned to the cave several times and found no sign of him. Balsu won't let her go ashore to search. She's not a prisoner, exactly. Only beholden. Yet isn't that similar? Chains in another form? She tugs her blond curl again, the one that always falls annoyingly over her eyes. Maybe the man died because he didn't listen to her about the rains. That might be a good thing. He could have been bad like those others. It's entirely plausible.

But her heart says otherwise. Normally, she'd scoff at this idea. Hearts aren't logical, and she was raised to believe only facts mattered. Numbers, not feelings. Now she's not so sure. Gaia has changed her. *Is* she still Alice? Shy Alice. Brilliant Alice. Weird Alice. The girl with the photographic memory. The woman who can't cry and hates hugging. Is she still herself?

She doesn't know. All she *does* comprehend is that she wants to see the man she saved just once, to know he's all right. Maybe then she can let him go.

ACKNOWLEDGEMENTS

I'm grateful to my writing groups for their fresh perspectives and honest advice. Thanks for holding me to account and asking good questions. Also, a big thanks to my cherished beta readers, Pete, Nellie, and Howard, as well as to my editor, Janette.